The Audacity
of an
Adirondack
Summer

The Audacity
of an
Adirondack
Summer

By L.R. Smolarek

The Audacity of an Adirondack Summer is a work of fiction
All characters appearing in this work are fictitious. Any resemblance to real persons, living or dead, is purely coincidental.

Audacity of an Adirondack Summer
Copyright © 2018 Linda R. Smolarek

Cover Design © Leslie Taylor BuffaloCreativegroup

Printed by CreateSpace, An Amazon.com Company
Available from Amazon.com and other retail outlets
Available on Kindle and other devices

PRINTED IN THE UNTIED STATES OF AMERICA

ISBN: 978-1719223386

DEDICATION

To my husband, Jim
My first love, my last, my one and only.

Also by L.R. Smolarek

Adirondack Audacity

Audacity On The Water

Not all girls are made of sugar and spice and everything nice…some girls are made of adventure and wine and all things fine…

Of all the paths you take in life, make sure some of them are dirt...

The breeze waffles through needles of balsam fir perfuming the air with the scent of the forest. My paddle pauses, droplets of water form a vanishing silvery trail on the surface of the lake. Off in the distance a loon's haunting cry echoes across the water. Deep contentment fills me, I'm home...

"Mom...Mom?" My daughter, Lani, breaks into my daydream, pulling my thoughts from the Adirondack Mountains to her tiny kitchen in California.

"What, what?" I shake my head to refocus. "I'm sorry, I wasn't paying attention."

"I see." She says, reproach in her voice. "What could be more important than my wedding plans?"

I give a slight shrug to my shoulders. I have no excuse. I must be the worst mother in the entire world. From the moment a girl is born, a woman instinctively begins to plan her daughter's wedding. As the first pink garment is buttoned and zipped on the baby girl, a mother dreams of long white dresses, towering cakes of sugary confection surrounded by flowers in subtle shades of pastel.

What is wrong with me?

A dull pain throbs in the back of my head, like the rumble of low-lying clouds on a humid summer afternoon. Pulsing, ready to unleash the potent power of a thunderstorm.

The antique clock hanging on the wall chimes six-thirty. Thin beams of weakened sunlight filter through the slats of the window shutters painting dappled stripes of early evening sun on the hardwood floor. The round mahogany table that dominates

1

the room is covered in the litter of take-out food containers, half full coffee cups and empty wine bottles.

My eyes glaze over at the pile of bridal magazines, a helter-skelter collection of periodicals scattered across the scarred tabletop. Some propped open, others have dog-eared corners that act as bookmarks. Ripped pages stand with jagged edges lining up to form a runway parade of fashion models, all dressed in white.

In my defense, I was excited until a copy of 'Weddings by Martha Stewart' became the gold standard for Lani's wedding ideas. My enthusiasm quickly became replaced with fear and trepidation. Everything that woman does is overlaid with precise attention to detail and elegance. It's terrifying that my daughter, Lani O'Connor has emotionally teamed up with Martha Stewart for her wedding. It is tantamount to a cyclone converging with a tornado. The ensuing vortex kicks up clouds of fabric swatches and seating charts, destroying practical thought in its path. The resulting aftermath is enough to make any sane mother seriously consider an extended stay in a cloistered convent.

I can do this, what mother doesn't want to help plan her daughter's wedding. It's a right of passage, a womanly ritual.

It's flipping driving me nuts.

We've been at this since morning; it's now evening. The sun has set. I need a walk, I need air, I need anything but lace and tulle, icing and floral bouquets. Tilting the wine bottle, I watch with disappointment as a ruby-red drop slides into the glass. Resigned, I line it up with the other empty bottle.

"The only pictures I'm finding are of men dressed in spats." Lani says, leaning back in her chair. She chews on her lower lip, her face a study of deep concentration. Ripping the photo out of a magazine, she pins it to the small corkboard propped on an easel. Almost every inch of the board is covered with pictures of ideas we've torn from magazines or printed off the fashion archives of the Internet.

"Spats?" I croak.

"Yes, gentlemen wore them to protect their shoes and trousers." She says with a defensive edge to her voice. "Most of the time they were black and white. They were the height of style

2

for men at the turn of the century."

"Seriously?" I ask. My face crimps into the expression one gets after eating a sour pickle. "Spats?" My energy zapped, leaving only enough stamina for one-word sentences.

"Okay," I nod slowly in acknowledgement. My mind a whirl of reasons why men shouldn't dress in spats, for starters, they look like something out of a vaudeville circus act.

I hand her a black and white photo of a man dressed in hunting attire, fashionable for a country estate gentleman at the turn of the century. Simple, elegant, and readily available from the L.L. Bean catalog. My kind of plan.

"Ummm...I don't know." Lani says, twisting a curl of her black hair around her index finger. "We should still consider the spats. I think they're kind of cute."

Inwardly, I groan and outwardly I smile like an indulgent mother. A mother thrilled to consider the possibility that the entire male population of her family will be walking down the aisle in front of everyone she knows, in spats. Where does she get these ideas?

Lani holds the L.L. Bean photo up for closer examination then wrinkles her nose and shrugs her shoulders. "I guess, maybe, that could work. We'll see." And she adds the picture to the growing pile of possibilities.

Hoping to cajole her, I point to the picture from the catalog again, "Jason would look so handsome in a tweed sport coat."

"Yes, I like the country gentleman's look with the tall leather boots and wool knickers. It would fit our historic Adirondack theme perfectly. But the spats would be so fun."

"Knickers?" I try not to sound incredulous. Where did knickers come from, what planet orbiting around her dark glossy head conjured up *knickers*?

Putting on a bright smile, I propose a dose of reality into her Hollywood fantasy wedding plans. "Honey, I don't picture your down to earth mid-western fiancé wearing spats or knickers."

"I know Jason loves me." Lani sighs, "But I guess asking him to wear spats would be too much."

"Ya think." I mutter, trying not to roll my eyes at the obvious. Lani lives in Los Angeles. She works as an understudy for one of the most talented costume designers in Hollywood, hence, the turn of the century wedding theme. She can't help herself; it's in her blood, she needs to create. As a little girl she had the most outlandishly dressed Barbie dolls in the neighborhood. She would rummage my rejected sewing projects to use as her wardrobe foundation. Her vast creative talents did not come from me.

"But if you do change your mind, please, pretty please, can I be there when you ask Jason to wear spats?" I tease.

"Sure, as long as I can be in the room when you try to put Vic in knickers and high socks." Lani arches an eyebrow, turning a sketchpad toward me. She has sketched out a rough drawing of a man dressed in woolen knickers, tall boots and a tweed blazer. "This is the perfect attire for a weekend in the country or a summer vacation in the Adirondacks at the height of the Great Camp era." She uses the eraser end of her pencil to pull a scrap of paper closer; on it is a pencil drawing of a woman. "This is more of a doodle than a design. How about something like this for you?"

I look at the paper and then look at her. Struggling with the certainty that my daughter is either hallucinating or enjoying too much of the legal marijuana California has to offer. The woman in the picture is wearing a dress with a high tight collar, long narrow sleeves, a corseted waist guaranteed to suffocate and a voluminous hem dragging on the ground behind her. *Is she nuts?*

"Sweetheart, are you trying to kill your mother? I would melt in that get-up. No wonder women years ago fainted, between the corsets and heavy dresses. It explains why they never smiled in the old black and white photographs. They were miserable." I raise my hand. "It's bad enough we have to wear high heels and Spanks, at least we can breathe."

Lani sticks out her lower lip in a feigned pout.

Seeking a compromise I propose, "I'm still caught up in the idea of Vic in knickers." I waggle my eyebrows up and down. "He is tall enough to pull it off, it might be kind of hot."

"Mom!" Lani admonishes with a giggle.

"Hey, it's been awhile." I mutter so low she can't hear me complain. "Try seven months of abstinence and then we'll talk."

I swirl the empty wine glass in my hand conjuring up the image of my six-foot three, tall, dark and gorgeous husband escorting me down the aisle in knickers and high socks. I snort and choke on a fit of laughter. Vic is Lani's stepfather and a good sport. He is willing to do almost anything to please us, but wearing knickers might test the limits. Vic came into my life and consequently the lives of my children by a serendipitous chance of fate, three years ago after the death of my husband, Jack. I was lonely, bereft and a widow. Perfect timing for an old sweetheart to swoop in, and swoop in he did.

Vic was my first love, my summer camp love. The man I never got over even after twenty-five years of marriage and two children. I was devoted to my first husband, but they say you never forget your first love…*and sometimes…how true.*

"Well, Vic won't be walking you down the aisle, so he can probably forgo the knickers." I say. "But I'm sure your Uncle Patrick will look divine in them."

Lani claps a hand over her mouth as she convulses into giggles. "Can you imagine? When I asked Uncle Patrick if he would stand in for Dad he said he was honored and willing to go anywhere or do anything I wanted."

"Really?" I comment, my voice wry with amusement. "Does he not remember the plays you put on as children? Where unsuspecting adults were captured and dressed as trees, beanstalks or clowns with curly red wigs."

"Apparently not."

To invoke a sense of her father's presence at the wedding Lani asked his brother, Patrick to walk her down the aisle. Patrick was Lani's godfather and closest in age and temperament to her dad.

With her wedding plans spread before me, I'm struck by the memories of the mother my daughter grew up with, and now how to reconcile that history into the new life I've created with Vic. When Lani and her fiancé, Jason decided to get married at our Camp in the Adirondacks, Vic and I were ecstatic. Since Vic and I were married at the Camp two years ago, I have experience in Adirondack weddings. I just prefer them to resemble a picnic, not a royal coronation.

But this is my daughter's wedding; I'm simply the assistant coordinator to whatever outlandish ideas she brews up.

As a costume designer she has a vision. She wants a wedding based on the Adirondack Great Camps at the turn of the century. The vision includes the bridal party dressed in period clothing, guests to arrive by carriage, guide boats or vintage automobiles. Tables will be set with linen, fine china and candles. The decorations inspired by a woodland theme.

I admit; I'm intrigued and overwhelmed at the same time. The guest list will be small so there is room in the budget for a few extravagances.

Almost every surface in her tiny California kitchen is covered; lists of things to do are held prisoners under an army of magnets on the refrigerator. A trail of torn pages leads into the living room, and a mobile of magazine brides sway and dance from the chandelier on colorful pieces of yarn. All the details needed to make Lani's wedding unique. She has been practicing for this since she was a little girl.

Her calico cat, Bergamot turns his head and regards me with tawny golden tiger-eyes. Unable to resist the temptation I toss a crumpled paper at him. With a flick of his tail he rolls into a crouch and pounces, batting the ball through the doorway into the living room.

With Vic away on location for his next film, I've spent more time visiting under the guise of helping with the wedding preparations than a mother-in-law in-waiting should. But the house is so welcoming, that warm lived in feeling brought on by small rooms and low ceilings studded with redwood beams. The furniture large and cushiony done in cool grays and blues to temper the searing midday sun. Lani loves spending her weekends scouting local yard sales and flea markets, her creative touch turns family hand-me-downs and rustic relics into decorating treasures.

The remodeled bungalow dates from the early 1900's. The outside stucco walls are painted sunny yellow. The brick chimney covered in climbing David Austin roses leads to a weathered gate that swings on squeaky hinges to a small garden. The profusion of flowers are home to a mix of colorful birds and butterflies.

An added plus for me, Lani's fiancé, Jason, for some ungodly reason seems to enjoy my company, repeatedly encouraging me to stay. Needless to say this has scored him multiple points on the potential son-in-law scale and so I've stayed. But spring is in the air and it's time to head east, home to the mountains. I'm longing for our Camp in the Adirondacks and I'm longing for my husband. I understood the nature of his profession when I married him but the extended away locations have put a strain on our 'still blushing from the altar' marriage. Only married for two years and he's been away on location for almost half of them. I put aside my teaching career when I married Vic because it made sense. It made sense when he was home, not when he is away. And I'm bored.

"Mom, do you still have your wedding dress, the one you wore when you married Dad." Lani interrupts my thoughts as she plunks down a bowl of freshly washed strawberries on the table.

"Oh." I pull myself out of my doldrums and chide myself for whining. Most women would die for my life, a loving husband who happens to be hot and rich. "I'm sorry, what was the question?" I sigh and stretch my folded fingers over my head.

"Do you still have your wedding dress from the first one? I mean the one with Dad."

"Yes, I do." I smile at her efforts to cover over the awkwardness. "In fact, I have the dress in storage at Camp. I couldn't bear to throw it out. Grandma Fiona made it for me. Do you remember her? She died when you were very young."

"Who could forget her? She was a scary old lady."

"She ruled the O'Connor family with an iron fist." I lean my elbows on the table reminiscing, "I liked her; it was a hard life growing up in Ireland during the depression. She raised her children and likewise her grandchildren to be strong and not afraid of hard work. Grandma Fi was kind to me, she made my wedding dress as a way of welcoming me into the family."

"So have you looked at it recently?"

"No, when I moved, I didn't even bother opening the box. The last time I took the dress out was after your father's death. I thought maybe I should give it away but I couldn't bear to part with it. At the time it was in good shape, the material intact, very little wear, no rips or tears. Why? Are you thinking of wearing it?"

"I don't know, the styling won't be correct for the time period, but I'm thinking of modifying or maybe using pieces from it."

"That's a great idea. You're a wiz with a scissors and sewing machine, just like great-grandma Fiona."

"I'm glad you've stayed connected with Dad's family after your marriage to Vic."

"Of course. They will always be my family, Lani. Just because your father died doesn't mean we'd stop being family for each other."

"Mom, do you still love him?"

I start, the hand holding a large strawberry stops midway to my mouth. "Who, darling? Your father?"

"Yeah, I know you found Vic again and anyone can see how much you love each other. But I can't help wonder if you still love Dad?"

I shove the strawberry, half the size of a small apple into my mouth nearly choking. To bide my time, I pour a generous splash of wine into a long stemmed glass. She had opened a new bottle, some California, Sonoma-Napa something or another wine. Thank goodness, I need a drink and a moment to compose an answer to her question.

I would never tarnish my children's image of their father, but bottom line, the man was a bit of a two timing philandering male whore. Jack was charming, devastatingly handsome in a Kennedy sort of way, a pilot with a smile that could knock a woman's panties off within a ten-yard range. Other than that he was a good husband and father. Yes, I did love him, and in his own way he loved me too. When confronted about his infidelities, he was remorseful; claiming the children and I always came first. But with no excuses offered, he claimed he wasn't made for monogamy. I never left him because, quite frankly, I had nowhere to go. My mother died young and my father remarried. My stepmother and I loathe each other, thereby, souring my relationship with my father and brothers. Jack's family was all the family I had, and I desperately didn't want to lose them. So I looked the other way. I didn't want to disrupt my children's lives and find myself in the divorce nightmare of spending holidays alone without the large Irish family I had come to love. In the end, I have no regrets.

"Lani, of course, I have feelings for your father. We were married for twenty-five years. You and your brother, Trey are proof of that love. Losing your father was an emotional blow for all of us."

"What about Vic?" She asks.

I shrug my shoulders. "Vic? Maybe Vic was supposed to come back into my life. Kismet? We fell in love fast and hard as teenagers, if I didn't get pregnant with your half brother, Josh, things may have turned out differently. I never forgave our parents for taking Josh and putting him up for adoption." I throw my hands up in the air, still bitter. "But the bottom line is, Vic and I were young and naive. I'm grateful we were able to trace the adoption records and find Josh. Thirty years later, but now, I have my son back."

"Do you think you and Vic would have married and raised Josh?"

"Who knows, fate did not swing that way for us. I married your father, and we were a good team; our strengths and weaknesses complemented each other." I raise my wine glass. "To Jack."

Lani's wine glass catches the light from the overhead chandelier, the pitched clink of the glasses resounds in the room. "To Dad."

The moment is interrupted by the distinctive Latin mamba ring tone of my cell phone. The ring tone alerts me that my sultry hunk of a husband is calling. "Speak of the devil, guess who's calling?" I say with a giggle.

My cell phone is muffled under the piles of magazines and fabric swatches. I scramble pushing aside coffee cups, lunch plates and half empty bottle of wine. "Where the hell is it?" I fume.

"Hello?" I fairly shout into the phone and hear Vic's voice coming through the static. "Vic?"

"Elle? Buttercup, is that you?" He sounds a million miles away.

"Yes. Vic, how are you? It's been so long. I was beginning to get worried."

"I know, I know. The communication lines on this island are crap. How are you?"

"I'm fine, it's so good to hear from you. But your voice is breaking up."

"Yeah, I have a lot of static on my end. Listen, I'll make it quick. I wanted to give you a head's up. I'm going to be"…the connection breaks off and his voice fades in and out.

"Vic, what did you say?" I wave my hand, standing up in frustration, moving about in hopes of improving the signal.

"I said, I'm going to be home in two…"

"Vic, I know, sweetheart, you'll be home soon." I pace the room, pointing to the phone, giving Lani thumbs up to indicate good news. "I can't wait."

"No, Elle, that's why I'm calling, I'll be home"…static…"Thursday. I'm getting on a plane to come home now."

"What! Vic, did you say *Thursday?*" I ask incredulous. "That is less than three days away. I'm still in Los Angeles!"

"The production company finished ahead of schedule… I'll be home sooner than expected. I'm not even stopping to see"…the phone crackles with static.

"What!"

His voice crashes through the estrogen driven haze of wedding planning and sends me in a panic. I'm still on the West Coast. I have to fly to New York, open camp for the season and be ready for his arrival! Vic wasn't scheduled to arrive home for another week.

Now with less than three days…*oh boy, giddup!* My mind is a whirl of preparations. His voice cuts through my panic; I stop pacing and listen intently.

"Elle, I just want to let you know…*chhhhhh…*" I can't hear him, the signal fades out and then his voice is back. "Elle, listen I don't want to shock you, but there have been changes." The cell phone goes dead, for good, he is gone. I try redialing his number…nothing. Aggravated, I clunk the phone against the table, damn cell phones never work when you need them.

10

"Damn it! Changes? What does he mean by changes?" I fume to Lani.

She scrunches up her face in bewilderment. "I'm sure it's nothing, Mom. Don't overreact."

"Overreact, who's over reacting?" Easy for her to say, she wasn't married to her father. Twenty-five years of marriage to Jack has left me riddled with insecurities.

Changes? What did he mean changes? What kind of changes? A new hairstyle, movie contract, different living arrangements, *or* my heart goes into wild palpitations…a new woman?

My subconscious wails. Every wife left behind is afraid of fading like an old memory in the face of the excitement, romance and danger of a movie shoot. The insecure, green-eyed shrew that resides deep in me raises her vicious head. I thought I buried her deep in some bubbling miasma of an endless sink hole, too far away for her ugly suspicions to rise and hang in the air like a fetid cloud of jealousy. Evidently, I need to dig deeper, much deeper because…*the bitch is back.*

May good friends and a good hike be on your side…

"You have got to be kidding me! What the hell!"

The Lazy-Dazy Market was quiet for a Tuesday afternoon. In addition to myself there is a retired couple and two young men picking up supplies for a backpacking trip. So when all three of them stopped and stared at me, I realized I spoken out loud, voicing my protest to the entire store. In the wake of Vic's abrupt return I flew from the West coast to the Adirondacks and currently I'm blitzing the local grocery store. I was moving along nicely until standing in the checkout line I'm stopped in my tracks by the celebrity tabloids.

With a shrug of my shoulders and an apologetic smile to the small group assembled; I turn my back and snatch the tabloid from of the newsstand. I read the headlines in disbelief. That's my husband on the cover, in the arms of another woman, for the whole world to see!

Outrage engulfs my body sending curling tendrils of fear and trepidation to snake and twist through my spine. Suddenly I can't breathe, my heart hammers, a faint buzzing hums in my ears. I feel a flush creep across my chest, spiraling through my torso bringing on nausea and dizziness.

My wonderful day vanishes, dissolved under the onslaught of words clamoring for attention, words that jump off the magazine cover cut straight through my heart.

"Ma'am, did you find everything you were looking for?"

The checkout clerk behind the register looks at me with an odd expression on her face, her words lost in my blur of fury.

"Ma'am, are you okay?"

"Umm…yes."

"If you are ready to check out, you can put your items on the belt." She talks slowly, enunciating her words as if talking to a slow-witted or elderly person.

She swipes my items one by one over the barcode scanner, *bleep, bleep, bleep,* the rhythm matches my racing heart. I close my eyes, attempt to deep breathe, anything to still my galloping panic and put reins on my temper.

The young clerk looks to be in her mid-twenties, long thin dark hair held back with a black elastic band into messy bun. I'm barely aware of her. Oddly, my eyes focus on the tattoo running down her arm. A great hideous multi-colored serpent, it feels like an omen.

"I know. Don't those tabloids get your blood rolling?" She nods her head in sympathy at the small newspaper. "I just can't resist picking up one or two each week, just to see what is *really* going on with the celebrities. I love to read the gossip sheets."

"Read?" I croak. Who would consider this reading material? I sputter to myself.

"Sometimes it makes you kind of glad just to be a normal person." She continues, "Does that one have any good stories? I didn't get a chance to look at this weeks' edition."

I gaze at the woman, dumbfounded. I think to myself. Really, you buy these pieces of trash with your hard earned money. The nerve of the publishers, creating insidious lies, it's like stealing. It should be illegal to print the slander they post on these gossip rags. Especially when it's my sweet husband on the front page! He is charismatic; people fall in love with him all the time. But some sexy, nubile young actress who happens to be his co-star better keep her hands off my man!

"Ma'am, I'm sorry I didn't hear you. Did you find everything you were looking for?"

In a supreme effort not to be rude, I paste a smile on my face and answer, "Yes, thank you." My face feels like brittle glass, threatening to crack and shatter in a thousand pieces. "I found everything I need and more." I look with growing alarm at the line of food, cleaning products and assorted household products on the checkout belt. Good lord, how much did I buy? A glance at the two-page list in my hand makes me realize, everything in that cart and on the belt in front of me is needed. This is Adele's fault, I pout to myself. If her mother hadn't gotten ill last winter she and Weasel would have cleaned and opened the house for us. I mentally chide myself for being so self-centered, knowing fully well her mother slipped and fell in January requiring Adele to hop on a plane and fly to Florida. And if my memory serves me right, I told her not to worry about a thing, take her time; nurse her mother back to health. Why not take Weasel with her so the two of them could enjoy winter in Florida? Vic and I paid for the airfare, a little added bonus for them. No worries, the house will take care of itself. They promised to be home by late April well before Vic and I were due back to our Adirondack Camp. But her mother had a serious setback, which required nursing home placement. Sadly enough, this left Adele and Weasel the task of selling the mother's house and sorting through her belongings. They wouldn't be back until June.

My response to that bit of news, "Absolutely, take your time, I've got it covered. I'll handle everything." Now I blow out a sigh and chew on my lower lip. I'm exhausted just looking at the amount of food to be put away and the amount of scrubbing mandated by the plethora of cleaning products purchased. *Damn*…this is my fault. Why did we buy such a big house?

I sigh…because we love it. We love the mountains, the wilderness and for me it's home. Our son Josh and his family live nearby and we would do anything to foster our relationship with the son we lost so many years ago.

"Ma'am," the casher's nametag reads, Gina. "Are you going to be taking that Starlight Gazette paper? I mean you have to find out the rest of the story, the cover only hints at the juicy details inside."

Her voice brings me back to the tabloid in my hand. I know the details of the inside story. Esteban Diago, Vic's movie alias is a happily married man. He is not having an affair with his stunningly gorgeous co-star who happens to be twenty some years younger than his wife. That's the true story, not this rubbish. Vivian Gust, my ass. And then I remember him warning

14

me... something about changes that he could not go into detail over the phone.

"Ma'am?" She points to the tabloid.

My conscious screams absolutely not! Don't you dare give those gossip mongers a penny of your money. But curiosity kicks in, those lies and misconceptions are about my husband! The picture accompanying the caption shows Vic and his leading lady, in the clutches of each other's arms, suggesting a romantic interlude. I chide myself; you know that picture was a publicity stunt. Vic would never cheat on me. We've been separated for seven months, that's not so long...right? My heart flutters. A lot can happen in seven months. *Oh holy long distance relationship.*

The filming company was supposed to shoot the movie in Hawaii. I was to join him on the big island at a convenient point in the production process. Then some nickel and dime accountant got the bright idea to film on a remote island in the South Pacific. An island so tiny and off the beaten path it didn't have a real airport or connecting transportation. The cast and crew signed a binding contract; there was no room to negotiate, unless Vic wanted to pass on the opportunity to star in the sequel of *Firebrand,* the movie that made him rich and famous. Not a good idea so...he was going to Pela Bunta Gorrda. *Whatever,* the name of that stupid island is. Families were not invited. There was to be a Christmas break but then a typhoon blew up over the ocean and dashed any travel plans. So for seven months our relationship has stalled to a standstill. Even something as simple as talking on the phone was next to impossible. Phone sex felt awkward and disconnected. I went so far as to download some trashy erotica novellas on my kindle, just reading them made me blush. There was no way I could say the words let alone text them to Vic. He was highly amused at my lame attempts at seduction, encouraging me to stick to the basics. Which means holding hands, dancing to music on our deck overlooking the lake, snuggling under a fluffy down comforter for a little early morning nooky. Not stumbling over words I don't even know the meaning of. It's was way too nuevo sexo for me...I prefer my men in the flesh.

So here I stand on the day he is to arrive home, holding a

15

gossip rag sheet with his picture plastered across the front page deciding whether to buy it or not. Seriously…can life get any crazier?

"Fine, I'll take it." I snap at Gina. The poor girl's face turns as red as her uniform apron at my rudeness.

"I'm so sorry. I don't mean to be rude. It's just that I know…." I start to explain and realize I cannot tell this girl my husband is Esteban Diago. One, she will think I'm nuts and two, I don't want to do anything to jeopardize our Adirondack hideaway.

"Just add the paper."

"Okay," the clerk clears her throat and looks at me oddly. "I have your groceries bagged, how would you like to pay for them? Cash, credit, or debit card?" The man behind me heaves out a sigh, a grimace of impatience distorts his face. To further demonstrate his annoyance, he loudly taps his credit card on the counter signaling, I've wasted enough of his time.

"Sorry," I apologize. Old men seem to be in such a hurry. Where in the world do they have to go? Aren't they retired, enjoying their golden years? I hand Gina my credit card and turn, I give the gentleman behind me a dazzling smile thanking him for his extreme patience. Turning, I thank Gina for her help loading the mountains of groceries.

"My pleasure," she gushes. "Enjoy your magazine. I can't wait to get home and read it myself. I just love that Esteban Diago!"

"Me too." I sigh. "Me too…" and push my overloaded cart out the door.

Happiness is hiking up a mountain…

The Adirondack Regional Airport is a small public use landing strip located four miles northwest of Saranac Lake. Vic chartered a private plane from Chicago to Saranac Lake rather than have me pick him up in Albany.

The digital clock on my watch reads twelve forty-five. I'm fifteen minutes early. With a grateful sigh I sink into a chair and look around the lounge reserved for guests who request privacy with their travel arrangements. The walls are painted in muted tones of green and covered with large framed photographs of the Adirondacks.

I'm amazed at how much I've accomplished this morning and still arrive on time. Though I did have to change my clothes in the ladies room of a coffee shop on the way. I take a compact mirror out of my purse and squint, making sure my makeup is in all the right places. Normally I wear little makeup and even less when I'm in the mountains. But I want to look my best for Vic's arrival so I used a slightly heavier hand applying foundation and concealer and enough blush and eye shadow to accentuate my cheekbones and wide set eyes.

Lani helped design the female equivalent of dating combat fatigues. In California, we found a pair of ocean blue stilettos, tall enough to be sexy but shy of being called 'do-me' shoes along with a dress of understated seduction. Even with express shipping the dress arrived at Lani's house, literally as I was walking out the door. I shoved it into my suitcase and forgot about it until this morning. It looked pretty on the model in the ad and was the perfect turquoise blue to match my shoes. Imagine my horror when I zipped up the dress in the rest room only to find the neckline too low, dangerously low. Not perky half-moons of cleavage peeking out low, but half my chest exposed low. The skirt is too short, too tight and everything about the dress is too much!

This is all Vic's fault for changing the schedule. I tried tugging the bodice up; but what I gained on top caused my butt to hang out on the bottom. So here I am sitting in the waiting room of the airport looking like an aging pin-up model.

Oh well, the only one looking at me is Vic, and he will *love* it, it's enough to cause male heart palpitations.

I tuck my legs under the chair in the waiting lounge and tug at the skirt in an attempt not to flash the security guard standing by the door that leads to the runway. I can't help but notice his eyes wander over then fixate on my boobs. He smirks with a satisfied expression on his face seeming to say, thanks for the show. At least there is no one else besides the two of us waiting for Flight 504 from Chicago.

I had played out the reunion with Vic in my mind over the past few weeks, envisioning a slow motion scene of us running into each other's arms across the runway tarmac. The security guard doesn't look like he'd be sympathetic to my romantic notions. His demeanor suggests law enforcement, ex-military following a stint with the Navy S.E.A.L.S. His body language reads, don't bother trying to mess with me. Close cropped hair, well-muscled body, carrying an extra ten to fifteen pounds of weight to make him look imposing.

"Excuse me," I venture. "I don't suppose I could go outside and meet my husband as he is getting off the plane?" I give a flirtatious toss of my head and only succeed in flipping my sunglasses off. Deftly catching them in my hand, bravely, I continue on, "We haven't seen each other for almost seven months and well, you know…"

The man's eyes travel over me, like I'm carrying a concealed weapon under this dress. I couldn't hide a nickel in this get-up. He is silent for a few seconds, I begin to chaff under his scrutiny.

"Ma'am." He says. Whenever a law officer begins a

conversation with 'ma'am' you know you're in for a lecture about some infraction of the rules you don't understand.

He begins again, "Ma'am, I'm sure you are aware that Federal Aviation Law does not permit un-ticketed civilians on the run way. It is a hard and fast rule, there are no exceptions." He raises his eyebrow and with a sneer on his face says, "If you've waited this long, a few more minutes aren't going to change things." The implication is, keep your panties on.

"Sure. Yes, I understand." I sit back down feeling chastised. For goodness sake, he acts like we're going to do it on the runway. *Geez…*what does he think I am? You look like a cheap call girl on a Saturday night parade to Hell. The inner Catholic schoolgirl subconscious that resides in the deepest recesses of my soul growls at me. Don't even start with me, I retort back. This didn't go as planned. I give the dress another defiant tug. Sorry I even mentioned it. And then all the vexing nuances of the day vanish as Vic's plane comes screaming down the runway coasting to an abrupt halt, turning and taxiing over to the terminal. Unable to control my excitement, I run up to the window and press both hands against the glass, bumping my nose. I feel like a five year old searching for Santa Claus on Christmas Eve. The plane comes to a halt and the door swings open, a set of retractable steps extends onto the runway. A crewmember steps out and holds a hand out to the passenger slowly making his way off the plane, some skinny old man using a cane as he carefully walks down the steps. I thought Vic was traveling alone. Wait a minute; I whack my nose against the glass, harder this time. That skinny hunched over old man? Nooo! That can't be? I wipe furiously at the window as if to remove an invisible fog. That's my Vic? What! Wait? *My Vic!*

I hardly recognize him. He has gray hair and walking with a stooped bent back…using a cane! He looks like he lost twenty-five pounds. "Oh, my God, what's happened to him?" I make a dive toward the runway. Just as I'm about to yank the door open and sprint out I feel a strong pair of arms hook around my waist and lift me off my feet. Twisting, kicking and yelling, I protest vehemently, "Hey, put me down! Can't you see? Something's wrong with my husband. He's hurt or ill or…something! I need to go to him. Stop it. Put me down!" I wiggle and squirm in his grasp. "Vic, Vic! Oh my God, are you all right?"

And this is how I greet my husband, after seven months of separation, he finds me struggling in the arms of another man, wearing a tight little pencil dress riding up my ass and the girls out sing the Gloria for the whole world to see…when will I ever learn.

The security guard hauls me back into the waiting room refusing to put me back on my feet until I promise to behave. "Lady, if you try to leave this room again, I'll be forced to arrest you."

And that's all the admonishment I need to shut up. The last thing I need is another run-in with the law. Through no fault of my own, I'm on a first name basis with the Old Forge Police Department, have been known to exchange Christmas cards with members of the S.W.A.T. team and the local FBI agent. The last thing I need is more law enforcement in my life.

With an aggravated sigh, I agree. I can hardly breathe with his arm holding my mid-section in a vise-like grip. As he sets my feet back on the ground, I swear he copped a feel of my ass.

My 'how dare you!' was cut short by Vic's entrance into the room.

"Elle, are you okay? What's going on here?" He leans heavily on the cane and I think my heart is going to break. "Mia bella?"

It's all I can do not to burst into tears. The long anticipated reunion I had foolishly played out in my head is dashed by the dingy surroundings of the airport and my shock over his appearance. My instinct is to fling myself into his arms but fear he is not strong enough to hold me. My strong fearless husband is a shell of his former self and I don't know how to react. He looks so feeble I hardly recognize him. In shock my arms fall to my side and I whisper "Vic, what's happened? Are you all right?"

"Elle," He breathes out my name, his lips curl into a smile and his eyes bore into mine. "Just the sight of you in that slinky dress makes me more than okay." He gives a slight nod, his voice somehow managing to be both deep and soft. "Everything is fine."

"But you don't look fine." I protest. "You've lost so much

weight. And…why is your eyebrow twitching? Did you catch some tropical disease, scurvy, berry-berry, dengue fever?" I rattle on and on, anxiety my fuel. "You look like you've spent three weeks in the jungle on one of those survivor-reality TV shows."

He laughs and the rich, deep timber of his voice comforts me. No matter how long or far we are separated, or how our appearances change, I'll always recognize his voice…and his eyes, no one has eyes like Vic. Deep brown, intense with golden flecks of amber in those dark irises fringed by the most sinfully long curling eyelashes. A girl could melt and lose herself in those eyes.

"Ella, Ella, my Mia Bella." He pushes himself up on his cane and his thumb traces the curve of my cheek. Our eyes lock on each other's face, thoughts racing back over the months, the dormant but still white-hot passion that has sustained our love over the years, rekindles like a flame into an ache of wanting. The attraction is powerful and predictable.

"Elle, let's go home." Vic whispers. "Trust me, everything's okay."

He leans in and his lips, parchment paper dry, touch mine. I, in the heat of the moment I swoon a little and sway toward him, longing for the comfort of his arms. I've missed him so much. Nights of lying awake in bed, restless, lonely, wishing he were by my side, irrationally fearful he would stop loving me and desire someone else. I've waited so long to let my guard down, to sink into his embrace, knowing he is home. My best friend, the one to share coffee with in the morning, long walks in the woods and contentment in his strong arms at the end of the day. I've missed him terribly. It's not good to be alone.

I stoop and sling his carry-on bag over my shoulder and extend my arm to him. "Let's go, I need to get you home and healthy again." I run a finger lightly down his arm in a teasing fashion. "So don't get any ideas about leaving Camp…for a *very* long time."

Vic chuckles and I hear the security guard snort behind me and mutter under his breath, "Fat chance with that geezer." I turn on my heel, scowl and give him a withering look.

"Vic, let me help you." I insist.

"Elle, really I'm fine." He says. I swear I hear the hint of laughter in his voice. He gives a self-deprecating smile that along with the smoldering eyes and hint of a dimple reminds me how he knocked my socks off years ago. "We really need to get phones with better connections." He says.

"What?" I ask, not comprehending his implication.

"I'll explain…later."

It is not the mountain we conquer but ourselves...

With Vic and the baggage safely stowed, I steer the Land Rover out of the airport parking lot and turn onto the highway towards Camp. The road curves through a tunnel of green pines under a ceiling of cerulean blue sky. Green ribbons of meadow dotted with purple lupine border the road pushing back the dense forest floor. The sight of flowers set against the monotone green is a welcome herald of summer. It's a beautiful day to be in the mountains, but my mind never registers the fact, I'm too distraught. In an attempt to quell my trepidation, I fix my eyes on the road, concentrating on my driving. Vic is breathing heavily from the exertion of leaving the airport. I steal surreptitious glances at him, chewing on my lower lip to prevent myself from screaming.

Vic senses my dismay and puts his hand over mine on the steering wheel. I can feel him on every inch of my skin. His touch is the warm, engulfing feeling of security. "Elle, turn the car onto the dirt road over there." He points. "We need to talk."

My foot trembles on the pedal. "Okay." My eyes well with tears and I choke back a sob. His face is tired and sharpened, he seems decades older. This is where he tells me he's dying of some horrible disease or has a young energetic lover who has worn him to a fraction of his former self. Just the thought makes my stomach clench in a tight knot of anxiety. I pull the car over, place the gearshift into park, and open the windows, hoping the fresh scent of pine air will ground me for the onslaught of atrocious news. I know it's bad, I can feel it in my gut.

Taking a deep breath, I steel myself, "Okay, Vic." I clutch the steering wheel in a white-knuckle death grip. "You can tell me. Whatever it is, I'll understand. I promise, I won't be hysterical." I close my eyes, willing down the anxiety that threatens to erode my crumbling composure. But impatience breaks through and I can no longer restrain the questions. "What happened to you? How did you lose so much weight? Why do you look so old and unhealthy?"

I see him flinch as if I slapped him. Vic has a *little* bit of an ego problem, probably brought on by his Hollywood smoking hot super star image. He gets testy when reminded he's getting older. "Sorry, I'm mean," I try to amend the question. "You know, you don't look like yourself." I shrug my shoulders and blow out a woof of air to relieve the stress.

Vic runs a hand through his grey hair and his scalp comes off in clumps.

"Oh my God, Vic!" I scream. "Your hair, you're losing your beautiful hair!" And then I notice his shining black locks pulled back in a short ponytail at the nape of his neck.

"What the hell!"

He proceeds to pull a putty like substance off his face in sheets, exposing an under layer of smooth skin. He looks at me quizzically. "Elle, did you not hear me the other day on the phone? I distinctly told you there were going to be changes in my appearance. And not to worry, it's a disguise to throw off the paparazzi."

"A disguise for the paparazzi?" I repeat like a dull child asked to repeat the multiplication table.

"After the encounter we had with them last summer, I wanted to make sure no one recognized me as Esteban Diago."

"This is a disguise…." I accentuate the 'd' and hiss the 's' in the word disguise, whirling my finger up and down to encompass his entire body. My concern for him is morphing into a smoldering temper tantrum with a molten lava center, bubbling and seething. *Kerpow!*…without warning a volcanic eruption has occurred. I slap his arm, infuriated at him for scaring the *bejesus* out of me.

"Ouch!" He feigns pain, holding up his arms in mock fear.

"Hey, easy, I've had a long flight."

"Makeup! This is all makeup?" I punctuate each word with a light slap to his arm. "So you are not old and decrepit!"

His voice sharpens and he protests, "No, of course not. I had the makeup department give me an old wig, and they showed me how to apply plasticine to mimic wrinkles on my face." He finishes by pulling off a long stream of facial putty, his face streaked with foundation. "The head of the costumes raided the company wardrobe and put together this outfit of oversized outdated clothing."

"You did this on purpose?" I continue to slap his arm in short sharp raps as my voice raises several octaves. "All I heard on that phone conversation was, and I quote, "Elle, there have been some changes"…and then the phone went dead." My eyes rove up and down his body for a closer inspection, not fully satisfied. I thrust my chin in close to his face and demand. "Explain why you are so skinny and what about the dark circles under your eyes?"

He opens his mouth to explain but I slash my hand in the air cutting him off. My boiling caldron of temper no longer held in check as I rage at him. "What about the weight loss? The makeup department worked twenty pounds off of your frame." I jump out of the car, march over to the passenger side and yell at him, "Get out!" When he hesitates, I bark louder, "Get out of the fricking car where I can see you." I stomp my foot in frustration.

"Stop stamping your foot," he admonishes. "You know that gets me hot. When you put those hands on your hips and your eyes start flashing, you look so damn cute. And as much as I want to, right now I don't have the stamina."

"Agh! I'll give you foreplay! Don't you dare change the subject. I'm angry! I want to hug you and smack you up the side of the head at the same time." I stand in the green shadow of trees for a long moment, every inch of me quivering with anger.

"Mia bella, I'm sorry. I didn't mean to frighten you." He unfolds his long frame and steps out of the vehicle to his full six-foot glorious three-inch height. And a part of me melts in relief.

"Maybe you should spank me. I've been a naughty boy." He does the samba with his eyebrows, wiggling them up and down.

25

"Obviously, you're not dying." I close my eyes and shake my head.

"You knew about the weight loss."

"No, I did not."

"Yes." He protests. "Remember I had to lose fifteen pounds for the movie."

"Yes, but this is more than fifteen pounds."

"Yes, but unfortunately, I got food poisoning. The food was terrible; everyone lost weight. Rumor was the production company did it on purpose so the cast would look like refugees. So in total I've lost almost twenty-five pounds. I didn't want to tell you until I saw you. I knew you'd worry." He shrugs out of the suit jacket and holds out the waistband of his extra-large pants, throwing off the old man demeanor with each movement.

"So you lost twenty five pounds, turned your hair gray, made your face up like an aging circus clown and dressed in old man hand-me-downs from a Salvation Army bargain bin. And threw in the cane for extra effect. And you *didn't* want to tell me because I would worry! Vic!" I burst into tears.

"I'm so sorry, Elle. I thought you understood when I talked to you the other night at Lani's." He folds me into his embrace and despite clothes, hair and makeup, remembrance comes in his arms, and this is Vic.

I stiffen against him and draw in a great, trembling breath. "I could hardly hear you." I whisper and exhale with a hiss. "I just heard the word, changes. I thought the studio gave you a new contract or something. I was never given the impression that you were going to get off the plane looking like something out of the walking dead. Oh my God, Vic, you gave me such a fright. Twenty-five pounds and food poisoning, to lose that much weight is detrimental to your health."

He squeezes me tighter and buries his face in my hair. I can feel his rib cage pressing against me. He is so thin.

"I'll admit," he says, "I thought I'd be feeling better by now. The dysentery knocked the crap out of me. I'm exhausted and still eating a bland diet. I'm not a hundred percent; in fact I'm barely fifty percent. I wanted to tell you in person." He takes one look at my crestfallen face and hastens, "Now that I'm home, I'll be fine. I just need rest and your home cooking. I'll be back to my old self in a few weeks."

I grimace in dismay, burrowing my head into his chest so he can't see my face. Oh boy…I'm not exactly known for my wholesome home cooking. My kitchen skills have improved since our marriage, but I have a long history with burnt pans and take-out food. I slip my hand under his shirt, tracing the sharp contours of his ribs comforted by the steady beat of his heart.

He leans down, kisses me, slow, and delicious, his hands skim my back and travel to the base of my neck, enfolding me in his embrace. I relax in his arms, but can't help but feel the lack of intensity that is such a vital part of Vic. Something is missing, I sense his passion has waned, either from his illness or the long separation. Time apart has never been a problem between us, upon reunion we reconnect instantaneously. Yet, this time I feel something has gone awry, a part of him lost, somewhere else or to someone else.

He kisses the top of my head and murmurs against my ear. "Elle, take me home. I just want to go home and sleep in my own bed curled up next to you."

I brush a lock of hair out of his eyes and feel the heat rise off him. I hold the palm of my hand against his forehead, the way I would check a sick child. "Vic, you're running a fever." I exclaim. "We need to get you to a doctor. This could be serious."

"I already had some blood work done and a complete physical. It's only a matter of time before I get my strength back. I hope you can be patient. I'm sure this isn't the homecoming either one of us were thinking of, but it's only temporary and I'll be back to my old self."

"Of course, I can be patient. I'm just happy to have you home." I lean back in his arms, cautioning myself to be patient. Time heals all wounds, and as desperate as I am to have him wholly back to me, I can wait. "I'll be the best nurse ever. In fact," I tease, "I saw a cute nurse's outfit online when I was scanning for something adventurous to wear for your home coming."

"Mia, you're killing me. I love you dressed in white." He inclines his head and appraises me, "Short and tight, I hope?"

I bite down on my lower lip and mutter under my breath, "Hopefully not too tight." I shouldn't have eaten that entire blueberry muffin this morning, a five hundred calorie grand slam right to my thighs.

Between every two pines there is a doorway to a new world…
John Muir

Vic fell asleep before the SUV reached cruising speed; his face relaxed in repose, snoring with soft little popping sounds, his skin a shallow yellow color. He slept the profound sleep of the exhausted as we traveled through the densely wooded forest toward Camp. I turn onto a gravel road marked by a tree covered with signs; all the signs are different colors, shapes and sizes, posted to demark the many Camps along the lake. We have no sign on the tree, preferring to protect our anonymity. The SUV slows as we pass the smaller roads that veer off to the right and left. We continue along the lakeshore the road narrows further as trees encroach and low-lying shrubs of hobblebush and saplings fill in the gaps. At last coming to a stone and timber gatepost with a length of eight foot high fencing that runs off into the woods for a quarter of a mile in each direction. I hate the fencing but it's meant to be a deterrent for the uninvited curious. I press in the key code and wait for the gate to lift and drive through. Not to wake Vic, I slow the SUV to a crawl. The road is rutted with potholes and bumps, we want to discourage visitors as much as possible so have purposely let it revert back to its natural state. Around the last bend a clearing comes into sight, the view dotted with tall mature trees, their branches arch out over the lakeshore like the fringe of a watery shawl.

Twin stone pillars flank the entrance to Camp. I drive through and pull the SUV up next to the back door on the circular drive. The engine idles then stills, as I turn the key to the off position. The afternoon light filters through the overhanging trees giving a sneak peek of the sparkling lake.

I'm grateful for the quiet to sit and take in the scene, finally able to breathe in the only place that truly feels like home. Aside from the rustling of the leaves, the only sound is the call of the loons. A benediction, a welcome home. I watch the loons trail small V-shaped wakes behind them, marring the smooth placid surface of the lake. They crisscross back and forth like two well-heeled sailboats only to dip, dive and disappear. Then pop up minutes later, repeating the process again and again stopping only to broadcast a location call to their mate.

The timber-framed house of our Camp sits atop a grassy hill commanding a stunning view of the stubby grass lawn sloping down to the small sandy beach.

The few houses visible along the lake stand out as bright spots in the forest, a harmonious blending of green, brown and blue-grey of the lake water.

Our house stands as a looming giant nestled against the backdrop of forest, constructed of timber, stone, bent twigs and branches. The porches and patios appear bare and colorless awaiting the chairs and cushions of bright plaid that herald the summer season. Tall stands of hemlock, balsam fir, and yellow birch throw long arms of dappled shadow across the roof. They stand as silent sentinels of the forest rising in quiet welcome.

Vic stirs in the seat next to me, rubbing a hand across his day old stubble, yawns, stretches and groans. "Wow, sorry about that. I didn't mean to fall asleep on you."

"Did you miss my fascinating company?" I tease.

"Buttercup, I missed everything about you, from the top of your head to the tip of your toes. By the way, what color are they today?"

I arch my foot in display showing off the vivid green shade. "Believe it or not, it's called Lush Wilderness Woman."

"Sounds kinky, wish I was feeling well enough for a little backseat foreplay. And speaking of backseat foreplay," he inclines his head toward the rear seat. "What did you do, rob a library? What are you doing with all those books?"

"Umm...." I steal a surreptitious glance at the mound of

books piled on the backseat. This is not the best time to unveil my latest summer idea. What with him being ill and all.

"Well, you see. I was thinking."

Vic lightly taps his head against the side window and mutters under his breath. "Whenever you start thinking, trouble usually follows."

"Trouble? How can you say any of my ideas lead to trouble?"

"Well, let me see." Vic holds up his hand and starts counting on his fingers. "Skinny dipping on a cold night in May requiring the Old Forge Police to rescue and assist you back into the house. An unsolicited ride on the luggage carousel at the LAX airport involving security, two incidents with the S.W.A.T. team, a canoe race with a coach who turned out to be a little bit more than we expected…" He pauses for breath. "Shall I continue?"

"Fine, fine." I frown and hold out a hand to stop him. "I get your point but those were not my fault."

"It never is, Mia Bella, it never is."

"Seriously?" I blow out a deep sigh; my bangs flutter from the force of the exhalation. "I've had a run of bad luck. It could happen to anyone."

"Yeah." He leans his head back against the headrest and chuckles, "But it never does."

"But this is different, how much trouble can I get into hiking? Just a few itty-bitty walks up a mountain, I'll tell you about the books later. You're exhausted, and now is not a good time to talk about it."

"No, I want to know. What scheme have you got cooked up in that little head?"

"My head is not little, don't be condescending." I stab a finger in his direction. "If you must know, the books are about hiking in the Adirondacks. Remember we thought we might try our hand at becoming 46R's. 46R's are that exclusive group of people who have hiked all 46 of the Adirondack peaks over 4,000 feet."

"Yes, vaguely." He yawns.

"Well, I stopped at the bookstores in Old Forge and Inlet, had a lovely visit with the owners. They were extremely helpful in recommending books to get us on track for our 46R quest."

"Imagine that," he teases. "A book store that sells books to people, what a novel idea."

I give him a withering look and pause, struck by a new thought. Wagging a finger up and down in the air, I continue, "You know I might need to visit the stores in Lake Placid and Lake George and see what hiking books they carry. One can't be too prepared."

"Oh boy," he murmurs, closing his eyes, he grumbles. "I'm exhausted already."

"Oh, Vic, sweetheart, I'm so sorry. You're not feeling well and I'm babbling on and on about hiking. We need to get you out of this hot car and into the house." I'm ashamed of my callous behavior. He is so ill he can barely stand up and I'm prattling on about hiking up some stupid mountains. "You are too ill to even consider such a silly idea. I'll take the books back to the stores. It's no big deal, really. The main concern is getting you healthy again."

"I wouldn't discount the hiking idea immediately." Vic smiles. He tips his head in my direction, giving me the old squint eye. "I agree with you, taking a few hikes may be fun and challenging, maybe not all 46 of them. We can start slowly. I'm sure I'll be back on my feet in no time and we can start with some moderate climbs."

Yes! A thrill of excitement courses through me, I love a challenge. Shifting in the seat I give him a quick peck on the cheek, pausing to run my hand over the smooth curve of his forehead and gaze lovingly into his eyes. "I'm so glad you are home. I can't tell you how much I missed you. I'm lonely when you are gone."

"Me too, Mia." He draws me into an awkward embrace, hampered by the armrest. His voice low and raspy in his throat as he whispers in my ear, "In fact, if I were you, I'd start resting…I have plans." His finger trails enticingly down my neck to skim with a feather light touch at the crest of my cleavage sending a shiver south that shocks me with its intensity and a moan escapes my lips. *Oh my*…it has been awhile.

"Okay, hombre, I think we better get you in the house and start the healing process before I hop over this armrest and put on a show that will make the wildlife blush."

"I hate to take a rain check on that promise." He opens the door and swings his long legs to the ground. "Here I'll help you carry the groceries into the house."

"Absolutely not." I protest. "Lani and I spent way too much time planning her wedding and not enough time exercising. By the way, are you hungry?"

"No, I ate on the plane from Chicago. I'm just tired."

"Why don't you take a shower, the new hot water tank takes only minutes to heat up, and then rest before dinner. Adele gave the house a thorough cleaning and changed the sheets on the beds before she closed last fall. I'll unpack the perishables and join you for a nap. I didn't get much sleep the last few nights with traveling from California."

Vic yawns, and smiles weakly. His skin is pale yellow-gray covered with a thin veil of perspiration. He grimaces a little as he turns toward the house the dark circles under his eyes look like faint bruises.

I hate to admit it but I can't ever remember him looking this bad. He looks good...always. Whether he is wearing sweats or decked out in well-polished Ferragamos, dress pants, a custom-made linen shirt under a well-tailored black blazer. I can never decide whether I like him best in a tuxedo...or nothing at all. Vic always looks good. But not today, I blink my eyes rapidly to stop the tears threatening to fall. An insidious fear worms its way into my heart...what if he doesn't get better? I lost him once, how can I bear to lose him again?

~~~

Vic

Vic closes the bathroom door and leans heavily against it. He steps over to look in the mirror and cringes. He runs a hand over his face, shocked at how the illness and weight loss has aged him. Wow, he doesn't look like a Hollywood box office leading actor now. He leans in and traces the lines on his face. At this rate he won't have to worry about leaving home, he'll never get hired again. Maybe as someone's aging father but never as a leading man in an action film.

All he could think about the past few months was getting home to Elle, and now so exhausted, he can't even summons the energy to make love to her. What kind of husband is he? The sorted business with Vivian Gust didn't help. He tried to discourage her attention but the woman was relentless, clinging to him, on and off camera, showing up at his room all hours of the day and night. She has a reputation for falling in love with her leading men. The last thing he wanted was an affair with that nut job. She is beautiful, but he recognizes her type: vain, ambitious to a fault, only out to further her own desires and career. For him, a quiet summer in the mountains with Elle and his family, maybe his daughter, Hanna, can come back east. No grand adventures, just rest and relaxation, that's all he wants. With a weary sigh he slides down to the floor, unable to stay on his feet any longer. He folds his arms across his knees and lays his head to rest. He can't remember ever feeling so ill in his entire life.

He tries to straighten up but only manages to lean his head against the doorframe. He winces, groaning to himself, "God, I feel like crap. When the hell am I going to get better?" Vic glances up hearing Elle downstairs, opening and closing doors as she carries in supplies from the car. He feels terrible deceiving her but he can't bear the thought of her worrying over him. No doubt she is suspicious, he thinks, but he can't let her know the extent of his illness. With a sigh he heaves himself off the floor hoping a shower will restore his flagging strength.

The woman who walks alone will likely find herself in places no one has been before…

I mount the stone steps to the entrance portico, a large porch-like structure supported by huge log beams. Entering the security code for the front door I step in at the *beep*, snapping on the bank of lights. Quickly scanning the room I take in the wide-planked floorboards, antique rugs and fireplace of rough-hewn stone. A grand staircase fashioned of bent twigs leads to the bedrooms above. I can't help but smile in pleasure at the sight of our beautiful mountain home. I've always found the lodge comfortably warm both in temperature and atmosphere.

After rummaging through our luggage I trade in my heels for sneakers and seven trips later, back and forth to the house, up and down the stairs, I've had enough of a workout. On the final trip I slam the SUV hatchback shut and notice a piece of yarn trailing out of the passenger rear door. What the heck? The line of yarn rolls down the road as far as the eye can see. Has that yarn been trailing the car since the airport? Most likely it fell out when I got out of the car at the gate. *Hmmm…*I pick up the end of the yarn wedged around the seatbelt and recognize it as a very expensive skein purchased in California. I had rolled it into a large ball and was planning to knit a shawl. I don't have the energy to solve this mystery at the moment. Stooping down, I find a rock, brush away the dirt and tuck the piece of yarn into a crevice, promising to come back and follow to the end some other day.

Staggering under the weight of the last two bags, I force the screen door open using my pinkie finger and plunk the groceries on the cupboard. Not wanting to waste time, I work quickly and efficiently putting the perishable food away. My gaze strays over to the sliding glass door leading out onto the patio and I spy a family of ducks nonchalantly floating by the boathouse dock. The temperature is warm for a day in mid-May and the breeze wafting through the open door is gentle on my bare arms.

All and all, the house is in good shape considering no one has been in it since January. Inside, every room glows with a greenish summer light pooling from a bank of windows that form a wall of glass facing the lake. French doors open onto a broad stone veranda and a terraced rock garden borders the gravel path to the water.

The focal point of the house is the large living room with its two-story fieldstone fireplace. The ceiling gleams under a wooden dome of pine planking intersected by log rafters. The furniture is large and cushiony, the colors leaning toward earth tones, with accents of yellow and red. The walls are decorated with antique pictures of Adirondack Camps in the 1890's, snowshoes, paddles and even a mounted deer head that came with the house. Color infuses the room from the rich jewel tones of oriental rugs scattered across the polished hardwood floors. The finishing touch; blankets so thick and luxurious, it is a little bit of heaven to curl up under them on a chilly night.

The only problem I can find with the house is a strange hole in the pantry floor. Unfortunately, the pantry light burned out over the winter so I'm not able to thoroughly inspect the damage. It looks like something has clawed its' way through the floorboards from the crawl space below, most likely a raccoon. A few of the food cans left on the shelf are dented and some appear missing. Sticking my head in the small closet, I wrinkle my nose in distaste, there is some funky smell coming up from that crawl space. With a shudder, I slam the door shut, making sure the latch is secure and mentally put the job on Weasel's to-do list. Tomorrow is another day.

Satisfied with my progress for the moment, I place the rotisserie chicken on the countertop along with a carton of prepared potato salad, a bag of salad greens and a bottle of chardonnay. This is the perfect menu for a casual welcome home dinner. Oh, I almost forgot, I reach into one of the bags and take out the chocolate layer cake, Vic's favorite dessert. It is so lovely I leave it on the countertop to admire. I may not be able to bake a cake, but I sure know how to buy one.

The German cuckoo clock in the foyer chimes three o'clock reminding me there is just enough time for a shower and quick nap. Josh, Claire and the children are due to arrive around six o'clock with Cyrus. I can't wait to see them. I must admit; I don't sleep as well at night without Cyrus curled up at my feet. I'm excited; tonight I will have both of my boys back in bed with me. Cheered by the thought, I charge up the polished staircase, eager for a hot shower. The last flight leads up to our bedroom on the third floor. It is an enormous room covering the length and width of the house built with vaulted beam ceilings, a stone fireplace, floors of gleaming old heartwood pine. Best of all, windows everywhere, perfect lighting for Vic to prop his easels and paint whenever the whim comes upon him.

Not wanting to wake Vic, I use the small guest bathroom at the far end of the house. After a hot shower I feel relaxed and refreshed. I creep quietly into our bedroom wrapped in only a towel planning to slip into bed next to Vic. Until his health improves, at least I can spoon with him, preferably naked. Just the thought of his warm skin against mine sets my body aglow.

At the bedroom door, I can see out the balcony window straight through the trees and the lake comes into view, glittering in the afternoon sun. Stopping for a moment, I pause and study my sleeping husband, his face thinner now, bordering on careworn. A light breeze ruffles the thin curtains and a dog's bark echoes in the quiet from somewhere down the lake. A low humming comes from the grass as the orchestra of insects tune up for the evening chorus.

Leaning against the door jam, I smile, lost in quiet thought. I know looks are fleeting but even as he ages, Vic is perfect, at least for me. It has been more than thirty years since we first met as teenagers, yet his physical beauty slices through me. Approaching fifty, his body remains firm and muscular; the wide shoulders splayed across the sheets take up half the bed with just the tantalizing crest of his butt teasing from underneath the tousled blanket. The raven dark hair skims his shoulders, still thick and luxurious, only slightly threaded with grey. My hands ache to get lost in its glossy locks. The spider web of smile lines radiating from the corners of his dark brown eyes are relaxed, the tension of his illness eased in sleep. Vic has that indefinable something that lights up a room when he enters, those gypsy eyes command attention and set every woman's heart aflame. He possesses a rare spark of charisma that only becomes magnified by the lens of a camera.

I wrinkle my nose. *Phew!* What is that smell? It's the same funky odor that was coming from the pantry downstairs. It's up here too. Has that nasty smell permeated all through the house? Taking a firm grasp of my bath towel, still damp from the shower, I bend over and start sniffing the room, investigating the source of the smell. Suddenly, a pair of brown eyes pop up from the other side of the bed, followed by a second set of eyes and two wiggling bodies of fur.

My limbs turn to water and all the breath leaves my lungs in a whoosh of panic. Oh, no, oh no. No! No! My vocal cords are paralyzed by fear. I can't speak. It's a miracle I don't start screaming at the top of my lungs. For lying on the bed next to my sleeping husband, who is terrified of bears…are two bear cubs rolling and tumbling around on top of the bedspread.

Without taking my eyes off the cubs, I gasp out in a raspy voice, "Vic, Vic, wake up. Sweetheart, you have to wake up now." If he sees those bears he will die of a heart attack on the spot. I have to get him out of the bedroom before he notices the two twin balls of fur. They are so adorable, but I'm afraid mama bear will not be pleased to see her cubs in bed with my husband. Walking on tiptoes, I creep over and shake Vic by the shoulders, trying to convey a sense of urgency without throwing him into a panic. Any nature loving person will tell you, if there are baby bears…that means mama bear is not far away. And on cue, I hear a bellowing coming from somewhere down on the main floor of the house. My blood runs cold and I give silent thanks for having the foresight to lock the pantry door. Hopefully, it gives us time to make an escape. Fear overwhelms me and I pull Vic from the bed by his feet, he tumbles onto the floor half asleep.

"Elle, what the hell are you doing!"

"Vic, get up!" With no time to be coy, I scream into his face. "We have to get out of here, there are bears in bed with you."

"What the f…? Are you crazy?" Vic leaps up and trips, his feet tangled in the sheets, his eyeballs almost pop out of his head when he sees the two cubs. The bears stop their personal rumbas on our bed to watch the antics of the two humans rolling around the floor half-naked, yelling and screaming. One cub sits back on its haunches and cries out in response to the bellowing of the mother bear below. The sound of splintering wood can be heard coming from the kitchen.

"Hurry Vic, we have to get out of the house. That's the mother downstairs trying to get in through a hole in the pantry floor."

The mama bear's roars echo through the house. Vic turns white, grabs my hand and we streak down the stairs, skidding on the hardwood floor as we round the corner to the door.

"Wait," I gasp pulling my hand out of his grasp. I sprint over and grab my cell phone off the table next to the door just as the sound of breaking wood reverberates in a sharp crack and snap. I look into the kitchen just as the head of the enraged mother bear emerges from the debris of my pantry door.

"Run!" I scream and slam the front door shut hoping to corral the baby cubs that started down the stairs after us. I pray the mother reunites happily with her babies before she decides to eat us first and ask questions later.

"Quick, into the car." Vic yells yanking open the SUV door while making shooing motions with his hands. I dive in the passenger seat and he rolls into the driver's side. We slam the door shut and sit there gasping for breath, as panic and adrenalin race through our veins.

"Oh my God, oh my God! How the hell did a bear family get in our house?" He asks.

"I think they came in through the pantry floor last winter." I finally manage enough air into my lungs to eke out. "I noticed the hole when I was putting away the groceries, but I never imagined a bear made it. I thought a raccoon had worked its way into the pantry after the canned goods. The hole wasn't very big."

"Very big?" Vic asks, his voice incredulous. "Did you see the size of that mother bear? She was huge. It's probably the same beast that chased us off our dock last summer."

"I think the cubs got in through the hole, got trapped in the house and the mother came looking for them and must have clawed her way in."

"And for this I'm so glad I'm married to a naturalist." He says his voice tinged with sarcasm.

"Hey, I got you out, didn't I?"

"Yes, you did, Buttercup. For that I'm grateful."

We lean our heads against the headrest and listen to the mother bear's roars still coming from within the house.

"Sounds like she's giving those cubs a scolding."

"No, it sounds like she wants out." Vic flinches. "We locked the door, so now they are trapped in our house."

"Well, I didn't want the cubs chasing us with the mother following. I thought slamming the door would give us a few extra seconds to make our escape."

"I hear you, it was a good idea. But now what do we do?" We look at each other and realize we are in a rather precarious situation. I'm naked with a towel and he is bare-chested wearing nothing but boxer shorts. The keys to the vehicle are in the house with the bears. I cleaned everything out of the car, so there is not even a blanket or a stich of food. And did I mention I locked the bears in my house. Someone has to let them out, preferably… not me.

Vic closes his eyes and suggests in a monotone voice that he has an idea he knows will not make me happy. "You have your cell phone?"

"Yes," I hold the phone up proudly. "I did have the presence of mind to grab it, a holdover from when I got locked out of the house two years ago."

"Guess what you are going to do with that cell phone?"

"What?" I ask, dreading the tone in his voice and knowing what he is going to suggest. "I'm not doing it." I insist.

"You don't know what I'm going to suggest."

"Oh yes, I do. You call."

"Why? You have a close relationship with them. Aren't they your, how do you call them, BCFFs, best cop friends forever?"

I groan inwardly. "Yes, but there is no way in hell I'm going to sit here wearing only a towel and call the Old Forge Police Department to rescue me, again."

"It's not like they haven't seen you naked wearing only a towel before." He closes his eyes and making a sucking sound with his tongue against his teeth. He leans forward and gives me a piercing glance. "Maybe you'll get lucky and your favorite BCFFs will be on duty tonight."

I groan and mutter, "I'd rather break in a new set of cops. Frank and Brian have had way too much fun at my expense."

"Oh yeah. They love you." Vic says with glee.

"Very funny."

"Well, it actually is but…" Vic says with the air of a long suffering husband or an exhausted one. "We don't have a lot of options. We are sitting in a car with no keys, no food or clothing. The sun will be setting soon and the temperature will drop. I have a fever and I'm not feeling very well. *And* did I mention we have three bears in our house we need to get out. Are you going to open the door and have an enraged mother bear come charging out at you?"

"No," I squeak in a quiet mouse-like voice.

"Well, neither am I." He closes the argument with a determined statement. "There are people who do this kind of thing for a living. So we need to call 911 and ask the police to bring a conservation officer with them."

I screw my lips up into a pout.

"Make sure you are specific, not one bear in the house, but three bears, a mama and two cubs."

I grumble, "Should have left the stupid phone on the table."

"Ellen." Vic admonishes. "We have to get the bears out before Josh and his family arrive."

"Okay, okay, okay. I'll call." I pick up the phone and hope the battery is dead or maybe we're out of cell range. But spending the night freezing in a car with no food while a trio of bears ransacks my house is not a better option. Swallowing my humiliation, I press the keypad on the phone. There is no need to call 911. I know the number to the police station by heart.

The station answers on the third ring and I recognize the voice, Officer Brian Domler, one of my BCFFs. "Old Forge Police Department, Officer Domler speaking. How can I help you?"

"Officer Brian, (we're on a first name basis.) Umm, this is Ellen O'Connor Rienz, up at Camp Sky Haven."

"Ellen!" he interrupts. "How good to hear from you. Welcome back to the mountains. How was your winter?"

"It was good." I hesitate, not knowing how to launch into my saga. Vic raises an eyebrow in impatience, and makes a circling motion with his finger, encouraging me to speed things up.

"We're good, happy to be back." I continue. "Vic is here with me and we can't wait to see everyone." Vic groans and leans back in the seat closing his eyes in resignation. "But you see…well…we have a little situation going on at Camp."

"Oh, what's up?" Officer Brian asks.

"Umm…well, we have three bears in our house."

"Seriously?" He barks out a laugh.

"Yes, a mama and two first year cubs. They came in through a hole in the pantry floor and chased us out. At the moment we are sitting in our car but we don't have the keys to the car. And we can't go back into the house because the bears are in there."

"Really," Brian's voice rises in complete and utter glee. "Hey, Frank, get over here. Ellen Rienz is back and you'll never guess what? She has three bears in her house." I can hear Officer Frank in the background, "No shit, you're kidding me?"

"Three bears, I did hear you correctly, Miss Ellen? Got in through a hole in the pantry?"

"Yes." I sigh. I don't know why they insist on calling me, Miss Ellen, makes me sounds like I'm their kindergarten teacher or some fussy old aunt. I stifle a groan of irritation. "Yes, the problem is I slammed the front door shut so they couldn't chase after us. The stupid doors on the house lock automatically and now the bears are locked in the house and we're stuck in the car and it's getting cold. And we're a little hungry." I finish lamely.

"Ask her what she's wearing?" Officer Frank has moved

closer to the phone and now wants details.

"Franks wants to know…" Brian starts to ask then thinks better of it. "I can't ask her that, are you crazy?"

I blow out of sigh of mortification. "Listen, I just got out of the shower and Vic was asleep when I saw the bears…so we're a bit *disheveled*?"

"Ellen," Vic snaps. "They don't need the details of our wardrobe." He snatches the phone out of my hand only to hear Officer Frank chortle in delight, "She's only wearing a towel. Tell her we're on our way!"

"Gentlemen, excuse me for interrupting your mental image of my wife…"

"Oh, sorry, Mr. Rienz." Officer Brian Domler is suddenly all business. "We will contact a conservation officer to meet us at your residence. In the meantime, please stay your vehicle. We will be there shortly to assist the conservation officer in removing the bears from your house."

"Thank you. The gate code is 1748." Vic responds sweetly, giving me a smug look, as if to say this is how it's done.

I lean over Vic and yell into the phone. "Don't use sirens. I don't want to scare the bears!" I bite my lower lip and run my hand up and down Vic's arm in apology. "Welcome home, I think, sorry."

"It's not your fault. Buttercup, with you, it's always an adventure."

"Do you want my towel? You're shivering."

"No, but why don't you climb over here and cuddle in my lap until the police arrive. We might as well get comfortable and share our body heat."

Into the forest I go…to lose my mind and find my soul.

Twenty minutes later, I hear the sirens off in the distance, and raise my eyes to the heaven. Oh holy hell, nothing like a grand entrance.

The squad car roars down the driveway and comes to a stop with a flourish of sliding tires and flying gravel. Right behind the police is the conservation officer who repeats the high-speed performance.

"Show offs," Vic mutters under his breath.

"Come on, let's see if we can help them get the bears out of our house." I clutch the towel tighter as I untangle myself from his long arms and legs. We sat barely clothed in a confined space with total body contact for over twenty minutes and he didn't try to get fresh, not even once. Boy, he is sick!

My eyes widen in horror as the law enforcement officers leap from their vehicles and pull out high power rifles.

"No…!" I scream in alarm, jumping out of the car. "Don't shoot them, please!"

"Ellen, are you and Mr. Rienz all right?" Officer Frank asks, his eyes scanning the house and surrounding grounds.

"Yes, we're fine." Vic responds. "Just cold and a bit shaken up after being run out of our house by three bears."

"Here, take this." Officer Brian hands Vic a duty jacket and shakes out a large woolen blanket for me. "We keep one on hand for you, Miss Ellen. Next time, we'll have it embroidered with your initials." He chuckles at his little joke.

I smile weakly and thank him for the loan of the blanket.

The conservation officer steps forward and offers his hand to Vic. "I'm Henry Humboldt, Mr. and Mrs. Rienz. I'm the local DEC conservation officer stationed in the township of Webb. I'm in charge of handling interactions between humans and wildlife in the local area." He scratches his head and thinks for a moment, "Well, I guess I'm the head of the wildlife situations but technically my boss at the Ray Brook office is chief of the total operation. But on the scene, I make all the decisions." He sees the confusion on my face and pauses, "Sorry about that, I sometimes go off on tangents. My wife reminds me to stay focused on one topic at a time. She is a great gal, and speaking of bears, you should taste her blueberry cobbler, boy, oh boy is that delicious. I was on my way home for dinner when I got the call to come out here. Sure hope we aren't having blueberry cobbler for dessert. Guess it's early for blueberries anyway. The bears sure do love them."

I hear the Old Forge Police Officers snicker in the background.

Vic interrupts, "Sorry about the inconvenience, Officer Humboldt, but we have a situation that requires your expertise. I'm sure your wife will keep your dinner waiting."

"Oh, I don't know about that. She hates to disrupt the children's routine, if they don't eat dinner on time it throws off their schedule. Then we have the darnest time getting them to sleep. Gosh, raising kids is tough these days. Back when I was a kid, well, if my old man…"

"Henry!" Officer Brian chimes in, "The bears. We have to take care of the bears."

"Yes, please don't shoot them." I plead. "It was our fault; somehow there was a hole in the pantry."

"Now, Elle," Vic protests. "It's not our fault the bears are in the house, well, maybe it's our fault, but not intentionally. You might say it was an accident, well, not exactly an accident. What the hell, now he has me talking like him!" Vic exclaims pointing to Officer Humboldt, "Holy hell!"

"Now in my experience, this is no one's fault unless you left food in the house over the winter months." Officer Humboldt says. "Now that's another story. Well, never, or almost never leave food in an unoccupied house. Those bears can smell food miles away."

Vic gives me a wry look and mumbles. "Some naturalist I married."

"It's not my fault. Weasel said it was okay to leave canned goods." I disagree and sneeze. The wool blanket makes me itch; I think I'm allergic.

"It's not necessary to quarrel." Humboldt advises.

"We're not quarrelling!" Vic and I turn on him, protesting in unison.

Out of the corner of my eye, I see the police officers give each other the high five. Officer Frank averts his eyes off the overflowing cleavage threatening to exceed the limits of my toga wrapped towel. "Man, I am so glad I was on duty tonight." He says looking way too happy for my comfort.

"Me too." Brian responds with a big grin.

Officer Humboldt scratches his head and blows out a sigh. "Here's the story, we don't want to go in and start shooting up the place, makes a terrible mess, gets all the animal rights activists up in arms…"

I squeak in protest, Vic squeezes my arms to hush me. "No, that would be a bad idea." Vic agrees, trying to lead the man toward a more harmonious solution.

Humboldt walks over and opens the back hatch of his vehicle taking out a long rectangular bag and extracts a rifle. "Now, this little number should do the job, well, not do the job. I'll have to shoot the rifle, unless someone else wants to shoot the gun." He scratches his head. "But that wouldn't work, as I'm the DEC officer on the scene. So, I guess I'll take care of the situation."

"What are you doing?' I ask, panic rising in my chest as he loads a cartridge into the gun.

"I'm going to march up to your front door, swing the door open and, hopefully, the mama bear will waltz out and lead her cubs back into the woods. If she comes out nasty, I'll have to tranquilize her with this dart gun and remove the entire family to a new location. That could take all night and I'll never get my dinner. Well, maybe not never, but it will probably end up being breakfast by the time I get home."

While the law enforcement officers confer on how best to stake out the house, a forest green Subaru comes around the curve of the driveway stopping next to our assembled group.

Josh, Claire, and the children. I had forgotten about them. They were invited to dinner and bringing Cyrus home.

As the car stops, the expression on their faces turns from pleasant anticipation to complete bewilderment. No one moves for several seconds, they take in the image of Vic and I standing in the driveway surrounded by police vehicles, shivering, half naked, dressed in clothing handed out by the police officers. And the mama bear continues to bellow her rage from inside the house.

"Mom, Dad?" Josh opens the car door, putting one leg on the gravel driveway while keeping the other in the car, not sure if he should get out or not. With his free hand he motions his family to say put until he figures out what his parents have gotten themselves into this time. We have a good relationship with Josh, our recently reunited long lost son from our teenage years. But relationships and trust take years to foster, so our family bond is still on somewhat tenuous ground.

I see his wife, Claire peer through the windshield of the car craning her head to get a better view; she looks at Vic and I, scanning her eyes up and down. Only Vic could look good in a pair of boxer shorts and police duty jacket. Me, on the other hand, wrapped in a wool blanket, I look like a Yoda character from Star Wars. They are never going to leave those grandchildren alone with us. We were going for the cute and quirky grandparent image...but have ended up with enough collateral damage to label us as strange and untrustworthy. *Damn...*

"Josh," Vic turns to his son. "Keep everyone in the car. We have a bear with cubs trapped in the house."

"Seriously?" Josh asks, his face incredulous. "You have a mother bear and her cubs in the house?" And he starts laughing, a deep belly laugh, soon gasping for air as the tears stream down his face. "You! Bears in the house."

"Josh!" Claire admonishes, but her face turns pink and a

giggle escapes. "You really have bears in there?" She asks in disbelief. "Oh, my goodness."

"A bear!" Ansel yells from the backseat, "Papa Vic, you have a bear in the house! Cool!" He starts climbing out of his car seat. "Let me out. I want to go see the bears."

"Me too, me too." Izzy begs, unbuckling her seat belt trying to wiggle passed Cyrus who is barking and clawing at the window in his excitement to see us.

"Whoa." Josh admonishes. "Everybody freeze, no one is going anywhere until the bears are gone."

"Daddy, Papa Vic needs my help! You know he's afraid of bears." Ansel cries. "Who is going to save him?"

Vic pokes his head in the window of the Subaru and gives Ansel a high five. "Thanks little buddy, but I think the policemen have the situation under control. They have a tranquilizer gun. If necessary, they will give the bears a shot in the butt and put them to sleep. Then they take them someplace where they will be safe. We just need to be patient."

"Aww…" Ansel pouts as only a four year old can, the long drawn out face, complete with sad eyes.

"All right, everyone but the law enforcement officers, I want in the cars with the doors locked." Officer Frank commands.

By this time Officer Humboldt is creeping up the path that leads to the front door. The Old Forge Police officers standing at point with their rifles trained on the door. As Humboldt hedges closer to the door, he raises the tranquilizer rifle to the stand ready position in the crook of his arm. The house is quiet. The mama bear has probably found the cubs and the entire family is stretched out on my couch eating the rotisserie chicken I left sitting on the kitchen cupboard.

In a blur of movement, Humboldt dashes for the door, grabs the doorknob and it's locked. He turns to us with an incredulous look on his face and yells, "Who's the idiot who locked the door?"

All heads turn to me.

"I didn't lock it." I protest. "You know that stupid alarm goes off and locks everything automatically. I just pulled the door shut."

"Here." Vic tosses the jacket at the police officers and sprints up the path in his boxers, the ones with little red hearts and 'I love you's plastered all over his butt. I thought they would make a cute Valentine's Day gift, not exactly bear chasing attire.

"Vic, be careful." I cry, watching as he reaches the keypad and enters the code. Humboldt swings the door open and both men streak down to the safety of the cars lining the driveway.

After a few minutes the mama bear comes to the entrance way, sniffs the air, looks back and grunts to her cubs. In mass, they shamble across the porch, down the steps and into the woods without a backward glance. Appearing, dare I say it, almost bored? Sure enough, as I look closely at the cubs I see one of the little stinkers has my bra trailing off its hind leg and the other is carrying the matching panties in its' mouth. They were in a bag Vic carried up to the bedroom. I bought them in California, expensive honeymoon quality lingerie, now off to be trampled into the duff of the forest floor.

As a group we watch the mama bear's large backside sway as she walks away, calmly down the path, the distance stretching...fifty yards... a hundred and then they are gone. We stand in silence, the only sound, a melodic hermit thrush calling from high up in the trees.

"Well, then." Vic says. He squeezes my arm and points to the open door, there strewn across my beautiful hardwood floors is the litter of take-out containers and the package that held my beautiful chocolate cake.

"It could be worse." He says.

I shrug. "I guess."

"Wow…" I hear Josh exclaim.

"Big bear." Officer Frank says.

"Good size cubs too." Agrees Officer Brian.

"Well, I don't know if I'd say they were good sized maybe just average." Argues Officer Humboldt.

"I'm hungry!" Ansel complains from the back seat of the car. "The bears are gone. Can we have dinner?"

I do a quick assessment of the damage done to my house and see eight hopeful faces looking at me. I wonder if the local pizzeria delivers this far outside of town. Something tells me, dinner is on me tonight…I better have a large tip for the delivery person. They look hungry.

"Ella-ma, why are you wearing just a towel? Did you lose your underpants?" Izzy asks.

My cheeks burn with chagrin, "Yes, Izzy. I guess you could say I lost my underpants."

"What happened to Papa Vic's pants?" Ansel asks.

Oh boy…

Sometimes you just need an adventure to cleanse the bitter taste of life from your soul.

Two days later, before the blush of sunrise has dried the sparkling morning dew, I hear frantic pounding coming from the front door. Someone below is calling our names. *Who? What? You've got to be kidding me!*

I kick and claw my way out of the strangle hold of bedcovers. Nights in the mountains are still cold. Rather than turn on the furnace, Vic and I choose to snuggle into the mountain of comforters covering our bed. And quite frankly spooning is the closest thing I'm getting to sex.

"Who is rude enough to come knocking on my door this early in the morning?" I grumble.

Once free of the last down duvet, I stumble toward the door...and recognize the high-pitched voice bellowing from down below.

Adele?

Why is she here today? She and Weasel are not due back from Florida for another three days?

"Mrs. Rienz, Mr. Rienz. Wake up!" The cry so strident it hurts my ears even through closed windows.

"Elle, who the hell is screaming out there?" Vic's tousled head pokes out from underneath a quilt. I plant a quick kiss on his forehead. "Just stay put. It sounds like Adele."

He groans and falls back on the bed. "Adele? Now? What is she doing here? I don't have the strength to handle Adele before coffee. I'm weak. I'm feeble. I thought they were coming on

Friday. It's not Friday, is it?" His grumbling fades as I skate across the shiny hardwood floor.

"Coming." I call and fling open the French door that leads to the outside balcony.

"Adele, what a pleasant surprise. You're not supposed to be back for..." I stop on the threshold of the door, momentarily stunned at the sight below me. Now the sight of Vic in the morning is perfection. Especially when he brings me coffee wearing just jeans, bare foot, no shirt, his black hair gleaming, soft and curling around his ears. That little bit of morning stubble scratches my cheek as he plants a good morning kiss. That is the image that gets a girl up and running in the morning, not the one on my doorstep.

Adele, first thing in the morning is a sight to behold. While in Florida she decided to dye her hair red. Lucille Ball-red, styled in a short blunt cut held in place with copious quantities of mousse. Her head is crowned with little red flaming spikes. The Florida sun has turned her skin the color of burnt shoe leather. She's gained twenty pounds, her faded blue jeans are stretched to bursting at the seams and her midriff spills over the waistband held in check by the spandex top she is wearing. Her shirt reads, "Florida is for Lovers" with a picture of two alligators locked in a passionate embrace.

"Morning, Mrs. Rienz." Weasel standing beside her nods and touches his baseball cap as a sign of respect. He's lost weight and resembles a great blue heron. A beautiful wading bird with a stature of nothing but long legs and neck. Whatever weight Adele gained, Weasel lost.

Vic joins me on the deck, yawning, rubbing a hand across his jaw trying to wipe the sleepy look off his face. "Hey, Weasel. Good to see you." He croaks in a raspy morning voice. "How's it going?"

"Good, good." Weasel replies.

"Morning, Mr. Vic." Adele interrupts. "Sorry, to wake you but Weasel's cousin, Joey, called and told us about your bear problems. So we put the petal to the metal and hurried home. We were going to stop last night and have dinner at that Cracker Box restaurant. They have the best biscuits and gravy. I swear I'm going into that kitchen and refuse to leave until the cook gives me the recipe. But, I says to Weasel, 'we got to get home. Mr. and Mrs. Rienz need us. Them bears got in and probably destroyed the house. This is our fault for not being there to watch over things this winter'."

"No, no." Vic and I protest in unison. "It was just an unfortunate mishap."

"Look we're fine." I add to reassure her. "I almost have the house straightened out from the ordeal."

Vic points to the side of the house. "We'll probably need to get a contractor in to look at the basement crawl space." Vic suggests to Weasel.

"Got just the man for the job, Mr. Rienz." Weasel takes a toothpick out of his mouth and nods.

"Mr. Vic, what's happened to you? You look like death warmed over. Didn't they feed you on that movie shoot?" Adele demands. "Mrs. Rienz, are you starving this man?"

"No, he hasn't been home long enough…" I object. "But…"

My reply cut off as Adele continues her assault on Vic's lack of proper nutrition. "Let me into that kitchen. We'll find something in the freezer, throw it in the crockpot, add a little BBQ sauce and I'll have him fixed up in no time. Nothing a little barbeque can't cure. It's the spices in the sauce."

I see Vic wince and his face pales. Anything other than bland food sends his stomach into a cataclysmic uproar.

"And Mrs. Rienz, what in God's name are you wearing? No wonder the man looks ill." She plows on in her single person narrative. "Is that any kind of outfit to welcome your husband home after he's been gone, what is it six or seven months?"

"I…" And she cuts me off before I can explain.

"Why, when my Weasel takes off on a road trip somewhere and comes home. I greet him at the door, proper. Don't I, honeykins?" She tickles Weasel under the chin, he looks down and shuffles his feet as his face turns beet red. "I have a few outfits from that Fredrick's of Hollywood store that will make a man stand up straight. If you know what I mean."

Oh, dear God. I feel faint. Just the thought of Adele in one of those crotch-less see-through, tassel-tossing pieces of lingerie is enough to bring on mental trauma. Vic's face turns even whiter still and he sways on his feet.

"I'll call them up when I get home and have them send you a catalog. Maybe, we can order together and save on shipping."

"It's really not necessary." I croak thinking of the Belgium lace panties and bra purchased to welcome Vic home, crumpled, lost somewhere in the forest. There is no way in hell I'm telling Adele the only reason I'm wearing pajamas with dancing moose on them is because my husband is either too ill or not interested enough to initiate sex. He seems ill and distracted for some reason, I can't figure out. In the mean time, I'm dressing in my Adirondack pajamas so as not to tempt him, give him some space to recuperate.

"Come on down here and open the door, Mrs. Rienz. I'll put the coffee pot on while you and the Mister get yourselves dressed. I can see just from the garden alone, we have days of weeding and cleanup to do."

I hear Vic whisper beside me, "And *vamonos* we go."

~~~

Dressed in what I call my 'daisy duke's' outfit, a pair of cut-off jeans and an oversized flannel shirt tied at the waist, I'm ready for a day of work. By the time I walk into the kitchen, Adele has the coffee pot brewing, a pan of sausages sizzling on the stove and her whole body in motion as she whisks a bowl of eggs for an omelet.

After a breakfast fit for a lumberjack, Weasel, Adele and I attack the house and gardens, organizing Camp for the summer season.

It's mid-afternoon by the time I go searching for Vic. We sent him upstairs to rest after he attempted to paint the pantry and started shaking. He is so weak. I'm worried about his health. The stairs creak under my weight as I trot up to the third floor, peek into the bedroom and find it empty. No sign of him in the bathroom. *Gee, wonder where he could be,* I muse, then notice the door to his office/studio is closed. Maybe he is feeling well enough to work on one of his projects. That's a good sign. I swing open the door ready to express an enthusiastic greeting of wifely good cheer. But as I step into the room he swings around from the desk where he is working on the computer, a look of surprise crosses his face and his nostrils flare in annoyance.

"Ellen, what the hell?" Vic barks. "What are you doing barging in here?" He swivels his chair around to click off the computer and hastily shoves a stack of papers into the desk drawer. "Can't you see I have the door closed? That means I want privacy."

"I…I…" I'm flabbergasted. Vic has never spoken to me with such anger and impatience. "I thought I would check on you. See if you needed anything?"

"I'm fine." He snaps and the little lines of tension form commas around his mouth. "I'm not a two-year-old to be coddled and watched over every waking minute of the day."

"No…" I agree, almost speechless over his outburst. The world through my eyes stills, moving in slow motion segments, clip by clip, blurred yet sharp and brittle around the edges. Small insignificant details of the room come into focus as if turning the lens of a camera. Half completed paintings are propped on easels clustered near the windows, flowers on canvas soaked in oil paint turned toward the sun waiting for completion. The countertop of a sink tucked into a corner is littered with paintbrushes laid on towels to dry. A single blade of sunlight slices into the room, dust motes dance in the beam. The air coming through the open window is perfumed from the garden below, flowering crab apple, lilies of the valley, and dames rocket. At one end of the desk, Vic's photographs are sorted into various slots on a sectioned shelf for organization. The room is neat, orderly, walls and shelves filled with photos of family and friends caught in moments of rare candor beneath Vic's skillful eye with the camera lens.

"But…but." I stutter, at a loss as how to rebuke his uncharacteristic behavior. "I just wanted to see how you were feeling. I noticed that you were trembling when you tried to help Weasel this morning."

"I don't need to be reminded of my physical limitations." He almost snarls at me. "I thought you and Adele had so much work to do. You don't need to come snooping around, checking on me and my business."

"Vic!" I cry. "What's wrong? I wasn't spying on you. I'm just concerned."

"Well, a little less concern is needed." He turns back to the computer. "Now if you will excuse me, I have work to do." He hunches his shoulders over the computer screen, dismissing me.

I back out of the room and shut the door behind me. My breath coming in short panting sobs as I try to brush away the tears streaming down my face. *Oh, my God. Who was that in there?* My sweet kind Vic would never act this way. Maybe he has some terrible tropical disease, one of those parasites or horrible little worms that enters his brain and eats away at his personality.

What if it's more than his illness, what if he's lost interest in me? How can I forget the picture in that trashy tabloid newspaper? The woman embracing my husband, her body plastered against him as if staking a claim, taking ownership. What was her name? Vivian, something…let me think, Vivian Gust, that was it. She is tall, dark and voluptuous. And young. Everything I'm not…

My gut says this is more emotional than physical, his health appears improved, slowly in small increments. What has caused such a bizarre reaction from my husband? Where is my Vic?

~~~

Vic

"Oh, damn it. I've done it now." Vic says leaning his head against the computer screen.

"How could I treat Elle that way?" He heaves a deep guttural sigh and runs a hand over his unshaven face. He shakes his head in disgust. *What the hell is wrong with me, yelling and screaming like that?* He picks up a coffee cup and flings it at the wall. The heavy porcelain mug bounces off, unbroken, leaving behind spattered drops of coffee dripping down the wood paneling.

He gets up and crosses the room, locks the door then returns and opens the desk drawer. Inside are several pieces of paper with patches of words glued to the sheets. He takes the pages out and arranges them in order of arrival to the house. He leans back in the chair, thinking, digesting the evidence. This whole thing is making me crazy. He taps a finger on the desk, deep in thought. The pieces are cut from magazines, newspapers and advertisements. He holds a letter up to the light, trying to decipher the words that dangle and dance on the paper. The ominous message slithers into his brain and sends a chill down his spine. There is no rhyme or reason to the letters, written by a person with severe mental delusions, the intent is clear, someone means to harm them. When he received the first letter he dismissed it as a disgruntled fan. When the second one came he gave the letters to Ike for further investigation. Ike, his best friend for more years than he can count, acts as his personal confidant and wing-man, so to speak. Ike contacted the security firm hired to protect their privacy at Camp but there was little hard evidence to start an investigation. When the third letter arrived, Vic thought the fever and his illness were making him hallucinate. This can't be happening. Someone had broken through his carefully laid privacy wall.

Furious over the lack of progress and offhanded treatment of his family's welfare, he picks up his cell phone. Searching his contact list, he finds the number and places a call to New York City. When the secretary answers he asks to be transferred to the head of the security firm immediately. He refuses to be put on hold and wastes no time in giving the company's CEO a piece of his mind. "I pay a huge premium for your services and this is what I get. Threatening letters arriving at my personal address, in envelopes with the letterhead of our favorite resort in the Adirondacks. This twisted son of a bitch knows where we live and vacation? How did they gain access to my private information? I need answers and I need them now. What kind of company are you running?" All the pent up anger and frustration spill out of him, leaving Vic hoarse.

After a lengthy assurance that his file will be pulled and investigated fully, an appointment was made to meet with a specialist in New York City three days later. Vic hangs up the phone and cradles his head in his hands, discouraged. Who or what is behind these letters, he doesn't know but the taste of dread lies heavy in his mouth. He realizes he owes Elle an apology. But what excuse can he give for his outburst without telling the reason. For the time being, better to let her place the blame on his illness.

Some woman want diamonds, others just want a hammock, a campfire and some peace and quiet.

"He ain't coming down for dinner, Mrs. Rienz." Adele announces coming into the kitchen.

I'm standing at the island counter busy chopping vegetables for a salad. "Why not, he needs to eat? He's lost so much weight." Worry clings to my voice like static on a soft blanket after a dry winter's night. After my unpleasant encounter with Vic earlier this afternoon, I was grateful Adele suggested she and Weasel cook and stay for dinner.

"Says he is nauseous and has a headache." Adele leans over to open the oven, stirring the pot of simmering meat inside. "He has no appetite and just wants to go to bed early." The rest of her reply is lost to the depths of the oven. I hear something about how he will feel better tomorrow and not to worry. I look at the meal Adele has created and wonder if Vic's refusal has anything to do with the menu. While well meaning, Adele is convinced that a good BBQ dinner will fix any physical or mental ailment. I have my doubts; meat, potato salad, coleslaw and beans not a diet for a person recovering from a stomach malady. I'll pop upstairs later and ask if there is anything he needs. Although, maybe it's best I leave him alone. He made it perfectly clear he doesn't need my assistance.

It was almost ten o'clock before Adele and Weasel left, declaring Camp officially open for the summer. Their presence helped ease the tense atmosphere in the house. I felt badly that Vic did not join us for dinner; it was awkward without him.

After locking the house and setting the alarm system, I slipped quietly into our bed and lay rigid next to Vic, barely touching him. He was deep asleep long before I came into the room. I tried to sleep but couldn't, tossing and turning, thinking about his behavior. It was so uncharacteristic of him. Drifting on the hazy edge of restless slumber, my mind fixates on the image of him with Vivian Gus. Or worse, a fear lodges deep in my gut, could he be seriously ill?

Once the gray edges of dawn steal through the bedroom windows, I realize there was no point in trying to sleep any longer. I slip out of bed and pick up the clothes I hastily tossed on the floor last night. Vic, sound asleep, is lying on his back, one arm flung above his head; a lock of hair covers his eyes. I long to brush it away, but hesitate for fear of waking him.

Motioning for Cyrus to follow me, we creep down the stairs and head outdoors. I disarm the security system and slide the door open to a glorious morning. Stepping onto the deck, I take a deep breath stretching my arms over my head, reaching to the sky and exhale. I pick up Cyrus's leash and decide it's a beautiful morning for a walk.

A good walk will clear my head and help me decide how to broach the conversation with Vic about what's bothering him. I look around our Camp with wistful eyes. I traded in my old life to be with him, I left my job, my home and family. I've been happy almost ecstatic at times with that decision. A life without Vic is unimaginable to me. Where would I live? Could I go back to teaching? Move to California to be closer to my daughter? None of those options appeal to me. Starting over, alone, without Vic, sounds hollow, empty and terrifying.

Don't let your imagination run wild and for once don't overreact. I chide myself. Every marriage has its ups and downs. Turning up the collar of my jacket I whistle for Cyrus and head down the path away from the house.

Twigs crackle beneath my feet, and the trees reach out their branches giving me a poke to say hello, welcoming me back to the mountains. As I walk deep into the shadows, I'm reminded of my Grandmother pointing out the beauty of the forest. She'd stop and point out clusters of jack-in-the-pulpit, brown speckled toads sitting among a green carpet of ferns and colorful fingers of mushrooms poking their spongy fingers up through the damp earth.

Gran taught me to honor the woods, to enter its wonders with respect. She was firm in the belief that we were never to intrude or cause any harm, saying we were stewards of the earth and to mind our manners.

An ancient yellow birch, shaggy with long strips of peeling bark stands along the trail. I can hear Gran's words in my ears as if it were yesterday, "A powerful healing force lives deep within these woods. Whenever you are hurting or can't make sense of things, just come out here and spend some time with the trees. Give their trunks a good pat. When you go home, you'll feel better." I press the small of my hand against the tree, look up at the sunlight filtering through the leaves, and desperately want to believe her. I miss her so much; a day doesn't go by that I don't think of her. As I gaze into the dense forest, I say a small prayer to accept whatever might come my way. Life has a way of tricking us just when we think we know where we are going.

I give a tug on the leash, moving us along an overgrown path edging its way through the woods and into a meadow. The air is alive with chirping and chirring of the animals waking from the night.

A flutter of movement catches my attention and I stop, hushed in awe of a young buck. He's standing not more than twenty feet away, tawny brown, and the dew on his back glistens in the early morning sun. The buck stands motionless, his eyes fixed on me, regal and unafraid. He watches me carefully, flicking his tail, showing the white under part like waving a flag. He steps forward and almost in reach, he stops. Small velvet buds of new growth antlers protrude an inch or more from the top of his head. The wind has picked up, and with it comes the hum of the forest, the steady trickle of a stream, the strident call of an ovenbird, the rustle of dry leaves. I make exaggerated shoo-shoo motions with my hands thinking the deer will dash off on a dead bolt. But it doesn't. In fact, the young male hedges closer and extends his neck smelling the air to get a better lock on my scent. His deep brown eyes watch my every move. This is bizarre behavior from a wild animal. Generally, you don't see deer up close. The minute they get the scent of humans, they're gone. I'm so intent on the deer that when Cyrus barks and lunges at the leash, he tugs it out of my hand. He takes off at a dead run, but not at the deer, in the opposite direction…towards home.

"Cyrus!" I call at his departing back. "You traitor! How dare you leave me alone with this crazy deer?" The deer, sensing its advantage, continues to take slow, halting steps toward me. Curiosity, not fear, in his eyes. I place one foot behind the other and start backing away. He's following me. I don't know what to make of it. Is it sick with some disease, can deer be rabid, most mammals can carry rabies. Perhaps, he's grown accustomed to someone feeding him, thereby losing its fear of humans. Whatever the cause, this little buck is acting strange. When an animal acts abnormal, it's a warning sign to be cautious. As tempting as it is to reach out and touch his velvety muzzle, I need to be wary.

The more I back away the more the deer follows. He's starting to freak me out. I make more shoo-shoo motions with my hands and yell, "Go away!" but nothing deters him. The urge to turn and run is strong. But when stalked by a wild animal never run, it sets off their predator-prey instinct. But deer are not predators; the only prey a deer wants is grass. So what do I do, the former camp nature counselor but turn and run, full out run, crashing through the woods in a complete panic. After ten minutes I'm winded and the deer still close on my heels. Why is it chasing me?

I back into a tree; the buck lowers its head threatening to nudge me with its antler buds. For lack of a better option I grab one of the overhanging boughs and swing myself up. The deer comes up to the tree, sniffs the bark and begins nibbling, teasing off loose pieces. Bored, he drops his head to graze the tufts of grass growing around the tree.

"Okay," I mutter out loud. "Now what? I'm stuck in a tree with a rogue deer holding me hostage. My dog took off for home. I think I'm lost because nothing looks familiar. I broke the first rule of survival which is-never leave the trail." I blow out a sigh. The second rule of survival is to stay put when you realize you are lost. A check of my cell phone shows I have no service. So rescue options are limited. Anyway, a helicopter airlift out is too expensive and dangerous with all the trees. And there is no way I'm calling the Old Forge Police Department, a woman can only stand so much laughter at her expense. After yesterday's outburst I'm not calling Vic unless hell freezes over. So I might as well climb higher and enjoy the view. Wiggling into a better position on the perch, I glance around to see if another branch would be more comfortable. Maybe I could drop to the ground and fight my way out? It's a young deer, the antlers are small, how much harm can it cause me? Then I remember the stories of how dangerous moose are in Alaska. At this point I'd rather take my chances with the deer instead of Vic. I wrap my arms around the tree trunk, and listen to the sound of nature's orchestra. To my ears no symphony on earth sends out a more glorious song. The twitter of a wren, a squirrel foraging for food beneath the fallen leaves, the distant sound of a near by-stream. I decide to wait the deer out. The only problem, I'm starving. Back home, safe in the closet is my backpack, loaded with emergency supplies. I didn't think to grab it because I was going for a short walk. I didn't plan on getting lost in the woods. In my pack I have food and water, a compass, signal beacon and a host of other necessary items. Hell of a lot of good they do me now. I tug on my lower lip, trying to remember Burt's survival training advice when I hear a dog barking. Cyrus?

"Oh crap." I groan. Off in the distance I hear Vic frantically shouting my name, a death gong. I look down at the deer and tell him, "Now look what you've gone and done? I'm in big trouble." Before Vic and Cyrus break through the underbrush into the meadow, a small dog burst out of the woods from the opposite direction. The dog makes a beeline at the deer; on short stubby legs the dog circles the deer snapping at its heels, barking furiously. The dog's small tan body is a blur, dashing back and forth across the meadow, teeth bared, ears flattened. I've been rescued by a twenty-five pound Tasmanian whirlwind. The deer turns tail and bolts, bouncing across the meadow on legs made of springs, disappearing into a shadowed stand of trees.

I peer down wondering who is worse, the deer or a crazed

dog? My fear is put to rest as I watch the dog trot over to the base of the tree, sit down, its little stumpy tail a wiggling extension of his body. He looks up at me, his tongue hanging out the side of his mouth, panting heavily and he appears to be grinning. I think he is some kind of Corgi mix. One of those dogs the Queen of England is so fond of with his buff colored coat, one ear cocked up and the other ear folded over like a tulip bud.

"Whooo…." I hear Vic call and decide it's probably for the best to answer. I may need him to call off the dog.

"Whooo…" It's our communication call when we are out of eyesight of each other. It's easier to hear than yelling names.

Vic bursts into the clearing, yelling, "Ellen, Elle, where are you?" He stops and leans over placing his hands on his thighs, his chest heaving as he gasps for breath. His t-shirt is soaked with perspiration, hair disheveled sticking out in all directions. He presents an outlandish sight in his faded flannel bathrobe, sweatpants and moccasin slippers. He is fresh out of bed and angry. Maybe I'll stay up in this tree and pretend I didn't hear him. My feelings come in waves of panic. Unfortunately, the dog is barking under my hiding spot, doing a fine job of pointing out my location.

"Ellen!"

Vic stands under the tree, peering up into the foliage. "Elle, are you up there?" He shades his eyes with his hands. His voice harried with worry.

"Ellen? Answer me!" From my lofty perch I see he is furious and exhausted.

I manage to eke out a weak. "Yes."

"Where the hell have you been? I wake up to find you gone, no note or message. I thought someone kidnapped you again."

"Sorry?"

"Sorry my ass! What are you doing hiding in the tree?" He asks, shaking his head in exasperation. "Get down here!

"I'm not *really* hiding, just enjoying the view." He will never believe my story about the deer stalking me. I don't believe it and I was there.

"Elle, I'm sorry I yelled at you. Buttercup, please come

down. When I woke up and couldn't find you, I panicked. I almost called the police."

"Oh God, no!" I protest. One appearance on the Old Forge police scanner for the summer is enough.

"I didn't call them when I saw you had Cyrus with you. But when I found him on the trail, I thought something terrible happened to you." His voice has an uncharacteristic catch in it, like he was choking back a sob. Awww…the soft sensitive side of me that loves him so, wants to reassure him that I'm fine.

"Ellen, get out of that tree right now or so help me God, I will climb up there and drag you down. I am so mad at you I can hardly speak."

Whoa, not loving him so much right now. "I'm fine up here." I declare. "I'll meet you back home."

"Ellen O'Connor Rienz, I'm not leaving without you. Get down now!"

"Not if you're going to yell at me." I retort. "I couldn't sleep so I took a walk and I got lost."

"Ella, Ella, mia bella." He calls out the old familiar nickname from our days at camp. He croons in the sweet singsong voice he used to lure me out of my cabin on hot summer nights, usually to land me in all sorts of trouble.

"Do I have to climb that tree?" He starts toward the tree. "Are you stuck?"

"No, no, stop." I command, pointing a finger at him. "Don't you dare climb this tree! You're too weak."

"I'm feeling better. I'll show you how weak I am."

He wraps a long leg around a branch, hoisting himself up, grunting with the effort. "Shall I climb higher?"

"Fine, I'm coming down." As I pick my way down the branches, I see Cyrus and the strange little dog rolling and tumbling, chasing each other like old friends.

When I get to the last branch, Vic is standing on the ground, arms open ready to assist me.

"I'm perfectly capable of climbing down without your help."

"I know." He agrees. "I just need to hold you. What possessed you to take off this morning without telling me? And what are you doing up in a tree and by the way, who is the dog?"

I stall, refusing to leave the last branch.

"I'm sorry." He apologizes, motioning me to keep coming with his fingers. "I won't ask any questions."

"Promise you're not going to yell at me?"

"Me, yell? What would ever give you that idea?"

"Yesterday." I retort, swinging down from the branch to land on my feet. Immediately, Cyrus and his friend descend on me, a mass of wiggling, licking and barking joy.

After returning the dogs affection, I stand up, immediately engulfed into Vic's arms. He pulls me in tight and close, nearly strangling me. He tucks my head under his chin and I feel his body trembling. "You scared me." He says in a quiet voice. "Don't ever do that again."

"Vic, really I'm okay. I took a walk and a deer chased me up the tree."

"A deer. A deer chased you?" He cranes his neck looking around the meadow in disbelief.

"There was a deer standing here two minutes ago. Cyrus and I were walking along when I heard something behind me, I turn and there is a young buck following me. Because it was acting so strange, I panicked and tried to run away, only to get lost in the process."

"Really, a deer? How close did it get to you?"

"At first he was about twenty yards away, but when I stopped, he kept coming closer and closer. He was freaking me out so I made shoo-shoo noises."

Vic interrupts with a grin on his face. "How do you make shoo-shoo noises?" He teases coming closer, backing me up against the tree.

"You know." I flap my hands impatiently at him, "Shoo-shoo!"

"And that didn't scare it away?" He laughs. "Shocker."

"Very funny." I sniff at his sarcasm. The rough bark of the tree chafes my back, and the jagged edge of meadow grass tickles my ankles. With the sun warm on my face, all of my senses are heightened as Vic moves closer; the very air crackles with expectation.

"Is that some nature secret Burt taught you? Deer shooing,

like a deer whisperer." He asks, placing his hands on either side of my shoulders, effectively pinning me against the tree.

"No." I can't help but notice the warm flush rising to his cheeks, a crooked lopsided grin crinkles the corners of his mouth. He's in an amorous mood. But the most telling of all, his dark eyes, the amber flecks glow, forming a halo of light around the iris. He leans in and breathes on my neck. When he is warm, dark and smoldering like this, I'm reminded of temptation, like a vanilla ice cream sundae covered in dark, warm, gooey chocolate, add a drizzle of luscious caramel and topped with a dollop of whipped cream. You know you shouldn't, but there is no way you can resist. As a teenager, Vic was the oh-so-bad boy wrapped in frayed denim jeans and a leather jacket. He was unlike anyone I had ever met. More experienced and worldly, he lived between Mexico and New York City. I was an innocent, naive sophomore in high school from a small town. My life dictated by the harsh rules of my stepmother and a social life, rivaled only by the members of the chess club. I rarely engaged in normal teenage activities. Lonely and essentially neglected at home, with my father's lukewarm blessing, I defied Helen and accepted a job in the Adirondacks as a camp counselor. My life a clean slate, with little experience, nothing in my world prepared me for Vic. He crashed through my poorly fortified defenses and laid me open to a force of love I never knew existed. Meeting Vic was the worst and best thing to ever happen to me. He was my temptation, the Adam to my Eve's apple, the opiate of my soul. Even now, some thirty years later, I still can't get enough of him. He turns those gorgeous eyes on me, pulling me against the length of his six-foot three-inch body and my arms find home in the hollow of his broad shoulders and narrow waist.

"I thought you were mad at me?" I ask, trying to decipher his mood.

"I'm very, very angry at you…" Instead of admonishing me, the reprimand comes out as a purr.

"So mad I think I need to punish you. You've been a naughty girl." He stares at me for a long moment and with my eyes still open, his lips seduce mine. His mouth traces a heated trail along my jaw and feather light kisses along my neck sending ripples of pleasure to echo through my body. A shiver of sensation bounces through me, waves of desire suppressed for seven months burst forth and rob me of speech. The longing for him, held in check for so long, breaks through a dam of need. My heart thuds and then his weight is pressing on me, as he traps my head between his hands, and his mouth sinks down onto mine.

"Uhhhh-mmmm." My breath ends on a moan. I melt under him. Completely.

His mouth is amazing, drugging, warm and gentle; he hasn't lost his touch. His hand cups my jaw. His lips, his tongue and the smell of him form the perfect pleasure as he grinds his hips into my pelvis. Whatever inhibitions I harbor vanish on the morning air. I made a vow I was done with naked outdoor adventures; they never end well for me. But how can I deprive myself of this? His hand slides up and under my shirt, cupping my breast, teasing the nipple. My body opens like a ripe bud in springtime, I wrap my arms tighter around his neck and pull him closer heedless of the consequences. I run my fingers through the tangle of his thick, silky hair. I can't breathe, and I can't move. I'm pinned to a tree and he is kissing me like he is drowning. And I love every second of it. Our tongues tangle, and our breath mingles, our legs and arms intertwine, as we struggle to become one.

"What the hell!" Vic cries out.

Our mouths tear apart when the yapping of the stray dog turns into a rumbling growl. The little dog sinks his teeth into Vic's sweatpants, rears back on its hind legs, pulling Vic's pants down. The crack in Vic's butt appears and my lust-addled mind deciphers that he has no tan lines. His body, burnished an all over golden brown. Nude sunbathing on a remote island location and with whom, may I ask?

He removes his hand from my breast and I feel bereft from the loss of his touch. He points to the dog. "Who the hell or what the hell is that?"

I wheeze, trying to catch my breath, my mind fumbles. "*What...?*" I gasp. My brain momentarily dumbfound because all reason has fled to places south.

"The dog." Vic frowns, trying to pull his pant leg out of the dog's mouth.

"I don't know. He came out of the woods, started barking and chased the deer away. Now I think he is defending me from you."

"Of all the stupid…" Vic mutters hopping around, engaged in a tug of war with the dog. The dog's short legs pump furiously to hold his ground, refusing to let go, and just when Vic is stretched out, leaning back with all his weight, the dog releases his hold. Vic tumbles to the ground landing on his butt. "Ouch, damn it!" Vic fumes. "The little devil!"

The dog trots over to my side and sits down next to me, acting as my bodyguard, daring Vic to come closer. I squat down and ruffle his ears, "Its okay, buddy. He's really not all that bad." I look over at Vic rubbing his posterior with a disgruntled look on his face.

I burst out laughing. "Hey, Amigo, you okay?"

"Not funny."

"Actually, it is." I quip, holding my mirth in check, lest I sour his disposition further. "Let's see if we can find out who this little guy belongs to." I turn the dog's collar over and read the tag, Porky Pellinger. Just a name, there is no address or phone number or any way to contact someone who might be looking for him. Odd.

"Look." I point to the collar and show Vic. "There is no contact information. Why would you put the dog's name on it but no way of notifying the owners?"

Vic joins me and pets the dog whose butt wiggles in appreciation. "He does look thin, maybe he is lost. Do you recognize the name on the tag? Pellinger?"

"No, I can contact the local dog warden and see if anyone is missing a dog. He seems like a friendly guy." I give a sideways hopeful glance at Vic. "I hate to leave him in the woods alone. I think we should take him home with us." I hasten. "Just for the time being until we can find his owners."

Vic nods his head and agrees. "Actually it might be a good idea to have another dog around. This dog obviously has protective instincts. He hasn't left your side and seems attached to you." The dog licks my hand signaling his agreement with Vic.

Vic continues. "I didn't tell you but I have to leave for New

York City on Tuesday. It will only be for a couple of days. I have some business to clear up."

I'm momentarily shocked. "New York City?"

He ignores me. "I think having another dog around is a good idea. You try and find the owner but in the meantime he can help Cyrus guard the house."

Cyrus, hearing his name, flops down and rolls over on his back. All four legs sticking straight up in the air as he scratches in glee.

Anger and frustration choke out my response; it takes a few seconds before I find my voice. "When were you going to tell me about this trip? What kind of business?"

He runs a hand over his face and looks guilty. "It came up quickly. I won't be gone for long. Nothing to worry your pretty head about." He plants a kiss on my forehead and ruffles my hair as if appeasing a five-year-old. Vic whistles for the dogs. "Come on, boys, let's go home. I'm starving. All this traipsing around in the woods has worked up an appetite. Elle, what do we have in the house for breakfast?"

I scowl, and narrow my eyes. Worry my *pretty* little head, my ass. What is he up too? I fume inwardly. Abruptly taking off to New York City on mysterious business without any warning. All my senses are on high alert and warning bells go off. I notice his face has a flushed look to it, like his fever is back and there is a slight tremble in his hand. Is he ill or adulterous? Will he be alone in New York City or will a certain young starlet be with him? *Damn*…I'm back in suspicious wife mode, I swore I'd never put up with a philandering man again. And here I am, questioning the fidelity of my husband.

"And by the way," Vic tosses the words over his shoulder like careless confetti. "Ike will be coming to stay with you."

"Absolutely not! Since when do I need a babysitter?"

The best view comes after the hardest climb…

"Elle, he's here. I hear the motorcycle." Vic calls from the veranda.

True to Vic's promise, at half past ten on Tuesday morning, the rumble of a motorcycle echoes across the lake. Ike is here.

I've resigned myself to Ike's visit. Vic refused to disclose the details of his business trip, citing some studio conference regarding an up-coming movie. He spent most of the previous day locked in his office or resting. Vic has always been a private person, keeping his emotions to himself. I understand the quiet and private part of his personality, but he has never been moody. The emotional outbursts and locking himself away are not part of the man I know and love. I don't understand this new Vic and feel uncertain how to approach him. Rather than start an argument, I agreed to Ike staying with me. It gets lonely in the mountains. It might be fun to have Ike keep me company, even if it means watching a lot of baseball and putting up with him in the garage working on his motorcycles.

Reaching into the kitchen cupboard, I grab two mugs and pour the coffee, one for Ike and one for me. I'm confident he stopped at the donut stand down the road and picked up fresh donuts for us. It's tradition.

Ike pulls up to the portico entrance and cuts the engine as I push the front door open with my hip, releasing the dogs in a rush of excited anticipation. Cyrus recognizes Ike, runs around the motorcycle, yipping excitedly, his tail waggling like a flag in a holiday parade. Porky Pellinger goes into attack mode, snarling and growling at the bike's tires, returning to my side, forming a protective circle between the bike and me.

In the past few days I've contacted the local animal shelters, put advertisements in the newspapers and stapled pictures of Porky on telephone poles and community bulletin boards. Nothing. It appears the feisty little guy has been abandoned. It was our intent to return him to his rightful owner but in all honesty, we're relieved when no one claims him. Porky has slipped into our household and our hearts, forming a special attachment to me. He never leaves my side, which Vic loves and hates at the same time. Vic has no faith in Cyrus's ability to act as a guard dog and often suggested we add another dog to our family. It appears that Porky showed up at our doorstep and applied for the job. Vic's only complaint is the dog never leaves my side, including nights when Porky wedges his body between Vic and me, no spooning allowed.

"Who is this little wildcat?" Ike asks, swinging his long leg over the bike to dismount. He pulls his helmet off, running a hand through his unruly russet red hair.

"Meet Porky Pellinger." I introduce.

"Scrappy little fellow." Ike says. "Amigo, how's it going?" He greets Vic, his eyes hidden behind dark aviator sunglasses. Ike engulfs Vic in a manly bear hug, clapping him on the back before turning to me with a roguish grin on his face. He holds his arms out, wiggling his fingers in a come hither motion, calling "Chica, Chica, come here and give a real man a hug." I set the mugs down and he sweeps into his arms and off my feet twirling me in a circle. Not exactly an unpleasant experience, being spun through the air in the arms of a handsome devil of a man. Ike Adamsen is six feet two inches of burnished Irish charm. His hazel eyes twinkle with mischief, he enjoys provoking Vic, who accepts the challenge in stride and their paybacks border on childish revenge.

"How was the ride over from Lake George?"

"The ride from Lake George was fine but that damn road of yours is so bumpy and rutted, my back is killing me." He winces and rubs his lower back.

"Sorry man, we'll make a single lane smooth for you."

"Did you have a nice visit with your daughter?" I ask, handing him a cup of coffee.

"Yeah, we rented a house on the water, visited the local sights and had dinner at the Sagamore Resort. What a place, if you've never been there, I think you'd enjoy it. Lake George is a pretty area, lots of shops and hotels. We had a nice visit."

"So your daughter is finished with school?"

"She graduated from college with her MBA and has an interview with some big accounting firm in Toronto. Her boyfriend came along on the trip. He seems to be a nice guy, works in the medical field, something with x-rays. She seems very happy."

"And Siobhan?" Vic asks, with an inquiring raise of his eyebrow.

"Ahhhh, don't ask, buddy." He unzips his jacket, tossing it and his helmet on a deck chair. "You know, women want commitment, show up on time, wear a watch, check a calendar, and send flowers. It's not that I didn't love her. I'm just not that guy." He looks at me, his face apologetic. "Sorry, Ellen. I know she's your sister-in-law. I did enjoy her company but I'm not one for long-term relationships."

Vic claps Ike on the back. "That's an understatement."

"But I'm lovable, right?"

"Absolutely," I say. "Siobhan hasn't learned to be alone after her divorce and she was greedy for your attention. I can't say I blame her. She knows a good thing when it," I giggle, "ends up in her bed."

"Well, thanks for understanding. And not to change the subject, but I'm starving. Am I too late for breakfast?" He stretches and yawns. "I busted tail to get here this morning so I didn't stop to eat."

"No donuts?"

"Sorry, didn't have time to stop."

"Fine then, no more coffee for you." I feign a pout and gather up the cups. It's not like I can't buy my own donuts. But when someone else buys them, the calories don't count. Oh well, my hips don't need them. I turn to Ike, "I'll go in the kitchen and whip us up some breakfast. Eggs, bacon, home fries, toast?"

"Chica, you are the best." Ike says bumping Vic with his shoulder. Despite Ike's long relationship with Vic, who is of Mexican descend and speaks fluent Spanish, he has only managed to pick up two Spanish words, chica and amigo. "You are a lucky man. Beauty, brains and she can cook." Then to Vic he whispers under his breath, "She can make eggs, right?"

"I can hear you, I'm in the room. My cooking abilities have expanded greatly."

"Eggs are her specialty." Vic pulls me into his embrace for a quick hug. "Elle, do you mind excusing us for a few minutes. There are a few things I want to go over with Ike before I leave." He gives Ike a knowing look and nods his head toward his office. "I need to be on the road by eleven-thirty to catch my plane to New York."

I study Vic as they retreat down the hall, taking in his polished luxury Italian Salvatore Ferragamo shoes, the sharply creased dress pants and custom-made white lawn of his shirt. I'm reminded how well he carries off designer clothing. It doesn't really matter what he's wearing, jeans, flannel shirts or haute couture, the drape and fit of the clothing, designer or not, flatters his lean tall, dark good looks. I'm not surprised his agent has been pressing him to book some modeling sessions with the major clothing designers. It would be great exposure for him.

He turns to give me a smile. "We won't be long. Thanks, Buttercup." His sleeves are rolled up to reveal lightly muscled forearms and the collar of his shirt opened to reveals a tempting patch of taut, tanned skin, I long to bury my face in his chest, anything to keep him home. And now all that loveliness is heading to New York City and possibly into the arms of another woman. I brush away a tear, my face and mouth prickled into a frown. I chide myself for being ridiculous; Vic would never cheat on me. Yet the image of him in the arms of Vivian Gust haunts me.

I watch them head up the stairs, talking in hushed whispers, Vic nodding emphatically over some point and Ike agreeing.

What is so secretive they can't include me in the discussion? This is unlike Vic to exclude me, odd, so odd. It only heightens my suspicious nature. I contemplate sneaking upstairs and eavesdropping at the door and realize that is childish, even for me. With a huff I stomp off toward the kitchen and slam the door behind me.

~~~

The next morning with Vic gone and no immediate plans for the day, I thought I'd sleep in…at least until eight o'clock. But a barrage of dogs and a towering Irish banshee have other ideas.

"Chica, chica. I let the dogs out for their morning walk and they miss you." Ike calls from the hallway, pushing open my bedroom door. The dogs charge into the room and leap on the bed, covering me in canine kisses before I open my blurry eyes.

"Get off me, you savages." I cover my face to ward off the slobbering attack but they are not discouraged. Cyrus laps my chin, leaving behind a trail of morning dog breath. Porky dances across the bed like a puppy, scratching and making a mess of the sheets.

"Can I come in? I have coffee." Ike asks, enticing me with the sweet promise of morning nirvana.

"Sure." I mumble, sitting up and making sure my clothing is properly adjusted. "What the hell time is it?" I groan. "It's not even six-thirty!"

"Time for you to get up." Ike hands me a mug of coffee and strides over to the French doors throwing them open to a blast of dew laden spring air. He plops himself down on a plaid armchair and pulls out a list. "Vic says I need to keep you busy."

"What?" I say, choking on the scalding hot brew, protesting. "I'm perfectly capable of amusing myself for a few days." I huff. "In fact, I did a pretty good job of it while he was away for seven months. If he cares to remember." I snort in derision

"Ouch…do I detect a tone of hostility?" He arches an eyebrow in question.

"Yes, I'm a little put out. He goes off for seven months, comes back sick then takes off for New York City with no warning and brings you in to babysit." The words tumble out of my mouth in a rush, a stream of disappointment and discontentment. "He's distant and preoccupied, locking himself in his studio and has an emotional meltdown if I interrupt him." I stab the air with a finger and harangue on. "*And* we haven't even had se…" I stop abruptly, stemming the tidal wave of hurt, clamping my lips together. Ike knows Vic better than anyone, but discussing our sex life or lack there of, with his best friend borders on betrayal. Made more awkward by the fact I'm sitting in bed wearing nothing but an oversized t-shirt, and little else underneath it.

"Chica, Elle." Ike takes a sip of his coffee, pausing for a moment. He lets out a deep sigh. "I've known Vic for a long time. We've been through our share of ups and downs but there is one thing I know for sure," Ike stops, looks me long and hard in the eye. "Vic loves you deeply. Whatever is going on in that head of his right now, you have to trust him. Don't doubt his feelings for you."

"What about that Vivian Gust? Those tabloid newspapers are plastered with pictures of them. Intimate, huggy-kissy pictures of them." I grab a tissue from a box on the nightstand and wipe away the tears welling in my eyes. "I'm sorry, Ike but I can't bear to lose him to another woman."

"Elle, Chica." He moves to sit on the edge of the bed, patting my leg under the covers while the dogs converged on me in a wiggling mass of sympathy.

"Elle, trust Vic."

"But Ike," I cut him off. "My husband, Jack swore he loved me, but he cheated our entire marriage."

"Vic is not cheating on you. You know those photos are publicity bullshit. He hates that crap but it's all part of the movie industry game. He has kept his relationship with you quiet to protect the family privacy. The best way to do that is to put up a smoke screen. Let him be seen with a young starlet or two, it's only hype. Look at me." Ike commands.

I shake my head, sniffling, refusing to meet his eyes, knowing he is going to lecture me. "No."

"Chica, Chica." He sighs and pulls a few tissues from the box and tosses them at me. "No one, and I don't think even you knows him as well as I do." Ike puts a finger under my chin and forces my head up to meet his eyes. "Listen. He never stopped loving you for all those years. He isn't going to stop now. And yes, he has a few things preoccupying him now. He has business to deal with in the City and then he's going to see a specialist on tropical diseases. He feels his recovery should be going faster so he wants to make sure there is nothing lingering in his system and that he is not contagious."

"Why didn't he tell me he was going to a doctor?"

"He didn't want to worry you."

"Why can't you tell me about the business?"

"Because he asked me not to."

I know the bond between them is a locked vault. Ike would sooner die than betray Vic.

Ike stands up and whistles for the dogs. He calls over his shoulder, "Breakfast in fifteen minutes, don't be late." He pulls a sheet of paper from his pocket and reads, "First thing on the list, Vic says we should hike Old Bald Mountain. Tomorrow we hike Blue Mountain, the next day then…what the hell!" Ike stops in mid-stride, paper in hand, a grimace on his face. "I'm a biker not a hiker. Is he crazy? Some of these hikes are over three miles! He is nuts!"

"We're training to become Adirondack 46'Rs."

"Forty-what? What crazy idea do you have your heart set on this summer? Does it involve any German trainers, guns, murders, and diamonds?"

"No!" I protest. "To become a 46'R involves just a little hiking through the woods and up a few mountains. And last summer, none of that was my fault."

"It never is, Ella, Ella." He tosses a pair of jeans at me. "Get dressed." He says as he leaves the room. "I'm going to attempt to make some breakfast."

"Wait a minute. Don't you dare go near my kitchen! You can't cook. God knows what kind of shape you'll leave it in when you're done. Adele will kill me if we mess up her clean kitchen. And I repeat, you can't cook."

"I know." He peeks his head around the door. "That's the answer I was hoping for…I'll go see if I have anything that resembles hiking boots. Call me when the food is ready."

"Vic's old ones are in the hall closet." I call after him. "You might fit into them. I ordered new ones, they should be in any day now." I lean back on the pillow and realize I've been had, guess who is making breakfast?

~~~

Even though Ike moaned, groaned, bitched and complained every step of the way, he turned out to be a capable hiking companion. After Old Bald Mountain, we hiked to the peaks of Blue Mountain and Ampersand. With elevations below four thousand feet, these mountains are not considered high peaks in the Adirondacks. While charging up a mountain is not his idea of fun, Ike has managed to stay fit. Very few people know his secret, to look at him you wouldn't guess he has a green thumb and enjoys gardening. The gardens around Vic's house in California and lately the plants and trees of our Adirondack house have come under his care. At first Weasel was irritated, feeling Ike overstepped his role as a guest and possibly causing Weasel to lose his job. With the reassurance of a long list of chores the upkeep of the house required, Weasel realized the help was welcomed. Weasel's comment was "Mr. and Mrs. Rienz, if your friend wants to come and do my work for me, I have no problem with it. In fact, I have a cord or two of wood that needs chopping." Ike had the wood split and stacked before lunch the next day, gaining Weasel's grudging admiration. And Adele's... Ike prefers to do his gardening in a pair of worn-down work boots, jeans and no shirt showing off his well-muscled shoulders and chest. Last summer, I caught Adele standing at the window, mesmerized by the sight of Ike in the garden, cleaning rag hanging limply in her hand. I heard her utter a low moan. I swear she was drooling. Adele shows appreciation in her own unique way. A few seconds later she drops the cleaning rag and charges out the door yelling, "Hey, you, Ike-man, put on a shirt; people around here trying to get some work done. What the hell, you think we're running a nudist colony!"

The past few days with Ike have been strange. It has been just the two of us. I guess I'm old school and being alone with a man who isn't my husband seems inappropriate. Yet with Ike, our mutual point of commonality is our love for Vic, the unspoken bond between us. I admit I find him attractive. A woman would be half dead not to appreciate his ruddy Irish good looks but it ends there. There is no sexual tension, more of a brother-sister relationship. Ike entertains me with humorous stories of the times he and Vic worked on the ocean freighters, shipping off to ports around the world.

I'm not sure why Vic had him come and stay in the house with me. There have been many occasions in the past where I've been alone with just Cyrus. Our son, Josh lives only twenty minutes away. Something is bothering Vic since he has been home. Before he left for the city, he sat me down and reviewed the alarm system of the house and grounds. He insisted I find my small handgun and put it in a safe place. Apparently he didn't feel my knitting basket was a secure location, forgetting that little revolver in my basket came in pretty handy last summer. I've noticed Ike's revolver to be conspicuous, often strapped to his body or nearby. Vic and Ike have pistol permits but only carry when a situation warrants extra caution. Since his arrival, I've never seen Ike without his gun; the whole thing is very unnerving.

*Somewhere between the start of the trail and the end is the
mystery why we choose to walk.*

I finish tidying up the kitchen from dinner and suppress a
yawn as I turn out the lights, tired after a long day of hiking. In
the living room I can hear the cheering of a baseball game on
television. Ike is a passionate baseball fan. His idea of a perfect
day begins with working in the gardens and an evening sprawled
out on the sofa with a cold beer watching a baseball game. I smile
affectionately in his direction. I think Vic's list of hikes has
exhausted both of us, I can't help but wonder if it is part of a
diabolical plan on his part. I woke up this morning with stiff legs
and a sore back. After the seven miles today, I need to drink
plenty of water and take a couple of anti-inflammatory pills if I
want to move by morning. Even the dogs are tuckered out,
instead of following me they are curled up on the couch next to
Ike having a male bonding experience over the game.

Glad for a few minutes alone, I pick up my glass of wine and
head for the guest room. Before Vic comes home tomorrow I
want to sneak into the spare bedroom and dig around in the
closet.

The other day Lani called reminding me I have a wedding to
help her plan. With motherly efficiency, I responded with a list of
calls and arrangements I have all ready completed. Then she
asked for the one assignment not checked off my list. When
would I have a few minutes to find my old wedding dress?
Apparently she wants to know the condition of the dress and
whether any of the fabric can be used in the design of her

wedding gown. I thought she was kidding when we talked about the dress in California. I'm delighted with the idea, now I just have to find it.

I shut the bedroom door with a faint click and flip on the light switch. Everything in the guest room is neat and in order, waiting for one of the children to visit. The room is well appointed with rustic furniture crafted in Adirondack birch bark and bent twigs. A handmade quilt covers the queen size bed. The pattern of the quilt is constructed of small carefully cut fabric pieces chosen in woodland colors to resemble the shape of a log cabin. A French door opens onto an outside patio offering a view of the shoreline and mountains off in the distance. Above the bed a row of small transom windows hug the ceiling and windows facing the driveway overlooking a rock garden covered in perennials.

I set my glass of wine on the dresser, careful not to slosh on the wooden surface. Porky pushes open the door and follows me into the room. He jumps on the bed and after several circles, flops down with a groan. He certainly has made himself at home.

To my horror, I've discovered he eats things. Like everything…especially expensive things…the other day I found half a pair of Lululemon yoga pants, one leg chewed off. When Vic gets home, he'll find a pair of his Italian Salvatore Ferragamo shoes destroyed yet his flip-flops untouched. Porky chewed the buttons off a Pendleton wool shirt, a Christmas gift from Jack years ago, leaving behind the inexpensive flannel shirt next to it. The buttons showed up on his morning walk. Unbelievable. He snubs his nose at bargain dog food and devours the organic sixty-dollars-a-bag brand in minutes. I'm thinking of buying baby-locks for my lower kitchen cupboards.

I took him to the veterinarian for a checkup and he was diagnosed with giardia. Giardia is a water-borne illness hikers can get from drinking untreated water. The veterinary bill involved an overnight stay with intravenous fluids and a bill of over five hundred dollars. The mystery of why no one claimed him is no longer a mystery. He's an expensive little guy to keep, yet loyal and affectionate to a fault. I stop and give him a pat on the head and he wiggles in delight and licks my chin.

Once I have paid homage to the canine king, I pad across the bedroom floor and drag a chair to the closet. In bare feet, I stand on it, groping along the highest shelf searching for the box with the wedding dress. Nope, instead I find a plastic tote with Trey and Lani's school projects and pictures. I step down and pause by the door, gnawing on my lower lip in thought before plunging into the small mountain of boxes stacked in the back of the closet. In a moment of haste when we moved in, I shoved all the 'too dear to part with' treasures from my old house into this dark corner, items that should have been donated to charity years ago.

Down on my hands and knees I sort through the collection of odd shaped boxes until finding the one I'm looking for, a large rectangular box at the bottom of the stack.

I run a hand over the once white box, now faded by age to a pale buttery yellow. A flood of memories overwhelms me. Jack's mother helped me shop for the material. Grandma Fiona needed a special lace to fashion the eight-foot train. Jack's mother loaded up the three of us and drove to the west side of the city, searching for a store that specialized in lace and fabric for wedding gowns. After an hour of combing through floor to ceiling shelves of fabric we found the coveted lace. Grandma Fiona declared it as beautiful as any lace ever made in Ireland. For the next month every second of our free time was spent cutting, pinning, and basting the dress together. Over countless cups of tea, the table in Grandma Fi's dining room covered with a thick pad to protect the surface, we created a dress. But more than that, memories were created for me, with each stitch on that dress, on each seam completed, a family was created. Jack's parents and siblings accepted me into their loving Irish fold without reservation and the painful memories of losing my mother, Vic and our baby faded into the past. Never forgotten, but the awful gaping raw wound, healed. My heart would always carry the scar, but I learned to love and move on with my life.

I lift the top off the box, pushing away the dark blue tissue paper, meant to prevent the dress from yellowing. Unlike so many brides of my generation, I didn't have the dress sealed in an airtight box. I'm not sure why. Of course, it was dry-cleaned but expensive preservation seemed extravagant at the time.

Tenderly, I lift the dress out of the box and lay it across the bed. It was designed in the style of the day, long sleeves of lace formed a triangle at the wrist, a high mandarin collar framed my throat, fitted tightly through the bodice and a wide sweeping eight-foot train trailed down the aisle behind me. The veil was a cascade of flowing tulle. At that time to be married in the Catholic Church a bride's shoulders must be covered for modesty sake. And there was no question, in Jack's family, their one stipulation was the sacrament of matrimony take place in a Catholic church.

Smoothing back the creases, I see the raised edges of the lace yellowed slightly, adding a patina to the texture of the pattern. The frayed edge on the hem brings a smile to my face at the memory of Uncle Sean moving across the dance floor, holding me tight in his arms then lifting me off my feet to twirl around and around like the white down of a milkweed plant spinning in the wind. Flipping the dress over, I trace the long line of tiny buttons and loops down the opening of the back and remember how tenderly Jack undid each one, with almost reverence the night of our wedding. For all of his glib faults, in my heart I do believe he loved me best. If I push the unpleasant memories aside, and what marriage doesn't have difficulties, we had a good marriage. We raised two amazing children and for the most part enjoyed each other's company. I read in a magazine somewhere if you are happy seventy-five percent of the time in a marriage, you are doing well.

I'm happy the dress has weathered the years after being packed away for over so long. While holding up the dress from my first wedding, I see hanging in a clear garment bag the one I wore on the day I married Vic. Pure, white untouched by the passing of time, at first glance it looks new, just off the rack from the store. I take a sip of wine and wonder, what will this dress look like in twenty-five years. When I wore it, I was so confident, the love of my life had returned, lifting the scar of the past and healing the raw wound underneath. Sighing, I finish the wine in one gulp, and wipe away a tear. I don't know what has gone wrong. Am I over reacting, seeing doubt and suspicion instead of trust and commitment to our marriage?

To dispel the gloomy mood, I switch on my laptop and log in to connect with Lani for a FaceTime visit. As luck would have it, she's home and we spend the next half hour going over the details of the dress and her options to use some or all of it in her design.

The effects of hiking with Ike and emotional memories of the past have exhausted me. I'm fading fast, and fatigue settles into my tired body. The problem with having a daughter on the west coast is, everything is three hours earlier for her. So I'm exhausted, ready for bed and she's chattering on non-stop about her plans, asking for my input. Trying to stifle a yawn, I cover my mouth when suddenly my eyes are distracted from the computer screen by a movement outside the French door.

My breath catches in my throat, my eyes widen and my heart bangs wildly with uncertainty, so loud I think it will burst out of my chest. The roaring in my ears nearly blocks the sound of Lani's voice calling, "Mom, what's wrong? You look like you've seen a ghost. Mom, Mom, answer me."

Her words slam into my consciousness. A ghost. I blink my eyes and shake my head in disbelief. For standing just outside my door, framed by the thin light of the moon, is the pale image of a slender girl dressed in a long white nightgown. Her fine, light hair hangs limp down her bony shoulders, her eyes are a pale watery grey. A blank expression on her face, a face made sharp by high cheekbones and long aquiline nose, her mouth a small rosebud of colorless lips. She appears to be about fourteen or fifteen years old. She smiles faintly, silhouetted against the black of the night, a pale glow by the dim lights of the bedroom. She presses her palm against the window, staring. We stay like that for a long moment. And for some odd reason, I want to press my hand against the glass, and hold her, there is something so compelling about her. I should be terrified, a strange vision outside my window, but instead I feel drawn to her, as if she were a child in need of help. Porky picks his head up and growls, at the same instant Lani screams from the computer, "Mother, what the hell is wrong with you? What are you looking at?" The girl startles, freezes like a deer caught in the headlights, then bolts and vanishes into the night.

I feel a snap within myself, as if coming out of a trance, the spell held tight by the presence of the girl. With reality comes fear, and terror floods through me. I start to scream. Seconds later, Ike bursts into the room completely bewildered by the chaos he finds there. I'm screaming and pointing at the door, Lani is screaming because I'm screaming and Porky is barking and then Cyrus is barking because Porky is barking. The room is like an insane asylum on cocaine.

"What the fuck?" Ike yells, banishing his pistol, not knowing where to point it. "What the hell is going on here? Elle, are you all right?"

I had climbed onto the bed, mindless of the wedding dress crumpled beneath me. Speechless, I raise a hand toward the door, unable to utter a word.

"Lani, what happened?" Ike commands, crossing the room in two quick strides, surveying the property in the dim glow of the outside lighting that surrounds the house.

"I don't know." Lani babbles, "I was talking to Mom and all of a sudden she goes still, and she looks weird as if she's caught in some kind of spell. Mom, what did you see?"

I have my knees pulled up to my chest and I'm deep breathing, gasping for air, trying to calm myself. *This is so bizarre. How do I describe what I just saw?* I glance at the empty glass of wine. Questioning myself, did I drink too much wine? I thought I only had two glasses. But I have the bad habit of pouring an inch, then another inch and maybe another so I don't keep an accurate account of the amount I've drank. I realize Lani and Ike are looking at me for an explanation. I shake my head. "You are never going to believe me." I stammer.

"Try me." Ike snaps.

"Ike!" Lani reprimands. "It's okay, Mom, take your time, obviously something frightened you."

I close my eyes and bite my lower lip. The image of the girl fresh in my mind, I know she will haunt my dreams for nights to come. She seems too sad, so lost and forlorn. I look at the screen filled with Lani's image on it and then back at Ike. "I saw a young girl standing outside the French door on the patio."

"Get out of here!" Lani exclaims.

"No shit." Ike scoffs.

I sit up straight, knowing what I saw and they can choose to believe it or not. "There was a young girl dressed in a white nightgown. She was tall and thin. She had shoulder length hair, very, very blonde almost white. She was barefoot and looked so sad."

"Ike," I implore him. "You need to go outside and see if you can find her. She may be lost."

"Chica," Ike says. "How in the hell would a young girl in a nightgown make it through all the security cameras and detectors we have positioned around the property? Does anyone else even live around here?"

"Mom," Lani asks, her voice stern, pointing to the empty glass on the dresser. "How much did you have to drink tonight?"

"Not that much." I snap, offended she would think I'm drunk.

"Elle," Ike adds, "Chica, I know you had a few glasses of wine with dinner, after all the hiking we did, maybe you are dehydrated and you just imagined the girl."

"No." I'm adamant. "Porky saw her too. He growled at her. If she was a figment of my imagination would he have growled at her?"

"Lani, stay on Facetime with your mother. Elle, keep your cellphone next to you. I'll go outside and check around."

"Take Cyrus with you." I suggest.

Ike snorts, "And why would I take him. Knowing Cyrus, I'll end up looking for him by the time the night is over." Ike ruffles the dog's head.

"What about Porky?"

"I want Porky to stay with you. Of the two he is more reliable to protect you."

"Ike," I ask. "Look on the window of the door, it looked like she held her hand against the glass, could there be a finger or handprint?"

Ike opens the door and swings the flashlight he's carrying around the yard and then bends to examine the window.

"I don't see any smudges on the window. We can look in the morning when the light is better, but it looks clean now."

86

Damn…now I do look like a crazy drunk. I thought if there was a handprint it would verify my story.

"Ellen," Ike says, "Come and lock the door after me and stay on with Lani while I canvas the property."

"Ike, be careful." I caution.

"Of what?" He laughs. "A pale little girl? I think I can handle myself."

"Unless you believe in ghosts." I mutter and with that thought I curse. "Damn Jack."

"Mom, why are you accusing Dad?"

"Lani, this would just be like your father. I pull out the old wedding dress and I'm besieged with memories of him and our life together. This would be his idea of a practical joke, sending down a little ghost angel to keep me company. He had a weird sense of humor at times."

"Mom, don't be preposterous!"

"I'm not. You explain what I just saw."

"You just had too much wine and you're over-tired. That's all."

"I didn't have that much wine and I'm not that tired." I raise an eyebrow in consternation at her.

Twenty minutes later, Ike appears at the patio door. I unlock it and let him back into the house.

"Well?" I ask, hoping he has some explanation.

He shakes his head, "Nothing, Chica." He shrugs his shoulders. "No girl, no tracks, no car…nothing."

I close my eyes and swear off wine indefinitely. I still think it was Jack.

"Let's take the dogs out for one last walk and then put on the alarm system. I'll spend the night outside your bedroom in a chair by the door."

"Oh, Ike, that's ridiculous." I protest.

"Yes, it is, but Vic will be home tomorrow and he is not going to like this one bit."

"Mom, are you going to be okay?" Lani asks, her voice cloaked with concern.

"Yes, I'm fine." I run a hand through my hair. "It's one of those weird things that happens. Maybe I'm phasmo-phobic."

"Phasmo-what's that?" Ike asks.

"Phasmo-phobia is the fear of ghosts, the feeling of eyes following your very move. The very chill in the air can suggest a ghostly presence." I laugh at the silliness of it all. "We are too far away from Halloween to be having such ghoulish thoughts."

"Okay, Mom."

"It's not my fault."

"It never is, this is a new level for Klutz-Ellen. Creating ghosts…?" Lani twitters. "And they say people in California are nuts. Sounds to me like a little too much of that fresh Adirondack mountain air or too much fruit of the vine." She nods in the direction of my empty wine glass.

I blow out a sigh and look at the French doors, knowing this is not some fabrication of my imagination. Someone or something was out there. Ask Porky…

*Leave nothing but footprints, take nothing but memories,
kill nothing but time.*

I wake from a sleep jumbled and riddled with dreams of the girl in the window. My bed, usually a place of sanctuary, comfort and rest became a wrestling ring of conflict during the night. Rolling onto my back I hear shouting, loud arguing, coming from downstairs and recognize one of the voices belonging to Vic. What time is it? The clock on the nightstand shows it is already ten o'clock in the morning. Gosh, how could I sleep this late?

Cyrus is gone but Porky is looking at me with anguished eyes. "Come on buddy. Let's get you outside." I pick up a plaid flannel robe lying at the foot of the bed and slip my arms into the sleeves cinching the belt over my nightgown. What is Vic doing back so early? He was scheduled to come home later this evening.

After letting Porky out the patio door I walk into the living room and see Vic and Ike glaring at each other. They never fight. I hesitate at the doorway, unsure of what to do. When Ike sees me, he silently points in my direction. Vic whips his head around and fixes a forced grin on his face. Ike folds his arms across his chest and appears to be sulking.

"Mia," Vic says with almost false sincerity. He holds his arms open wide and I slide into his warm embrace.

"What are you doing home so early? I thought your flight was scheduled for later tonight."

I feel his body tense as he kisses the top of my head. "I got an earlier flight out. I missed you."

I tilt my head back to meet his lips. "I missed you too."

"If you two will excuse me, I'll be moving back to the boat house if my services are no longer needed." Ike says, his voice tight and clipped.

"Ike, what about breakfast? I was going to make stuffed French toast for you this morning."

"I'm not hungry." He says and walks out of the room.

I turn to Vic. "What's going on? The two of you never argue. I don't understand. Is this about last night?"

Vic gives an impatient shake of his head. "Well, yeah, hell, I leave him here to keep an eye on you and next thing I know there's a strange woman on the porch looking in the windows." Vic's eyes meet mine, direct and piercing me. "He thinks you had too much to drink."

"Vic, it was bizarre. There was nothing Ike could have done. The doors were locked and he always has that gun with him. Anyway, I was on Facetime with Lani, we had been talking for about a half an hour, I look up and there was this girl standing at the window. She was so pale and sad. At first I wasn't afraid, she looked so lonely then Porky started barking, and she vanished. I freaked out and started screaming, in comes Ike banishing his gun."

Vic runs a hand through his hair and paces the room, agitated. "Elle, there have been a few odd occurrences lately. I'm sure it's nothing." He turns to me and holds up a hand. "But in the meantime, promise me, Mia bella. Please be careful. Stay close to Ike or me. Make sure Cyrus or Porky are with you." Vic looks around for Cyrus, nowhere to be seen, and gives a dismissive nod. "Well, at least we have Porky."

At the fearful look on his face, I capitulate to set him at ease, even though I don't believe the words coming out of my mouth. "Vic, I'm sure I had too much wine to drink and with the hiking, I was probably dehydrated and my imagination ran away with me." I look at Porky lying at my feet, he cocks his head and barks. He knows I'm lying. He saw it too.

"You think?" Vic looks so hopeful; I can't take back the story.

"Absolutely. Now how about that breakfast? Why don't you

go and patch things up with Ike. He was wonderful while you were gone, hiking and hanging out with the dogs and me. He deserves a thank you."

"First, I want that welcome home kiss you promised me on the phone yesterday." He lifts my face in his hand and kisses me again long and soft and searchingly, on my mouth. I can feel my lips tremble and distort under his searing touch.

His lips caress and nibble my chin, nipping and pulling at my upper lip. "While I was in New York City, I saw a specialist on tropical diseases." He leans down, his lips warm and insistent. His tongue parts my lips and flicks over my teeth moving insistently in my mouth as he deepens the kiss. His hand strokes over my breast and slides down my waist and full hips.

"Oh really?" My breath coming in short panting gasps.

"Yeah," the nuzzling trails down to my throat and his tongue find the hollow of my collarbone. "I was afraid I had something contagious and I didn't want to infect you. I wasn't feeling well so I kept away from you. The doctor assured me I have nothing contagious, just a bad case of food poisoning and fatigue. I do think my health is improving. I'm ready to start hiking…and…" he licks the hollow at the base of my neck, his hand moves to undo the belt on my bathrobe, pushing it aside, pulling my body up against him. Pressing against the thin material of my nightgown, I can feel the proof of his desire.

"Oh…" I groan as his fingers slide the hem up, he caresses my bare bottom. "Ohh…oh my, I thought…"

"What did you think?"

"Well," My mind barely able to form a coherent sentence, addled by repressed desire, sweet heat rushes through my body, saturating every pore of my being with want…and need.

"It's just whenever I go into a grocery store, every tabloid newspaper on the stand has my husband wrapped in the arms of his new co-star. It tends to get your attention. I try to ignore it, but it's eating my insides away."

"Elle, Elle, its all publicity crap."

"Vic, I know. I shouldn't pay any attention but you were gone for so long, I can imagine the temptation."

He silences my worries with a kiss that literally has me

standing on my tiptoes and he lifts me off my feet. I'm floating in his arms on a euphoric cloud of lust.

"Ella, Ella, my Mia bella. How many times do I have to tell you? Only you...always only you."

He sweeps me up into his arms and heads toward our bedroom, stopped in his tracks by the sound of...

"Mr. Vic, Mrs. Rienz, where are you two? Weasel and I have a passel of work to do today. We need to ask you a few questions. Yooo-whoo." She's standing at the doorway of the kitchen. "There you are." She grins triumphantly. "I got the coffee on, so go dress and then get your sorry butts down here."

"No, no, no." I moan into Vic shoulder. I forgot it was Adele's day to clean. This is killing me, abstinence does not make the heart grown fonder, it causes you to lose your mind.

"Hold that thought, Mia." He pushes a lock of hair back from my face. "I've planned a romantic evening for us."

"Ohh...really? I like the sound of that." I lean back in his embrace, rubbing my finger against the rough stubble of his chin.

"I had Juls contact one of the best restaurants in the city, and they prepared a feast for us. It just needs to be reheated. I have a bottle of your favorite Rombauer wine from California. I thought we'd dine down at the little rustic lean-to cabin on the lakeshore. The weather forecast is for a beautiful evening and tonight is the full moon. A little food, music, moonlight and..." That roving hand of his moves to the small of my back and presses me closer, I can feel the rivets of his jeans pressing into my soft tummy. He leans me back over his arm, "Later, Buttercup and wear the 'daisy duke' outfit...with heels."

The General Lee is back and ready to roll...*yehaa!*

Every mountaintop is within reach if you just keep climbing.

I spin in front of the mirror for one last inspection. I'm dressed in a short, cut off denim skirt, a plaid flannel shirt knotted at the waist and my favorite red high heels. Add a little sexy underwear and I'm ready for a night of seduction. My husband is back, emotionally and physically.

The aroma from the pans heating in the kitchen is enough to make me swoon. The food Vic brought home looks fabulous. Who knew classy, expensive restaurants in New York City did take-out? I guess if the price is right, anything is possible.

Down in the kitchen, using a large wooden tray I stack the aluminum pans and cover them with an insulating blanket from the restaurant. With my heels in a canvas bag along with a sweater, I slip on my hiking boots for the walk down to the lean-to. The path leading down to the water is rocky and uneven in places, not high heel terrain. I give each dog a bone and hug, trying to ignore their disappointed faces as I lock them in the house.

The night is cool, post sunset in the mountains, chilly with a hint of green balsam in the air. I work my way down the path following the glow of the brazier heater and candles Vic has lit in the rough log lean-to cabin for warmth. He went down to the lake earlier to create, as he called it, the love nest.

He meets me halfway and carries the food down to the lean-to. Climbing the steps to the diminutive building hugging the lakeshore, I stop, enchanted with the decorations.

"Oh Vic, how lovely." I spin in a slow circle, taking in the linen draped table with three forest green pillar candles of varying height surrounded by small branches of balsam fir. The tall crystal glasses refract the light from the candles like a prism, splintering, multiplying setting the table aglow. He chose vintage china plates, decorated with pinecones on a white background. We found them on the back shelf of a local antique shop last summer. On the underside of the plates is a stamp identifying the china from one of the grand hotels on Lake Saranac. One of the many historic buildings that provided food and lodging to tourists escaping the oppressive heat of the cities in the late nineteenth century.

He'd woven strands of small lights and pine boughs between the roof rafters, creating a ceiling reminiscent of the forest canopy on a star lit night. White candles are spaced on the ledge that separates the walls from the ceiling to form a circle of shimmering light. Two chairs pulled up to the table are draped with soft blankets, in case the evening becomes chilly while dining.

The shelf bed tucked in the corner is made up with our sleeping bag, big enough for two. The inner lining of plaid lays open, unzipped and inviting. A collection of throw pillows are scattered along the wall like a row of brightly colored marshmallows. Soft music fills the air with a mixture of tunes from the 1940's era. Music from our parent's generation created to soothe the soul.

Vic sets the food on a pine shelf covered with a white linen tablecloth. He turns to me with a shrug. "I thought if the temperature doesn't drop too low, we'd spend the night down here.

"I love it." I laugh. "The pine branches and candles are so romantic, you never fail to amaze me."

Pleased by my admiration, he picks up my hand, turns it over and gently kisses the inner palm, like a gentleman from a by-gone era. "And I have so many more surprises planned for you, my dear."

"Ohh…I like the sound of that." I hold up a finger. "Wait, I haven't finished the Daisy Duke ensemble." I rummage in the canvas bag and dangle the red heels under his appreciative gaze.

Slipping them on my feet I twirl around. "So…what do you think? Pretty skimpy attire for a night by the lake."

"I like it very much and you won't have any trouble staying warm, if I have anything to say about it." He runs a finger, lifting my chin for a kiss. "But if you stand there any longer, sashaying that sexy behind of yours like a wanton temptress, the expensive dinner from New York City will be wasted."

"Dining will only build the anticipation, sort of like culinary foreplay?" I tilt my head at a coquettish angle.

"Madam, please have a seat." He instructs, pulling out a chair and placing a napkin on my lap. He wiggles his eyebrows up and down. "Let the foreplay begin."

I shiver with pleasure; here I am, watching my very non-domestic husband serve our dinner in the most splendid of Adirondack settings. I'm so happy to have Vic back to his old self I hardly know what to say, fearful of ruining this beautiful spell of enchantment spun over our humble little lean-to. When I realize he is watching me, my cheeks grow warm. With our plates laden with the most delectable food on earth, he takes his seat and smiles, his eyes hold a glimmer of amusement as he holds up his wine glass, he salutes, "To my Ella. My most precious Mia-bella."

"To my husband, welcome home."

A light breeze moves through the pines and a few wispy clouds hang low in the indigo sky, stars slowly appear on the midnight blue canvas of the heavens, hanging like bright orbs of pearl strung across the night.

Our dinner begins slowly as Vic and I go through the re-acquaintance transition that happens when a couple reunites after a long separation. Awkward tentative exchanges aided by a lovely wine turn into a wonderful, relaxed evening of great food and conversation lasting well into the night.

Vic stands and holds out his hand. "My lady, may I have this dance."

Suppressing a yawn with a giggle, I throw off the blanket and the cold air hits me in a rush, only to be pulled into the warmth of Vic's body. I love the fact that Vic enjoys dancing. He is so graceful, moving with slow, easy movements, no complicated dance steps, just swaying to the beat of the music. Our bodies adjust to the nooks and crannies of each other, the rise of heat as our skin makes contact. Our breath mingles in the cold air creating soft plumes, drifting slowly up to the sky. He tilts my chin up so our eyes lock, the amber flecks of his iris glow, a mirror of the radiant embers in the fire pit.

"Thank you for a lovely dinner." My arms fold around his neck.

He chuckles, his breath warms my ear. "The evening isn't over yet. May I kiss you?"

"I thought you'd never ask." I murmur against his chest, my fingers work the top button of his shirt, his skin warm through the open V, the collar scratchy against my forehead.

Taking my face in his hands, he looks deep into my eyes and the world falls away.

"I love you." He whispers. He takes my breath away with the words, along with my heart. It's not fair that I love him so much, the moment I laid eyes on him in that dusty parking lot on my first evening in the Adirondacks, I was smitten. I was only sixteen.

"I love you back." My eyes fill with tears and my throat closes up. He takes in my emotion and gives me a fierce kiss. His mouth leaves mine and traces a heated trail along my jaw, using his hands and mouth, making ripples of pleasure echo through my body. We stand still, swaying to the tempo.

He trails his finger over the hollow at the base of my neck. Heat flares in my belly, and goose bumps crop up on my skin. His finger travels lower still, and grazes over one of my nipples. The nipple hardens under his touch. His eyes meet mine with a smoldering gaze. He unties the daisy duke's knot on my flannel shirt. Slowly the buttons come open, cool night air caresses bare skin tempering the heat kindled deep in my belly as his fingers travel upward, button by button, branding me with his touch, laying claim, taking ownership of my body once again. At my bra, he stills, and bends his head pushing aside the lace, raining a line of fire with his kisses until he takes one of my nipples in his mouth, flicking his tongue slowly, sending a flood of electricity through my body. The hand at my back that held me so tenderly when we danced slides down to the edge of my skirt, slowly lifting it up, caressing my thigh as he moves higher.

I tug at the top button of his jeans…drowning in the wave of passion coming off his body.

"Vic! Vic!" Ike's voice comes over the intercom, insistent, commanding. "Sorry to interrupt. But you better get down to the boathouse right now. Something is going on across the lake. Hurry up!"

What!!

Vic swears under his breath. "You have got to be kidding me." He groans, leaning into my hair. "Now?" He straightens and points to the house. "Elle, get up to the house right now. Get the dogs, your gun and lock yourself in the bedroom."

"What? Why?"

"Just do as I say!" He barks, bending down to pull his forty-four caliber, fourteen round Glock from his backpack lying next to the sleeping platform. He checks the safety on the gun and tucks it in the waistband of his jeans as he buttons up his shirt. "Go!"

"No! If something is going on, I'm not going up to the house by myself." I kick off my heels and jam my feet into to the hiking boots discarded in the corner.

"Ellen!" He growls.

Oh boy, he's mad. He only calls me Ellen when he's angry. "Too bad. Don't you 'Ellen' me. I'm going with you." With a tug and a wiggle, I pull on a fleece jacket, drag my hair into a ponytail and take off before he can protest. "Come on, Ike's waiting." I sprint down the path leaving him behind.

I hear Vic cursing as he takes up the chase after me. "Son of a bitch. Damn woman is going to be the death of me! Ellen! Get back here. Wait for me."

"Catch me if you can! Hurry!" I taunt, trotting toward the boathouse.

Miraculously, we make it down to the lake without tripping over a rock or tree root in the dark. Ike is standing at the top of the stairs, holding the door open to the second floor living quarters.

"What's going on?" Vic asks Ike, breathless. Leaning over

before Ike can answer, he growls at me, "I'll deal with you later."

I stick my tongue out at him. "I'm not afraid of you."

He shakes his head fuming. I swear steam is oozing out of his ears.

Ike motions us over to the balcony off the front of the building, overlooking the lake. "Check this out." He holds out a pair of binoculars. "There is something odd going on across the lake."

Vic takes the binoculars and studies the shoreline in the direction Ike pointed. "What the hell?" He exclaims.

I cup my hands forming makeshift binoculars with my fingers, straining to see the opposite shoreline. At most I can make out the flickering of a campfire. "What?" I tug impatiently at Vic's arm.

He hands me the binoculars and turns to Ike. "Who do you think they are?"

Once I have the lens focused for my eyes, I can see what looks like a young man and woman in the light of the campfire, preforming with glowing hula-hoops and ninja nunchucks. If I didn't know any better I swear I was on a corner in some city watching a pair of street performers. They are dressed in black, she has on red leg warmers and I can make out slashes of brilliant red and purple in her hair. It's difficult to make out many details in the dark, but I'm coming up with black, leather, chains and a lot of body piercing. "They don't look evil as much as eccentric." I suggest. "Goth mixed with Cirque Du Soleil." I watch, fascinated, as glowing objects whirl and twirl back and forth through the black night.

"How did they get there?" Vic asks, "Can I see the glasses again?"

Silently I hand them over to him, mystified by the couple.

Vic scans up and down the shoreline. "I don't see any kind of boat or water craft. That shoreline is inaccessible by road. I don't think there are any hiking trails or old logging road. Elle? Do you know the area?"

I shake my head. "That is part of the state forest land protected by the Forever Wild clause. I'm not sure they are allowed to have a campfire there. To my knowledge there is no way in and no way out except for bushwhacking your own trail."

"Maybe." Vic shrugs. "What do you think, Ike?"

"I've been watching them for a while, and they don't appear to be doing anything harmful. Just playing with their 'toys'." He makes quotation marks with his fingers around the word toys. "It looks like a couple of kids out in the woods at night playing with glow in the dark sticks. Weird." He leans against the doorframe. "I thought you should know."

"Yeah," Vic chews on his lower lip. "I don't know if we need to get the boat and go over there. I'd like to find out what they are doing. But it's state land so I don't have the right to chase them off or even call the police…" Vic's voice trails off.

"Oh no, don't call the police." I interject quickly. "The last thing we need is for the police to come flying out here with their lights flashing. Those kids would vanish into the woods and you and I will look like a couple of overreacting fools."

Vic grins, "Stupider than we already look."

"I'm not sure that's possible." Ike mutters to himself.

"Do you think they could be Porky's owners? If they're moving and camping out in the woods, it would be easy for them to lose him."

"Well," Vic takes the binoculars and watches the couple for a few moments. "If they are his owners, I think Porky is better off with us."

"He was awful skinny when he came to us. It would kill me to give him back to someone who neglected him."

"I agree." Vic says. "If they wanted him back they would have come looking for him. A phone call to the local dog warden isn't that difficult. We left our contact information with just about everyone in the area."

"I don't want to give him back. The little guy has grown on me. And Cyrus would be devastated, he loves having a doggy buddy."

Vic nods, "What do you think Ike? Should we charge over there and demand to know their business?"

"I think we can wait until morning." Ike says. "You and I can get up at the crack of dawn, take the fishing poles and act like we are out for a morning on the lake. I'll keep an eye on them through the night, set my alarm on the hour." He looks over at Vic, "Or whatever you think we should do."

Vic runs a hand over his jaw. "I don't know what I think. How much wine did we have to drink tonight, Buttercup?" He asks. "There have been some strange goings on this summer: mystery dog, ghost children, hippies dancing in the night. Makes you wonder if it's time to give up alcohol."

Ike chuckles.

"Very funny." I retort, not drawn into their little jest.

"If you don't mind Ike, keep an eye on them and we'll go over in the morning. They don't appear to be practicing satanic cult rituals or anything bizarre. They look like a couple of street performers practicing their new act."

"I agree," says Ike.

Roses are red, dirt is brown, let's go hiking and get out of town.

Vic

At first light, Vic slips out of bed and stops to pick up his clothes carelessly tossed on the floor from night before. So as not to disturb Elle, he steps into the hallway and dresses. Always cautious, he holds his handgun up in the pre-dawn light checking the safety before tucking it in the waistband of his jeans. Satisfied everything is in order he starts down the stairs. A glance over his shoulder shows the dogs decided not to follow, too early in the morning for them. Good, the last thing he needs is a pack of yappy dogs.

Once outside he sets off down the path to the lake at a swift jog. Talk about lousy luck, he fumes. Last fall after much procrastination on his part, he finally installed a sophisticated security system. One that covered the house and surrounding property, he thought his security issues were solved. Wrong, it remains a mystery how three bears ended up in his house, followed by a stray dog, a ghost girl on the porch and now who knows what kind of crazy camping on the lakeshore.

And those are the least of his concerns. When in New York City, he handed over four threatening letters to Karl Whitman, the chief detective of the security firm. After an unsatisfactory meeting with Whitman, he had a lunch with a friend of Ike's, a retired investigator for the New York State Police. The bottom line, no one had any answers, both investigators dismissing the anonymous letters received to his personal address as harmless.

They concluded the evidence pointed to an obsessive fan, but rarely do these individuals act on their threats. The letters don't implicate a direct threat or cite the intent of physical harm. What Vic finds disturbing is the amount of personal information the letters contain and the implied veiled malice toward his wife. Which is why the security firm feels the letters are coming from a fanatical, probably female fan jealous of Elle. The entire situation leaves him frustrated and uneasy over the safety of his family.

In the feeble morning light Vic trips over an exposed tree root; falls to his knees, clutching a bruised knee, cursing.

"Son of a bitch." He barks, angry. He could be home, curled up in his warm bed next to Elle, instead he's crashing through the cold, damp woods before dawn trying to kill himself. With a groan, he staggers to his feet and heads toward the lake limping slightly. Those kids camping along the lake had better be legitimate. The mood he is in, it would give him great pleasure to call the cops on illegal campers. He stops to catch his breath and wipe the sweat from his brow, realizing he is weaker than he thought. This is not how he planned the summer. The romantic dinner last night, ruined, wasted to marauding raccoons. He realizes he has been as ornery as a hungry grizzly bear after a long winter of hibernation, short and snappish with Elle. The dinner was his attempt to make up for his bad behavior. Yet, he may as well join a monastery for all the sex he is getting lately, or not getting. He knows it's his fault for being ill, but now he is finally feeling better and this happens. Poor Elle…not the romantic husband she expected after seven months of absence.

In the mist rising off the lake, the creeping edge of morning approaches. Vic breaks out of the woods and sees Ike standing on the dock, waiting. Ike's loyalty to him is never in question and Vic realizes he needs to apologize for the harsh words spoken the other day. He had no right to attack Ike. It's not Ike's fault for the bizarre incidents. The entire situation has pushed Vic to the limits of his patience. Without regard to Ike's schedule, he had asked Ike to come and watch over the house and Elle. And Ike without asking a question; came. Vic chastises himself for being such an ass.

Elle…she should know about the letters, for her own safety,

but he hates to ruin her bubble of faith. The past few years have given them plenty of reasons to become distrustful and paranoid. He enjoys seeing her happy and engaged in a new venture. They had spent so many years separated; most of their lives apart, that the thought of any intrusion on their idyllic existence terrifies him. Even though his strength is in question, maybe getting away and hiking in the mountains is a good idea. He's avoided committing to another outdoor challenge, last summer the 90-mile canoe race was tough and strenuous. This year all he wants to do is lounge around the house and be lazy. But if anything, getting out and hiking will make Elle happy. He makes a resolve; it's time to hit the first peak of the 46'R challenge, a smaller summit, nothing too vigorous. We'll load up the car and head to the wilderness, away from everyone and anything hostile.

Love is, bring me coffee, take me hiking and tell me I'm sexy.

I know without opening my eyes it's past sunrise and the other side of my bed is empty. I reach over and touch his pillow. Cold and empty. Sitting up I see the sheets creased and rumpled from the imprint of his body. How did Vic manage to dress and slip out of the bedroom without waking me? I wanted to go out in the boat with them to meet the couple camping across the lake. He has been so paranoid lately, I'm sure he thought it was too dangerous for me. He's making me crazy with his worry.

I throw back the quilt, yawn and stretch. Only to have my feet run into the soft rump of a dog, I lean up on one elbow to see who is in bed with me. Cyrus. Where did Porky go? I flop back on the mattress with a sigh, too tired to go searching for him. It was well past two o'clock in the morning before we made it to bed last night. On our way back from the boathouse we stopped at the lean-to to gather up the leftovers and found two young raccoons feasting on the remains of our dinner. The inside of the lean-to looked like a nursery school after a shipment of free finger paints. The outline of a small child's hand, the classic paw print of a raccoon covered the floor, table and half-way up one wall. The white linen tablecloth was stained crimson red from a bottle of pinot noir, knocked over in the skirmish. We spent an hour picking up scattered wine glasses, plates and silverware. The wooden floor littered with broken glass and shredded aluminum pans of food. The little bandits wasted no time in taking advantage of our carelessness. I know they're hungry after a long winter but do they have to make such a mess.

The Audacity of an Adirondack Summer

Our romantic notions of the evening vanished and banished, replaced by reality. If we didn't dispose of the remaining leftovers, it would be an invitation to the bears. There have been no sightings of Mama Bear and her cubs, but unattended food would be like putting out a welcome banquet for them. By the time we finished the cleanup Vic was still upset and preoccupied with the couple camping across the lake. Before going to bed he went on-line to check the local police blogs searching for any reports that matched the description of our mysterious campers. Falling into bed exhausted, we exchanged a chaste kiss taking comfort in the warmth of each other's body and the promise that tomorrow, come hell or high water, nothing will keep us apart even if we have to lock the doors and bar the windows.

As I pad across the floor to the bathroom, I'm more angry than amorous with him now. I feel like giving him a piece of my mind. The nerve of him leaving me behind, the sneaky devil. The couple camping on the lake looked interesting if nothing else. I wanted to meet them.

Nothing I can do about it now. I'm not going to chase them across the lake in the canoe so I may as well enjoy the morning. After our adventures last night a hot shower would be heaven. Humming, I turn the water jets on full blast and step into the shower, relishing the stream of warm water sluicing down my body. The smell of lavender body wash fills the steamy air and the warm fragrant steam wakes up my tired muscles and rejuvenates my spirit. Even though I'm miffed at Vic for leaving me behind I decide to take advantage of the time and prepare a romantic breakfast on the terrace. The vegetable bin of the refrigerator is brimming over with peppers, fresh herbs, brown eggs and a lovely slab of bacon I bought at the farmer's market the other day. Everything I need to make the frittata recipe from a cookbook I hide from Adele because she calls it 'nuts and berry' food.

I shrug my shoulders under the spray of hot water feeling the stiff muscles of morning, loosen and relax. I step out of the shower, towel off, apply moisturizer and step into the bedroom taking a white eyelet sundress from the closet. Feeling like a pampered princess I don the pretty dress I've been saving for a special occasion. With a tug and a shimmy, I smooth it over my hips and slip my feet into a pair of strappy sandals. A little understated elegance. The cut of the dress enhances the illusion of full body curves and shows off my long legs. After brushing my hair and pulling it into a sleek ponytail, I put on earrings; apply concealer, a touch of blush and a sweep of coral colored lipstick. I purse my lips, looking at my reflection in the mirror and dab at the corners, blending in the edges. A spritz of perfume finishes me off, and in less than five minutes I'm trotting down the stairs to the main floor.

Once in the kitchen I throw a tea towel over my shoulder and take a spray bottle of cleaner out to the terrace. Across the still waters of the lake, the early rays of sun peek their way above the treetops. Stepping outside, the air is saturated with the fragrance of early summer, trees and flowers, a full orchestra of perfume for the senses. The birds join the chorus, and my daisies are mini white flags waggling in the breeze. I breathe deeply, feeling alive and whole. Yet a nagging worry mars the perfection of the morning. Should I be worried about Vic and Ike out on the lake visiting our mysterious guests?

As if on cue, the loons move out of the cove where they spent the night and glide over the lake, only to disappear under the surface of the water in hunt of breakfast. I wipe down the patio table and add a bouquet of fresh flowers to the table.

Returning to the kitchen I prop the recipe book open on the countertop, put on an apron and assemble the ingredients needed for the frittata. With a great deal of banging I rummage through the cupboards searching for bowls, a whisk, and measuring cups. Using two hands I lift the cast iron pan from the bottom shelf nearly giving myself a hernia. Damn thing weighs a ton. Twisting my hair into a knot at the base of my neck, I blow a stray bang out of my eye and take a deep breath.

This will be delicious. I assure myself as I reposition the recipe book against the canister set and carefully begin to follow the directions. Cooking has never been high on my list of talents, but with extra time on my hands, a little patience and a hungry husband who appreciates good food, I've managed to produce some delectable meals. Twenty minutes later I ease the breakfast casserole into the oven and set the timer. Breakfast should be delicious. If Vic gets home later then expected I'll keep the frittata warm on the back of the stove. When he returns I want the kitchen to look neat and tidy so I gather the leftover ingredients and head to the pantry.

Struggling to open the door with my arms full, I stop in my tracks struck with the thought, what if he brings Ike home with him? I tug on my lower lip, a frown on my face. Oh well, we'll just include Ike and then make some excuse to send him on his way. I switch on the pantry light using my elbow and methodically put everything back on the shelves. Weasel did a wonderful job in repairing the damage from the bears. You'd never know a three hundred pound bear wedged herself and her cubs through the floorboards. Humming a nameless tune off key, I categorize the spices on the shelf, potatoes in the wooden bin, onions and garlic in the smaller one. Oh, I better grab a jar of salsa. Vic loves hot spicy salsa on his eggs. As I turn to leave, my eyes light on the box of Green Valley Organic Natural Flax and Bran Goodness Cereal, a box Vic would never dream of opening. In his opinion whole grain foods are nothing but roughage best feed to cattle. Whenever I try coaxing him into trying a healthy cereal, after one bite, with a derisive snort, he hands the box back to me saying, "I wouldn't feed that to my horses." And Adele treats my 'nuts and berries' hippy food as she calls it, like it was rat poison.

Temptation creeps into my soul, I glance around feeling guilty. I'm the only one who knows that box doesn't contain cereal. I cleaned it out and made it my secret Twinkie stash. Vic doesn't mind what I eat, and Adele would approve, saying I'm finally eating "normal" food. But training for the canoe race last summer, I got a little holier than thou about healthy, organic eating. Thumbing my nose at anyone who'd put toxic chemical laden foods into their bodies. Bottom line, I was obnoxious. Reality has knocked some sense into me but it's too early for me to completely fall off the preverbal healthy food bandwagon. For the most part, I purchase local sourced foods treating chocolate and coffee as the 'other' food groups. Once I attempted to make Twinkies from scratch using wholesome ingredients. The result was a gooey flop. There is just no substitute. Don't mess with perfection. Right now, perfection would be a Twinkie and a cup of coffee while I wait for Vic. Slowly without taking my eyes off the box, I creep over to the shelf and take out a Twinkie, pause, steal a glance over my shoulder to ensure no one is watching and take out another one. It could be a long wait. I rip off the wrapper and take a bite. Ummm…those little golden morsels of junk food heaven, I love them. Pilfering one more bite I turn to leave the pantry as the dogs come running around the corner, chasing each other like puppies, slamming into the walls, ricocheting off the cupboards and skidding to a stop. With their noses in the air, sniffing, they eye the Twinkie in my hand, licking their chops. Damn, I don't want to share with them, I don't have many left and I'm sure Twinkies aren't good for them. "Sorry guys." I apologize, stepping back into the pantry and pull the door shut to avoid the agony of their begging faces. Pausing after the last bite, I lick my fingers and brushing away the crumbs then turn the knob. The door is locked…from the outside!

"What the hell. Oh my God, I'm locked in the pantry." I panic. I have food cooking in the oven and no idea when Vic will be back. I frantically wiggle the knob, jiggling it back and forth. Muttering, "No, no, no! This can't be happening." I start yelling and pounding on the door, my fists balled up in tight little hammers of fear. I hear one of the dogs whine and scratch at the door, probably demanding his share of the Twinkie.

I blow out a deep sigh and slide down to the floor, breathing: think, think. I cajole myself. No need to panic. There are worse things in life, but I can't help thinking about the casserole in the oven, baking away, headed toward becoming a charred cinder. What if it explodes inside the oven filling the house with smoke and sizzling embers land on the hard wood floor. The whole house goes up in flames with me locked in a closet? What about the dogs? The dog door is open so hopefully they can get outside.

"Oh, God," I moan. Who has a pantry with a lock…on the outside? For heaven's sake, who locks their pantry? Stupid people who have bears break into their house *through* the pantry and tell their handyman to put a lock on the door. And knowing Weasel he bought the cheapest lock he could find because he thought it was a dumb idea. In his mind, there was no way any bear was getting through the reinforcement work he did underneath the house. And there was no way a puny door with a lock was going to slow down a hungry three hundred pound bear. No one stopped to think of the crazy lady who lives in the house sneaking in to raid her hidden Twinkie stash and pulling the door closed behind her. And now I'm trapped. I moan, "Klutz Ellen strikes again…oh God, I hate that crazy bitch!"

"Okay, Elle." I sigh, square my jaw and firm my resolve. I give myself a mental chiding. You are not a stupid woman, think of a way to get out of here. Searching the pantry I wonder if I can find a thin piece of cardboard to use like a credit card and jimmy the lock open.

Fifteen minutes later, having tried every conceivable option I can think of I'm still held captive in a three by eight foot cell and smell my breakfast cooking. It needs to be out of the oven in ten minutes or it will be burnt.

Without the strong claws of a bear, there is no way out of here. Sinking down on the floor, I try not to give into despair. It's one thing for Vic to find me locked in a closet; it's another to find me crying my eyes out like a frightened five year old. I squeeze my eyes shut and sniff. I've been in worse situations than this, hey, no big deal. I'll be patient and just wait it out. Then I remember the remaining Twinkies tucked in the box on the back shelf, I'm starving. I might as well enjoy the wait. Wish I had carried my mug of coffee in here with me. Oh well, I muse and unwrap the Twinkie. A half an hour and four Twinkies later, I smell the raw charred stink of a forest fire in my oven. The stench of smoke so thick, it would summons Smokey the Bear to the rescue.

God, I hate being patient. I start chewing on my thumbnail. Where the hell is he? Now I'm worried that something happened to him and Ike. Those kids looked innocent enough, playing around with their hula-hoops and batons. But you never know, strange things happen. If I hadn't locked myself in, I could call him on the phone. No, that won't work, no cell reception on that side of the lake. And somehow in the midst of my worrying I managed to doze off, waking to the sound of Vic bellowing my name from upstairs and the sound of the smoke alarm. I wipe the drool from my chin. I must have really fallen asleep. Leaping to my feet, I start pounding on the door, "Vic, Vic, I'm in here." I hear his feet clattering down the stairs.

"Elle, where the hell are you?"

"Here."

"Here where? I can't see through the smoke. Are you all right?"

"I'm fine. I'm locked in the pantry."

"Hold on, let me get some of this smoke out. I can't see a damn thing. Are you sure you are all right?"

"Yes!"

"What the hell happened in here?" He asks, moving about the kitchen opening the doors and windows, flipping on the switches for the exhaust fans.

"Get the frittata out of the oven." I yell to him.

"What!" Then I hear him open the oven door, "Wow! What a mess."

I hear coughing as he carries the burnt pan outside onto the deck.

"Okay, got that mess out of here." He says, his voice muffled through the door. "Now, where are you?"

"I'm in the pantry."

"What are you doing in the pantry?" He opens the door and finds me sitting on the floor surrounded in Twinkie wrappers. Not my finest hour.

"I got locked in."

"How the hell did you get locked in here?" He reaches down to help me to my feet and the wrappers roll off my lap.

"It was an accident."

"I bet it was," he says. "Lucky you had an emergency supply of Twinkies to help sustain you through your ordeal." He chuckles, brushing the crumbs off my dress. His hand lingers a bit too long over my breasts.

"It wasn't my fault." I protest. "The dogs came running around the corner and slammed the door shut. We made Weasel put that stupid lock on the door and it clicked into place with me on the wrong side."

He starts laughing, "Ella, Bella, Bella." He nuzzles my necks. "You crack me up."

I allow myself to be folded into his embrace, wishing I thought I was as hilarious as everyone else did. Quite frankly, the mishaps and Klutz Ellen mistakes are trying my patience. My life at times looks like a Lucille Ball rerun. Instead of a Cuban husband, I have a Spanish Don Diago…

"What happened with the campers?"

"Disappeared without a trace."

"Oh, that's disappointing."

"Ya know." Vic whispers in my ears. "Our romantic dinner was rudely interrupted last night and we promised, no matter what, to continue today." With that pronouncement, he licks my ear lobe and everything down south turns to molten lava.

I murmur against his cheek, "I couldn't agree more."

"Well, it's morning." His hand goes to the zipper on the back of my dress and starts inching it downward as his hand moves up my thigh.

"Hey, Amigo, where's that breakfast you promised me?" Ike booms, walking into the kitchen. "Phew, what happened in here? Oh…" He hesitates seeing us literally intertwined in each other's arms.

He backs away, hand on the door handle, "That's okay, I'm not really hungry." He turns ready to bolt.

"Ike, wait." I call after him. "Come back."

I untangle myself from Vic's embrace and straighten my clothing.

"My first breakfast burned to a crisp. Why don't I start over again? I have plenty of food. Get in here and help me cut the cantaloupe. Now where did that melon go?" Tucked in the corner, with his head facing away from us is Porky, gnawing on the melon rind.

"Porky, you ate the whole thing. A cantaloupe? What dog eats a cantaloupe?" This dog never ceases to amaze me. His capacity to eat the strangest things without any intestinal distress is mind-boggling. I shrug and point to Vic. "You, make coffee and set the table on the patio, we'll eat outside." I bark out commands, attempting to cover the trembling that has invaded my body, the unhinging of self-control, a total loss of inhibitions. Vic looks at me, a little smile playing around his mouth, I'm smitten by two days' worth of knee-weakening stubble, dark hair tousled, and those eyes, the amber iris smoldering with passion. He, alone, has the power to seduce me, the intensity frightening after all these years. But first things first, breakfast…

"Ike, forget the cantaloupe, make the coffee!"

Mountains have a way of dealing with over confidence.
Hermann Buhl

An hour later a clutter of dishes litters the patio table. Ike, literally, ate and ran. I see him jogging down the path toward the boathouse with the vehement assurance he had *big* plans for the day and likely to be gone for the night.

"Soo…" I look at Vic over the edge of my coffee cup, taking a sip of the now tepid brew. "Those kids were gone when you got to the campsite?" I ask, running my foot up and down his calf under the table.

"Yep." Vic's habit is to kick his shoes off the minute he steps in the house; his bare foot takes up the chase and moves up to lift the hem of my dress. "Not a trace of them, all of their camping equipment packed up and gone. The coals in the fire pit were still warm. At least they were responsible campers and doused their campfire."

I lean across the table, giving him ample view of my cleavage, enhanced with a little "secret" help from my friend, Victoria. The toes of his foot inch higher. I dance my fingers over to meet his on the tabletop, he picks up my hand and traces a line up my wrist, followed by his lips placing delicate kisses, first on each fingertip and then progressing to my wrist and forearm, at this point his face is mere inches away from mine.

His voice husky with desire, "Elle, if I don't have you soon, I will explode."

"I may self-combust." I whisper back. "It won't be pretty."

He stands pulling me up from my chair; "We don't want to

be a fire hazard, now do we?" He cajoles, lacing his fingers through mine and twirling me around lightly. The heat ignites between us, the fever of abstinence course through our bodies, setting off an inferno, not sweet, not tender. Clothes are flung in every direction across the patio, we are mindless to heed our vulnerable location, and I pull the shirt from his back, literally ripping off the buttons in the process. He unzips the delicate sundress, catching the zipper, he yanks and pulls the dress over my head with an impatient tug, leaving me to kick it aside in my haste. I spring up on my toes and straddle him, wrapping my legs around his waist eager to feel the warmth of his skin against mine. I want him, fast, hard and furious. Our mouths nip and tug. Kisses turn greedy with a starving for union. He anchors the back of my head with his hand and his mouth ravages mine, a foreshadowing of pent up lust, barely held in check. My hand fumbles to his waistband, excited to undo the top button of his jeans, my need and desire so great. As I slide the button free, my hand slips lower. He groans and rears back his head with a hiss of exquisite pleasure.

"Elle," He gasps. "Stop, stop, I can't take it." Just as he leans to lower my body down onto a chaise lounge and rip my panties away, we hear a voice from around the hedges. "Yoo...hoo!"

"What?" I mumble in the hollow of his neck. "Yoo-hoo?" Ike doesn't Yoo-hoo. Who the hell is calling Yoo-hoo! We have a state of the art security system, complete with lasers, cameras and alarms and someone is in my yard calling, "*You-hoo?*

Vic lifts his head, the expression on his face incredulous as he darts a glance over his shoulder. His response, "What the f...?" is cut short by another 'Yoo-hoo', closer this time.

"Quick." I instruct him. "Get in the house. We're like, naked!"

"I don't care if I'm buck naked and a Chippendale stripper all rolled into one." Vic fumes, "Who is in our Camp? I'm firing that security company tomorrow. What the hell!" He grouses. "What kind of incompetent idiots did I hire?"

"Hurry, we don't want her to see you." The voice was definitely female layered with a hint of southern accent in the 'yoo-hoo'. "What if she recognizes you?"

"Damn it." Vic says, his voice dripping with irritation as he hitches me higher on his hips, trotting toward the house with my arms clutched around his neck.

"There you are." The voice comes closer. "Well, well, looky, here." The voice twitters as she gets a ringside view of Vic's departing ass. "Why, darlings, excuse me, did I interrupt something? Whoo-Eee!"

Using Vic's neck as leverage, I peer over his shoulder to see a parody of a living human Barbie Doll standing on our patio. She giggles and waves as we duck into the dark interior of the house.

"You all, take your time, get your nickers on." She calls out. "I don't mind waiting. Get yourself decent or not. I like what I see. Ohhh...my stars!" She croons.

"What the hell!" Vic swears again as he puts me down and leans over to peer out the window, staying in the shadows to avoid being seen. "Who or what is that standing on my porch?" He demands.

"I haven't a clue." I respond pulling up the front of my dress, twisting and turning to adjust my plundered undergarments. "Zip me up. You stay here. I'll find out what she wants and send her on her merry little way." I wag my finger under his nose in admonishment. "Don't come out. If she recognizes you as Esteban Diago, our happy private little life in the mountains is gone."

He zips my dress up half way. "Good enough, you go get rid of her and we'll pick up where we left off." He gives me an affectionate slap on the butt. "Be careful, stand by the door and I'll hide behind it. Just in case she's a nut case."

"Careful?" I scoff. "Did you see her? She's tiny. I don't know if I've seen a full grown woman that small." I cock an eyebrow at him. "I think I can take her."

"She might be packing heat." Vic cautions.

"You've been watching too many crime shows on television. Packing heat." I jest, straightening my skirt and smoothing out the passion pressed wrinkles.

"Yoo-hoo, are you all coming out or do I have to come in there and drag you by the seat of your britches. If you're wearing them." She crackles in unabashed amusement at her own joke.

"Persistent little bitch, isn't she?" Vic mutters under his breath.

"I was hoping she would take the hint and disappear." When I open the door, no such luck, there she stands. A pixie with Barbie doll blonde hair pulled back in a severe ponytail, wearing spandex running capris, a pink t-shirt and matching headband. I recognize the Warriors in Pink Breast Cancer Logo printed on the shirt tightly plastered to her chest showing every inch of her overwhelmingly exuberant, probably silicone breasts. I have the same shirt from a race Lani and I participated in last February, Lani ran seven-minute miles and I...well, I made it across the finish line. It's not the time that counts, as long as you finish the race for a good cause, right?

My eyes travel down the length of her, nearly popping out of my head at the sight of her obscenely expensive Danner hiking boots. The very boots with the red shoelaces I've secretly coveted but couldn't justify the expense. Instead of the traditional red laces, her laces are pink, wow...Barbie gone wilderness? I look behind her almost expecting the pink camper and Ken.

"Well, there you are." She stands with hands on her hips. "I was beginning to think you all didn't want to meet your neighbors."

"Neighbors?" I ask. "You live around here?" My mind befuddled by lust.

"Yes, ma'am," Her voice has a childlike chime to it. "I live just down the road a bit. And I was out walking and came across this length of yarn leading down the road and into your driveway. Seeing as how I can't resist a good mystery I started reeling it in to see where it leads me. And here I am, ta-da!"

I hold in a groan that threatens to explode and shatter my insides. The yarn that fell out of my car the first day we arrived, I meant to go pick it up but got busy and forgot about it. Now, look what it brought to my doorstep. A petite parody in pink tossing a dirty ball of yarn back and forth between her hands, chattering away. "I am a little early getting up here this year. I wanted a head start on opening the Camp for summer. Usually we arrive just before the 4th of July except for the last year or two, cause I've been battling the cancer." She points to her t-shirt with pride. "I'm a survivor. It will be two years next month." She extends her hand. "Hi, I'm Twinkie Wannamaker."

My eyes widen in astonishment and an involuntary shiver dances up my spine. I hear Vic give a strangled snort of laughter behind me. I'm momentarily struck speechless. Twinkie Wannamaker…Twinkie, like in the golden nuggets of deliciousness that I crave and covet. This can't be true. Who names their kid, Twinkie? For a moment I have a twinge of regret, disappointed I didn't think of it first. It would make a cute nickname or name for a pet. As if on cue, Cyrus and Porky Pellinger come barreling around the corner. Cyrus falls at Twinkies feet fawning and pawing at her leg. Porky sets up a howl, obviously not in love with our new guest. I hear Vic mutter behind me, "Good job, Porky. Tell her to beat it. An extra biscuit for you tonight."

But Porky's fierceness doesn't faze Ms. Wannamaker, she continues…"I'm so glad to see someone my age living up here. I'm fair parched from loneliness these last few years since the kids have grown, gone away to college and jobs."

I nod, apparently a response on my part is not required. She prattles on. You'd think the fact that I'm half hiding behind a door indicates I'm not interested in her company. But no…

"The house looks nice, you've kept it up well. It's been a while since I've been back here." Twinkie cranes her head and surveys the house. "The Bellamys, well, they weren't too neighborly if you know what I mean." She gives me an inquiring look. "I heard they sold the house, I assume you are the new owners? Where did that handsome man go? Wouldn't mind another look at him. He was some kind of gorgeous." She gives me a wink. "Now my family has summered in the Adirondacks since, let me see, since my great grand pappy built the Camp in the early 1930's just after the stock market crash. He was able to scoop up the property real cheap after all those poor folks lost everything. Pappy always said put your money in real things, land, cattle and lumber. Only a fool would invest in a piece of paper."

Up to this point in the conversation I haven't said a single word. I'm using the door as a block, only the upper half of my body visible to Twinkie, hiding my semi-undressed state and my husband. Who, by the way is becoming bored with Twinkie's one-sided conversation. I can feel the zipper on my dress lowering, tooth by tiny zipper tooth. When the zipper can go no further, I feel something tickling my spine. I squirm trying to keep my composure as Twinkie rattles on about her family and growing up in the mountains.

I give an involuntary shudder and realize a feather is running up and down my back, he's tickling me, the ratfink. He's pulled a feather out of the floral arrangement that sits on the drop leaf table in the foyer. I can't believe him, crouched down, hiding behind me, having fun at my expense. Just wait until I get him alone, visions of him tied to the bed with *me* in command of the feather come to mind. No, he would enjoy that way too much.

"What?" I ask, pulled out of my reverie, realizing Twinkie has asked me a direct question and is waiting for a response. Trying to compose myself, I apologize. "I'm sorry, what did you say?"

"Darling, are you and that tall gorgeous hunk of man going to be spending the summer here or are you one of those showcase landowners who come once a year just to brag about their mountain property."

"Umm…" I hesitate, not wanting to give too much information away. I hear Vic hiss behind me, "Don't tell her anything."

With a bright smile on my face, I answer, "Our schedule is very erratic." Waving a hand in front of my face, I add, "We come, we go. Who knows, we are like the wind." I can't help but notice she appears to be looking for something. Her eyes are darting from me to various points around the house, her eyes moving as much as her mouth and that's saying something.

"Are you looking for something? Or someone?" I ask, raising an eyebrow.

"Oh, I…" Twinkie stammers.

I lose her reply as my body tightens and tingles in pleasure. Apparently the feather was getting humdrum, so Vic replaced it with his tongue. I feel a burning trail down my back as he stops to nip or, oh dear God, *swirl*, his tongue into the little hollows on either side of my spine above my butt. Heat flushes my body, raising a fine sweat in its wake. A wave of desire slams into the pit of my stomach and I fear my knees will collapse. I cringe, knowing I'm in trouble. I wave my hand blindly behind me trying to swat him away. No such luck.

"Actually, I was out for a walk, looking for…a…umm." Twinkie fumbles, biting down on her lower lip. "Our cat!" She produces the word almost triumphantly; leaving me with no doubt, she's lying.

Gathering my senses and exerting extreme willpower to ignore Vic, whose hand has crept up the hem of my dress to caress the outline of my butt, gently kneading. The roving hand reaches my underwear and pushes it aside, and…I hear him whisper, "Bella, Bella," and he breathes, "Mia" into my back. He knows what he is doing to me. He *knows* when he's been gone for so long my response to him is intensified. I could jump him like an out-of-work jockey at the starting line of the Kentucky Derby. Oh, he's going to pay. I take a deep breath and concentrate on Twinkie. She has a quizzical look on her face as she watches me. Through a clenched jaw I blurt out, "Oh gee, sorry, no cat around here. We did find a dog but no cat." I wave and start closing the door. I thought she followed my ball of yarn to the house, where did the lost cat come from, what a strange woman. It's time to say good-bye. "Good luck on your search. It's been great meeting you. Maybe we can get together some time, do lunch." The minute the words *found dog* and *do lunch* left my mouth, I regretted saying them. Porky has been a strain on our budget, what with the expensive yoga pants, shoes and vet bills but we've come to love him and don't wait to give him up.

I admit, the offer of lunch with Twinkie was made in haste, simply to get rid of her. But it's an intriguing idea. I love her name, she likes to hike, and she is a cancer survivor, lunch might be interesting. Since marrying Vic, I've lost connection with my girlfriends and miss the camaraderie of female companionship.

I adjust my mental attitude, smile, and ask, "What is the cat's name, should we find it?"

She looks befuddled, thinks and says, "Why, Kitty, of course." She looks at me like I'm stupid. "What else would you name a cat?"

119

Taken aback, I say, "Of course." Vic surreptitiously presses a card into my hand and whispers in my ear, "Give her the card, she can call the number on it next time she loses her cat. That way she doesn't have to come wandering through our property. Got it?"

I give a slight nod and thrust the card at Twinkie. "Here, take our card." I say abruptly. "It has our number on it. You can call and let us know when your cat is missing. That way you don't have to come all the way over here looking for, umm, oh yes, Kitty." *Hint…hint.*

Twinkie takes and examines the card. "Why, I do declare, that is so sweet of you. But I enjoy the walk and the pleasure of your company."

"Sure, sure, we'll get together real soon." I inch the door shut, almost tripping over Vic. "Great meeting you!" I chorus and shut the door literally in her face.

Twinkie calls out. "Hey, I have two tickets to a Breast Cancer Fundraiser next week. Come with me. I'm donating three baskets for the Chinese Auction. We'll have lunch with the girls, a few cocktails. It will be fun. I'll pick you up next Thursday at ten-thirty."

"Sure, sure!" I yell, leaning against the closed door. I'm engulfed in Vic's arms no longer caring who or what is on my patio as passion overwhelms reason. We fall to the plush oriental carpet on the hall floor. And then, nothing remains but the heat of desire, the passion of his body fusing into mine. Twinkie who…?

The higher the mountain, the deeper the valley…
An Alsacian saying

We lay sprawled on a makeshift bed in front of the fireplace. Embers crackle and pop from a glowing pile of coals, flames flicker in shades of yellow, blue and garnet, the only light in the darkened living room. In the gloom, the outline of his body, a piece of the dimness except for the flash of his white teeth. He smiles down at me and I spoon closer, basking in the warmth his skin gives off. Using my fingertip I trace our names on his chest, Vic & Elle, forever, branding him as mine. The remnants of a simple meal spread across the coffee table, now pushed off to the side.

"Why is it after making love, you want breakfast food?" Vic runs a gentle finger across my lower lip.

His voice echoes in my very blood, deep, sonorous, blurred with the edges of a Spanish accent. I would, I think, know his voice anywhere. "It's comfort food, simple, satisfying and the only thing I have energy to make."

"Umm…" He mutters contentedly.

"This is nice, isn't it?" I snuggle deeper into the crook of his arm. "As our new friend, Twinkie would say, I'm as content as a coon dog on a hot day in July. I couldn't move if I wanted to, I'm fair to middling plum wore out."

"Maybe I could change your mind." He teases. His finger traces the hollow of my throat showing though the V of his half buttoned flannel shirt, the only thing I'm wearing. His chest bare, taut corded muscles flicker golden in the shadowed light. He's wearing my Christmas gift, a pair of navy blue boxers with moose figures printed on them. He looks adorable with his tousled hair, dozing in the firelight.

"Vic?" I ask, my ear pressed just above his heart, the slow rhythmic thudding soothing to my soul. "Are we okay?"

He cocks his head and looks at me quizzically. "What do you mean, Elle?"

"Well, when you first came home, you seemed upset. I know you were ill, but I thought you were mad at me."

"Elle, Elle, Mia-bella." He places a finger under my chin and turns my face up to meet his gaze. With a gentle kiss on my lips, he murmurs, "I'm so sorry. I've not been at my best. I didn't feel well and there are a few issues I needed to work out. Forgive me?"

"I'll always forgive you, no matter what." I breathe against his lips. His kiss starts my heart pounding and every nerve ending in my body hums. Because I know, no matter what the consequences, there is a direct line from my heart to him. I sometimes wonder what would have happened if I had met him before Jack died. I don't dwell on the thought too long, fearful of what the answer might be.

I tighten my arms wrapped around his neck and persist. "But I need to understand. What made you so preoccupied? I was afraid there was another woman."

Vic groans. "Buttercup, I'll prove to you that I'm not interested in other women. Especially the ones I meet on a movie set or in Hollywood."

I close my eyes and nod. "I know. I try to ignore the gossip columns and for the most part I do well. But on the way to pick you up from the airport, I stopped at a grocery store and there screaming at me from every newsstand were tabloids, covered with pictures of you and Vivian Gust. After being apart for so long, I was insecure and jealous."

"Mia," his voice so gentle it hurts my heart. "Why didn't you talk to me about it?"

I swallow and look away. "You were so ill and, I don't know, distant. I didn't want to act like a baby and trouble you even more." I pause for a breath and ramble on, "And why can't you tell me what is on your mind, what is troubling you? You can't deny it, but there's a shadow hanging over you."

"I'm sorry." He kisses me, sweetly, gently and stares at me for a long moment. "I behaved badly when I came home." He says. "But that is no excuse for how I treated you." He stares into my eyes. "Elle, I love you. Please, trust me." His eyes are solemn, completely sincere, and the knot of dark suspicion in my chest releases, leaving me limp with relief. I chide myself for being so apprehensive.

"So I shouldn't be upset over the pictures of you hugging Vivian Gust?"

"Nothing but Hollywood PR, hype for the movie."

I harrumph, "What a stupid business."

We sit in silence for a moment. He weaves his fingers through mine, willing me to understand. "I'll admit I'm still concerned with the breach of security around the Camp. That's why Ike is staying here. We need to be vigilant about our comings and goings, monitoring the cameras and doing background checks on the people surrounding us."

"Why are you so suspicious?"

"Elle, shall I review the past two years. I have good reason to be careful." He rubs a hand over his chin, now covered in a three day stubble, looking very pirate like, if I do say so myself. "We need to be cautious, based on my celebrity status and your propensity for getting into trouble, a little extra security is a good idea."

"Are you going to check out Twinkie Wannamaker?"

"Definitely. She was on our property, uninvited. That alone makes her suspicious."

"She was looking around, as if she was searching for something." I add, "She was acting a little strangely."

"I'll have Ike run a profile on her first thing in the morning."

"It's probably a good idea."

"Yes," he adds, "And in case you were so engrossed with the titillating talent of my fingers and didn't hear her, she invited you to lunch. Something about a fundraiser for breast cancer."

"What!"

"I think that's what she said." He shrugs.

"But, but, I don't even know her." Suddenly uncomfortable, I sit up. "What if she calls, what will I tell her?"

"Why don't we wait and see what Ike's background check digs up on her. She's a little wacky, but you could use a few friends up here. You said you missed your girl friends back home. Maybe it's time to make a few new ones."

"I guess." Uncertainty clouds my voice.

"Anyway, wait and see what we find on her before you make a decision." He stands up and throws another log on the fire. "Stay right here, I'll be back in a minute."

"Where are you going?" I feel bereft without his warm presence next to me. "Come back." I whine.

He tosses another blanket at me. "Cover up. Brrr, it's freezing away from the fire." He picks up a fleece jacket from the pile of hastily discarded clothes.

I watch his retreating back go down the hall and hear the wood creak under his weight as he goes upstairs. Pulling the blanket up over my nose, I wonder what he is doing.

I must have dozed off because before I know it, he's back carrying a box loaded with books and pamphlets. It's the box of books I ordered to help us hike the high peaks of the Adirondacks, details on all of the forty-six peaks.

Now wide-awake, I scramble into a sitting position. "What are you doing with the hiking books?" I pat the floor next to me, inviting him to sit down, trying to hide my excitement. Could he be interested in hiking or did he bring down the box of books only to burn them in the fireplace? I had pushed the idea of becoming a 46R to the back of my mind. Vic's illness and plans for Lani's wedding took precedence, I decided I was being childish, wanting to spend time chasing after such an outrageous goal.

"First close your eyes." He instructs, sitting with his legs crossed in front of him, facing me.

Eager to comply, I obey. Usually when my eyes are closed good things happen.

"Here," he says gently placing a box in my hands. "Okay, open your eyes."

A large shoebox size package rests in my hands. I let out a

squeal because in my hands is a vintage Danner box, the logo of a company, established 1932 to create a boot described as 'close to being the ideal hiking shoe'. The exact boot was used in 1995 when Cheryl Strayed set off to hike 1,100 miles of the Pacific Crest Trail. Inside the box are the iconic Danner hiking boots with handcrafted stitch-down construction made popular in the early 1970's. These boots are believed by many to be the greatest backpacking footwear of all time.

I open the box and reverently lift out the boots. I run my hand over the buttery tannin colored leather, soft and supple. The inner soles so well padded my feet will be floating over the rocky trails. They are gorgeous; I will probably wear them on non-hiking days as well. I love the vintage look, the high quality leather and especially the red laces.

"Oh Vic, they are stunning! These boots are the Cadillac of hiking gear."

"And hopefully worth every penny." He waves his hand in exaggeration, "They were smoking expensive, but after my poverty years working on the freighter ships, I've come to appreciate the beauty of quality shoes. I was paging through the outdoor gear catalogs and couldn't help notice you had a large red X marked next to these boots, in every single catalog. It's worth it to keep those cute feet of yours happy and on the trail."

Even though Vic earns a *very* healthy income, being raised on a ranch in Mexico and working on the ocean freighters for a good portion of his life, frugal habits are in-grained and he spends his money prudently. I undo the laces and slip the boots onto my bare feet, wiggling my toes. "With socks they will fit perfectly. They remind me of the cowboy boots you bought me for our first date at the ranch. Remember?"

"Some men buy jewelry, others buy boots." He grins, his dark eyes transformed. "I seem to remember that first date was very successful." He waggles his eyebrows up and down in a sexy rhumba. "I have a vivid memory of you down by that mountain stream, wearing nothing but the boots. It was very nice."

"There were thorns, I had to protect my feet." I protest and swat a hand at him, embarrassed how easily I lose my inhibitions, loving him without hesitation and reservation.

"Look, there's more." He points to the box.

"More? You spoil me." I complain while digging through the tissue like an eager five year old on Christmas day.

"Socks and more socks! You are the best husband ever!" I throw my arm around him and plant an enthusiastic kiss on his lips.

"Gee, if I had known buying socks would make you this excited, I'd have bought a few pairs sooner." He grins and reclines against the couch, watching me decide which pair to try on first. There socks with stripes, polka dots, and floral prints. He drawls, "From my research on hiking gear, socks are just as important as the boots. You need sturdy comfortable socks that have thermal and moisture wicking properties and in addition be loyal, faithful and true."

"What? Loyal, faithful and true?" I give him a quizzical look.

"Okay, I made up the last part, only our dogs can fulfill that promise." He shrugs, a bemused smile on his face. "I included heavier socks to keep your tootsies warm in cold weather and lighter cushioned ones for when we hike in hot weather."

I shake my head at his silliness, happy to see him carefree and teasing. I kick off the boots, add a layer of socks then lace them up again before hopping up and waltzing around the room. "How do I look?" I ask him, pirouetting around in just the boots and his shirt.

A wicked gleam comes into his eyes and he growls; swings on to all fours and starts stalking me like a wolf. "Come here, my little pretty." He creeps toward me, a lock of his dark hair falls across his eyes; his barred teeth shine in the firelight. The sight of playful Vic sets my heart racing...in a good way. With a lunge he grabs and takes me down to the floor with him. Held captive in the vise of his broad shoulders, he slowly uses his free hand to unbutton the shirt and proceeds to raspberry my stomach with very loud and wet enthusiasm. My feet pinned by the heavy hiking boots tangle in the pile of blankets and I have little defense against the onslaught of kisses and his wandering hands. He rolls onto his back, dragging me on top of him. His fingers trail down to my butt, pulling me closer. Then he kisses me again, deeper and thoroughly, there is no talking, except for "Oh, don't stop."

The coals in the hearth burn to small winking embers and extinguish, the fire forgotten as sparks of another sort ignite, and expensive hiking boots join the pile of clothes tossed aside, flung in all directions. Nothing has ever felt as right as being with him. When I feel his hot skin against mine, the delicious weight of him on top of me, his mouth, his hands, I know our love is safe and all is right within our world.

How glorious a greeting the sun gives the mountains!

The following day dawns clear and bright, cotton puffs of clouds dot the pale blue sky. A faint breeze riffles through the tree branches but the lake remains calm, barely a ripple on the smooth water.

We spent the night entwined in each other's arms, our faith and commitment to each other rekindled atop a small mountain of throw pillows and soft velvety blankets. The ache, that craving, gnawing hunger brought on from months of separation finally quelled.

Somewhere in our post-love making bliss, our thoughts turn to hiking. The mountain of books and camping equipment strewn across my floor leaves me faint. Last night, as we lay relaxed, lulled into that drowsy haze of slumber we decided to take a hike today, something quick and not too difficult. A look at the load of gear littering the living room floor suggests anything we attempt today will not be easy or quick.

I've unleashed the competitive monster in Vic. He wants to start hiking, not one mountain but two. I have no one to blame but myself. Someone needs to lasso and curb my enthusiasm. Experience has taught me that it's not the handsome man sitting on the couch engrossed in hiking books, maps and pamphlets. By nature Vic is laid back, if anything he is a procrastinator, leaving what should be done today for tomorrow. But in spirit, when someone challenges him, he rises to the dare with a vengeance.

So here sits my knight of modern times, dressed in gym shorts and a t-shirt. His long lean legs stretched out, propped on a footstool, a cup of fresh coffee still steaming in his hand.

"Elle, add this map to the pile." He waves a folded waterproof map above his head. "We're going to need it." As I take the map from his hand, he adds, "Do you mind, could you get my GPS, it's in the top drawer of my desk." The gauntlet has been thrown and the knight is preparing for battle.

"Sure." I toss the map onto the pile of backpacks, hiking poles, rain gear, water bottles, boots, packaged food, hats and jackets. The two dogs are sprawled in the middle of the mess, making sure they're not left behind. We've even gone so far as to purchase monogramed puppy-packs for each dog to carry their own food. *Holy jumping mountain.*

Do I really want to be a 46R? This is starting to look like a lot of work. The equipment looks heavy and we haven't added the overnight camping gear. I chew my lower lip and glance over at Vic, consumed by hiking fever. I should know better, look what happened last year when I proposed the Adirondack Canoe Classic. One minute he thought it was a ridiculous idea and the next: we were on a 90-mile river course with him at the helm barking orders. Our coach, a mysterious German, we ended up with more adventure than we bargained for.

"I got our hike." Vic yells from the couch. "Mt. Porter, outside of Lake Placid, in terms of elevation it is one of the 46 high peaks of the Adirondacks but not the steepest or more difficult climbs. And Mt. Cascade is on the same ascent if we want to do two mountains in one day."

"Sounds good." I comment and plop down next to him. I slide an arm around his shoulder and lean in to read the book in his hand. "Porter Mountain, elevation four thousand and fifty nine feet with an ascent of twenty-seven hundred feet, 7.6 miles long with a hiking time of approximately 5.5 hours." I nod in agreement of his decision.

"We're in reasonably good shape." He folds the map. "I don't think we'll have any problems knocking off this hike."

I mutter under my breath, "Speak for yourself." Grateful I took those hikes with Ike to prepare. He may be in good shape but I am still a work in progress. "Do you think Ike wants to join us?" I ask.

Vic starts laughing and laughing until tears leak out the corners of his eyes. "Yeah, right."

"What?"

"Well, the first thing Ike said to me when I got home was, Thank God, you're back! There's nothing worse than a woman who thinks it's *great* fun to drag your sorry ass up and over some godforsaken mountain for the sake of a *challenge*." Vic makes quotation marks over the word challenge. "In his opinion that is why God invented gas combustible engines.*"

"Fine," I huff. "I thought he was enjoying himself. He didn't have to go if he didn't want to, it's not like I forced him."

"I did." Vic says, giving my forehead a quick kiss, his cheek raspy against my delicate skin. His three-day stubble has turned into the beginnings of a trail beard. It's customary for male hikers on the Appalachian Trail to grow a beard; by the end of their two thousand mile odyssey they've sprouted a beard that would make an Alaskan hermit proud. Vic has a good start.

"I asked him to stick around and keep you company."

"Well, he's a big faker. He acted like he was having fun. How does he stay so thin?" I complain. "It's not like he does any exercise."

"He gardens, lifts weights and avoids monogamous relationships like the plague."

"Poor Siobhan," I sigh. "I thought they'd be good for each other."

"I'm not sure the relationship is entirely over. It's not just Ike." Vic says. "I don't think Siobhan is ready to commit either."

"She had a difficult time with her ex-husband. I can understand her reluctance to settle down so soon with another man. I hoped they'd enjoy each other's company and see what the future brings."

"Speaking of the future, if we're hiking, we better get going. We have a drive ahead of us and we want to finish in daylight."

"*Vamanos!*" I chime, standing up to grab the notebook on the end table. "We'll need this to record our hikes, dates, times, location and other pertinent information. To be official we need documentation. Last one to the car is a..." My response cut off as he leaps up and gives my butt an affectionate slap.

130

"Loser drives," he calls out running down the hall.

"Oh holy hell." I mutter, watching his retreating back. Between his long legs and natural good looks that require little to no grooming, I'll never make it to the car first.

The reward is not always the summit view when we climb. Sometimes it's what we see along the way that leaves us with a sense of awe.

Sometimes serendipitous or spontaneous decisions don't translate well into reality. Through lack of planning and a misunderstanding of the variables involved in a strenuous hike, our first attempt at the Adirondack High Peaks was delayed. By the time we packed the car and drove to Lake Placid it was too late in the afternoon to start hiking. The trailhead was six miles east of the village of Lake Placid at Cascade Pass overlooking Cascade Lake. Vic and I decided a better option was to spend the night at the Pine Tree Lodge and start off early the next morning. And who am I to argue with a plan that includes a stay in a five star hotel?

Armed with a good night's sleep and a hearty breakfast, we pulled into the trailhead parking lot by six-thirty the following morning. A light frost covers the grass along the highway and I can see my breath in the forty-degree air. A swirling mist billows over Cascade Lake hanging like a bale of cotton stuffed between the steep rock walls of the narrow valley.

With a tummy full of pancakes, eggs and coffee, there is little need for Vic to coax me out of car. With a weather forecast promising mild temperatures and brilliant blue skies, I'm excited about our first climb together, confident in our ability to complete the seven miles by sundown. Due to the fact that both Porter and Cascade are in designated Wilderness Areas the dogs are not allowed to come with us. We're disappointed but wilderness rules state no mechanized vehicles, tools, no dogs, no fires above 4000 feet and a carry-in-carry out policy.

Vic and I retrieve the gear for the day and close the back hatch of the SUV with a *slam*. Wiggling the packs into place, we adjust the straps and retie the laces of our hiking boots. With a beep from the key fob the car is locked and we're on our way. Because we are only doing a day hike, our packs are significantly lighter than if we were carrying the equipment for an over-night camping experience.

A short walk down a set of log steps and across two wooden bridges brings us to the wooden box where we stop to sign in on the trailhead logbook. Vic takes the stubby pencil and enters our name, date, time and hike destination. He shuts the box turns and gives me a high five, the first of our 46 high peaks. Look out mountains, here we come!

On our way up to the trail, I stop and read a sign. "Carry-A-Rock to Cascade. These rocks will be used by the Summit Stewards to build cairns and define trails."

"Vic, look at this sign." I take off my gloves. My hands are freezing in the morning cold, and point to the sign. "What a great idea."

Vic reads the sign and warily looks at me, contemplating what he wants to say and how to say it…without getting into trouble. "Umm, Elle, I love the idea but do you really want to add any weight to our packs this being our first hike?"

"I'm sure I'll be fine." I reply with false bravado and confidence. "I want to take a big one."

"I could carry two rocks, one for each of us."

"Absolutely not!" I protest. "Let's compromise, I'll choose a smaller rock but I want to carry my own. In fact, I just saw a pretty one back on the trail a little bit. Hold on while I run and get it. Find one for yourself." Vic groans as I lope away…in the wrong direction, down the hill.

Minutes later with a rock in my hand, we leave the open area and enter the trail under the canopy of trees. The temperature drops and becomes noticeably damper. Trees act as nature's umbrella during a rainstorm, shelter from the howling snow and wind of winter and a natural sunblock in summer. Due to the moist dense micro-climate of the Adirondack Mountains a carpet of greenery composed of ferns, mosses, wood sorrel and Canada mayflower covers the hardwood forest floor. A forest at lower elevations with less damp conditions would be blanketed in a bed of leaves, a much drier cover.

"Watch out for hobble bush." I caution.

"What?" He asks.

"Hobble bush or witch hobble is a woodland shrub," I hold up the branch of a low growing shrub. "The branches take root where they touch the ground and trip or hobble passersby, giving the plants its name. See the large heart-shaped leaves of light green. Once they were used as toilet paper. The fruit when ripe, supposedly it is edible."

"You been reading those field guides again, haven't you?" Vic accuses. "Toilet paper, huh? I don't think so."

"City boy." I taunt.

"You bet and look where you have me. I'd be quiet if I were you. And quit while you're ahead."

"Okay." I say meekly. "But isn't it interesting?"

"Mia-bella, you are always interesting. And trust me nothing is growing on these trails, they are worn down to the bare rocks and tree roots."

When hiking in higher elevations one must be prepared for fluctuating weather conditions. The weather can range from a hot sultry day to rain drenched night or an early snowfall.

Circular red plastic markers are nailed to trees at regular intervals; the trail is well-used and has an elevation gain of 1,940 feet. Steep but fairly gentle for an Adirondack peak. The surface of the path is covered in worn tree roots that form a matrix, like that of an obstacle course and rocks, and rocks, and then more rocks. Aside from the rocks set in a stair formation, the path resembles a streambed.

Along the edges of the trail a verdant pasture of green moss covers the forest floor like a thick carpet, shimmering under a thin veil of dew. I lean down to inspect the moss and discover at least four different varieties. At this lower elevation with dappled sunlight the vegetation is composed of bunchberry, moss, Salomon Seal, and the promise of aster and goldenrod in the fall.

"I thought you weren't going to wear your new hiking

boots?" Vic asks, craning over his shoulder to look at my footwear.

"I wasn't, but I thought why not break them in on a day hike, we're only walking six or seven miles."

"Okay," he answers dubiously. "I packed moleskin and duct tape if you get blisters. That's why I choose the sneaker-type of hiking boots; they never need breaking in and are lighter on my feet."

"I'm sure I'll be fine." I quip and proceed to trip over an exposed root, falling onto my wrist. Lucky for me the incline of the hill took some of the momentum out of my fall.

"You, okay?" He stops, lending me a hand up.

"Yeah, I'm good, need to keep my eyes on my feet." Muttering to myself, "And not on his ass."

We walk through a paper birch forest that cloaks much of the mountain, a legacy of the 1903 fire, which destroyed the old spruce and fir cover.

After an hour and a half of walking we reach the junction between Porter and Cascade Mountains. A wooden sign with yellow lettering points in the direction of Porter, the first decision of the day. Do we hike Porter or Cascade first? Because it's shorter we choose the Cascade trail.

A large boulder sits where the path winds around to the right but we head to the left for the summit of Cascade. In spite of the large breakfast I ate only three hours ago my stomach is growling with hunger pains. Our original plan was to hike straight through to the top of the mountain and have lunch. I wish I had taped a few Twinkies to the side of my pack, just to keep up my strength. I hate to admit it but I'm already getting tired.

A group of younger hikers pass us just before we break out of the tree line. The last girl in the group, a tall brunette whose long legs dance across the rocks on the trail lopes by us, calling back, "Are those Danner hiking boots you're wearing?"

Feeling pleased that someone noticed my sweet boots, I call, "Yes, they are a gift from my husband."

"Aren't you the lucky girl?" And she gives Vic the once over and licks her lips.

Really, I frown and shake my head in exasperation.

135

She says, "I love the red laces."

I bet that's not all you like, I muse. Answering her, I call out, "Thank you. Today is their maiden voyage."

"Congratulations, I've always wanted a pair. Hope you broke them in." She waves and moves on up the trail. "Go Cheryl Strayed!"

"You bet." I call after her, buoyed by her approval and referencing me in the same sentence as Cheryl Strayed from the book, *Wild*, like we were kindred sisters of the trail.

"Who is Cheryl Strayed?" Vic asks, stopping to pull his water bottle out of the mesh pocket on the side of his pack. He takes a sip and hands it to me.

"Thanks, hon." I take a drink and wipe my mouth on the back of my sleeve. "Cheryl Strayed was the woman who hiked a portion of the Pacific Crest Trail, the West Coast equivalent of the Appalachian Trail. She wrote a book about her amazing trip called *Wild* and it was turned into a movie."

"Oh, the one that Reese Witherspoon had the lead role."

"Yes."

"I always liked Reese, sweet girl. I think you look like her."

"Whoa, you know Reese Witherspoon?" I ask blown away by the fact he knows this super Hollywood actress and that he just compared me to her.

"Yeah, I did a movie with her about ten years ago. I had only a minor part but she was nice to everyone."

"How cool is that." I slap him on the butt and say, "Let's go." Under my breath I mutter, "And you are as blind as a bat, my sweet husband, even on a good day I don't look anything like Reese Witherspoon. I'm way too tall."

And because the girl mentioned it, I feel the beginning of a small nagging sore spot where the back of my boot rubs my heel. I think she cursed me. The boots felt so comfortable when I was walking around the house; I thought for sure they would be fine on the hike. I'm beginning to regret my decision to wear them. There is still a lot of mountain to climb. And climb we did, up and up and up some more. Many of the guidebooks describe the climb to Cascade/Porter as an easy hike, with great views at the top. But we found the trail rocky, steep, and at times treacherous,

136

never ending up and over rocks, up, up and up. Where the hell is the top? I groan, huffing and puffing to keep up with Vic's long legs. There is a short plateau to stop and take a rest but then it's on to chug up the remainder of the trail, no complaining allowed. *This is an easy one…?!*

Finally, we scramble up the steep slope of the mountain and break through the tree line only to step into a biting wind from the north. Dropping back into the shelter of the trees we quickly don a windbreaker over our fleece jackets, adding hats and gloves. We follow the cairns and rock trails with yellow dots to the crest of the summit. Before we forget, we look for the sign and add our rocks to the growing pile used for building cairns and trail maintenance. Carrying a rock up a mountain is silly but forgetting to empty your pack and carrying the rock down the mountain is downright stupid.

A climb up the short wooden ladder and we step out onto the open face of the summit. The wind is fierce but the vista from Cascade is magnificent, it is a bare rock summit with a 360-degree view. The sun burned off the early morning fog and spread in front of us is an unending panorama of the village of Lake Placid. Scenic vistas of the forest, mountains and lakes are as far as the eye can see. It's worth every gut-wrenching step we took to reach the top.

"Elle, go stand over there so I can take your picture."

Vic is something of an amateur photographer. He has even won a few awards with his work. Eager to comply with his request, I take a few tentative steps backwards while keeping a cautious eye on the steeply sloping edge. Heights make me queasy.

He holds the camera to his face and says, "Cheese." I strike a silly posture with my hands in the air, and shout, "Look at me; our first Adirondack High Peak."

"Yahoo!" And a gust of wind whips around the corner of the mountain knocking me off balance. I teeter; I totter and hit the ground hanging on to the granite rock surface for dear life. *Holy kricky…*

"Help!" I blurt out.

"Elle, stay down." Vic yells, scuttling over to me on his

hands and knees. "Wow, what a gust. Are you okay?"

"Yes, just help me move back from the edge."

Vic leans over me, blocking the wind so I can crawl over to the leeward side of the mountain.

I fall onto my back, gasping, "Okay, that wasn't fun. I think we should eat lunch at a lower elevation."

"I agree," Vic says. "Are you all right?"

"Yes. But give me your camera. I want to take a picture of the survey marker on top of the mountain to commemorate our accomplishment." Vic hands me the camera and stands behind me holding onto my shoulders, anchoring my body to the mountain. I frame the marker between my feet and take a few pictures. A survey marker is a small round metal plate embedded to mark key survey points on the Earth's surface, found from sea level to the highest peaks.

"Why do you want a picture of the marker?" Vic asks.

"Many people collect photographs of these markers. I thought it would be fun to have a documentation of each mountain with its name, elevation, latitude and longitude."

"Would you like us to take your picture?" One of a trio of college students asks us. They are lounging on the flat rock surface near by enjoying a snack and soaking up the view.

"Do you mind?" Vic asks handing over the camera. "This is our first peak, we hope to hike all 46 of the high peaks."

"Great," says the tallest of the three. He has dark eyes and reddish brown hair. "My name is Ryan and this is my twentieth peak, Joel has done fifteen and Marcy has summited five mountains."

Directing my question to the girl, I can't resist quipping, "Marcy, have you hiked Mt. Marcy?" But she isn't paying any attention to me; she is too busy ogling my husband. Her face has that 'isn't he dreamy' look on it. I wave a hand in front of her, restraining myself from pointing out that he is old enough to be her father.

"Oh, I'm sorry. Did you say something?" She at least has the grace to flush. I repeat the question.

"Yes, it actually was my first peak. I had to hike the namesake first." She laughs.

Over lunch we exchange pleasantries and pass cameras back and forth to document the moment. Marcy slyly asks us to sign her trail book; she collects signatures of people she meets along the way. I have a suspicion she recognized Vic but was gracious enough to respect our privacy. The beard, sunglasses and battered hat fool some fans, but not all. Too bad her autograph reads, *Vic Rienz*.

After summiting Cascade, we hiked back down to the trail junction and turn left. The trail descends slightly into a pass before climbing in elevation again. The trail climbs gently on the ridge as we reach the summit of Porter Mountain. Day one of our Adirondack 46R quest, two mountains down…*and my feet are killing me!*

The wind has finally calmed down and we stretch out on the rocks enjoying the view, the top of Mt. Porter offers a nearly 360-degree view.

Welcoming the chance to rest, I flop down on a rock and kick off my boots. As I peel away my socks I suck in my breath at the sight of a huge angry red blister on the back of my heel.

"Whoa, babe." Vic says, picking up my foot and examining the blister. "Ouch."

"I know, I know." I say, waving my hands in frustration. "I should have broken the boots in more, I was so excited to wear them I didn't use good judgment."

"Here, let me kiss the boo-boo." He tenderly kneads the ball of my foot, then bends and kisses the blister.

"That feels good, don't stop." I moan. No one gives a foot massage like Vic. This pleasure might outweigh the pain.

"Gladly," he smiles, running his hand up to rub my calf.

"Oh you're good."

"So I've been told." He runs his hand farther up my thigh slipping under my pants leg. I slap it away. Undeterred, he leans in and breathes, "I don't have to stop…" and he flicks his tongue across my earlobe causing a shiver to travel up my spine.

"But not good enough for you to seduce me on top of a mountain in front of God and anyone else who comes around the corner of that trail."

While I'm very aware that Vic possesses many talents, I

didn't realize first aid was one of them. With practiced ease he
bandages my blister with a piece of moleskin and duct tape. In no
time he has me back in my boots ready to climb down the
mountain.

Rested, a few snacks under our belts, dry socks and the
promise of a soak in the hot tub and a meal in a four star
restaurant is all the motivation I need to endure my blister and
get down the mountain. There is glamping, which is pampered
camping, this is hikamping, pampered hiking. It almost seems
unfair to count these mountains if we don't rough it and camp
out. Actually, from the research I've done, it's almost impossible
to complete all 46 of the high peaks without some bushwhacking
and camping out.

While hiking up a mountain is strenuous, the hike down is
treacherous. The downward angle of the slope puts pressure on
the knees and joints while adding momentum to slips and slides.
A proving ground for a good hiking boot is its downhill
performance on descents. So far I appreciate the sturdy
construction of my boots, holding my feet stable as I use my
hiking poles to maneuver through the maze of rocks and tree
roots. I repeat to myself, "Slow and steady, as she goes. If Vic
gets ahead of me, that's okay, it's a hike not a competition."

As we descend the trail, the noise of civilization intrudes on
our mountain solitude. The roar of motorcycles winding through
the valley, the sound of cars on the highway, and the friendly
chatter of hikers mar the pristine silence of the woods. Up to
now it has been fairly quiet on the trail and mountain summits
due to our early departure, but as the day moves on, more and
more hikers hit the trail. The hike up Cascade and Porter is
popular due to the magnificent views and short distance, making
it a well-liked destination for hikers.

As the noise increases, the road comes into view. We stop at
the wooden box at the trailhead and fill out our exit information
then trudge out to the vehicle. At the car we indulge in a quick
embrace congratulating ourselves on a hike well done, knowing
this is only the beginning. If we expect to complete the 46R
challenge, we need to put more miles on the trail, spend nights
camping out in the open, endure cold, rain, heat and even snow.

Today was simply a warm up for the real event. There are no delusions that hiking up 46 mountains with steep rocky assents over 4000 feet will be an easy task. It's back to training mode for us, beginning with healthy eating, weight training, rest…and pure grit.

I heave a sigh of relief as I slip the pack from my shoulders, wiggling out the kinks in my muscles. The moleskin and retying my lace helped lessen the pressure on my heel, overall I feel good. Vic tosses the packs in the back of the Land Rover and that's when I see them. The ones, that couple camping across the lake from our house with the whirling hula-hoops and nunchucks. The girl is twenty yards away from me, a vision in glossy black Goth, almost everything black. Her hair is black, she's wearing black pants, black shirt, and tall black lace-up work boots with huge buckles. I can even see the black liner etched around her eyes. Everything black except for the red buffalo plaid shirt she is wearing, with a tulle ruffle underskirt over her leggings. Very interesting hiking attire, if I do say so myself.

Every stitch of clothing on the young man is black. His hair is a knotted mass of dreadlocks reaching half way down his back; making the ones Vic grew last summer for a movie look like a shaggy dust mop. These are serious dreadlocks from years of growth. The young woman's hair is caught up in a ponytail of glossy cornbraids. The ends of the braids are capped in beads which swing, catching the sun in a cascade of rainbow glitter, her dark hair shimmers in the light like a water fall of black ink. Then the tattoos start, exotic swirls of color running up and down their arms, on any exposed surface, making it difficult to distinguish what is truly skin from perhaps, a piece of fabric.

"It's them." I hiss at Vic, staring in disbelief. "The mystery campers." At first I wasn't sure but then I catch a glimpse of a hot pink hula-hoop in the back of an apple green Westfalia van. Painted on the van are swirling images of twirling hula-hoops and fire breathing nun-chucks intertwined with musical notes.

"It's those kids who were camping across the lake from us. Vic, look, quick!" I grab his arm, tugging him in the direction of the van. The young man stops to tighten a bungee cord that holds a dozen or more hula-hoops of varying sizes and colors to the roof. Before we have a chance to call out, they climb in, slam the door and swing out onto the road doing a U-turn.

"It's them." I cry, hopping up and down on my toes.

"Them, who?" He asks, straightening up from stowing the packs in the SUV.

"The couple from across the lake, the mysterious campers from last week." I dash out from behind our car to get a better view of the departing van.

Vic follows me. He squints and takes in the apparatus strapped to the roof of the van and curses. "What the hell, hey you, stop!" He calls out running after the van.

The dark haired man in the van toots the horn, waves, pulls onto the highway and drives off.

"Son of a ..." Vic yells, throwing his hat onto the ground. "Did you get a license plate number?" He asks, his voice rife with frustration.

"No it was too small. It looks like a European license plate, small and more rectangular than ours. I couldn't make out the numbers."

"Damn it." He mutters, picking up his hat, slapping it against his thigh to dislodge the dust. At this point we've attracted the attention of the other hikers, loitering around as they prepare to hit the trailhead or depart from the parking area. I give a weak smile and wave in apology motioning Vic to get in the car. Once in the privacy of our vehicle, we look at each other and shrug.

"Maybe I'm getting upset over nothing." Vic says, rubbing the stubble on his chin, which has gone from two day sexy to homeless vagrant. "They're probably just kids doing their own thing and I'm blowing this way out of proportion."

"Did you notice the van was painted with hula-hoops and nun-chucks? Maybe an advertisement for acrobatic performers?"

"Yeah, here in the Adirondacks? I don't know, Elle." He drums his fingers on the steering wheel and bites his lower lip.

"I'm not sure why they upset you. They look harmless, if nothing else, rather exotic and interesting."

"I have my reasons." His voice clipped and response short. His lips thin to a fine line, his face taking on a guarded expression and he closes up. Discussion over.

"And you won't discuss those reasons?"

He shakes his head and refuses to talk any further when I question and probe. I settle back into my seat with my hands folded as we drive to the hotel...in silence. What the heck is going on in his mind? Why is he so upset over what appears to be an innocuous couple of hippies?

When life gives you mountains, put on your boots and hike.

"Elle, I told you so." Vic calls, slamming the front door shut, the dogs frisking and jumping around his feet excited from their walk to the mailbox, close to a mile away from Camp.

It's been a week of peace and quiet at Camp since our hiking trip up Mt. Cascade and Porter. No Malibu Blonde Twinkies barging in to ruin our privacy. No mysterious campers on the lakeshore. Ike was gone for six days to visit his sister in Montreal. Just Vic and I, sleeping in late, relaxing on the porch, swimming in the lake and basking in the summer sun, it's been heaven. The summer Vic always wanted, a go-nowhere, do-nothing kind of summer. But even paradise can become too quiet.

"What's up?" I ask, glancing up from the task of pulling out the seams of my old wedding dress. Lani wants to incorporate pieces of it into the gown she's designing for herself. I was so excited she'd consider using my old dress that without a thought I charged in and made the offer to rip it apart.

"Ouch!" I stick my thumb in my mouth, sucking off the drop of blood. I must have pricked myself a million times by now with the stupid seam ripper. Sharp little sucker. I look up to see Vic standing in front of me holding a pink envelope under his nose, sniffing it appreciatively.

"Perfume." He says, a goofy grin plastered to his face.

"What are you doing with a pink perfumed envelope? New girlfriend?"

"It's not for me. It's for you from your friend. I told you she was going to contact you."

"What are you talking about?" I laugh, snatching the envelope out of his hand.

"It's from your friend, Mrs. Hamish Carlton Wannamaker, *the* III."

"Who?" I look at the large pink envelope. It appears to be an invitation of some sort.

"Your Barbie hiking sister, Twinkie!" He beams with glee, smug in the knowledge that his prediction was correct.

"You're kidding?" I exclaim.

"I told you she was inviting you to some fundraiser thing."

"How did you hear her say that and I didn't? At the time you were very busy tormenting me."

"That shows how good I am, darling. I can multitask, pleasure my woman and keep tabs on everything going on around me."

"Bite me."

"Gladly."

I scoff at him and tear open the envelope; a handwritten note in delicate script is attached to an invitation. It reads, *Dear Ellen, I would surely be delighted if you'd join me as my guest for the annual Lake Placid Breast Cancer Awareness Luncheon this coming Thursday. You may email your reply to sugartwinkie@gspace.com.*

Vic comes to peer over my shoulder. "That's only three days away."

"A good excuse for me not to go."

He massages my shoulders "I think you should go. With precautions, of course."

"Why? I thought she was a bit strange."

"I thought she was cute, in a perky Barbie doll kind of way. And it might be good for you to have a few friends up here. You always say you miss your girlfriends back home."

"Yes, but that's different. I've known those women for ages; it takes time and commitment to develop a friendship. And besides I have you. It's harder to keep you a secret if I'm out socializing with people."

"I'm not going to the lunch. I'd look stupid sitting with a bunch of women wearing pink." Vic says. "What would we have to talk about? I'd look like a dog out of water."

"The saying is a 'duck out of water'." I shake my head and roll my eyes. I can imagine the reaction if he showed up at lunch. Once the jaws stopped hitting the table and the ladies put their eyes back in place, the room would break into bedlam. Oh baby, there would be plenty to talk about, trust me.

"Before you give her an answer, give me the invitation and I'll research the event to make sure it is legitimate and run a background search on Twinkie. I'll check out her family, husband's business and any particulars I can pick up on the Internet. I was going to do it last week but got distracted by our hike. Ike should be back, I'll have him help me." He goes over to the coffee pot, pours two mugs; adds a generous splash of cream. With a grimace he drops a spoonful of sugar into one of the mugs for me. He walks around the kitchen island, hands off the coffee and leans against the countertop surveying me. He chews on his lower lip, nodding his head up and down, in his customary 'thinking' pose. A loose lock of hair falls across his forehead and I can't help but notice how adorable he looks, forehead wrinkled in thought, lips scrunched up, drumming his fingers on the granite surface.

"This is how I think it should go down." He finally says.

I laugh, sputtering my coffee. "You sound like James Bond or a military commander planning a campaign. It's only a lunch."

"I agree. But you remember what happened last year when we invited a stranger into our lives without thoroughly investigating him. The encounter with Herr Schmidt should be a warning to us, we were lucky to escape with our lives."

An involuntary shiver runs up my spine at the mention of Dieter Schmidt's name. I still wake at night in a cold sweat thinking of how close we were to falling into the clutches of that man. And I'm the one who hired Herr Schmidt, maybe I should listen to Vic.

"If she checks out, you email her your acceptance of the invitation but insist you drive. Tell her your brother-in-law, who will be Ike, needs to go to Lake Placid on that day so he would be delighted to drive the two of you to the event."

"And you think Ike will agree to this idea."

"Not at first, but I have ways of convincing him. It's worth a try, right boy?" Vic leans down to scratch Porky behind the ears. "By the way have you seen my cell phone?"

I shake my head no and cast a dubious glance at Porky. "You might want to ask him. I told you to be careful about leaving stuff lying around. He chews and eats just about everything."

Vic sighs looking around the room for his lost cell phone.

"Back to our conversation," I say. "I don't see Ike agreeing to drive two ladies to a society charity event."

"He will when I tell him he can turn the garage into a workshop for his motorcycles. He's been hinting around about putting out some bids on jobs. I'd like him to stay up here with us in the summer. It would help if he had something to occupy his time."

"You're going to allow strangers with motorcycles to come into our Camp?"

"Absolutely not. He'll insist on picking up and delivering the bikes. That way no one has to come onto the property."

"Okay, if you think so, lunch with Twinkie might be fun. It's time to dress up, put on a little makeup, and break out something other than shorts and flip-flops. Let me see, what should I wear? I don't know if I have anything appropriate in my closet."

"All those clothes and nothing to wear?" He raises his eyebrow in question. "You look beautiful in anything, Buttercup." He grabs two biscuits out of the cookie jar and calls for the dogs. "I can't believe I'm saying this but, Porky, Cyrus, let's go check out Miss Twinkie." He stops to place a kiss on my forehead and heads toward the stairway. "Come on, boys."

"Oh, damn it, Porky!" I hear him cry from the living room. I think he found his cell phone and from the tone of his voice, it's not in one piece.

Chuckling to myself, I go back to ripping out the seams of the dress, stitch by stitch, such tedious work. I smile at the thought of Lani walking under the birch trees down the lane to the lake, in a gown made from the remnants of my wedding dress. With renewed determination, I jab the seam pick into the material and stab myself, again. A drop of bright red blood spills onto the material, leaving a crimson stain on the dress…

Vic

Vic strides down the path to the lakeside boathouse, pondering the wisdom of sending Elle off with a strange woman. He realizes she needs friends and the strain of his chaotic lifestyle makes social relationships difficult. "Damn it. Why is life never simple?" He fumes. Porky tugs at his pant leg so he stops to throw a stick for the dog. Lost in thought he fails to notice Cyrus waiting patiently for his turn. Vic gazes off into the woods trying to outline a plan in his head. If he sends Ike with Elle, that's as good as having an armed body guard. Ike has a permit to carry a concealed weapon. *What can happen once she is inside a charity event?*

Two weeks have passed since the last ominous letter arrived at Camp. Generally, celebrity stalkers grow weary of the game and move onto other targets. Or is this one simply laying low, bidding their time until he *or* she strikes without warning.

"Damn it." Vic swears under his breath, he is at a cross roads with indecision. He wants to protect Elle and yet let her lead a normal life. At least as normal as possible with his movie star fame status, but the situations of the last two years have had nothing to do with him. One was a ghost from the past and the other just a simple fluke of fate. He doesn't want Elle to turn into a fearful woman, paranoid that everyone she meets is out to harm her. He prefers to keep the disturbing information to himself, protect her from the ugly underside of his lifestyle. The first letters came through his fan mail base and followed the classic celebrity stalker profile which generally is more bluff than intent. But the letters received at Camp have been more personal in nature, and more disturbing.

The unknown element in this scenario is Elle. Historically, his delightful wife has been disobedient. It makes him furious when he tells her to be cautious for her own good. She doesn't listen, following him into dangerous situations or taking off on her own. How can he convince her to stay in public areas and keep Ike close without telling her about the letters? He needs to tell her, but how, without disturbing her sense of security.

"Elle, Elle...I love you, but you're killing me. I could throttle you sometimes." He muses. "Bad enough you have me canoeing and hiking all through this forsaken wilderness, not that I haven't enjoyed it, but now we need body guards? How do I tell you with out alarming you." Vic sighs and starts walking only to trip over Cyrus and fall to his knees. "And I need to stop talking to myself and pay attention to where I am going." Cyrus yips in joy, rolling on top of Vic, thinking this is a great new game.

The well-worn path from the house to the lake ends at the sandy beach, Vic climbs the steps of the boathouse calling out for Ike. Ike lives in the boathouse during the summer. The little house snug on the shoreline keeps him close to us and in visiting distance with his family. Between Ike, the security firm and private investigator, he fervently hopes he's taken the necessary precautions to keep his family safe. Lifting his head to the sky he adds a prayer under his breath, "Dear Lord, if you have any extra guardian angels just lounging around up there, please send them down. It would be much appreciated."

*Over every mountain there is a path, although it may not
be seen from the valley.
Theodore Roethke.*

While I assumed a nonchalant air about the charity lunch
with Vic, I'm excited about the invitation. I even Googled 'what
to wear to a charity luncheon'. The advice offered by the fashion
gurus on the Internet is as follows: a business or networking
event requires a skirt suit or sheath dress. But a social or charity
event, flowery dresses, flouncy skirts and pretty blouses are
suitable options. Armed with this information and a fashion
consultation call to my daughter, Lani, I raid my closet to select
an outfit suitable for an outing with a woman called Twinkie. I
chose a floral sheath dress with a flouncy skirt and a modest
scoop bust line. Plundering my accessory wardrobe, I found
matching high heels, earrings and under the bed, a bangle bracelet
lost three weeks ago. How it escaped Porky's unwarranted
attention remains a mystery.

The morning of the luncheon, I'm putting the finishing
touches of my makeup on when I hear Ike honking, impatiently
waiting down on the driveway.

Vic stands by the car, holding the door open for me. He has
a meeting at Camp with his press agent later in the day. Dressed
in perfectly tailored black slacks and a white shirt open at the
neck, he looks delicious. The corners of his mouth turn up in a
smile, as he looks me up and down. He approves of the dress.
Taking me by the arm, he looks intently into my eyes. I feel a
change in the air pressure and time stands still for a couple of

beats. I get a hot flash at the close proximity of his body.

"Now promise me. You will stay close to Ike or in public areas. No wondering off by yourself."

I stand on tiptoe and kiss his cheek. "You worry too much."

He leans back and raises my chin, "Ellen, I'm not kidding. Promise?" His voice is low and hard.

"Whoa, serious man. Yes, dearrr..." I can't hold back the sarcasm from creeping into my voice and for extra effect I put on an exaggerated 'good girl' face.

Vic shakes his head and cups my face between his hands, his eyes locked with mine, he tilts my chin up kissing me full on the mouth, the way he devours my lips belies his anxiety. My arms circle around his neck and his hand moves to the back of my head, holding me firm, beseeching me to be careful.

We jump apart as Ike beeps the horn. "Hey Amigo, enough all ready. Chica, let's get this party on the road before I come to my senses and refuse to chauffeur two blonde daft Miss Daisies."

With a warning look and a squeeze of my arm, Vic helps me into the front seat, clips my seatbelt in and shuts the door. With a wave we're off.

I settle into my seat, smooth out the wrinkles of my dress and glance over at Ike. "You're looking particularly handsome this morning." I comment.

He grunts, not taking his eyes off the road. "That Twinkie lady, is she going to be ready when we stop by to pick her up?"

"Yes, she emailed me accepting our offer to drive and will be waiting at the gate."

"Perfect. I don't have time to sit around waiting for some lady to decide which pair of shoes matches her dress," he grumbles.

I giggle, "Careful, she's going to take one look at you and forget about her shoes. You clean up well."

He gives an exaggerated sigh, drops his sunglasses down to give me a direct glare.

Well, I appreciate the effort because he looks great. Ike is wearing black dress slacks, a matching sport coat and a white button down shirt open at the collar. The contrast between the black and white clothing only enhances the copper hue of his good looks. He handles the SUV with practiced ease; body stature relaxed yet alert, should the need for action arise. I've often thought of him as a throwback to an Irish Warrior, the pagan king banishing the marauding Roman invaders. But today he reminds me of a sleek, sinewy tiger, taunt, on edge, alert and ready to spring into action.

I start humming tunelessly to myself. I can't wait to see his expression when he meets Twinkie; he's going to make Vic pay for this favor, big time.

And true to her word, Twinkie is standing at the entrance to her Camp. A wrought iron sign spells out the name, Camp Georgia North.

"Why the hell is she waiting at the road?" He gripes. "We could have driven down to pick her up. And what is that pile of claptrap she has with her."

"I don't know why she insisted on being picked up at the gate. And those are her baskets for the Chinese auction."

"Chinese auction." His eyes widen. "I thought this fundraiser was for breast cancer. What do Chinese people have to do with it?"

"No, no, a Chinese auction is kind of like a raffle where you buy tickets and then use them to bid on items you want to win." I pat the sleeve of his jacket, reassuring him. "It will be fine, we have plenty of room in the hatchback."

"Whatever…" He says pulling the vehicle to a stop and gets out to help load Twinkie's baskets.

"Hi, Twinkie." I say, hopping out of the car to welcome her.

"Hey, you all. Thanks for the lift." She walks to the rear of the car, takes one look at Ike and squeals, "Ewww…weee. Would you look at that gorgeous piece of manhood!" She extends her hand to Ike, batting her obviously false eyelashes at him, "Hey there, sugarbear, my name is Twinkie Wannamaker. It's surely my pleasure to meet you. Darling, you can drive me anywhere."

Ike reaches over and shakes just the fingertips of her hand, making as little body contact as possible. "Ummm…yeah sure." He says. "Pleasure is all mine." He rivets me with a glare that is locked and loaded with pure venom. I stifle a grin realizing that today maybe more fun than I anticipated. Just watching Ike squirm under the attention of Twinkie may prove hilarious.

Twinkie sitting in the back-seat is a parody in designer pink. Everything about her is pink: pink dress, shoes, accessorizing jewelry and expensive handbag. Her lips are outlined in matching pink lipstick. She is Malibu Barbie in pink, and a naughty thought comes to me, in the world of Barbie, she never wore underpants. Would Twinkie go commando?

While the outfit has potential to be garish, I must admit, Twinkie has an eye for fashion and looks well-polished and chic. I, on the other hand, have the appeal of a cute puppy, failing to enter into the realm of smart sophistication. I'm suspicious it has something to do with breeding and a whole lot of money. I have the genetic strains of a hippie mother and a working class father running through my bloodlines. I do the rustic woodsy girl look well but left to my own devices fall short of chic or elegant.

Twinkie keeps a running dialogue for the hour and fifteen minute ride to Lake Placid. It is a beautiful day for a drive, blue skies with puffy white clouds, temperatures in the mid-seventies. Impassively, Ike chauffers us through the hamlets of Inlet, Eagle Bay, Saranac Lake as she describes in detail her surgery, the course of chemotherapy and breast reconstruction. Or as she puts it, how she beat the cancer. At one point I thought Ike's ears were going to fall off as she educated both of us on the how and whys of reconstructive breast surgery.

"Y'all, first they make a slit here." She demonstrates by pulling the low V of her dress bodice to the side. "Then they take what looks like a soft squishy bag of Jell-O…"

While I admire her courage and honesty, I'm not sure all the detailed specifics were warranted. I see Ike's eyes rapidly blinking, his lips pursed and his breathing resembles panting, coming out in short puffs of annoyance. There is way too much estrogen floating around in the vehicle and it's killing him. Personally, I'm enjoying his discomfort. He needs to get out of his man cave now and then, experience a bit of feminine energy.

As we enter the outskirts of Lake Placid I look for the giant Viking statue that stood guard over the putt-putt golf course for years. He's gone!

"What happened to the Viking statue?" I cry. "When my

children were younger we came every summer to play miniature golf under the Viking."

"Oh, they took him down years ago." Twinkie says nonchalantly. "I heard someone over in Lake George bought him but he was in such bad shape they put him in storage and he hasn't been seen since."

"Oh, too bad." Everything changes. Sigh.

The two-lane road leading into town is lined with hotels, restaurants and a plaza, building after building angling down the steep hill towards Mirror Lake, the tiny lake surrounded by the Village of Lake Placid.

Circling around to the east side of the lake, we drive under a stone archway affixed with the name, Lake Placid Club and down a winding driveway to the clubhouse where the luncheon will be held. Ike opens the car doors for us like a perfect gentleman and assures Twinkie he will be back in plenty of time to drive us home. To me, he leans over and in a low voice whispers, "I'll be in the parking lot with my phone if you need anything, call or text."

"Sure." I place a quick kiss on his cheek and quip, "See you later, good luck on your prostrate examination."

Twinkie stops in her tracks and wheels around to look back at Ike, her face contorted in sympathy. "Oh lord, honey, glad I'm not in your shoes today. That makes a trip to the gynecologist sound like fun. But I never thought I'd be envious of a proctologist." She gives him a lewd wink, giggles and propels me, loaded with her Chinese auction baskets, toward the clubhouse door.

I hear Ike growl, the heat of his glare threatens to scorch a hole in the back of my dress.

Immediately we are swept into a gaggle of chattering women who welcome Twinkie with a round of hugs and kisses. I stand off to the side, not wanting to intrude.

"Ladies," Twinkie trills to the group. "This is my dear friend, Ellen. She lives just two camps down from me on the lake. She and her husband bought the Bellamy Camp. I was purely devastated when Julie and Phil moved away but I cannot tell you how excited I am to have a new friend. We just hit it off like two peas in a pod. Isn't she the most beautiful thing you have ever seen? I would die for this honey ash blonde hair." Twinkie runs a hand down my hair...and the hand travels down my back to rest quite *intimately* on my butt. Uncomfortable with the effusive introduction and close proximity of her body, I squirm away under the guise of searching for a table to set down the baskets. Good Lord, I've just met the woman, you'd swear we're best friends from kindergarten.

A raven-haired woman steps forward, her smile sly and her eyes cool. She extends her hand. "Hello, I'm Sara Miles, it's a pleasure to meet you. Here, let me help you with those baskets."

I hand Twinkie's donation over to Sara and the group of women line up to welcome me. I try pairing names with some identifiable feature, be it hair color, jewelry or clothing to help me remember each of them. But by the fifth handshake, I can't remember if Martha had the madras skirt and white shirt or the one with the close-cropped pewter grey hair.

Twinkie leads us toward the back of the room to an open veranda overlooking the golf course. The air is scented with a mélange of expensive perfume, the tinkling of crystal goblets, and waiters circle the room passing silver trays filled with artfully arranged hors d'oeuvres. The aroma of sizzling shrimp reminds me I'm famished, it's been a long time since breakfast. The veranda is large enough for a hundred or more guests. Cheerful bouquets of yellow and pink flowers form the centerpiece of tables covered in pink check tablecloths. Matching napkins folded into a fan shape sit atop white plates while tall stem crystal goblets and gleaming silverware complete the festive air. A large striped awning protects the entire affair from sun and any potential threat of rain. The view of Lake Placid and Whiteface Mountain in the horizon is magnificent.

Before sitting down, I snag a glass of wine and an appetizer *or two* from the circling waiters. I'm starving. Choosing a seat at the table I try making conversation with the women in closest proximity. I nod and smile, politely answering the potpourri of questions peppered at me.

Yes, I love the mountains. And oh, my husband travels extensively for work. How many children do we have and etc...etc...etc. But truthfully, I'm enjoying the company of other women, exchanging stories, common interests, joining in with the ladies. Twinkie dominates the conversation on my right, her arm around my shoulders and she's twirling my hair with her fingers. I find the unwanted attention distracting, and impossible to stop with out-making an awkward scene. I don't think she even realizes she is doing it. To diffuse Twinkie's attention I engage the woman on my left in conversation and to my delight discover she has hiked many of the high peaks in the Adirondacks. Her husband is a member of the 46R club.

Nadine Williams, a cancer survivor herself, is tall and pencil thin. Her salt and pepper grey hair is short, verging on almost masculine and her skin tanned a light bronze from spending time in the outdoors. Glacial blue eyes dominate her face, piercing in their intensity. At first I feel intimidated but soon find myself drawn to her honest and direct demeanor as she answered my bazillion questions on hiking the high peaks. We found other commonalities in addition to hiking. Nadine's daughter also lives in California, not far from Lani. We lamented the pitfalls of having adult children living so far away from home. Nadine's family has owned a camp on one of the islands in Lake Placid for generations. Kate Smith, a famous singer back in the fifties and sixties was one of her neighbors.

When lunch is served Twinkie gives up her fondling of my hair in favor of eating. The lobster bisque and grilled chicken salad are excellent and I enjoy them immensely. A good portion of the food served is from local farms. The host club supports the local agricultural community by serving fresh food directly from the farm to the table.

Dessert is a luscious raspberry cream tart. It is so good that I have to restrain myself from licking the plate. A dark-haired woman named Janet from our table stands signaling to the other ladies that it's time to start the presentation, leaving me alone at the table with Twinkie.

"What a lovely event." I comment to Twinkie as the waitress pours coffee. "Thank you for inviting me."

"Well, of course, sugar darling. What do you think of my gals? Most of them are fellow breast cancer survivors."

"They're charming," I say, taking a sip of hot coffee, scalding my tongue, a reward for my haste.

Twinkie leans back in her chair and appraises me. "So do you and your hunky husband get out much, do any entertaining?"

I squirm in my seat. "Well," I hesitate. "We're kind of home bodies. His work involves so much travel that when he's back in the States, he's content to stay home."

"International?" She drawls, "How interesting."

"Sometimes." I answer. "What about your husband?" I make a blind stab at diverting the conversation toward her.

"Hamish?" She shrugs and feigns a pout. "Hamish parks his butt in Atlanta and thinks it's heaven, nowhere else on God's green earth is worth visiting. In the last few years he has developed political aspirations, running for local office. I have a difficult time getting him up here even for a week since his recent election to the county legislature."

"Oh, that's too bad."

"But…" Twinkie rounds on me and gives me a full on stare, her eyes flair with a wicked gleam. "When he does come up, ohh…eee. We sure do have a good time, if we have the right couple to join us." She arches an eyebrow and gives me a knowing look. "If you get my drift?"

"Umm…sure." I'm momentarily confused, squirming in my seat. "It's nice to have people to do things with," I add hastily, lest she gets the wrong idea about our desire to socialize. "My husband is a bit of a loner. I mean, you saw him at the house, he's not very sociable." I sigh with great dramatic effect to put my point across. It's a good thing Vic's the actor and not me, there is not a drop of thespian talent running through my veins.

"So you're saying…" Twinkie pauses, running a finger across my lips, a cat got the mouse cornered look on her face, "That you don't swing?"

"Swing?" I ask, confused. What in the world is she talking about?

"You know, honey child." Twinkie leans in so close I can feel her breath; she waggles her eyebrows up and down. "Swing…"

Still confused, I reply, "Well, yes, we do have a swing out

back on the old tree behind the house. V…um, I mean, *my husband,* he likes to swing the grandkids on it when they come over." I shrug my shoulders, "Sometimes I like to go outside, especially at night when the sun is setting and just glide back and forth. So, yes, I guess you could say I like to swing."

"Oh, my gosh." Twinkie breaks into gales of laughter. "You are so sweet. I just love you!" She lowers her voice. "You honestly don't know what swinging means?"

I shrug my shoulders in askance and make a swinging motion with my hand. "No?" I question her.

She pulls me into an awkward hug and whispers in my ear, "Honey child, *I mean,* do you and that hunky husband of yours like to indulge in the sweet nasty with other couples, ya know…swing." And with that statement she *licks* my ear!!

My eyebrows shoot up and my face turns beet red. A momentous hot flash slams through my body like a wildfire blazing out of control. I flounder in embarrassment. Oh, dear God…swing! How did the conversation go from the pleasant niceties of everyday life to kinky encounters with our husbands? And since when did the word 'swing' not mean a piece of playground equipment? I open my mouth to speak but no words come out because I'm flabbergasted. Imagine me, speechless. And Vic doesn't believe in miracles.

In a panic I look up and spy Janet, the dark-haired lady giving me a quizzical look and she smirks with a knowing look on her face. Does everyone know about Twinkie and her little sex games and realize I'm her latest victim. I'm mortified. I spot the exit sign and wonder if escape is possible. If I excuse myself to the Ladies' room, climb out the window and make a run for the car, Ike is waiting in the parking lot. I start to get up from my seat intent on making a get away.

Twinkie sensing my reaction to her proposal, sums up my horror at the idea in a flash and retreats. She removes her arm, gushing with good old southern humor. "Got ya!" She laughs, as if this was some kind of joke. "I couldn't resist teasing you a little bit. My daddy always said I have to be careful about pulling peoples' legs, one day that leg is going to fall right off in my hand." She giggles. Her giggle reminds me of the tinkling of a wind chime in a strong wind, pervasive and annoying.

"I'm teasing you. It's just that husband of yours is some kind of delicious."

I look at her aghast. What woman in her right mind makes a blatant play for another woman's husband, in broad day-light to her face? "My husband is very private." I respond stiffly.

"Well, maybe he and Hamish can go golfing sometime. I was joking about the swinging thing. The only thing my husband ever wants to do when he comes up here is swing a golf club. You would think Atlanta doesn't have enough golf courses. Sometimes I'm amazed he took off time to have the children, business, politics and golf are his passions."

She pouts.

Desperate to change the subject, I ask, "How many children do you have?" I grab the water glass in front of me to still my trembling hands and smile brightly.

"Four…eee…three." She stumbles over the number of children and then recovers, odd. "But all of them are in college and off on their own. I had them when I was a mere baby myself. Now I have time to devote myself to other activities." While she gives a dismissive shrug of her shoulders, her lips tighten as if she is holding back emotion. I sense a lonely woman with too much money and time on her hands.

"Empty nest syndrome. I can understand that." I pat Twinkie's hand and reprimand myself for wanting to ditch her. It would be mean to leave her stranded in Lake Placid without a ride. We'll stay until after the speeches then hit the road, deliver Ms. Twinkie to her doorstep and be home before dinner.

Wait until I tell Vic about my foray into the boundaries of female friendship. I'm ready to go home, I miss Vic and it's a long drive back to Camp.

I hike to burn off the crazy...

Unfortunately, Twinkie has a plan that doesn't involve returning home immediately.

"Just a quick ten minute stop, you *have* to meet Jonas and Arthur and try the magic brew. It's the best. I swear it helped me beat the cancer. I never come up to Lake Placid without stopping to pick up a gallon or two." She races on without stopping for a breath. "You will just *love* it."

I start to protest. "I'm not sure, we should be getting home." Paying no heed to me she charges on, grabbing a hold of Ike's arm and implores him with a pleading glance.

"Ike, darling, sugar. You don't mind if we stop for just a teensy-weensy little bit. The shop is on Main Street. We drive right pass it on the way home."

I swear she rubbed her breast against him shamelessly, reconstructed or not, Twinkie knows how to use her 'tatas'. To my astonishment, Ike blushes yet doesn't pull away, he fixes me with a deer caught in the headlights glare before responding, "Sure, but make it quick."

"We'll be in and out like greased lightning." She agrees, hopping in the back-seat, locking herself in with a click of her seatbelt.

The cell phone in my purse chimes, a text from Vic, if I was counting, this would be number twenty. They have been coming with regularity, about every twenty to thirty minutes. Asking innocuous questions, how was the drive, did we arrive on time, what was for lunch, overly interested for my sweet laid-back husband. His caution is bordering on the point of paranoia.

"Vic?" Ike asks with a glance at the phone in my hand. I nod yes. He shakes his head and blows out a long sigh. "How many texts have you received? Ten?"

"Try twenty." I respond.

"I thought he had a meeting this afternoon."

"It must have ended early or he's bored." I shrug and smile back at Twinkie who gives me a giddy wave. Maybe I won't rush home, let him fret, wallow awhile in his non-existent worries. Secretly, I'd enjoy the opportunity to do some shopping. I love Lake Placid with its string of charming shops along Main Street. The bookstore is holding a few books for me. A quick pop-in will save me a trip to pick them up and I need a birthday gift for my friend, Kat. We'll find a bar that serves beer, burgers and sports television for Ike, a man's version of heaven on earth.

Ike drives along the backside of Mirror Lake. The southern end of the lake is bisected by a beach, tennis courts and a toboggan ramp. Mirror Lake Drive meanders along the lake beneath a leafy green canopy of trees. The shoreline is peppered with beautiful residences and restaurants sporting outdoor patios overhanging the water's edge. I jot down a few names imagining a romantic dinner with Vic at some future date. The marina on the larger lake of Lake Placid comes into view. I wonder if the vintage tour boat is still in operation. Fond memories come to mind of the day Jack and I took the children out on the 'Dory'. It was a beautiful day with a clear view of Whiteface Mountain. I remember playing a game where we decided which of the palatial Camps we'd choose for a summer vacation. Trey wanted Camp Dakota because it had a huge stuffed bear on the porch. Lani loved a cottage built in a modern design. The building was all jutting angles with a wall of glass facing the lake. Most importantly, she loved it because there was an access road to town. She was horrified so many of the camps on Lake Placid were boat accessible only. She couldn't imagine being trapped in the wilderness without transportation to civilization. Her current residence, living in California outside of Los Angeles is simply an evolution of her DNA.

I chose a camp on a forested island at the far end of the lake.

An imposing lodge constructed of cedar bark logs and stone stands on a bald outcrop of granite overlooking the lake. A cluster of cabins, built as miniature replicas of the main building dot the shoreline, playing a game of peek-a-boo between the trees and the lake. I was charmed by the idea of an island, a sanctuary bound by water, a hidden get-away for friends and family.

Jack chose a large house covered in white birch bark that was once the home of Johnny Weissmuller, an Hungarian-born American competition swimmer turned actor best known for playing Tarzan in over twenty films of the 1930's and 1940's. He had one of the best competitive swimming records of the twentieth century. He won five gold medals and set 67 world records in the 1920's.

Around the next curve of the road the white façade of the Pine Tree Inn comes into view, profuse gardens of flowers spill over stonewalls onto the sidewalk. A riot of colorful blooms accentuates the white hotel jutting out of the hillside. Balconies framed in flowering window boxes offer a world-class view of the lake and High Peaks, a vista rivaled only by the Swiss Alps. The hotel invokes a sense of Europe with its grand staircase and lobby of ornate wainscoting and massive fireplaces.

With expert ease Ike parallel parks the SUV along the business district of the village, and refuses to leave my side. He says he already ate lunch and would be happy to tag along while Twinkie and I do our shopping. *Liar, liar...*

Before I have a chance to duck into the bookstore, Twinkie grabs my arm in a vise like grip and drags me into a small boutique shop. The words, Elixir of Health are painted in a scrolling script of green, gold and burgundy on the sign. Ike stands next to the doorway, assuming the classic bodyguard stance, hands folded behind his back and waits.

The window case shows an array of bottles and jars, all containing the miraculous Agaricus Wondrus. A bell attached to the door tinkles announcing our arrival and from the back of the shop a man's voice trills, "Twinkie, darling!" A large rotund man dressed in a pink shirt and matching plaid Bermuda shorts sails out with his arms outstretched. "Ma chere, how are you, it's been ages since we've last seen you." He enfolds her in his arms, rendering her tiny body virtually invisible in their matching pink embrace.

Twinkie giggles in delight, squealing, "Jonas, you're going to squeeze the life out of me, you silly oaf!"

"What better way to die, than in the arms of this hunk of burning love." He jokes, pulling her off her feet and swinging her body in circles. She erupts in gales of laughter.

"Jonas! Put her down," admonishes a tall man carrying a large cardboard box with Agaricus Wondrus scripted on the sides. He sets the box down on the counter and places his hands on hips; he surveys our little group shaking his head. "She is one of our best customers, don't break her."

"Oh hush yourself, Arthur. We was just having a little fun. Right, Jonas?" Twinkie says breaking away from Jonas. She primly presents her cheek to Arthur for a kiss.

"Arthur, you are as stuffy as ever." She trills, "But I love you just the same." As Arthur leans down to give Twinkie a kiss on the cheek, she turns her head and gives him a full on the mouth kiss. He reels his head back in a violent protest.

"Twinkie!" He purses his lips in disapproval.

She cackles, "Oh, you old prude. Like you've never been kissed by a lady on the lips before?"

"I try to avoid it like the plague." He says drily.

I look between the three of them in confusion and suddenly a light bulb goes on…you can take the girl out of Kansas but sometimes you can't take the Kansas out of the girl…*they are a gay couple.*

Upon closer inspection, with his blonde hair, perfect Malibu tan and sparkling green eyes, Jonas is a flamboyant enlargement of Twinkie, effusive, happy, and openly affectionate, the opposite of his partner. Arthur is tall, whippet-thin with a shaved head but sports a black mustache and goatee. His eyes are flat and calculating until he looks at Jonas, then soften with obvious affection. Talk about an odd couple…

Twinkie turns toward me and pulls me into their little circle. "This is my new friend, Ellen McCauley. We're neighbors," she gushes. "I found this little treasure right down the road from me. And you should see her husband, eeeww-eee!"

Puzzled over how I am a 'little treasure' as I tower over Twinkie, I extend a hand in greeting, Jonas' grip is warm and moist, and Arthur's is cold and dry.

Not knowing what to say, I spread my hands to encompass the entire shop, "Wow, I'm impressed. What is Agaricus Wondrus? I've never heard of it."

"Well, sugar you have come to the right place, let us introduce you to our miraculous tonic." Jonas gushes.

"Oh, Ellen, you've opened a can of worms with that question." Twinkie giggles. "Don't say I didn't warn you."

"Are you familiar with the medicinal properties of mushrooms and herbs?" Arthur asks.

"Ummm…no." And silently curse Burt for not adding mushrooms to his edible plant hikes back at Camp High Point. Burt's philosophy was, kids and mushrooms don't mix.

Jonas not missing a beat starts the monologue. "The use of medicinal mushrooms dates back to the ancient Egyptians and Chinese, these cultures used them to promote general health and longevity."

Arthur chimes in, pointing to the framed mushroom charts decorating the walls of the shop. "The difference between medicinal mushrooms and the ones you order on your pizza are medicinal mushrooms contain immune activating bet-glucans."

Jonas picks up the line. "These complex carbohydrate polymers are stored in the liver and muscles ready to be converted into energy."

"They protect and support your immune system." Twinkie chimes in. "There is good evidence that mushrooms are among the most powerful functional foods in a growing cancer-fighting and cancer-preventing arsenal. I swear Agarius Wondrus helped me beat the cancer."

I'm waiting for the three of them to break into song and dance, their cadence and chorography well orchestrated by repetition and practice.

"So what type of mushrooms do you use in your brew?" I ask with caution, interested but fearful of starting another lecture.

"Commonly we use a combination of rishi, maitake, agaricus blazei murill, and turkey tail mushrooms."

"So…?" I shrug. "Can't you just eat them instead of drinking a mushroom cocktail?"

"Cocktail?" Jonas' face turns red and he sniffs, offended by my label. "We have customized a specialized formula using exacting standards, obtaining only the finest fungi from trusted sources both here and in Asia." He looks down his nose at me and reprimands, "It is the Elixir of the Gods."

Arthur puts a calming hand on Jonas' arm. "There are several ways to ingest mushrooms. We prefer a liquid by a hot water extraction."

I nod to be agreeable. "I can't wait to try it." I say brightly, "Do you make your formula here, on site?"

"No," Jonas scoffs. "We have a specialized production facility at a hidden location. We employ highly trained professionals under maximum security to prevent a leak of the secret formula."

"Wow, very impressive." I say, thinking to myself, hope your security system works better than ours, we found Twinkie on our doorstep.

"I need six half-gallons, four for myself and I want to treat Ellen to her first installment." Twinkie links her arm through mine as I start to protest. "No arguments, my treat."

And who am I to argue with this tiny woman warrior in pink? "Sure, thank you."

As Arthur rings up our purchases, he calls over his shoulder to Jonas, "Tell Twinkie our latest news."

"Oh, my stars." Jonas exclaims, clapping his hands to his face. "You'll never believe it. Two days ago we received a call from the staff of Oprah Winfrey. They are compiling a list of products to be included in Oprah's favorite things list this Christmas. And guess what?"

Twinkie shrieks, "No way, shut up!" She squeals jumping up and down.

"Yes way!" Jonas beams. "She wants to add the Agaricus Wondus to her favorite things list." The two of them grab each other's hands and start jumping up and down in unison.

"Jonas, that is wonderful."

"Amazing!" I chime in, not wanting to be left out of the

cheerleading squad. Oprah's show has been off the air for years. I didn't realize she still compiled a list of Christmas favorite things. One of my girlfriends actually scored a ticket for Oprah's Favorite Things Christmas show. It was weeks before we tired of asking her to describe every detail of the show and her gifts.

"Do you know what this means?" Twinkie gushes. "The two of you will be uber-rich, you can open boutiques in every major city. People will be standing in line to be part of your franchise. Once you are on Oprah, your product goes viral."

Jonas and Arthur don't say a word; they nod and smile, looking like the cat that swallowed the proverbial canary. I swear Arthur preened his mustache in a gesture reminiscent of the Cheshire Cat in Alice in Wonderland, gloating over the tightly held confidence of forthcoming wealth.

"I hope you have a patent on your formula; it would be a shame for someone to copy the Agaricus Wondrus." Twinkie says.

"Oh, darling, our formula is so unique that no one and I mean, no one can duplicate the complex chemistry of our recipe. In fact, we add a secret ingredient that is nothing but the pure essence of the Adirondacks." Jonas responds with a giggle. Arthur's eyes harden into a glacial stare, he tilts his head in an infinitesimal nod at Jonas, and the emotional temperature in the room plummets, the implied warning hangs in the air.

~~~

Twenty minutes later, Ike places two pretty tote bags loaded with six half-gallon containers of Agaricus Wondrus into the back of the SUV and closes the hatch with a thud. Four of the bottles are for Twinkie and two are for Vic and me. I eye the clear glass bottle with trepidation; the mixture is slightly cloudy with a greenish tinge. Jonas says the coloring is from the high-grade matcha green tea used in the extraction process. What I do know, Vic will take one look and refuse to drink it. He tolerates my 'nuts and berries' ideas but that cloudy looking concoction sloshing back and forth crosses his line of tolerance. I'll do some research on my own when we get home before I fully commit to…*four* doses a day! *Holy snake oil.* That's a lot of elixir at twenty-five dollars a bottle. Wait until Oprah's followers enter the market place, prices will double.

The copious amount of literature Jonas handed me spills out of my oversized handbag onto the car floor. Who knew how much knowledge went into creating a microbrew that promises to cure everything from cancer to toe fungus? The claims of Agaricus Wondrus remain dubious. I doubt Arthur and Jonas developed a highly sophisticated pharmaceutical formula. Did they purchase the recipe for Agaricus Wondrus? From where and how much did it cost? And is it a truly legitimate health food or just something they wiped up in their basement.

Twinkie pats the seat next to her and insists I sit in the back so we can chat. I protest and Ike, with an evil grin on his face, places a firm hand at the small of my back and propels me into the back seat. Before I know it I'm belted in and off we go, *with* Twinkie's hand resting on my knee. If that hand moves one inch higher, I swear I'm jumping out of the car.

One would think after a busy day of lunch and shopping, Twinkie would be tired. I know I'm exhausted. Like the tireless hummingbird never seeming to rest, Twinkie chatters all the way home. From my perch in the back seat, I see the muscles in Ike's jaw twitch and his nostrils flair with the effort of trying to remain calm. I swear my ears are going to fall right off.

An hour later I pop off a text to Vic. *Hooray! Dropped Twinkie off and just turned onto the dirt road to Camp, be home soon!!*

His response, *I'll be waiting at the door. Miss you.*

My response, *XO…XO.*

Good travelers leave no tracks…

By the time Ike swings the car under the portico of the house Vic is waiting at the bottom of the flagstone staircase. He looks impossibly handsome in low-slung jeans and a tight-fitting weathered grey t-shirt. His hair falls in dark glossy waves tucked behind his ears, long enough for a bad-boy ponytail. He's growing his hair for a movie shoot in Hawaii; his character is an undercover detective posing as a surfer to ensnare marine poachers. Apparently surfer dudes wear their hair in man buns, who knew? Personally, I'm looking forward to the trademark physique of a serious surfer, broad shoulders tapering to a narrow waist *and* the golden bronze tan. *Yum-O.*

His smile grows, his dark eyes turn a warm whiskey color and the worry lines fade from his face. Ike pulls the vehicle to a halt under the portico, jumps out and unloads my purchases, including the Agaricus Wondrus dumping the entire pile on the flagstone steps.

I exit the car in slow motion, my legs stiff from a day of too much sitting and talking. Vic pulls me up the steps into a bear hug and holds me so tight it hurts. He kisses me fiercely. "I missed you." He whispers in my ears.

"I missed you too, but first I need to get out of this dress, dump the heels and have ten minutes of silence before I can tell you about my day. Open a bottle of wine, start up the hot tub and I'll grab a bathing suit."

"Don't bother with a suit." He says nuzzling the back of my neck. At my lack of response, he loosens his embrace, a look at my face has him questioning. "Everything okay?"

"Yes, let's just say, I don't know if I can handle the pressure of a girlfriend in my life right now, especially Twinkie. Please help me out of this dress; it's killing me. Whoever invented Spanx is a hideous, sadistic monster. *Errrr*…first it started strangling my hips, then worked its way up to cut off the circulation in my chest. I can't breathe."

"I should wait until Ike leaves before…" Vic pouts, casting a glance in Ike's direction.

Ike slams the rear hatch of the SUV. "Please! I can't wait to get out of here. I've had enough female chatter to last me 'til I die. If you need me, I'll be enjoying some peace and quiet with a beer and the double header baseball game on television tonight." Sliding into the driver's seat, he continues complaining, "Thank God, this day is over, way too much crazy pink lady shit. Buddy, you will never send me out with that nut case of a woman again!" Ike twirls a finger next to his temple before slamming the door shut with a *woomph!* The tires send a spray of loose gravel across the driveway as he whizzes by Vic extending his arm out the window…it's not a fond farewell gesture, he's giving Vic the finger.

"Hey!" Vic yelps, "Did Ike just shoot me the bird?"

"Maybe." I shrug. "Justifiably so, he's had a long day." I feel remorseful over Ike having to spend his day driving Twinkie and I.

"Oh, no!" Vic exclaims, confusion clouds his face then his eyes widen in horror.

"What's the matter?" I ask.

He closes his eyes, a look of pain crosses his face, "Elle, this is not what it looks like…" he starts to say, only to be interrupted by a female voice.

"Esteban, honeybuns, you left me out in the cold. What did you do with my clothes, you bad boy?"

The hackles on the back of my neck rise, fueled by a deep sultry voice and the sly staged exclamation of, "Oh my, your wife is home."

"What the hell?" I wheel around and standing on the path leading to our house is none other than Vivian Gust, female co-star from Vic's last movie, sans clothing. She is wearing only a towel; the towel slips from her grasp and falls to the ground.

"Oops!" She shrugs her delicate sculpted shoulders and doesn't look contrite. Her eyes glitter with arrogant confidence as she gives Vic a full body scan and licks her lips, a lioness stalking her prey.

"What the hell is she doing here?" I impale Vic with my eyes. "I thought you had a meeting with your publicist? You never mentioned Vivian Gust was invited. Did she come along and stay for the fun? Forget to send her home, did you?" A deadly rage seizes my body, words spill out of my mouth in a green haze of jealous vapor, "You said I could trust you, said she meant nothing to you." I stab him in the chest with my finger, wanting to inflict pain. "You lied to me!"

"This is your wife? Wow, you were right when you said she was older. She looks like my mother." Vivian taunts as she picks up her towel but doesn't bother covering herself.

"Agghhh…what did you say? You, you Hollywood hussy!" The events of the day catch up with me like a freight train careening down a hill out of control. I make a lunge for her, heedless of the consequences of accosting a major Hollywood celebrity. Vic manages to grab me by the waist and swing me over his shoulder. I land on his back with a *whoosh*, knocking the air out of my lungs, momentarily silencing me.

"Vivian, what the hell are you still doing here?" Vic turns to her, his face red with anger.

"You invited me."

"What? You invited her! What the hell is she doing in my house, with no clothes on!" I yell, kicking and beating my fists against his back.

"Esteban, darling, this is awkward. Maybe I should check into a local hotel, until you can straighten this out with your wife, then I'll come back or you can meet me at the hotel."

"Vivian, you need to leave, now!" I can feel Vic's chest heave with anger.

"Darling, I need a ride. You can't expect me to walk back to town."

Vic sets me down, holding on to the back of my dress and

squares off with Vivian. "You got yourself here. Now figure out a way to get off my property before I call the police and have you arrested for trespassing." Vic pulls the towel out of her hand and tosses it in her face. "Oh, by the way, don't forget your towel. Hit the road!" He jerks his head in the direction of the driveway. "I'm calling Gary Jenkins and telling him he's fired. If this is his idea of a publicity stunt I'm not amused."

"Esteban, are you kidding? This stuff I just shot is gold." A small squat man steps out of the bushes holding up a long lens camera. "Every tabloid in the country will pick up these pictures. The shot of your wife's ass hanging off your shoulder alone will set me up for early retirement."

Vic turns, his face a mask of disbelief. "August Findley, how the hell did you get here? You son of a bitch, give me that camera. I'm going to kill you first and then I'm going to kill that slimy bastard, Jenkins." Vic leaps at the man and knocks him to the ground. Vivian starts screaming. Unable to resist, I turn and give her a shove, landing her pretty little ass right into my rosebushes.

"You bitch." She screams. "You're going to pay for this, wait and see!"

It's worth it; those thorns are going to leave a mark.

Vic and August scuffle on the gravel driveway until Vic ends up on top, holding the swearing man down by the throat.

"What in the holy name of Jesus is going on here?" Ike yells running up the path from the boathouse, pistol in hand. He shoves the pistol in the waistband of his jeans and grabs Vic by the shoulders. "Vic, buddy, back off. That's enough."

Vic rolls off August, panting, wiping the blood from a cut at the corner of his mouth. "Get that son of a bitch out of here and make sure he takes her with him." Vic points to Vivian, scratched and bleeding from her tumble in the rosebushes.

"I'm suing, that woman assaulted me." Vivian cries, pointing at me. "Esteban, honey, we had such a good time on the movie set, come on, baby." She sidles up to Vic. "Don't you remember?"

Vic turns in disgust, "Where is your car?"

"We don't have one. Gary left us here. He thought leaving

us stranded with you in the woods had the potential for a new reality show." Vivian gushes trying to angle her body closer to Vic's. I think I'm going to gag. It's all I can do not to toss her into the bushes again.

"It could be fun." She croons.

"You broke my camera, you asshole!" August curses, holding up the smashed camera in one hand.

"You're trespassing on my property." Vic threatens. "And if you or any of your slimy friends show up at my home or those pictures go public," Vic takes August by the throat and slams him against the house. "You will be sorry." He hisses between clenched teeth. "I'm not your average pretty boy, I will make your life a living hell. Do we understand each other?"

August nods mutely, terror shimmers in his eyes.

"If you aren't off my property in ten seconds, I'm calling the police."

I groan, not the cops, anything but the Old Forge Police department. God, would they love finding Vivian here. My naked towel experience of two years ago would pale in comparison to the show she is putting on today. Instead, maybe we can call the State Forest Rangers, I understand they are authorized law enforcement officers.

"Vic, catch." Ike says, tossing his pistol to Vic. "I'll go get the car and get this trash out of here. Chica, go get some duct tape. Either they go willingly or we'll tape them up and I'll drop them off at the police station in town. We take trespassing very seriously up here, folks."

"I was invited." Vivian whines, pulling a skimpy t-shirt dress over her head from an oversized handbag stashed on the patio. "Don't you dare touch me with duct tape!"

"No, you crashed a meeting, uninvited." Vic says, "Vivian, don't mess with me, you'll be sorry. Go find someone who appreciates your attention."

Ike pulls the car up, skidding to a stop. He flings open the rear door and motions for Vivian and August to get in. The expression on his face is thunderous and brooks no argument. Celtic Warrior in full fury… glad that look isn't aimed at me. Although when Vic and Ike's tempers flair, it is kind of *hot*…

Vivian, in one last stroke of revenge, reaches into her purse pulls out a handful of photographs and flings them at my feet. "Believe what you want, but a picture is worth a thousand words." Scattered on the ground like the crumbled pieces of my heart lie a dozen pictures of Vivian, in Vic's arms in what can only be described as compromising positions.

"Elle," Vic says, "I can explain." He holds his hands out in a pleading gesture.

My composure crumbles at the sight of the pictures, turning I stumble up the steps to the house. "Leave me alone." I whisper, my voice strangled by sobs. Before he has a chance to respond, I'm running up the stairs, blinded by tears.

~~~

Vic

Ike swings into the driver's side of the SUV and pulls the door shut with a slam. He leans out the window and says, "Buddy, you don't pay me near enough to put up with the shit I've gone through today. We need a small army of mob hit men to put up with all this crap. You are my best friend and I'd do anything for you, but this is getting ridiculous." Ike puts the car in gear and pulls away. Vivian pokes her head out the window, blowing kisses at Vic.

"If you change your mind, Esteban, you know where to find me." She waves.

Good grief…

Vic runs a hand over his mouth and shakes his head, doubting the intelligence of Hollywood actresses. Talk about never giving up, Vivian has a reputation for falling in love with her leading men. He feels totally spent by the whole experience. A small line furrows between his eyebrows as he spies his wife's purchases scattered across the entrance to the house. He picks up a bottle of Agaricus Wondrus and inspects it, "What the hell?" Vic mutters, "What kind of vile witches brew did Elle find this time? This day just gets better and better."

He bends down and picks up the photographs Vivian threw

across the driveway. He wonders how he is going to convince his wife of his fidelity. It seemed like a good idea at the time. Elle goes off with Twinkie for a girls' day in town while he took care of some public relations business here at the house. What he didn't plan on was Gary Jenkins bringing Vivian and the paparazzi into his home. Vic has zero tolerance for that kind of behavior. Gary has been Vic's publicity agent for years, he trusted him. What made Gary think this stunt with Vivian would work.

Vic sorts through the pictures Vivian tossed at Elle's feet. The pictures are from a scene that was deleted at the final cut of the movie. The producer decided to down play the violence and sex to secure a PG rating and attract a younger audience to promote after-market movie goods. Vic was relieved the sex scenes were deleted. Elle knows enough about the movie industry to understand he's only doing his job, what he gets paid for, but it's difficult to watch the one you love in the arms of another person. He knows for a fact if the situation were reversed he would be wild with jealousy.

He massages his forehead to ease the tension of a headache brewing in his temple, wondering if a stiff drink is in order before he apologizes for this mess. The image of Vivian standing naked on his doorstep accusing his wife of being an old lady is enough to bring on a migraine. Vivian's lucky she only got tossed in the rose bushes. When aroused, Elle's temper over-rides her common sense and caution. If she had her way, Vivian would be tied naked to a tree, smeared with honey and left for the bears. He stops at the bar, pours a Jack Daniels neat and tosses it back. He grimaces as the bitter liquor burns down his throat and into his belly. And to make matters worse, he received another threatening letter in the mail this morning. This one riddled with personal information, information only someone close to them would have privy to know. The entire situation was making him crazy. And now he has to deal with the aftermath of a day with Twinkie and Vivian Gust. He envies Ike down in the boathouse with nothing more complicated than a beer and the ballgame. He heaves a deep sigh and heads for the stairs.

Climb the mountains and get their good tiding. Nature's peace will flow into you as sunshine flows into the trees.
John Muir

To help relieve the tension in our house over the 'Vivian incident', it was decided to take a hike. In our naivety, we thought since our bodies are fresh and unbroken; why not take on one of the most treacherous of Adirondack Mountains. Check it off our list of high peaks early on. Ask any seasoned 46'R what was the most challenging climb and often the answer is Mt. Allen.

What sets this hike apart from the other mountains is a 1700-foot slide, slick with rainwater as well as slimy, slippery red algae.

At the moment my mind is focused on revenge. I haven't quite forgiven Vic for the "Vivian" incident. The atmosphere in our house is chilly bordering on sub-Arctic. I understand the situation with Vivian was not entirely his fault. But the brazen sight of her naked body, taunting me with her youth and beauty sends a crimson haze of rage coursing through my veins. The utter gull and audacity of her to show up at my house and throw those pictures in my face, oh, he is going to pay. I know it's childish, but the thought of him struggling to climb a slick, slippery mountain covered in red algae sends a shiver of delight down my spine. The only downfall, I have to go with him.

Vic understands that fidelity is a raw wound for me. Poor Vic fights an uphill battle every day to prove his faithfulness. And to be honest, I do trust him. It's just my crazy head gets in front of my heart and I lose my mind.

To make amends, a new Osprey backpack arrived yesterday, shipped overnight. The card was signed simply, 'With my love, always, Vic'. The word always was underlined twice. Some women get jewelry and flowers, I get hiking gear. He knows the way to my heart. When the gift arrived, I insisted my old backpack would be adequate. Then I opened the box, took one look at the magenta blue beauty peeking out of the package and it was love at first sight. The backpack is designed specifically for a woman's frame. It took me an hour to figure out what all the straps, zippers and compartments were for.

With my new little blue beauty sitting by my side, we decided to table the hike up Mt. Allen for a later date. Hikers reference the mountain with a groan, prefaced by four letter adjectives that start with F... Not only is Mt. Allen slimy and slippery, it's difficult due to a long hike through a confusing maze of forest and logging roads just to reach the base of the mountain, and then the climb begins.

Instead we choose the Great Range Traverse for our first over night hike. Known as an extra-long day hike, the Great Range Traverse was listed as one of the toughest hikes in America by Backpacker Magazine back in 2005. The hike scored a 90 in difficulty points for 25 miles that included an elevation change of 17,600 feet and an X-factor of endless up and downs. The route scales nine peaks, including six 4,000 footers along with numerous cols, false summits and heinously eroded trail beds to wear you down physically and psychologically. The murderers' row of peaks includes Big Slide, Rooster Comb, Hedgehog, Lower Wolf Jaw, Upper Wolf Jaw, Armstrong, Gothic, Saddleback, Haystack and Mt. Marcy. Gut-wrenching moments consist of a half-mile of teetering above a 700-foot drop on a knife-edge between the two Mt. Wolf Jaws-inevitably followed by a scary-steep climb, followed by an exposed descent over open slab rock. The mountain face used to have cables to aid hikers, but they've since been removed to make the hike more adventurous and in accordance with Wilderness Guidelines. Hikers need to carry an ample supply of water as streambeds are often dry. So why hike Mt. Allen when we could do the Great Range Traverse, one of the most difficult hikes in America? It was a no brainer…and the operative word here is *no brains.*

Vic and I will break the Grand Traverse into a three-day hike instead of trying to conquer it in one day. That's just insanity, even three days is plain nuts. Ike will be on standby as our bail-out point man. *Holy mother mountain…*

~~~

I open my mountain journal, glance at my watch and write 5:42 a.m., barely dawn. I enter the date and weather conditions, knowing it's important to keep a record of the dates and mountains we climb.

The sun slowly breaks over the horizon; the gloom of night clings to the forest like a blanket. If we want to become 46'Rs, we need to backpack and camp in the Eastern High Peaks range. This positions us to summit many of the highest peaks without taxing our physical limitations. That would be my limited abilities, not Vic's. He looks capable of hiking all of the highest peaks in the Adirondacks without breaking a sweat. I, on the other hand, may require a helicopter and emergency mountain rescue team.

At the moment he's leaning against the car, he and Ike are studying the map. The wind rifles his hair, longer now, pulled back in a ponytail that only he can make look masculine. I watch his hands trace a line on the map…long tapering fingers, tanned a golden bronze.

"Elle, ready?" Vic questions, effortlessly removing our equipment from the trunk of the SUV.

"Let's hit the trail." Standing off to the side I adjust the straps on my pack as Vic and Ike go through the checklist of gear one more time. The parking lot is busy with groups of tall muscular hikers preparing for the day. They look like they live and breathe to hike the mountains, making my 5'9" weak and semi-out-of-shape body feel humbled.

Our original plan was to pull into the "Garden" at 5:00 a.m. placing us in perfect position to launch our overnight camping experience. The "Garden" in Keene Valley is a parking area run by the town of Keene with a shuttle out from the village and one of the more popular access points to the High Peaks region.

But we decided to start at the St. Hubert's trailhead on the Adirondack Mountain Reserve. The Ausable Club maintains the Adirondack Mountain Reserve, an organization rich in the history. Upon the initiative of William George Neilson, the AMR was formed in 1887 to save the lands around Beede's Hotel from the lumber industry. The land was eventually sold to the state of New York to be part of the Adirondack Park.

"Are you sure you want to carry so much weight? Vic asks his arms folded across his chest. The smile I give him flickers on my lips but ends in a yawn.

"Yes, I've gone over the list and everything is essential." I shove my hands deep in my pockets to stave off the early morning dampness, remembering the endless sorting and resorting of my gear, not wanting to be "that" person. "That" person is someone who is under-prepared, over-confident and doesn't respect the wilderness. The person, who overestimates their abilities, underestimates the mountain, puts themselves and those who have to rescue them at great risk.

"Holy shit, what do you have in this thing?" Ike swears, lifting my pack off the ground.

"Mostly water," I respond, a defensive edge to my voice. "Here, give it to me." I grab the straps of the pack and drag it off to the side, leaving behind a line of grooves in the gravel of the parking lot. Water weighs approximately 8 pounds per gallon and I have at least a gallon in my pack.

"All the guide books tell you to bring lots of water; there are very few resources on the trail. I don't want to run short."

"Mia, Mia, I'm sure we will find water. It's early in the summer the streams are still running. And I can help you carry some of that."

"No, I need to pull my own weight." I respond with a stubborn tilt to my chin.

"Hey Chica, this pack feel like you are carrying about half your weight and then some." Ike offered to come along, acting as our shuttle service. Vic will carry a satellite cell phone should we need to contact him for emergency purposes.

"Ready, Mia?" Vic asks, shouldering his pack with ease.

"Absolutely!" I stagger and shrug the heavy pack to my back, swaying on my feet. I teeter to the left and totter to the right, Ike grabs my arm to steady my balance. "Chica, are you sure?"

I gesture forth with my hand in a tally-ho salute. "Come on, Amigo, let's hit the trail!"

Ike claps Vic on the back in farewell, raises a hand to do the same to me, but pauses in midair for fear of knocking me over.

The parking area of St. Hubert's Trailhead is just off Rt. 73. We walk up the golf course road to a wooden gate marking the entrance to beautiful Ausable Lake grateful to the Club for their permission to use it.

By the time we reach the registration box and fill out the self-assigned hiking permit I feel the straps digging into my shoulder. The weight of my pack is pressing into my back like a small elephant. A half an hour into the hike and I'm beginning to regret the folly of carrying a pack too heavy for me. Ike was right but I'd rather die than admit it. I take a sip from the nozzle of my camel pack reasoning that the more I drink the lighter my pack will get.

The sun has creped over the horizon turning the woods a dusty gold. The forest floor nourishes various species of club moss, woodferns, trilliums and hop hornbeam that grow on humus soil with a high ph. The trail glistens a shiny brown with the sheen of morning dew upon it. Everything smells fresh and clean in the dawn of a new day. I feel energized by the cool temperatures and the euphoria of a new challenge. Gripping my hiking poles I forge on repeating my hiking mantra, "Algonquin, Allen, Armstrong, Basin, Big Slide, Blake, Cascade, Cliff, Colden, Colvin, Coushsachraga…

Vic stops and turns around, his right eyebrow shoots up, "Elle, what are you doing?"

I give a lopsided grin. "It's my High Peaks mantra, a distraction from the pain of hiking."

"Elle, if we look through the trees, we can almost see the parking lot. It hasn't been that hard."

"I'm getting an early start; it will help setting a pace."

He nods sagely. "And what is the mantra?"

"I have memorized all 46 of the High Peaks in alphabetical order, starting with Algonquin and ending with Wright."

"I'm impressed." The corner of his lips quirk in a half smile, and his eyes twinkle with amusement. "Maybe you can sing and keep the bears away."

"Sure," I bat my eyelashes and continue in a singsong voice to the tune of Frere Jacques. "Dial, Dix, Donaldson, Emmons, Esther, Giant, Gothics, Grace Peak..."

We begin climbing immediately at a steady pace to a beautiful little brook. The water sparkles in the sun and I'm careful to avoid the slick algae-covered rocks as we cross. The next few miles pass without need of my mantra, up and down the steep slopes of the Three Brother Mountains, up the first brother, until the summit of second brother, the climb traverses open ledges providing continuous views. The trail is steep and we do some scrambling, but barely notice because we're too busy trying not to fall off the mountain and the views are fabulous. We stop and give into the splendor of the beauty, whipping out our cameras to snap a shot of the 360-degree views. Once we exhaust our shutter mania a steady climb brings us to the mostly wooded summit of the third Brother.

The final ascent up Big Slide is steep, and half way up I feel a small river of water drenching my back through my pack.

"Agggh..." I shout, dropping my pack to the ground.

"What's wrong?" Vic asks, hurrying to my side.

"I think my camel pack broke or there is a rain storm in my pack. I'm soaked." I look down and see all that beautiful, *heavy* water running down my legs, forming a puddle at my feet, what a waste.

"How did that happen?"

"I don't know. A good thing I packed my clothes and sleeping bag in plastic or everything would be drenched before the first night."

"Let me see," Vic unzips and fiddles around in my pack pulling out the damaged bladder. He holds the bladder up in one hand and a knitting needle in the other. "What are you doing with knitting needles in your pack?" He shakes his head, not sure if he should be angry or amused. He nods politely to a group of hikers passing by. One of the girls yells as they race by, "Last one to the summit buys beer at the Cottage tonight in Lake Placid."

I watch the group trot past us and sigh wistfully. Gosh, a cold beer would hit the spot right now. But Vic stands with his arms crossed patiently waiting for an explanation. Why am I carrying knitting needles?

I shrug and point at a zip lock baggie packed with a ball of multi-colored sock yarn and four needles nestled deep within. Apparently, one of the needles thought it would be great fun to puncture the plastic bag and demolish my camel pack. "I brought needles and yarn to make socks."

"Socks?" He asks, dumping everything out of my pack and wiping it down with a small wicking towel. "Why?"

"Well, my feet might get cold, extra socks."

He gives me a withering look.

I help him arrange the articles from my pack on a tarp neatly set on the ground. "So, the nights will be long, and there are no campfires allowed in the Eastern High Peaks. I thought the yarn would give me something to do. I can use a headlamp to see and knitting is relaxing and productive at the same time."

"I guess. It's a shame to lose all that water." He complains, looking at the puddle surrounding my feet.

"I know. Well, at least my pack won't weigh as much."

"Yes, that's true. What else do you have in here that I don't know about?" He asks, rummaging around in my pack.

"Nothing." I pull the pack out of his grasp and finish organizing the parcels. "Everything is essential."

"I bet." He chuckles and points to the ladder leading up the steep slope of Big Slide. "This is a perfect time to regroup. We'll leave the packs behind hidden in the bushes and make a run up the summit, and pick them up on the way down."

I take one look at the set of ladders leading up to the summit of Big Slide and hastily agree. No way in hell do I want to climb that steep slope on a ladder with a pack. Without the heavy pack I can effortlessly climb hand over hand up the ladder and pull myself onto the rock face. Your hands come out to meet the rock and by the end of the climb your hands and feet become one with the earth.

Before we know it, we've run out of mountain and are standing on the summit of Big Slide, the twenty-seventh highest peak of the Adirondack Park.

The open ledge presents a glorious view from Hurricane and Giant in the east all the way over to Algonquin and Wright in the west. The precipitous cliff face begs you to admire the view from a few feet back because the south face of the mountain has peeled away in several major slides thus giving the mountain its name, Big Slide.

Even though the sun is at its highest peak of the year, daylight is waning and it's time to head down the trail, pick up our packs and find a campsite. Designated camping sites in this area are limited and few. The rule of no camping above 3400 feet was put in place to protect the fragile ecosystems that exists only in higher elevation. I've noticed the summit of several mountains is a patchwork of color: beige, brown, green and rust due to the delicate lichens growing on the stone face. Off to the side where traffic is less, the lichens form a thin crust-like coating on the rock surface of the summits. Very little can survive the harsh mountain environment and we take care to stay on the trail and avoid walking on the delicate high peak ecosystem.

The trail down to Johns Brook Valley crosses Slide Brook many times, seven to be exact. It would be tedious except that it breaks up walking over exposed rock and tree roots. By stream number four, my legs, tired and shaky from all the up and downs have met their Armageddon in the form of a downward slippery slope, slick from overuse leading into the stream. I take a step, my foot rolls on the loose gravel and the behemoth pack pushes me forward. Without warning I lose my balance, gain momentum and slide down the bank out of control, my arms flailing and *splat*… I land face first in the stream onto the rocks and muck. I can't move, pinned as the water rushes passed my face causing me to cough and sputter. I'm drowning in six inches of water! Vic is ahead of me, already climbing the trail. He can't see his pathetic, floundering fool of a wife drowning in mere inches of water. He doesn't know I'm in peril. Only an idiot would slip and fall in such a tiny stream. Using my forearms I push my upper body up and scream, "Vic! Help!"

His head whips around and he sees me mired in a stream buried beneath a pack he pointedly told me was too heavy. In a move reminiscent of his heroic character in the movie, Firebrand, he drops his pack and dashes down the bank. He reaches in and picks me up with one arm, my arms and legs thrashing like a turtle held out of water.

"Elle, are you all right?"

"No, I'm not!" I gasp, coughing and sputtering. "I almost drowned!"

Still holding me with one hand above the flowing stream he reprimands, "I told you the pack was too heavy."

"Don't yell at me."

"I'm not yelling. I'm just concerned. I turn around and there you are thrashing about in the stream like a beached whale."

"I am not a whale. Put me down!"

"No."

"Come on! It's not my fault."

"Yes, it is. Elle, I told you not to carry such a heavy pack. I appreciate your desire to pull your own weight but realistically it doesn't make sense."

He plops me unceremoniously on the bank and stands over me with hands on his hips and starts laughing.

Really? I'm soaking wet rolling in mud squashed under a colossus backpack that's intent on killing me and he's laughing. "Okay, I give. Help me get this thing off." But he can't hear me, he is sitting on the ground overcome with laughter; laughing so hard the tears are running down his cheeks.

"Hey, over here, wife in need of assistance. Cold, wet, Big Behemoth is trying to crush me." I try scrambling around in the mud but succeed in only digging deeper. He waves a hand in front of his face, gasping for air, he's laughing so hard he's got the hiccups!

"Come on!" I whine.

"I've missed Klutz-Ellen. She's been on sabbatical."

I wince, "That two timing, double-crossing, no good conniving witch who takes great delight in causing me untold embarrassment." I mutter under my breath, aggravated by the awkwardness that has plagued me most of my life. "Good riddance, I thought I got rid of that bitch for good."

"She is one of my greatest joys in life." He chortles.

"Easy for you to say." I sniff. "You're not the one lying in a cold stream covered with mud."

"Hey, I've got your trail name. Splish-splash! It's perfect." He's referring to the custom of long distance hikers on the Appalachian Trail or Pacific Crest Trail who adopt nicknames often based on something they did while on the trail.

"Really, I was thinking of Forest Pixie."

"At five foot nine, Buttercup, you're no forest pixie."

I give him a sour face. "Well, if I have a trail name, you need one too."

"Sure, we have time to find one. I was thinking of Tarzan, because he always has to rescue Jane."

"Very funny."

"I'm hysterical." He mops the tears off his face with a hiking bandana. With a final snort of laughter he reaches under me to unclasp my straps. "Here, let me get this pack off you. Good thing it's the end of the day. The camping area is just a few miles down the trail. We'll get you out of these wet clothes and boil some water for a hot cup of tea."

Who am I to refuse such a tempting offer from a man who looks like he stepped out of a Ralph Lauren advertisement? Even if he doesn't think I look like a forest pixie…

Life is better in hiking boots…

By the time we arrive at the camping area of John Brooks Lodge, the lean-to has been taken by a group of hikers. So we smile, exchange greetings and move off to another designated campsite.

Prior to this trip we spent hours practicing how to set up our tent. We timed ourselves, even went so far as to put on blindfolds, mimicking a night set up in the dark. As a result we established camp quickly and looked like seasoned hikers.

With a grateful sigh, I sink down on a log, slowly undo the laces and take off my boots. I groan in pleasure peeling the socks off my feet, a feeling of euphoria ripples through my body. My feet are killing me and I remember every mile is 2200 steps.

"You okay?" Vic asks, straightening up from staking down the rain tarp over the tent.

I glance at him with a guilty look, not wanting to admit my feet hurt on our first day out. "I'm wonderful. How about you?"

"Good. How are the boots, are your feet blistered?"

"Na, just sore." I rub the arch along my instep to encourage circulation. I pat the log next to me, an invitation to come sit with me.

"To be expected." He flops down and leans back, rubbing his back against the scratchy bark of the log. I swear I hear him groan.

"Back sore?"

"Not really." He tilts his head to the sky and closes his eyes. "Hey, I'm really proud of us. This is our third high peak, and we did it in under eight hours."

"It's not like we hurried, I can't imagine how many pictures we took between the Three Brothers' and Big Slide. The views were amazing."

"I'm glad it was a clear day." He adds, motioning for me to slide my feet in his direction. Not needing a second invitation, I scoot my butt over, positioning my feet for him to rub.

He pulls from his pack a delicious concoction smelling of sage, sandalwood and a hint of menthol. He starts rubbing my foot in small circular motions, concentrating on the reflex points.

Oh my…this feels divine, suddenly my exhaustion evaporates and everything south of my naval tingles. My feet feel every single one of those miles but if this is the treatment, it's worth every mile. I groan and then I moan…

Vic laughs, holding a thumb firmly on the ball of my foot. "Does this mean I'm forgiven for the Vivian episode?"

"Vivian who?" I groan even louder.

"Careful, the people at the next campsite will get the wrong idea."

"Who cares?" I whimper. "This feels amazing. Where did you learn to rub feet like this and why have you been holding out on me?"

"The women in Thailand are genius at…"

"Stop!" I hold up a hand. "I don't need to know anymore."

"It wasn't like that." He leans in to kiss the hollow of my neck. "You have such a dirty mind, my dear."

"Oh, be quiet and keep rubbing before I remember why I'm mad at you."

Somehow the touch moved up my calves to my thighs and north. He's kissing me, devouring my lips. I'm intoxicated by the antics of his tongue; the way he tastes, the way he smells. My hands curl in his thick hair and my cheek against his beard is tickling and titillating. And I want more, with Vic it's like going up in flames and before I know it…we're in the tent testing out the sleeping mats.

The sleeping mats work well. In fact, they work *very* well. And while the foot rub was delicious…what came after was *schrumdelicous*. Thoughts of Vivian and revenge fade in the throngs of passion. Finally, I have a trail name for Vic…*Captain Magic…oh my… to infinity and beyond!*

~~~

After a dinner, tummies full of dehydrated noodles we snuggle in our sleeping bags and watch the stars pop out one by one. Under a dome of constellations we listen to sounds of the night: the shuffle of nearby campers getting ready for bed, the rustle of leaves picked up by a stray gust of wind, the hoot of an owl, and then silence, deep, all encompassing silence. A silence so deep and pervasive it almost hurts the ears. A silence to quiet your senses, quell anxiety and still the empty restlessness of the world. This is the mountain experience, an escape from clutter and chaos to a simpler world, a world filled with essentials of life but not the untidiness.

*Wilderness is not a luxury but a necessity of the human spirit and
vital to our lives as water and good bread.*
Edward Abbey

There is something about waking up to the pitter-patter of
raindrops on the roof of your tent. It's comforting in that you are
warm and cozy, not exposed to the rain, and yet distressing
because at some point, you have to leave the sheltering cocoon of
your tent and brave the wilds of outside.

Late night after cleaning up the campsite and securing our
food and toiletries in the bear canister, we fell into a deep and
rejuvenating sleep. The type of slumber earned by a day of pure
physical exertion and the euphoria of crisp clean mountain air.

In the confines of our tiny two man tent we scramble around
trying to get dressed, giggling like school kids as we entangled in
each other's limbs and end up dressing one another. Usually
we're ripping the clothes off, not putting them on, a reversal for
us. At last, with clothing zipped, buttoned and secure we step out
into a light, misty drizzle. Vic pulls the camp stove under his
Siltarp for protection and soon has a fire started. We have a huge
hiking day ahead of us. The plan is to leave our camping gear and
large packs behind and return to the same camp tonight.
Hopefully, there shouldn't be a problem in maintaining our
camping space for the night.

A light daypack with the essentials of rain gear and food
allows us to move quickly up the trail. The first objective of the
day is Saddleback Mountain. A quick climb up Andover, a
wooded summit, a rest stop to check out the cliffs and this is our

turn-around point as neither of us wants to descend the cliffs.

Onto the col between the two mountains and we begin the ascent of Gothics, by the time we reach the approach there are several groups of hikers alongside us waiting to use the cables. This is my first experience with cables; in dry weather conditions the cables are not necessary but due to the early morning drizzle using them is a good safe-guard. A side trip takes us over to Pyramid and our second breakfast of the day. Hard-boiled eggs, thick pretzels for salt and a granola bar for sweet, washed down with water and weak tea. Required sustenance, for the trail between Pyramid and Sawteeth is rugged; first we drop 1000' in elevation before climbing 600' to the summit of Sawteeth. The trail starts moderately, but zigzags through some very steep pitches before finishing the climb.

We find a stream and fill our water bottles, taking time to treat the water with a steriPen. The last thing we need is Giardia; all water in the Adirondacks must be treated to remove water borne pathogens.

Up one mountain and down another, my body begins to feel the pain and so the hiking mantra continues. "Haystack, Hough, Iroquois, Lower Wolf Jaw, MacNaughton, Macomb, Marcy, Marshall, Nippletop, and Nye."

From the Range Trail we reach the summit of Gothics careful not to mistake the false summit for the real summit. The great, soaring slides of both the east and west arms of Gothics are awe-inspiring. From our vantage point they really do seem to curve like gothic arches above the valleys far below. The summit, at 4736 is the very threshold of the alpine zone. There are twisted confers, stunted from their battle with wind and cold, these dwarf forests are known as *krummholz*, a German word meaning 'crooked wood'. Artic alpine communities live on about a dozen of the highest Adirondack peaks.

On the summit of Gothics, a group of hikers are celebrating a member's 46th hike and admittance into the coveted 46'R club. Amidst cheers and hugs and a champagne toast, the hiker is presented an official ADK 46'R badge.

I eye up the badge with envy, just like my Adirondack Canoe Classic pin, I covet the 46'R badge but Gothic is only our fifth peak and we have a long way to go. I realize what an accomplishment it is to hike all 46 of the high peaks. Vic and I have hiked in the West and deem the hiking in the Adirondacks as some of the most challenging we have ever done. The worn packed trails scarred with exposed tree roots and hard scrabble climbs over rocks and boulders make each peak a hard won victory.

Wanting to bag Armstrong and the Upper and Lower Wolf Jaws Mountains we push off after a quick snack. Soon we reach the ladder on the north side of Armstrong, not a grand view, but worth our time to summit. A short climb down brings us to the Wolf Jaws. The Upper and Lower Wolf Jaws are named because of a series of knobs that resemble teeth in a strong jaw that grips the heights above Johns Brook Valley and the Ausable Lakes.

Along the trail a common sign near the tree line reads, "You are entering the Arctic-Alpine Plant zone. The plants are rare, fragile, and very much endangered. Walking and sitting on them will kill them! Please walk only on the trail or on solid rock surfaces."

From about 2800-4000 feet, much of the forest in the Adirondacks is the boreal forest, named for Boreas, the Greek god of the north wind. The trail to Upper Wolf Jaw is rugged and puts our training to the test. Huffing and puffing we reach the summit and are rewarded with our fourth peak of the day. Not to waste daylight, we take off for Lower Wolf Jaw, the thirtieth highest peak in the Adirondacks.

We've met the same group several times today, this is more than just hiking and checking off the names of mountain peaks on a list. It's about meeting people along the way, sharing common interests and goals. We were witness to a young couple, Jessica and Mason getting engaged on top of one of the peaks. It was so romantic to watch the young man get down on one knee in front of God and the heavens above and propose.

On the hike back to camp, while tired from the long day I'm jubilant over our success, hiking in the high peaks area is difficult. Cold, wind and ice are the dominant factors controlling life on the open summits. We noticed places where the bedrock or boulders are open to the ravages of the elements; only moss and lichens can colonize their surface. Pincushion-shaped clumps of diapensia grows in pockets and mountain sandwort is common where thin glacial soils fill shallow depressions in the bedrock. It is impossible to ignore the tenacity of the plants and animals clinging to life in these harsh high elevation environments.

And for us, five peaks in one day, I start singing my hiking mantra to help counter the hiking fatigue… Panther, Phelps, Porter, Redfield, Rocky Peak, Saddleback, Santanoni…Between the euphoria of the peaks, hiking the cols and dips between mountains with nothing to look at, except nice Adirondack woods, trail boredom set in. My feet feel the ten plus miles I've put on them. I can't wait to get these boots off, the word footsore doesn't begin to describe the burning, aching of my poor tired feet.

~~~

We barely have energy to boil water and gobble down our dehydrated noodle meal. Dessert was a bar of dark chocolate and a flask of bourbon Vic had stowed in his pack. The five peaks and bourbon hit around ten o'clock. We're sound asleep before the stars pop and litter the night sky with bursts of scattered light.

I fall asleep haunted by the "Don't look down" warning running through my head. The view from many of the slides was nothing but air below and a steep cliff drop off. Drifting asleep I'm jerked awake several times, feeling like I'm falling off a cliff only to find myself snuggled next to Vic in our double sleeping bag.

But in the middle of the night, I'm jerked awake by the sound of sticks breaking outside the tent, and then I hear the most offensive snort in the world. My nose is pressed into Vic's chest and the snort came from outside the tent. Could it be late arriving hikers? We did go to bed pretty early. I hear something or someone rustling around in the campsite. I roll over and call out softly so as not to wake Vic, "Hello?" No answer…again I call, "Hello?" Still no answer and the rustling continues. I fear my husband's worst nightmare is about to happen; we have a bear in our campsite. Almost everyone camping on the trail has encountered black bear. I thought our luck would hold out; then I hear the familiar shuffling grunt of a bear as he searches the campsite for food. We had placed the bear barrel with our food well away from the campsite but the smell of food clings to the immediate proximity of the tent. *Crap*...feverishly I crawl out of my side of the sleeping bag, hoping not to wake Vic. I pull on my pants, grab a headlamp and bear whistle, slowly ease my way out of the tent.

As if we haven't had enough trouble with bear cubs this year, there stands a pair of young black bears frozen in the beam of my headlamp. The bears are juveniles, old enough to be on their own but have not developed adequate hunting skills to ignore the promise of easy campsite pickings. I start yelling, "Shoo bear!" and the closest bear growls back.

Yikes....and double yikes. I jump back.

Vic comes crashing out of the tent in his boxers brandishing his pistol. "Elle, what the hell is going on?"

"It's a pair of bear cubs."

"Oh shit!" He cries. "Not again! What the hell!"

Before he panics and starts shooting his gun, I blow long and hard on my whistle.

"Bears!" Vic turns to me with an incredulous look on his face. "Bears...not one but two."

"It will be fine, they're little bears."

"Oh fuck, we're going to die!" He yells. "Fuck, fuck, fuck..."

"I thought you weren't using that word anymore. We agreed it was offensive."

"Hey, I save it for fucking dire circumstances. Like now when I'm going to die!"

"So that's going to be the last word you utter on this earth, fuck?"

"Seriously, Ellen," he hisses at me. "This is the time you going to lecture me about my language. We are going to die at the hands of two man-eating bears and you're worried about my cursing!"

"They're not man-eaters, they are just young juveniles trying to snitch an easy meal."

"Listen, Miss Nature Nancy, I don't care what the fuck they

are, just make them go away!"

"Okay, okay. Help me make some noise." I pick up a couple of sticks, hand them to him and grab our pot. We yell, scream, wail, whistle and crack sticks against trees to scare them away.

Eventually, the cubs wheel around and take off for the woods.

"Hey, what's all the racket going on out there?" Calls an irate voice from a neighboring campsite.

"Just a couple of young bears scrounging around the campsite." I yell back.

"Cool, good luck chasing them away. Call us if you need help."

I suspect the young men sleeping in that tent aren't going to be much help. There was the strong smell of marijuana coming from their campsite earlier in the evening.

"It's fine." I grab Vic's arm and make soothing motions across his chest. "Just baby bears and they are gone. You can put that big old bad gun away. No bears to shoot here."

"But if those are babies, where is the mama?" He squints his eyes scanning the edge of the woods, monitoring for signs of movement.

"They were young bears probably not with their mama anymore. I'm sure they're gone."

"They'll be back, the monsters." He remains unconvinced.

"Let's go around camp and make sure we have picked up all the food related items including our dishes, stoves, and cleaning products." After collecting what was already not safely stored we moved the entire stash farther down the path.

"Okay, all bear attractants are removed." With a yawn I point to the tent. "Let's go back to sleep, I'm exhausted."

"How can you be tired when two bears almost viciously attacked us?"

"Sweetie, they were only curious little cubs."

"Little? They looked to be about three hundred pounds."

"More like a hundred," I mumble through a yawn.

Once back in our tent, slowly drifting off to sleep, the snorting and grunting begins again. This time Vic streaks out of the tent ahead of me. "Don't shoot!" I yell scrambling after him.

"I'm not, I'll just scare them away."

I switch on my headlamp to find him standing in boxer shorts covered with little black bears (how apropos is that) with his gun pointing into the air.

"Vic, don't shoot. If you shoot that gun you'll freak out all the hikers in the area."

"Well, Ellen, maybe they should be freaked out. There are freaking bears running around our campsite in the dark." He swears, "Jesus H. Christ."

"No, they're not God, just bears."

"How can you be funny at a time like this?"

"Sorry, panic sometimes makes me inappropriately giddy. Let's do some more hooting and hollering."

I start whistling and banging sticks together, whooping and hollering, wearing nothing but leggings and a grey t-shirt with little black bears printed on it. I purchased his boxers and my t-shirt at the same time. I thought it funny, sort of a good luck talisman to keep the bears away. Unfortunately, better in theory than reality. At some point, all my dancing and hollering caused my all-purpose stretch bandana to fall down over my eyes, blinding me. You know the one, the bandana that promises to keep your hair off your face, warm your ears, act as a scarf, repel bugs, function as a tourniquet or sling, works as a rope if you need to hang off the side of a cliff, even the vivid coloring acts as a beacon to attract rescue crews. Well, apparently that bandana can also blind you.

"Mia, they're gone." Vic takes my hand and pulls the blindfold off my eyes. He's chuckling.

"What!?" I ask defensively.

"You're funny."

"I'm chasing the bears. I don't want you to shoot them. I thought you were afraid of them."

"I am, but I maybe more afraid of you. That war dance you got going was impressive, girl."

"Hey, they're gone. I got bear juju!" I do a happy dance around the tent.

"Maybe. But the way I see it, the only bear juju we have tonight involves me sitting up with the whistle and revolver until daylight. I don't see us packing up and hiking out in the dark, we don't have a lot of options. Do we?"

"Mmm-hmm…we could take turns. I hate to see you sitting up all night. You're tired, too."

"Buttercup," he pulls me into his arms and plants a kiss on the top of my head. "I'll be fine. After two adrenalin-producing episodes, there is no chance of me sleeping tonight."

"I'll stay up with you."

"No, get some rest, you're shivering."

"Are you sure?"

"Yes. Tomorrow will be an easier day. We'll hike Haystack and be on our way home."

My fingers nearly numb with cold fumble with the zipper of the tent, and I hear a spraying sound, like an aerosol can, followed by the smell of pepper spray. The odor fills my nostrils with fire. I can't breathe; choking and gasping for air I rocket out of the tent to find Vic standing with the bear spray in his hand.

"What?"

"*What* are you doing?"

"Spraying the tent. If the bears come back and try to eat us they end up with a mouth full of pepper spray."

My normally levelheaded husband has morphed into an idiot by the threat of another bear attack. Slowly with patience, I say, "I don't think it works like that; it's not a repellent. It's a weapon. I can't see, my eyes tearing from the intensity of the pepper spray."

"I was going to make a circle around the campsite. Stake our boundaries, you know, like how the animals scent mark their territory."

"Give me that, Amigo." I grab the bear spray away from him. "Your scent marking days are over, unless you plan on peeing in a circle around the campsite." He purses his lips in thought looking around, assessing the area he'd have to cover.

"You think that would work?"

"No! Just come to bed, there hasn't been a fatal bear attack in this area in the last hundred years!" I'm losing my patience. At this rate we're not going to get a wink of sleep, between the bears, the spray and Vic marking his territory like an alpha male.

After the aroma of the pepper spray faded, exasperated, I crawl into the tent, intending to lie down for a few minutes, but the moment my head hits the pillow I fall into the deep sleep of the exhausted.

One climbs, one sees. One descends, one sees no longer, but one has seen…
Rene Daumal

I find Vic sound asleep against a tree the next morning, so much for Tarzan saving Jane. If we don't get a move on, the morning will be wasted.

A hasty breakfast and a last glance around the campsite to make sure we've left no traces, it's on to Mt. Haystack.

To say my body isn't aching and sore would be a lie. Dog-tired by the climbs of the previous day and a night of poor sleep, I'm exhausted. My thighs burn with the pace. Each step I feel the cartilage and ligaments in my knees grind and strain, struggling to counteract the pull of gravity. With each step the pack pushes into my shoulders and my back aches. A sports bandage wraps one knee and I can't feel my feet. I won't be sorry to see the end of the trail today. I put my legs into hiking mode, autopilot, moving one in front of the other. Sometimes it's easier to keep moving, find a rhythm rather than taking frequent rest stops. When stopping the muscles stiffen and the desire to move on vanishes.

Using the slender hiking poles to distribute the weight from my legs to upper body I pull myself, step by step, over rock, exposed tree roots, through streams and waist deep boulders to the top of Mt. Haystack. At the summit we pause and view one of the most concealed recesses of the High Peaks: Panther Gorge. The vista is spectacular and unobstructed except where blocked by Mt. Marcy, the tallest mountain in New York State.

The hike out is mellow, the path meanders and traverses through the forest. The Adirondack Park was formed in response to concerns about trees. Early settlers began harvesting the Adirondack forest before the American Revolution. The government sold acreage to lumberman to discharge war debts. The resulting depletion of the watershed woodlands reduced the soil's ability to hold water, hastening topsoil erosion thus beginning an exaggerated period of flooding. In response the New York State legislature created a state park in 1892. But to achieve meaningful protection a forest preserve was established in 1895. Henceforth, the Adirondack Forest Preserve would be 'forever wild'.

~~~

"Hey, I was beginning to get worried about the two of you. I thought you'd be done by mid-morning. It's four o'clock in the afternoon." Ike runs a hand through his hair, causing it to stand on end. The worried look vanishes from his face. "Everything, okay?"

"Yes, aside from a little incident with bears last night and a wrong turn on the trail this afternoon, we did well. Right, Elle?"

"Absolutely, we mistook a streambed for the trail and took a detour. Thanks for waiting for us." I point to a cooler next to his folding chair, hunger pains in my stomach prompt my enthusiasm. "What's that?"

"Surprise!" He says opening the cooler to reveal a bottle of champagne and three glasses propped on a bag of ice. I have never loved him more. He even picked up those darling little cheese canapés I love from the local deli. I'm sure we look ridiculous lounging in a trailhead parking lot but this is a momentous occasion for us, especially for me. We climbed six Adirondack High Peaks in three days. Why not celebrate? There are some odd looks from hikers as they trod back and forth passed us. We offered to share but no one accepts the invitation. One young lady looks wistfully at the bottle but rather than break the purist code in front of her friends she moves on.

~~~

Lulled by the quiet conversation between Vic and Ike, I slept on the way home. Once back at Camp, I took full advantage of the luxuries of domestic life. After a deliciously long hot shower, I sank into our king size bed and groaned with sheer pleasure. Vic, already asleep, sprawled out on his stomach took up most of the space. There is something about sleeping in your own bed, it's akin to an animal's nest or burrow. While other beds may provide comfort, there is something about home and your own personal den. I think part of the allure of a wilderness experience is the removal of anything civilized and learning to depend on your own resources and skills. The remote expression of just being, to slip into the silence of your soul coupled with the sheer joy of a mountaintop, nothing but the trees, mountains and sky. These experiences take us out of ourselves and our petty existence and problems, opening us to renew, refresh and foster a new perspective on life.

In every walk with nature one receives far more than he seeks. John Muir

I'm standing in the kitchen waiting for the coffee to perk. I need sustenance. Last night on the phone, after giving Lani a narrative of our hike I promised to finish the wedding preparations, and I quote "Bright and early tomorrow morning". It's eleven o'clock and I'm still in my pink moose pajamas. A small mountain of lists, from limousine service, caterers and bakeries need my attention. And I'm tired, leaning against the counter-top I stretch the stiff muscles in my legs and back. It's going to take a few days for my body to recover from the beating it took traversing up and over those mountains. Ike knocks and walks in.

"Morning." He stops, dropping a pile of mail on the counter. "Coffee ready?"

"Perfect timing. Just finished brewing a pot."

He pours a cup and adds a splash of cream. After taking that first satisfying sip, he points to the mail and says, "There are a couple of personal letters in there. Old-fashion, real mail addressed to you."

"Really?" Vic says walking into the room, his face clouded with suspicion as he reaches for the mail. "There are very few people who have our address."

"Yeah well, I'm sure that circus train of clowns you employ for security is on top of it. Thought you were going to look into changing firms."

"Right, it's at the head of my things-to-do list. Until I find a replacement firm, I hate to fire this company."

Ike and I exchange glances, we both know Vic is a habitual procrastinator and while his intensions are good, sometimes he needs a prod to get things done.

Ike holds up an envelope. "This one, apparently from Miss Twinkie, hand delivered, was placed in the mailbox with no stamp. And the other looks like it's from your brother, Ellen." He leans against the open door frame of the patio sipping his coffee.

"Wow, we never get mail. I'll finish up the wedding details later." Does it really matter if the check marks are placed next to the caterer, bartender and limousine service this morning or this afternoon? I need confirm the R.S.V.P.'s before starting the seating chart. Now what I need is a break. I toss my pen down and pick up a plate of muffins from the cupboard. "Grab up the coffee pot and let's go out on the deck. It's a beautiful morning and I made muffins."

"You learned all that information without opening the letters?" Vic asks.

"Of course, I didn't open your mail." Ike appears offended by the comment that he was snooping. Vic chuckles and slaps him on the back as we file out to a gorgeous summer morning. The sky is clear blue filled with puffy white clouds.

"He's only teasing you. I like that you look out for us." I say, putting a muffin on a plate for him

"Hey." Vic says, putting down the coffee pot and tossing the newspaper he was reading onto the patio table. "How's that chopper coming? The one that guy in Lake Placid wants painted to look like the mountains with a pack of wolves."

"Tedious, but the design is unique. I think he'll be pleased."

"Twinkie strikes again, I wonder if she's planning another road trip." I laugh holding up the pink envelope.

Ike and Vic look at me in question. "I'm not driving." Ike says with a vehement shake of his head.

I rip open the letter. "Actually, it's a letter from one of the women we met at the luncheon. Apparently, she wanted to get in touch with me but didn't have our address so she sent a card for Twinkie to deliver. Oh, it's from Irene Krackower, she was very interesting." I search for my glasses to better read the small print.

"She's a clothing designer who owned her own boutique in Boston before she retired to Lake Placid and Florida. She seemed very conventional, married with children and all that. But what I found so fascinating about her is that she and a group of friends rode motorcycles cross-country stopping at National Forests along the way to raise awareness for wild open spaces. We hit it off immediately."

The men nod politely and resume their conversation, no longer interested. Ike eyes the muffin on his plate surreptitiously, carefully pulling it apart into small pieces examining them as if expecting a bug or something disgusting to pop out.

"What are you doing?" I exclaim, offended. "What are you looking for? It happened once!"

Ike flinches with a guilty look on his face. "Umm…nothing."

Vic takes a large bite of his muffin and chews with relish. He has a wolfish grin on his face. He takes the other half and waves it under Ike's nose. "Yum. Here, Ike, have a bite."

Ike scowls at him. "You can't blame a guy for being careful after the last time she made muffins." He accuses.

"You weren't supposed to get that one." I explain, exasperated. "It was an accident, it wasn't my fault."

"Right." And he picks the muffin apart even more.

I sigh. Last time I made muffins I thought it clever to put a pair of tiny thong panties in the bottom of one of the giant muffin cups. Of course, clean, brand new ones. The muffin with the thong panty inside would be warm and golden right out of the oven, I'd serve it to Vic with his morning coffee. He'd peel off the paper, find his present, take the hint and peel me out of my clothes. One of those little surprises that help a marriage stay fresh. Unfortunately, it wasn't my best idea and didn't go as planned. As the muffins were cooling on the counter, Ike came in and helped himself to one. His howl of disgust echoed through the house. And to make the situation even worse, he threw it on the floor only to have Porky Pellinger come charging in, gobble up the muffin…and the thong. So for the next two days we paid close attention to Porky's "outdoor" activities, ensuring the offending panties didn't lodge deep inside of him resulting in a very expensive and embarrassing veterinary visit. Some ideas are better in theory than in reality…thong panties being one of them. What sadistic male invented them, anyway?

I scan the letter wondering why Irene wanted to contact me. "How cool!" I exclaim with delight after reading the note.

Ike and Vic stop talking and look at me expectantly.

"Irene is on the board of the Adirondack Council and they have a volunteer position for an outreach children's education coordinator. Irene brought my name up and they discussed my teaching experience, googled my name and saw the Outstanding Environmental Educator award I had won years ago. They want me for the position. She explains in the letter that much of the work can be done online during the off-season and as long as I make the main meetings, which are held in the summer, I can fulfill the obligations of the position. Oh Vic, could I? I miss teaching and would love to be involved in environmental education again."

"Buttercup, of course you can. It sounds perfect. I know children and outdoor education hold a special place in your heart. We'll work it out. Find out more details and then give your answer. I'll support whatever you decide."

"I'll go online, research the organization and give her a call later today. I'm so excited."

Vic smiles, pats my hand and resumes his conversation with Ike.

The other piece of "real" mail gives me a jolt of shock. The return address on the upper left-hand corner is from my brother, Rory. Aside from a few emails and holiday cards, Rory and I have very little contact. He and his wife attended our wedding two years ago, it was the first time I'd seen him in years. We had a wonderful time but he lives in Nebraska so our paths rarely cross.

Ripping the envelope open in haste, curiosity fueling my impatience, I scan the handwritten note inside. "Well, I'll be a monkey's uncle."

I have Vic and Ike's attention.

"What's up, Mia?" Vic asks and Ike helps himself to another muffin, he gave half of his first one to the dogs. Cyrus is upside down on his back, all four paws waving in the air, hoping this act of submission will garner him a reward. Porky wiggles in delight and licks Ike's hand. He is in full mouch-pouche posture; body sitting perfectly, eyes huge in a point-blank stare trying to hypnotize Ike into his personal feeding machine. The dogs stayed with Adele and Weasel while we were hiking. Since picking them up, they've given us the cold shoulder, pouting for leaving them. They lay on the floor, watching us with huge sad eyes not raising their heads from their paws, rescue dog orphan mode. You'd think we locked them in the local dog shelter. I can only feel so bad because I swear there were traces of BBQ stains around their muzzles from Adele's generosity.

"Soo…?" Vic asks. "What does the letter from your brother have to say?"

"He and his wife will be in the area and want us to come for drinks and dinner this weekend. A business colleague of his loaned him the use of a house in the Forest Alliance. He has some old family pictures of Aunt Karen, Uncle Bill and documents from when our grandparents immigrated to this country from Germany that he thought I might enjoy." I wave the invitation in front of Vic. "What do you think?"

"Sure, why not. I've always been curious about the Alliance properties. Now we can visit with an invitation."

"What the hell is the Forest Alliance?" Ike asks.

Vic waves his hand dismissively and shrugs, "The Alliance is an organization that owns a large parcel of wilderness land in the Adirondack Park. I think it is some kind of privately owned club that got started back in the 1890's for hunting and fishing. You are only granted admittance to their land through invitation as a guest or a landowner who was approved for membership."

"Sounds a little too rich for my blood." Ike sticks his nose in the air as if mimicking an aristocratic swell.

"Mine too," Vic agrees. "Members include some former presidents, actors and business tycoons. The club recently found itself in the news after a series of mysterious break-ins that are still unsolved."

Ike shrugs his shoulders to indicate indifference. "I'd rather go to a good bar with a wide-screen television."

"I'm curious." Vic says. "Do you want to go, Elle?"

"Yes, I'd love to see Rory and Sharon again. We didn't have

much time to visit with them at the wedding. There is a map and phone number listed on the card, I'll call and let him know we can come."

"It's a date," Vic says.

"I'll stay home with the dogs." Ike replies.

My brother's voice comes on the voice-mail when I place the call. I'm disappointed not to speak with him personally but leave a message stating that we will see them on Saturday night.

"Ummm…now what to wear." I get excited when I have a chance to change out of my hiking clothes into something a little bit more formal. Yet an evening in the Forest Alliance doesn't necessarily call for high heels and bling. A quick perusal of my closet shows a cute summer plaid dress that I can pair with my jeans jacket and wedge heels. Jack's sister designs funky artistic jewelry. I have several bracelets and necklaces from her; one of them will match the outfit. I'm looking forward to the evening. It will be fun.

I was eleven when my mother died and assumed much of the responsibility for my brothers. My father was mired in grief, barely able to care for himself let alone three children. But once our stepmother, Helen moved into the house, she took over the care of my younger brothers and pushed me out of the picture. Helen planted a firm wedge between my brothers and I, severing the bonds of our early childhood. I give a little shudder; it's taken years for me to over-come the imbedded scars from her evil meddling. In her mind, I represented my mother and she despised my mother. She married my father and purged our home of anything reminding her of my mother. The only thing she couldn't purge, was me. Mean spirited, she tormented me, ripping or staining my favorite clothes, pointing out to my father how careless I was. It got to a point that I'd hide my clothing and do my own laundry when she wasn't in the house. She stole things from my brothers, then hide them in my closet, dropping subtle hints where to find the lost articles. I was the one to blame, a deceitful, lying thief. When I protested to my father, he always took Helen's side, claiming I was acting like a spoiled little girl and resented Helen's presence in our house. My brothers learned to distrust me. Over the years I've invited them to the significant events in my life and until my wedding to Vic, neither of them had accepted or reciprocated. This invitation from my brother has sparked my curiosity. And I can't help but wonder, what brings Rory to the mountains?

Sometimes, you find yourself in the middle of nowhere and sometimes in the middle of nowhere, you find yourself.

We arrived ten minutes early for our dinner with Rory, which was a good thing. The security guard at the entrance gate checked a list for our names, examined our I.D. and placed a call to Rory confirming our invitation to enter the property.

Once through the gate we traveled several miles along a heavily forested road passing driveways and gated entrances spinning off like a spider leading to the heart of a web. Not a house was visible, only signposts or gates with address numbers for emergency responders, cleaning and maintenance crews. Around the bend we find a gate with the number 4235 etched in a granite pillar.

"This is it." I point out after consulting the directions Rory had sent to prevent any confusion in locating the house on Alliance land.

Vic nods, putting on the turn signal. He makes a clicking noise with his mouth and says, "Boy, it's very quiet back here. No one is out and about. We haven't seen one car or a person walking a dog or anything."

"The weather doesn't help either." A summer squall had rolled in over the mountains, coating the forest in a blanket of drizzling fog. I shiver wishing I had put on pants instead of a skirt. The temperature dropped from the high seventies to a rainy fifty degrees. I flip on the heater to take the dampness out of the car. Maybe Rory will have a fire going in the fireplace. A glass of wine in front of a crackling fire sounds like a pleasant way to catch up on family gossip. In the invitation Rory said to come hungry, Sharon was planning to cook dinner for us.

After a short distance we arrive at the house, pull through the portico and park the car off to the side. A porch light is on but no one comes to the door.

Vic comes around to open the door on my side of the car. "I'm sure they are in the back of the house and didn't hear us arrive."

"Yes." I agree, shaking off my sense of unease, chalking it up to the strained relationship with my brother. I'm anxious for this meeting to go well. I gather my purse, along with the flowers and wine I brought for a hostess gift. I picked the flowers from our garden earlier this morning. The vase is a garage sale treasure I found last summer. A lovely glass vase in blues and green that set off the colorful blooms I had painstakingly arranged.

I give Vic's arm a little squeeze as I slip my hand into the crook of his elbow. His warmth penetrates my hand. "You look exceedingly handsome this evening." I compliment him. He is dressed in a pair of pressed dark khaki pants with a button down plaid shirt under a fleece jacket. I slip my hand around his waist, then into the rear pocket of his pants and squeeze his butt. I gaze up at him, looking all wide-eyed and innocent, he grins at me, one eyebrow cocked in wry amusement.

His mountain man beard, fully grown in, covers his face in a thick blanket of crisp curling black. A stray strand of hair escapes his man bun and he tucks it behind his ear.

He leans down to kiss me. A simple brush of lips but the soft pressure of his mouth melding into mine combined with the earthly smell of the forest, sandalwood fills my senses and I feel my body relax.

"I'm having my doubts about this evening. If it wasn't rude to leave, I'd rather go home and spend the night in front of a crackling fire with…" He stoops and kisses the tip of my nose, "just you."

"Later, my ardent amigo, later…" My voice a breathless whisper as his hand starts at the small of my back and travels south. I cuddle deeper into his embrace and his touch chases away the damp chill of the night.

"I'll be waiting, Buttercup." he croons.

"I never doubt you." I smile at him affectionately and ring the doorbell.

A minute or so passes before we hear any movement in the house. We've rang the door bell twice beginning to think we had the wrong address when the door swings open and there stands a woman, someone I've never met.

"Oh, I'm sorry," I apologize in haste. "We must have the wrong house. I was supposed to meet my brother and his wife here." I hold up the invitation for validation. "I must have confused the directions. Can you help me find…?"

"No, no this is the right house. You must be Ellen and Vic." She gushes, ushering us into the foyer. "I'm Rachel, Sharon's sister, visiting with them. Rory and Sharon were detained at a meeting and asked that I greet you and get us started on cocktails. They will be along shortly." She is a tall woman with broad shoulders, her body blocky and solid, almost masculine. She stands just a few inches shorter than Vic and he's 6'3". Her brunette hair is short, verging on a military cut. She wears black trousers and a tailored white blouse, ballet flats, minimal to no makeup, a pair of reading glasses dangle from a chain around her neck. She shakes Vic's hand and then nearly crushes mine in her vigorous grip.

"You know how Rory is, a stickler for details, he was unable to leave his meeting early but wanted to make sure everything here was in place and perfect."

I politely laugh, shaking my hand to restore circulation. "Yes, I remember when we were children, Rory would line his stuffed animals up in his crib, according to height and color." And in the dark corner of my mind I remember how furious Rory became when Helen would go into his room and scatter his belongings, claiming I was the one to maliciously ruin my brother's room. She'd invent some story saying I was angry over some slight. For the longest time I was convinced Rory hated me, because nothing I did or said swayed him from his opinion of my guilt. I hope this evening goes well. I know it would break my mother's heart to see us estranged from each other.

I hand her the wine and flowers. "Here, just a little

something for our hosts."

"Oh, thank you, how lovely. Come in, come in." Rachel waves her hand in an effusive gesture, leading us into a beautiful living room with high vaulted ceilings and a fire cheerfully crackling away in the hearth. She sets the flowers on the center of a coffee table glowing with an amber sheen. A tray holds an assortment of cheese, crackers and nuts next to a row of wine glasses. A bottle of wine is propped in a decanter, beads of dew cling to the chilled bucket, the bottle waits, open for our pleasure.

"Sit down." Rachel beckons to a couch covered in pillows. The décor of the house is sleek, modern with lots of windows, simple furniture with a few throw pillows for color. The house screams rental property, not a sign of personal effects or family connection. It has obviously been staged for rental or sale. The walls clean, devoid of pictures or memorabilia except for a scrapbook on the coffee table. I recognize the scrapbook. My mother made it years ago before her death. Helen told me it was lost, nowhere to be found

"Sit here." Rachel points to the couch while picking up the bottle. "Rory insisted you try this wine. It is from a little winery south of Rome. Did you know he and Sharon vacationed in Italy last summer, and fell in love with the cuisine? He had several cases of wine shipped home, and he insisted this was a special occasion to celebrate. You must try a sip even if you're not a wine connoisseur, but don't be surprised if you're converted to a wine snob."

"Sure," Vic says flashing his dazzling, panty-dropping smile at her. Unlike most women, she doesn't flinch, wilt, simper or break out in a heat rash. How unusual, I think to myself. Instead she dismisses him and turns her attention in my direction.

"Ellen, how is it that you and Vic manage to live in the Adirondacks for the summer? You seem young to be retired. Don't you work? What about children? You have children, don't you? How can you leave them?" Her deep-set brown eyes widen in expectation of my answer, the pupils slightly dilated.

"I...." I stammer at her eagerness to explore my private life, unaccustomed to such direct questions that border on rudeness.

Vic chimes in, "Ellen retired from teaching a few years ago

and my business is sporadic, often requiring a great deal of travel. So we have chosen the Adirondacks as our place of residence in the summer. I come and go as needed. And you, Rachel? What brings you to the mountains?"

I love how he hands the question right back to her, directing the focus away from us and onto her. I'm thankful for Vic's burly beard, which covers a large portion of his face, effectively disguising his identity. We don't know if Rory or Sharon recognized Vic as Esteban Diago at the wedding. It was never mentioned. They didn't stay long or mingle much among the other guests. In the past, Vic dismissed people's prying questions by citing a mistaken identity based on resemblance. If a person is directly involved with us such as Adele and Weasel, then we need a legal non-disclosure agreement in writing. Tricky business…

Rachel squeezes my shoulder as she leans over to take the bottle from the ice bucket. "It's so good to have you here." She smiles warmly at me. "Rory and Sharon are excited to see you."

"Yes, so are we, there are few opportunities for us to connect with them."

"Oh, what a pity." Rachel says with an odd look on her face as she hands me a glass.

I wave it away protesting, "Shouldn't we wait? It seems a shame to drink this lovely wine without them being here to enjoy it with us."

"Nonsense." Rachel thrusts a glass at me, and turns, handing one to Vic. "It may be a while so there is no point in waiting. We'll nibble on the munchies then go into the kitchen and put the finishing touches on dinner." She holds up her hands in askance. "If that is all right with you?"

"Sure, I love puttering around in the kitchen. I'm happy to help." I sniff the air and can't help but notice, there are no delectable cooking smells wafting through the house. We may be doing more than putting the final touches on dinner. My stomach growls in protest. I didn't eat lunch this afternoon, knowing we were going out for dinner. From the looks of Rachel I'm guessing she's not a culinary goddess. I pat Vic's knee adding, "He's pretty good with a knife and chopping block. What are you serving?"

Rachel gives me an odd look and her mouth tightens. She

looks vaguely familiar but I can't place where I would know her. "Oh, just some silly recipe Sharon dug up on the Internet. Drink up." She holds up her glass to toast. "To new beginnings and tidying up the past."

Vic twirls his glass looking uncomfortable. I sense he doesn't care for Rachel. She is abrupt, her manner suggests she is used to giving commands and expects to be obeyed. She reminds me of his father in her arrogance. I'm shocked at the memory, as I've not thought of his father in years. Smiling brightly, I clink my glasses with hers, already regretting the evening. Rory and his wife have yet to appear. I glance at the clock on the mantel registering the hour, six o'clock. I plan to be out the door and home by nine-thirty. I feign a yawn, a warning signal of my pending exhaustion.

I take a sip of the wine and think to myself, this is quite ordinary. If anything it tastes like cheap spoiled wine with salt added. I wrinkle my nose; guess I'll never pass for a wine snob. I take another sip to be polite and place the glass on the table. Now there isn't even a nice glass of wine to look forward to.

After a few sips of wine, Vic's face grimaces in distaste. "What the hell?" He holds the glass away from his body, examining the contents. His eyes widen in comprehension and horror. "Ellen, stop!" He yells, knocking the glass out of my hands. "Don't drink it!"

But it's too late; I feel the effects of the wine. After the first sip I thought it was due to the fact I hadn't eaten since breakfast. But the room is spinning; the dizziness makes me feel nauseous. My stomach rolls and I want to throw up. I've never felt so disoriented after just one sip of alcohol. I look at Rachel in alarm.

Vic roars, "What the hell did you do?" He lurches forward, trying to grab Rachel by the arm. Vic's reflexes are quick, his brain engages faster and his instincts are superior to an average man, but he sways and his body crumbles to the floor with a crash. Even my superhero is no match for the powerful drug she's laced into our drink.

I scream and lunge toward him but my legs won't work, it's like I'm frozen. I hear a maniacal cackling laugh coming from Rachel, her body a blur in the periphery of my vanishing vision.

The world before me spins and fades before my eyes go to black. Rachel leans over and whispers in my ear, "Welcome home, my dear, Ellen…come into my parlor, said the spider to the fly…"

Jobs fill your packet, adventure fills your soul…

"Vic," I whisper, opening my eyes. There is nothing but darkness before me. I'm lying on something soft, a mattress or a bed? I can hear the steady drip of a leaky faucet, not another sound, just suffocating silence.

"Elle," Vic's voice rasps out. "Elle, are you here?"

My mind is working, but my body refuses to respond. I'm having a hard time focusing, my head clouded from the drugs. My voice strangles his name out on a sob. "Vic? Where are you?" I struggle to move. My hands are tingling, asleep. I roll and shift my weight, trying to stretch my aching arms. With a metallic rattle they move and then I can move them no farther. *My wrists are chained together.* I struggle, twisting, kicking, fighting against the chain. My ankles are chained, too.

I fall back on the mattress with a sickening thud, little sparks of light explode in my head, a throbbing pain so intense it feels as if my head will split in two.

With a moan I ask, "Vic, where are you?"

"Here," I feel his foot connect with my calf. "Can you hear me?"

"Yes." My eyes adjust to the low level of light and I barely make out the shadowed form of his body. "Vic," I whisper. "What happened? How did we get here?"

"Elle, I don't know." I hear Vic trying to get to his feet; the chains around his ankles clank and rattle as he moves. "We're chained to something. I can't move."

"Me, either." I wiggle over onto my stomach, trying to twist against the chains, and realize, I'm naked. A chill starts at the base of my spine. Someone has taken my clothes. "Vic, my clothes are gone!"

"Yeah, me too." He says, his voice hoarse with emotion.

"Why would someone take our clothes and chain us to the wall?" My heart pounds in my chest like a jackhammer and the roaring in my ears drowns out Vic's words. My worst nightmare has come to life. And I've taken Vic along with me. The captor has imprisoned my liberator.

"Oh my God, I can't believe I let this happen to us." Vic crouches over his knees, swaying back and forth.

"Vic, what are you saying?"

"Elle, I'm so sorry."

"What are you talking about?" A snaking dread curls along the fog of panic that threatens to overwhelm me.

"I can't believe this is happening? Son of a bitch!" Vic curses and bangs his fists against the wall. He blows out a deep sigh of regret. "Over the last few months," he says, barely able to talk, overcome with emotion. "I've received in the mail suspicious letters. I didn't want to alarm you and take away your sense of security. After the kidnapping I know how hard it was for you to feel safe again. So I thought Ike and I would handle this on our own. I hired the best security company in the country, had Ike living with us for extra protection. The general opinion was, the letters were sent by a crazy fan, who would lose interest and go away."

"Oh, Vic…why didn't you tell me?"

"I thought I could be vigilant enough for both of us."

"Do you think this is a celebrity stalker?"

"No, Elle…. someone who knew us lured us here."

"Rachel? I didn't recognize her, did you?"

"No, but there must be a connection to her and your brother."

"I can't imagine Rory doing something like this."

I huddle close to him seeking out his body warmth. The cold damp air penetrates clear through to my bones. "Vic…" I squeeze my eyes shut to keep the tears from leaking out. "What are we going to do?"

He leans down and kisses my hair. "Who ever that bitch is up there," he whispers against my ear. "We're going to out smart her."

"How did she get a hold of the family information? It was Rory's voice on the answering machine. She knew about my aunts and uncles. Did you see the pictures on the coffee table? There was one of my mother, Vic, I'm scared."

"I know, Baby, I know. Shhh…" He molds his body closer to mine. "We have to talk in whispers. She probably has the room wired for sound; it looks like one of those panic rooms or doomsday shelters."

"What are you talking about?"

"Sometimes, wealthy or very paranoid people have panic rooms put in their houses. In case of a home invasion or a nuclear holocaust, they have a safe protected area that cannot be broken into and the basic essentials of life to wait out a cataclysmic event."

My eyes have adjusted to the dim light. I see we are sitting on a small twin bed jutting out from the wall. A simple kitchen occupies the opposite wall along with a small lavatory. The open cupboards are stocked with the basic essentials for a person to survive in times of adversity.

I look around the stark enclosure barely making out images in the pale light. There are no windows or doors allowing natural light to seep in, it must be night, but I have no idea how long we have been here. Has it been hours or days? My stomach rumbles with hunger and I'm terribly thirsty. A salty metallic taste lingers in my mouth. Then I notice a faint halo of light from underneath the cabinets along the wall. Just out of reach, sitting on the countertop is a pitcher of water.

"But how will anyone find us?" I lower my voice to a bare murmur.

Vic takes my hand and traces the letters…I…K…E… on it, and then he closes his fingers around my palm sealing the imaginary letters into hiding. He runs a hand through my hair and leans his forehead against mine.

I huddle, shivering against Vic and close my eyes, praying this nightmare ends soon and I'll wake up, safe in my own bed. I close my eyes and pass over to unconsciousness rather than dreams.

~~~

I'm awakened by a clawing thirst; my throat scraped raw. I've never been so thirsty in my life. Vic moans next to me and we're both soaked in sweat. The temperature is sweltering, where it was freezing before, now dry hot heat is spewing out of the air ducts mounted on the floor. It must be close to a hundred degrees in the room.

It is so hot I can hardly breathe.

"Vic, Vic?" I shake his arm. "Are you all right?" His body lies limp next to me, his breathing rapid and shallow.

He struggles to open his eyes. "I'll be fine." He rasps, his voice hoarse, trying to reassure me but I can hear the effort in his voice to maintain consciousness.

"We need water." I squeak out. "I'm going to try and reach the pitcher."

The pitcher gleams in the shadowed light, looking like a small oasis held captive in glass. I scan the small space frantically searching for something, anything I can use to pull the water pitcher closer.

I have to try again, even if it means pulling my shoulder joint out of the socket. Vic is too far away; it's up to me. I wipe the sweat from my brow; the salt burns and stings, mixing in with my tears.

I'm chained to Vic, so I extend his arm, holding it high as I creep forward, leaning my weight against the chain, pulling for every fraction of an inch. My hand brushes the pitcher, but I can't grasp the handle. I close my eyes and will my body to stretch, pulling with every fiber of my being against sinew and bone. I try exhaling, to minimize the air space in my lungs, hoping to gain even a mere fraction of an inch. I heave my body and grasp frantically at the pitcher; my fingers hit the side, knocking it to the floor. I feel the spray of water and splinters of glass splash against my leg. In despair, I grab a fistful of broken glass and throw it at the walls, screaming, "What do you want from us?" The shards of glass pierce my skin, a cruel stabbing into my flesh. Suddenly, a hidden switch is thrown and the room bursts into light. The harsh light blinds me, I shriek and throw my hands up, shielding my eyes from the glare. With a rumble the air ducts kick on, a blast of cold air pours into the room. The vaporous steam feels like a cloud of dry ice pushing back the heat, replacing it with a bone-numbing chill. And then the dead bolt rattles and slides, the door swings back on its hinge. I don't know who or what I expected…but the image standing at the door confirms it. The devil has slithered out of Hades, writhing its outstretched hand to grasp and snare, pulling me into the depths of the netherworld. What other explanation can there be? Standing before me is none other than Helen, my dead stepmother.

Mountains teach that not everything in this world can be rationally explained.
Aleksander Lwow

When alive, she was a small, compact woman, barely standing over five-foot tall. But in death, her stature looms large taking up my entire field of vision. Larger than life stands…Helen, the stepmother of my tormented youth. The woman who turned my father and brothers away from me destroying anything I ever held precious. A nightmare reincarnated to life. Before me stands the cunning bitch who ripped Vic and me apart and adopted out our son. I never understood the word 'hate' until Helen came in to my life. My mind whirls in a disarray of confusion. She's dead. Isn't she? I haven't seen her in almost thirty years. I disassociated myself from her and my father. I never wanted to see her again. I seem to remember Rory telling me she died. But where is Rory? We were to meet Rory for dinner; instead some deranged woman lets us into the house and poisons us. Is this a setup where Helen gets the last revenge?

"No…" The denial escapes my lips. I never doubted the depths of her evil.

"Hello, Ellen." Helen croons. She flashes a smile that is overly cheery, a madwoman's grin of self-congratulation. Her voice pleasant, meant to be soothing, makes my skin crawl.

There is the sound of metal, a faint click and the heavy door swings shut closing her in the cell with us. She moves toward the bed but stands out of arm's reach.

My heart races and instinctively I stiffen. "Helen…?" The words brush the air crackling with panic as I exhale.

Vic's voice is harsh as he exclaims, "Helen!" He shifts his weight to get a better view. "What the hell?" he swears. He nudges my leg. "I though she was dead!"

"That's what I was told." I hiss.

She laughs, although it's more like a giggle, a weird high-pitched giggle. "I see you woke up from your little nap." She says. "I was beginning to think I gave you too much of our magic elixir. I don't want to kill you, just when the fun is about to begin."

"Who are you?" I ask, almost afraid of the answer. "You can't be Helen. She died years ago."

"Some people never die, they just live on and on." She laughs and twirls around and around, dancing like a marionette puppet on strings, awkward with jerking movement.

"What did you put in the wine?" Vic demands.

"Why, darling. Just a little bit of that sweet old date rape drug, worked very effectively don't you think?"

"Are you crazy! Why would you do that to us?" I cry out. "Why are you impersonating Helen?"

"Don't tell me you've forgotten who I am after all these years." Her voice hardens. "So typical of you. You never appreciate any generosity that was done for you. It was always about Ellen. Ellen doesn't want to play the game. Ellen doesn't want to spend the night. Ellen doesn't want to be friends. Ellen, Ellen, Ellen without a thought of anyone else." Her face stretches into an evil grin. "But not anymore, my pretty," She thrusts her face in mine, "You and your fancy husband are mine. Did you think we would forget about stuck-up little Miss Prig?"

"Careful Elle." Vic hisses in my ears. I don't need his warning to realize I'm in the presence of crazy.

I clear my throat and run a tongue over dry parched lips deciding how to play her game. "Hello, Helen. How are you? It's been a long time."

"It has been a long time, Ellen." Her moods are mercurial, shifting back and forth between manic and deadly calm.

She pulls on the chain, hauling me to my feet, until my face is mere inches away from her. She has amazing strength for a woman.

"Too long. My dear, Ellen." She runs a finger down my cheek. "I went to a great deal of trouble to find you. I hope you appreciate my efforts. We are going to have such fun."

"Helen, why don't you take these chains off and we can talk. I'm sure this is some kind of misunderstanding." Vic tries placating her.

"Shut up, no one is talking to you!" She kicks Vic in the leg.

I hear Vic suck in his breath and groan.

"Helen, how did you find me? And why?"

"I have my ways and military experience. I was in the Maritime Security Team of the Coast Guard. I joined right out of college, enlisting in the Coastal Forces Program of the Reserves. I was one of the few females to make the Coastal Forces, we are the Seals of the Coast Guard." Her voice glows with pride, "Not many women can train to such a high degree in these very specialized areas."

I grip Vic's hand and shake my head slightly. This makes no sense. Helen wasn't in the Coast Guard, what is this woman talking about? In the recesses of my befuddle mind, a memory begins to click, a grove in my brains hits upon a familiar track. Something about this sounds familiar, but my mind is too feeble to connect the dots. To appease her, I agree. "You must be very proud."

"In the course of a day, I can run 5 miles with a full pack, spend hours in the water, do 2-3 hours on the mats in hand to hand combat before hitting the books for academic assignments." She brags. "I'd like to see you do that. You always acted like you were so smart. Ellen, Miss Goody-Two Shoes. I showed you. I did it all, until that stupid kid died on the water rescue. It wasn't my fault, but they blamed me. It was just an excuse to discharge me from the military. They said I was too old to be of service anymore. Look at me now! I handled the capture of you and your smart-ass husband without a hitch. He thought he was so clever with his high tech security system. Those idiots running that security company couldn't patrol a playground."

Vic whispers under his breath. "Stupid, stupid, stupid, I can't believe I didn't see this coming."

Even though she's wearing the same Chanel suit Helen wore to all dress-up occasions, the woman in front of me is not my stepmother. Overall she is too tall, Helen took great pride in her tiny bearing, endlessly taunting me about my height. Her favorite nickname for me was scarecrow because of my long legs and arms. This woman isn't old enough, Helen would be in her eighties now. The haircut was the same, but the black color looked dyed, not natural. I recognize the jewelry. My father had given that particular necklace and earrings to Helen for Christmas one year, early on in their marriage. The pumps and handbag dangling from the crook of her arm matched the suit perfectly; even the shade of nail polish was Helen's brand. Obviously, this was the woman who let us into the house. But why would she impersonate Helen?

"I'm sorry, Helen, I never meant any disrespect. I apologize for not understanding you."

"You think you can right thirty-five years of wrong with a false apology?" She slaps me across the face, knocking me to the floor. Vic roars and leaps for her but she pulls a Taser from her pocket, jams it onto his leg in a lightening blur of movement. A sizzling sound fills the air. Vic's eyes roll back in his head and he slumps onto the cot, unconscious.

I scream and leap at her. With a careless toss she flings me back onto the bed.

"What are you doing? Why are you doing this to us?"

"Not to him, my dear. He is just a byproduct. It's you, Ellen." She hisses. "Only you, my dear." She caresses my cheek. "All those years, you never played with me. Always going off by yourself, you were too good for us. Helen told me how much you hated me, how it was you who broke my toys and ripped the pages out of my diary. You sent the letter to Jenny Tillman, telling her that being my friend was dangerous. You made terrible accusations."

She thrusts her face in mine, "You told her I was mentally unstable, that I stole things and cut the heads off my dolls. Her mother never let me play with her again. All of the kids started calling me 'crazy girl'. I never had any friends. It's your fault.

Aunt Helen told me how you laughed at me, called me a pathetic dike."

What in the world is she talking about, I never did any of those things, and then the pieces of the puzzle fall into place. "Maltby…?" I gasp, recognizing her.

She laughs a deep, rich laugh, full of malice and glee. "My, my, you are not as stupid as you look, dear Ellen. So you do remember me."

"Yes, but Maltby, I never did those things to you. Why would I?"

She roars, "I know what you did! I spent two years taking care of Aunt Helen as she lay dying. No one else came, not you or your ungrateful brothers. She told me everything you did. She made me promise to make you pay. And here we are." She croons, running a hand down my leg. "Just the two of us, at last."

"No! Please, Maltby, let's talk. I would never hurt you. Helen was lying. She did the same things to me. It was her not me. Please, believe me." The depth and extent of her deception comes crashing through my consciousness. Maltby and I had nothing in common except for Helen. Any attachment is illusionary, coiled like a blind worm in her imagination. This is not a simple kidnapping. From what Vic whispered to me, she has been stalking us for months. The clever use of family connection was our undoing. In my desperation to reunite with my brother, we never saw her coming.

"No more time for talking." She says, whipping the wig off her head and tossing it into a corner. "We have to move." She pulls the plasticine away from her face, and with each movement I see the image of Helen fade and the mature face of Maltby emerge.

"It's time to get going." She says, aiming the Taser at me and I feel a jolt of electricity sting my leg, traveling through my entire body before darkness envelopes me.

L.R. Smolarek

I took a walk into the woods and came out taller than the trees.
Henry David Thoreau

I wake gradually but don't open my eyes, fearing what will come with the admitting light. My first conscious thought, why is my body lurching and swaying back and forth, moving and bouncing over something rough and uneven. My eyes spring open, and are met with nothing I recognize. Where am I? Where is Vic? The chains are gone but I'm still tied and held captive.

I wiggle, rolling, anything to lessen the cramping in my arms and legs. Everything hurts. It hurts even to breathe. I'm lying on what feels like a rubber mat and can feel the weight of Vic's body next to me. We are still naked but some kind of blanket is thrown over us. I feel the cold air on my face where my skin is exposed.

"Vic, sweetheart, are you awake?" I nudge him with my toe.

He groans and flips over on to his side facing me. "Yeah," he whispers. "How are you doing?"

"About the same as you, I suspect."

"Then not very good," he answers grimly.

"What are we in, it sounds like a plane."

"And it looks like a plane." Vic says. The shifting shadows of sunlight filter through the small windows of a two-seater passenger plane. Craning my neck for a better view I see a carpet of trees spreading below as far as the eye can see, nothing but trees. The air becomes increasingly humid and moisture soars through the air. Jolts from the air pockets send shockwaves of pain through our bodies.

"If I didn't know any better, I'd say we are in a seaplane. This looks identical to the interior of the ones I've used to fly in and out of the Adirondacks."

Vic's life experiences are more worldly than mine, this is my first seaplane ride and I would do anything not to be here.

"Who's flying?" I ask.

Vic lifts his torso in a vain attempt to see into the cockpit. "I can't be sure, but I think Maltby."

I flick my wrists, wincing at the tender areas on them. "At least the chains are gone, our wrists and legs are tied with what feels like plastic zip ties."

"This is so bizarre." He says. "Maltby is clearly deranged. Where can she be taking us in a plane?"

"We have to stop her!" I whisper. "We can't let her get away with this, kidnapping, poisoning, and attempted murder."

"What do you propose, jumping three thousand feet?"

"Of course not!"

"Shut up back there." Maltby calls from the cockpit. "No talking. We're almost there. We're going to land and then take a little walk. Hope you feel like stretching your legs."

I hate flying. I've always hated flying, even though my first husband was a pilot and we were granted unlimited air miles. My stomach pitches as a wave of nausea surges into the back of my throat. The lack of food and water has left my brain sluggish and slow. How can she expect us to walk, no clothes, tied up and dehydrated? And what terrifies me-where is she going to land this plane? There is nothing but forest below.

The plane swings wide as she banks a turn to the left, over the drone of the engine the wings creak and the plane lurches and plummets in altitude. How can we land in the middle of the forest? Lower and lower the plane floats, pitching as we hit air pockets then *bump* and a sharp jerk. The plane bobbles and sways back and forth and I can hear the splash of water on the pontoons. The landing confirms we are in a seaplane and our runway is some distant wilderness lake.

Maltby steps out of the cockpit to the main body of the plane and with a powerful thrust of her arm she pushes open the hatch door. Cool mountain air washes over us as she snatches off the thin blanket. I feel goose-bumps rising on my skin and shiver

225

involuntary. God, I miss my clothes. I love my clothes, soft, warm and comfortable. Maybe Eve ate the apple in the Garden of Eden just so she could start a wardrobe.

Hanging onto the edge of the door, Maltby swings out of the plane with a jump, we hear her splashing in the water. Tying off the plane, anchoring it to shore? She sloshes back to the door and with a vicious yank pulls me out into the water. My body sinks below the surface and I fear this is how I will die. I come to the surface, sputtering and coughing, as she hauls me onto a beach. It takes two hands for her to roll Vic into the water and drag him up the small spit of sand.

From my limited vantage point I see this is not a well-used portage or crossing point for happy hikers looking for easy access to mountain trails. No wooden signs nailed to the trees listing the names of hiking paths and mileage printed in yellow nor any rough skid marks from canoes dragged across the beach. Untouched, pristine wilderness.

The brilliant orange of a monarch butterfly catches my eye. It glides by, carried by the gentle breeze. A wave of longing and jealousy overwhelms me, to be so free and in control of your destiny. The butterfly stops and rests on the petal of a cardinal flower before dipping its proboscis deep into the blossom. And in a fleeting moment it moves on leaving me behind, bereft.

With a swift deft movement, Maltby slices through the ties on our ankles. She stands over us, a primitive, earthy presence commanding, "Get up! It's time to get moving. Let's see how tough you are now, Ellen. You loved spending time in the woods. This should be fun for you." I cry out in pain as her heavy boot connects with my thigh.

"Quit whining." She barks. "Sit up and wiggle through the ties on your wrists. I left them loose enough so you can pull your legs through and your hands will be tied in front. The trail ahead is going to be rough and you'll need the use of your hands."

Faint with exhaustion Vic and I struggle to thread our legs through the restraints on our wrists and maneuver our hands to the front of our bodies.

How could childhood miscommunication evolve into such a diabolical hatred? I don't understand. I never hated Maltby; I just didn't want to play with her. I remember her as being bossy and overbearing, more at home with the boys than girls. When no one was looking, she'd punch or trip me then claim I was so uncoordinated I couldn't stay on my feet. My brothers, young and gullible thought everything was in great fun. I hated going with the family for these weekend trips. I tried inventing excuses not to go. But Helen claimed I was too young to stay home alone. Now I see why. She insisted the visits were a family outing and everyone must go. The seeds of deceit and deception she planted in Maltby's mind, just another cog in Helen's master plan.

Maltby? Who names their child, Maltby? Supposedly, it was a family name from England. The poor girl was doomed before she even had a chance.

The weather today is overcast, the sun obscured by clouds and the shrouded cover of forest, a perfect day to dump someone off in the woods. I stumble to my feet, moving unsteadily down the faint remnants of a trail, fearful of the Taser in Maltby's hand. Vic places himself between her and me, as if trying to form a human shield. It feels like morning because the fresh feel of dew clings to the air. The birds are quiet except for the repeated call of the red-eyed vireo, calling high in the leaf canopy. Short, monotonous phrases endlessly asking and answering the same question. "Where are you? Over here. Come see me." The vireo call is constant during nesting season, even on hot summer afternoons.

Maltby pushes Vic in the back, causing him to stumble. "Pick your feet up and get moving. We haven't got all day."

"Where are you taking us?" Vic protests. "What do you want? Money? Revenge for something that happened years ago? Why don't you just turn around and leave us. No one will be the wiser. By the time we get out of these woods you can be long gone."

"Nice try, it'd be interesting to see how much the fans of your latest movie would pay to have you back on the screen." She chortles. "Yeah, I know who you are for all your disguises and cover-ups. It wasn't difficult to piece the identities of Esteban Diago and Vic Rienz together. I took care of Helen for months as she lay dying. Between the information she provided and hacking into your brother's Facebook account, it was child's play to find you."

"Maltby…" I start to say. "Why don't we…"

"Be quiet." She barks. "Turn here to the left."

"But there is no trail." I protest.

"I know." She chuckles. "This is where it gets interesting. We are going off trail and do us some bushwhacking."

"Bushwhacking?" Vic asks incredulous. "You mean just wander in the mountains without a trail?"

"We could be lost …forever." I exclaim. "We have no shoes, clothing, food or water."

"And that my dear Ellen, is the plan." Maltby crows. "I have a GPS. I'll be marking off the path as we walk through the forest. I've chosen the most remote portion of the park to start our little trek. We're going to hike deep into the backcountry and then I'll be leaving. You always acted so smart about knowing everything about nature. This will be the ultimate challenge for you. You and your husband will be naked and lost in the deep forest of the Adirondack Mountains forcing you to rely upon your skills as a woods woman to survive."

Vic and I turn as one to stare at her, astonishment written on our faces. Before I can stop my mouth, out bursts, "Have you lost your mind?"

"Ellen!" Vic reprimands me. "Don't antagonize the crazy lady." He hisses in my ear.

I shake my head in disbelief, not sure I'm elated she's not going to murder us and dump our bodies in the woods or terrified over the prospect of being 'naked and afraid' in the wilds of the Adirondack Mountains. But the next words out of her mouth leave me no doubt of her intent.

"I'm going to walk you so far back into the forest, it will be impossible for you to find your way without a compass or map. Then I'll hike back to the plane, give you a twenty-four hour head start before I stalk you with my bow and arrow. Make no mistake, I'll be hunting you…and I intend to kill you."

~~~

We hike for hours off the trail, climbing over downed snags of trees, the remnants of a blow-down years ago, up mountain slopes and down, working painstakingly over the tangle of roots, tree limbs and protruding branches.

"Having fun yet?" She asks, stopping to take a drink from her water bottle, guzzling the water and spilling it onto the ground just to torment us.

I stop my tortuous crawl over the logs to look back at her. My tender feet accustomed to pedicures and soft slippers are swollen, cut and bleeding. Welts stand out red and angry on my skin, torn and bruised from the punishing trek through brush and thorn thickets. I'm stunned to silence, no energy left to wail and scream at her, my body depleted from lack of food and water. It's as if she knows just how much nourishment we need to keep going, and doles it out accordingly, tossing food and half filled water bottles. A half a mile back on the trail, Vic charged her, head bent bellowing in rage, his act of defiance earned him a jolt from her Taser. As she baits us, he stands silent, smoldering in fury and frustration.

"Did you hear me?" She turns her head and spits. A disgusting habit she developed between childhood and now. "You loved to play in the woods, Ellen. Let's see how good you are at surviving in the wilderness with a predator stalking you. I've been training for years, spending weeks at wilderness survival schools, learning to track and live off the land. Now I'll have a prey worthy of my talents. Maybe I'll give you longer than twenty-four hours, I don't want the game to end too soon." She runs a finger down my arm. "Where would the fun be in that?"

In that moment, a spark of anger ignites; a flair of red, causing my vision to haze over. Her dare, the challenge to pit her dominance over me brings back all the memories of her bullying me as a child. I thought my stepmother was dead, but from the grave, the thread of her resentment has seeped like an evil noxious poison. She used Maltby as a vessel for her hatred. Maltby was always odd, off kilter and emotionally charged. She was the only child of older parents. Her mother was in her forties when she was born, she and Helen would whisper, calling Maltby a 'change of life baby' a mistake. Her parents not used to children in the house, already set in their ways, immersed in their careers, misunderstood and often neglected her. If Maltby weren't so mean, I'd have felt sorry for her.

And somehow in her dementia-addled mind Helen found a way to use Malbty, her caretaker, to fuel a childhood resentment into a murderous tool from the grave, the perfect crime.

In a swift movement, Maltby reaches down and yanks me off my feet, clasping the Taser in her hand, she aims and a jolt of electricity courses through my body and the world goes black.

One may walk over the highest mountain one step at a time.
Barbara Walters

"Elle, Elle, wake up, *quierda.*"

"Vic?" My body aches, but my heart quickens when he calls me, *quierda*. It means 'darling' in Spanish.

"Vic?" In the darkness, I reach out a hand searching for him. The cool air stings my exposed skin. Bewildered, why am I in the woods, cold and hungry and without clothes? As consciousness returns the reality of our situation comes flooding back to me.

"Elle, come on, we have to get moving. We need to put some distance between Maltby and us. Can you stand up?"

Vic hooks a hand under my arm and hauls me to my feet. I wince at the pain from the zip ties cutting into the tender flesh on my wrists.

"Wait," I implore him. "We need to get rid of these ties. We'll move much faster without them."

"How?" He asks holding up his bound wrists. "Maybe we can smash them?"

"Lani and I took a self-defense course last winter. The instructor showed us how to break the clip that holds them together."

"Well, hurry up and show me. The farther away from that crazy she-devil the better." Vic scans the woods looking for any movement. The stars are barely visible through the thick overhead canopy of the forest. But the moon is high and casting the trees in full shadow.

"Watch." I demonstrate, holding my wrist as far from my

body as the bonds will allow me. With a sharp jerk I smash the plastic ties against my hip. The force of the blow is supposed to crack the clasp. Unfortunately my snap was feeble and weak.

"Are you sure that works?" He asks, his voice clouded in suspicion.

"Yes, the instructor showed us several times. Lani and I both did it. If you snap the ties at the right angle they break right off."

"Okay." Vic nods his head and takes a deep breath. He purses his lips in concentration, raises his arms and with a sharp crack smashes his wrists against his hipbone. *Pop…*the tie breaks and falls away.

"Yes!" He cheers, shaking his hands to restore circulation.

"Okay, I'm going to try again." I say, willing my strength into one fierce downward thrust of my arms. I wince as I slam my wrist into my hip but the tie snaps and drops to the ground.

Vic runs a hand through his hair; the long strands fell out of his man bun long ago. He looks like the romance novel version of a prehistoric caveman. Even with tangled and snarled hair hanging past his broad shoulders, what cave woman wouldn't be humming a happy tune at the sight of his chiseled abs standing at her cave door?

Seriously, I scold myself mentally. I'm in a life and death situation and I'm ogling his ass. At least the scintillating thoughts are warming me up. Damn, it's cold out here for a night in July. Along with hunger pangs, I'm having clothes envy, yearning for shoes, thick socks, flannel shirts, yoga pants. There is nothing like deprivation to make you appreciate the simple things in life.

"This is on you, Elle." Vic says folding me into his embrace. "You know me, I'm the city guy with next to no survival skills. I'll follow your lead." I burrow into the warmth of his body, grateful for any heat. His breath when he speaks wafts across my cheek. His voice somehow managing to be deep and soft, tinged with exhaustion. He kisses the top of my head and asks, "Can you get us home, *quierda?*"

This would be a good time for a super hero to show up…I look around…no Wonder Woman, Bat Girl or even Lois Lane standing in line to help. *Damn…*

I nod, realizing he is right, an outdoor skills survivalist, he is not. I wrinkle my brow in concentration trying to come up with a plan. The feeble light of dawn announces the coming of a new day. "Maybe one of us can climb up a tree and get a perspective on our location?" I suggest, pointing to a nearby hemlock, the branches strategically sprouting out of the trunk.

"Good idea." Vic grabs a branch and shimmies about half way up the tree, cursing as the bark scrapes his exposed skin. "We seem to be at the highest reach of a mountain range." He calls down from his vantage point. "I can't go any farther up, the branches are too thick and I can feel the tree beginning to sway."

"We could head down toward that stream." He suggests, pointing, his arm protruding out of the foliage. "If we follow the watershed it should lead to a larger stream, river or lake. And where there is water in the Adirondacks, there are people." He drops out of the tree with the grace of a man much younger, the benefits of staying fit under the supervision of a personal trainer.

"Unfortunately, that is exactly what she will expect us to do. It also gives her a direct path to follow." I squint my eyes looking for clues as how to proceed knowing time is of the essence. "We need to start moving and now."

"There is nothing but trees and mountains for as far as the eye can see." He says with a shrug of his shoulders, batting away a pesky mosquito.

Pausing to assess our survival situation, I nod in agreement, calculating our odds of survival in the wilderness verses escaping Maltby. "I hate to leave a water source but the mountains are littered with streams and small ponds. I think we take our chances, pick a direction and walk a straight line in the hopes we encounter civilization. The key is to leave as little tracks as possible. We'll move in a zig-zag direction."

"Okay, but which way?"

"Traveling in an east or westerly direction will be easier because we can use the sun as a navigation tool, keeping it ahead of us to the left or right."

"But without a path will that be enough to keep us on a straight course?"

I dig deep into the memories of my summer at Camp High Point where Burt and I took the older campers into the woods

on over-night camping trips, teaching them survival skills. I grope
for the tidbits of knowledge and techniques Burt patiently
mapped out on how to survive in the wild. In later years as a
teacher, my students learned the concepts of English, math and
science using the natural world as a backdrop. Our classroom was
populated with aquariums, a touch table and bird mobiles flew
overhead suspended on clear fishing line. My students' studies
were augmented with field trips to local parks where they learned
what plants are edible, the importance of water and how to build
a shelter. Now I needed to draw on those experiences to survive.

"We'll start heading east. Burt taught me how to walk a
straight line in the forest. First you head toward the left side of
one tree and then the right side of the next tree. This will keep
your bearings in line."

I hold my hand out to him, "Come on, Amigo. We've got
traveling to do."

"I trust you, Elle. We can do this, let's go home."

Holding hands, shivering in the early morning air, hungry,
our bodies bruised and battered from the trek over the
mountains, we resolve to escape the deranged woman possessed
by the spirit of my dead stepmother.

Werifesteria-Old English (v) To wander longingly through the forest in search of mystery.

We stumble through the forest stopping only to forage for edible bits of nourishment along the trail. The days melt one into another, my mind a blur, coherent thought lost in a haze of hunger and exhaustion. Our stomachs cramped, begging for more than the little green sprigs of sorrel and Indian cucumber roots we managed to find. At the edge of a marsh we dug deep into the muck and pulled up the roots of nutrient rich cattails. A meager faire but at least we are putting a few calories back into our bodies. Since leaving home, aside from the pitiful pickings along the trail, and the energy bars Maltby tossed at us, we are slowly starving to death. To escape Maltby, we keep moving but moving requires calories of which we are sorely lacking.

At night swarms of mosquitoes plague us, flying in our eyes, up our noses, biting the most sensitive places. To protect our blistered and battered skin, we slathered ourselves with mud, thick, black odiferous mud. And to think at one time I spent good money on a mud wrap when the local wetland offered up this rejuvenating goodness for free. As much as I love the outdoors, this mud bath is a far cry from the sensuous pleasures of a five-star spa.

When exhaustion overwhelms us, we find temporary shelter in a thatch of bushes or under the sweeping boughs of evergreen trees, sleeping only in short snatches. Always on the alert for the snap of a branch or the crunch of a footstep; there has been no sign of Maltby. If she were near I find it difficult to believe she wouldn't succumb to the temptation of finding her prey, helpless and open to torment. Is she lying in wait, vigilant, ready for us to stumble across her path? Or quite simply is her plan that we perish from starvation and exposure, lost in the mountains?

Ever-present in my mind is the survival rule of threes, three hours of exposure to die of hypothermia, three days without water and three weeks without food. The end result always the same-death. Lucky for us, the nighttime temperatures have not dipped much below fifty degrees. While cold, our bodies have adjusted to the cooler temperatures. We huddle together for sleep and push our bodies to move, generating body heat under the warming rays of sun in hopes of chasing away the frigid ache that resides in our bones.

One morning in predawn mist, when the sun is the barest whisper of lavender, caught in the shadows of dawn; we saw a bear. A large black bear with a patch of white on its front paw is following us, almost leading, a benign soothsayer, intuitive almost magical in our imagination simply by its mere presence. Vic at first was terrified, but the bear did not appear malevolent, never approaching us, disappearing as the sun rose in the shadows of the woods. For three mornings, the bear transpired from the grey leavings of night, and out of our hesitation to avoid crossing paths with it, the bear has inadvertently acted as a trail guide through the woods.

Along with the quest for food, the search for water consumes us. We are always thirsty, hesitant to drink from the streams and small ponds we encounter due to the fear of giardia. On top of all the other abuses our bodies have sustained, I shudder to think of dealing with the cramps, bloating, nausea and diarrhea that accompanies the infection. Up to this point we have been able to obtain water from the abundance of moss growing on the forest floor. Sphagnum moss can hold up to twenty times its dry weight in water. Instead of roots, sphagnum moss has large dead cells in its stem and leaves that hold water. We quench our thirst by pulling up handfuls of moss and squeezing the excess into our mouths, gritty at best but pure sweet water.

Be fearless in the pursuit of what sets your soul on fire.

"You can do it."

"No, way in hell am I putting that thing in my mouth."

"It will be fine."

"No."

"Don't be a baby."

"I'm not being a baby. It's a worm for God's sake, Elle!"

"It's a little bitty worm, just open and swallow. We need the protein."

"No, look at it. Ugh…it's all slimy and gritty."

"We'll wash them off in the stream."

"You can't make me."

"Yes, I can, now man up."

"Don't try to pull the macho card on me."

"If the shoe fits then wear it, weeny boy!"

"I'm not doing it."

"Since when are you so squeamish?"

"Always."

"We need the protein, our bodies are starving!"

"No way. Where are those little red bunchberries? I'd rather eat them."

"Here, just open up."

"No."

"Yes."

"Not going to happen."

"Watch. I'll go first." I take a deep breath and hold the wiggling earthworm by it tail and steel myself. Oh yuck. I repeat my mantra, "I can do this...I can do this...I can do this." It's a matter of survival. I watch the worm dance and struggle to escape. I feel a pang of sympathy for the little guy. I like earthworms; they are industrious creatures, prodigious tunnel makers and enrichers of our soil. On rainy days as a kid and even now, I stop to pick them off the wet pavement tossing their wiggly bodies back on the grass so they don't dry out and die.

"Sorry buddy," I mutter. Once I pop the worm in my mouth, I'm not sure what do. The texture is foreign, should I swallow or chew? How to I force down the urge to gag? I chomp down a few times and swallow, a shudder 'worms' its way through my body.

"Oh God, Elle, that was disgusting." Vic groans, screwing his mouth up in a grimace of revulsion. He wipes his grime stained hand across his chin leaving behind a streak of dirt.

"Here," I hand a big, fat, juicy one to him. "Just pop it in and swallow. It's fine."

"Oh, I don't think I can do this," he grumbles, holding up the worm. "Doesn't this qualify as cruelty to animals, what if those animal rights people, PICA, PETRO or PETA, whatever they call themselves find out? I could be put in jail." He holds the dangling worm and suddenly, *pop*, it's gone. "Ouch!" Vic cries, wringing his hand as an arrow wizzes through the air, imbedding into the trunk of a tree behind us. Instinctively, we dive for cover in the heavy brush.

"Oh, did I interrupt your snack, Esteban? Where are your fans now, pretty boy? No one to come rescue you? Boo, hoo, such a shame."

Maltby.

The whoosh of another arrow rips through the still air, slicing into the rough bark of a tree, quivering from the force of impact. She yells down from a rise on the path. "Ellen, honey, I thought you were so competent in the woods. It only took me two day to find your trail, not so smart anymore are you?" She cackles and taunts us.

"Oh holy hell, she found us." I hiss. "What are we going to do?"

"Just what we planned," He says. "We are going to draw her

out, remember there are two of us and only one of her. And hopefully, she is armed with just the bow and arrow." He points. "There was a rocky summit back about a half a mile. We'll lure her out onto the open ledge. I'll be the decoy and distract her then you smack her over the head with a rock or tree branch."

"Jeez, it sounded better in theory." Though the plan was simplistic, our brains are blank, save for the pure animal urge to flee.

"I seem to recall you have experience in smacking assailants over the head and knocking them off a cliff." Vic says, reminding me of my ordeal with Jolib Freeport, the crazed hermit a few years ago.

"Gee, thanks for the vote of confidence but I had the S.W.A.T. team as backup."

"Buttercup, I have confidence in you."

Oh, boy…

"At least I didn't have to eat worms." He says, always one to find the silver lining in a situation.

"Seriously, that's what you have to think about now."

Whamp…an arrow with an evil steel barb lodges in the tree above our heads. Drawing on whatever courage or resilience remains in our battered bodies, we bend low and run in rapid leaps, hops and spurts. Stepping on exposed rock and thick underbrush, even a trained eye would find it difficult to notice where a foot had trod. We move quickly and swiftly on tiptoes so not to give our position away. Breaking out of the forest we bushwhack to the bald face of the mountain and climb higher as the rocks rise in a mound against the base of the cliff. There is a great expanse of veined granite running across the top ridge forming a slippery slope. At last we reach a narrow ledge that slopes upward to the right behind a row of birch trees. I peer over the edge down to the rock-strewn ground far below. It was a sheer drop. Halfway up the eastern side of the slope, shielded behind three stunted and twisted pines, I stop to listen. Vic silently motions me to find a weapon and take cover. Forcing my breath to quiet I drop to the ground and crawl to a vantage point behind a clump of trees. Vic crouches behind a small boulder close to the path, and we hold our breath, silently praying, waiting for Maltby…and wait…nothing but silence. I huddle motionless, eventually I hear her footsteps, soft and stealthy muffled by the trees. I pick up a large rock and toss it back and forth between my hands, trying to get a feel for it. Torn between the need to listen and the desire to run, I remain crouched behind the trees, ears so open they fairly ache with the effort. Then we see her, Maltby, her hair and makeup done in an exact replica of Helen. She steps onto the granite, silhouetting herself against the gray sky, and she is naked, not wearing a stitch of clothing. What is with her and the 'naked' thing? There is crazy and then there is insane, Maltby falls into the latter.

Resisting the need to keep Maltby in sight I duck behind the trees. Just as Vic crouches, ready to spring, the sound of breaking twigs heralds the approach of a large animal crashing through the woods. From across the open expanse of rock, a bear lumbers out onto the ledge. Our bear, the bear with the glistening black coat marred only by a patch of white on its paw. The huge black bear was swaying back and forth, weight shifting from paw to paw, head moving in slow arcs. The great head turns in our direction. The nostrils flare and its huge paws twitch. Even from a distance we can see the claws, four-inch nails, dull white against the dark fur of the animal's belly.

Brown eyes look at us, and then lock eyes with Vic, he moans with fear. The urge to run makes my legs tremble, but I ignore it, hoping Vic doesn't do anything stupid. The worst thing one can do when confronted by a bear is to run. The bear shifts its attention away from us, growling, huffing and snorting, making sounds like an unhappy pig. For an instant it looks as if it would turn and go, but then swings its massive head in Maltby's direction and bellows. Maltby, so intent on tracking us, stumbles in shock and fright not expecting a charging bear.

I'd never believed an animal that large could move so fast. The sun dyed its coat a burnished bronze and the fur ripples, beautiful and shining. He is enormous and intent only on Maltby. He rises up on his hind legs looming over the top of her. We can hear the labored *whuff* of breath. A scream cuts through the air, before Maltby has a chance to cock her bow, the bear drops to all fours and reaches with its huge paw slapping the bow from her hand causing her to stumble and fall on her wrist. She tumbles to the ground, rolling up like a pill bug, her arms covering her ears, hands clasped over the back of her neck, knees pulled up to protect her more vulnerable parts. Tucked in the fetal position, she holds her wrist, the lower half of her arm bent at an awkward angle. She howls and rolls in agony, scooting on her backside to escape the bear, paying no heed to the slippery drop-off behind her.

The bear begins batting at Maltby, the way a cat would taunt a mouse before the kill. She shrieks and skidders closer to the edge like an upside down spider using her two legs and one good arm. A quick jab from the bear sends her over the edge. Her scream of outrage ends with a soft thud as she lands on the rocks below.

Vic looks at me, an expression of astonishment fixed on his face. I crawl to him on hands and knees, one hand, one knee, one hand, one knee flinging myself against the solid wall that is his body, weeping with relief.

"Shh…" Vic shushes me pointing to the bear disappearing back into the woods. "Holy shit, what was that?" "I think, you have just been saved by a bear. Maybe your *abuela* was wrong about bears because we just got our butts saved by one of the biggest, blackest ones I have ever seen. Personally, I will be eternally grateful to *uris americanus* for the rest of my life."

"Yeah," he swallows hard, his face taut with fear. "Maybe, just maybe, I'm going to rethink my position on bears. That was amazing!"

"And it just disappeared, like a ghost bear. It's so bizarre, I don't know what to think."

"We should go check on her." He pulls me to my feet.

"Do we have to?"

"We need to see the extent of her injuries. Whether she is in any kind of condition to be a threat to us."

Off the bald face side of the mountain, a small stand of trees tenaciously clings to the edge held by a tangle of exposed roots. Not sure what to expect we peer over the ledge through a screen of green leaves. Lying sprawled out on the rock tableau is Maltby. She fell on her back, limbs outstretched, spread eagle not moving, unconscious or is it a trick?

"Oh, my God, did we kill her?" I breathe into Vic's ear.

"I don't know, we can skirt the slope over there," he points to a ridge of terraced rocks, "climb down and check her out."

After ten minutes of scrambling over rocks and tree limbs we stand next to Maltby's inert body. Vic leans down and checks her pulse.

"Weak, but she's still alive."

I don't know whether to be relieved or horrified. As long as Maltby is alive, our lives are in danger.

"What do we do?"

"I don't know." He says, running a hand through his beard, shaking his head in doubt. "I'm afraid to leave her. If she regains consciousness, she's still a threat to us."

"What if we tie her up?"

"Yeah, but with what? We don't have any rope or duct tape."

"No," I say slowly, thinking. "But we do have grapevine and box elder." I point to the long vines growing profusely along the edge of the woods. "We could tie her up with them, and while not as effective as rope, it should work."

"Sure, why not."

"Okay, you gather the grapevine over there." I point to the eastern facing slope where woven tendrils of grapevine curl through the leaves and branches, effectively blocking the sun and eventually starving the trees beneath a carpet of vines. "I'll gather the box elder over there."

Using yards and yards of the thick tangled vine, we bound Maltby's hands and feet together being careful not to jostle her broken wrist. She moaned once or twice but gave no other resistance as we dragged her body into the shade.

"Not bad for our first kidnapping." Vic straightens and stands back to admire our handiwork.

"I agree. I don't think she's going anywhere. Without her following us we can post S.O.S. signals and try to alert rescuers to our whereabouts. We'll start with an S.O.S made out of rocks on the open ledge over there."

"I'm sure Ike has alerted the authorities. It's just a matter of time before they track us down."

"Hopefully soon, and we'll send someone back for her."

"Well, lets get a move on," he says. "I'd like to put some distance between us and her before sunset. I swear she's the devil possessed, I don't want any more trouble with her."

"Wait," I say, stooping to pick up the bow and arrows scattered around her. "We don't want to leave these behind in case she regains consciousness."

"Good idea. Here give me the arrows, I'll break them over my knee." He takes the arrows one-by-one and cracks them in half. "There, the bow without the arrows is worthless to her."

Now that the niceties have been observed and Maltby trussed up securely, we turn our attention to finding our way out of the woods.

After creating an S.O.S sign on the ledge, we worked our way down the mountain following a streambed. Finally, luck was with us and we found a partial print, a scuff, a wrinkle in the mud that told of a shod footfall.

"Look Vic, a track."

"Really, where?"

I squat down to the ground for a closer view. "Here," I trace the track with my finger. "You can see the outline of a boot, at least the heel." Sure enough, someone had followed the path of least resistance, traveling downhill on a flat rock studded skirt at an angle to the mountain. Keeping to the curve of the mountain, we follow the faint scuff of a mud print into a stunted forest of pine. At last this was a genuine direction toward civilization, a waffle cross-tread hiking boot print leading us home.

When it seems we have the strength to go no farther, Vic holds up a hand. "Wait." He stops and sniffs the air. "What's that smell?"

"What smell?"

"That smell. Sniff." He insists walking in a circle "Whatever is in the air, doesn't smell like the forest. That's the smell of civilization. Come stand next to me." He motions me closer with his hands, excited.

I stand next to him, sniffing the air and he looks at me with suspicion. "Wait a minute, maybe that odor is coming from you."

"Me?"

"Yeah, you with the worm breath."

"I don't have worm breath."

"Well, something smells."

"I beg your pardon, I find that accusation offensive."

"Did you or did you not eat worms?"

"Yes, but…"

"Look what happens after you eat garlic, people stink."

"I don't stink. Well, actually I do stink. It's been a long time since we've seen soap and water."

"No, that odor isn't coming from us. It's more of a rotten egg smell."

"You're right, I smell it too."

He moves, waving the air in front of him, trying to get a better read on the location. "That smell is people, that's not a natural smell."

"You're right." My nose is twitching like a rabbit on a hunt for clover. "It smells like rotten eggs. It must be coming from somewhere near by."

Vic glances toward the sky. A bank of heavy gray clouds have moved in, turning the sunny afternoon dark with the promise of an impending thunder-storm.

"You lead," I instruct him. "Your sense of smell is better than mine."

Vic points his nose in the air like a bloodhound on the scent of its next meal. After a half an hour of crawling our way through the undergrowth the smell of sulfur is distinctly stronger.

"What do you think is making that smell? It's disgusting." I ask as we stop to catch our breath.

"I haven't a clue. I hope it's some kind of logging camp or forest industry."

With the approach of an on-coming storm, the light in the forest has grown dim bringing an early dusk.

"Let's hurry. I don't want to spend another night out in the woods."

And here we make our first mistake, in our haste to out-run the storm and elude Maltby, we unwittingly step into a cauldron of danger. In front of us, the bear appears, standing in our path, its black bulk in silhouetted relief as a flash of lightning cuts through the inky gray light of the forest. We circle around the bear and follow a path into the compound. The bear bellows a warning and fades into the forest.

*The mountains reserve their choice gifts for those who stand
upon their summits.*
Sir Francis Younghusband

Crouched in the protective cover of the tree line we peer into
a small cluster of buildings, dim in the artificial glow of lights
powered by the low hum of a generator. The entire compound is
painted a dark brown, swirls of green and beige camouflage the
buildings making them barely discernable from the tree trunks.
The buildings melt into the canopy of the forest. Thin rising
wafts of steam come from three giant stainless steel cauldrons,
spouting coils of copper tubes that drain into huge pots. The
miasma of sulfur odor hangs heavy, a light fulminous vapor of
noxious fumes.

Off to the side of a U-shaped compound sits a shed housing
a narrow row of cages. I can't make out what is in the cages but
the dank ominous shadows hovering over the buildings give me
the shivers. What is this place? But before we have a chance to
contemplate the situation a clap of lightning crashes into the glen
illuminating the forest with a blast of light. I scream and clutch
Vic's arm in panic.

"Come on," he says pulling me to my feet. "Whatever is
down there can't be any worse than what Maltby has planned for
us."

Holding hands, pelted by raindrops and pea-sized balls of
hail, we make a run for the buildings. The sky opens up in a
deluge of thunder, lightning, slashing rain and hail.

We duck into the nearest doorway, our chests heave with

exertion, momentarily still we watch the storm play out.

"Vic, look." Shivering with cold, I point across the gravel yard to the cages. My mind refuses to register what my eyes are seeing, for locked behind wire mesh bars, is cage after cage of loons. There must be at least a dozen. The speckling of their black and white feathers glows in the illumination of the nearby lightning strikes.

"Those are loons in the cages." I hiss. "This can't be good."

"What? No way." Vic says, craning his neck to get a better look. "Holy crap, you're right."

"Capturing and penning loons is totally illegal. We have to get out of here."

"Maybe it's a conservation project, raising them up and releasing them into the wild."

"I doubt it, let's go before someone finds us."

"A little late for that, my friends." A bare overhead bulb clicks on, washing the shed in a flood of light. Before my eyes have a chance to focus in the harsh glare I'm looking down the barrel of a shotgun, not one but two. Slipping in behind us using a back entrance are two men. Both are round and portly, overweight bordering on obese, dressed in bib overalls. The material so pock marked with holes the pants border on obscene. The once white t-shirts are dingy grey with sweat and grime. Cut off sleeves complete the hillbilly ensemble.

"What the hell kind of naked hippie running off into the woods bullshit do we have here?" The taller of the two shakes his head with disgust.

"I'll be a sum' bitch. Peaches, the boss ain't going to like this one bit." His partner laughs, the laugh is high-pitched and crude. He has a lazy eye, but his good eye rakes over my body.

Vic gives a growl, pushing me behind his back. "Listen, we were drugged and kidnapped. This crazy lady took our clothes, dropped us in the middle of the wilderness and stalked with the intent to kill us. We've been wandering for days. No food, no water and obviously, no clothing."

"Now, if that isn't the most cockamamie story I have ever heard." The one called Peaches scoffs. "Rooster, do these people think I was born yesterday? I ain't stupid, ya know."

"Please, sir." I duck beneath Vic's arm. My husband is telling the truth. We haven't eaten in days. This Maltby is a distant relative of mine. She is ex-military and insane. She wants to kill us. If you could just give us a ride to the nearest town, we can pay you. Anything you want."

"I want you not standing on my property. Sticking your nose into what ain't your business, little lady." Peaches raises the barrel of the shotgun higher, lining his eye up with the sights, aiming to shoot. 'Rooster," he directs the other man. "Go get some rope; we need to tie these fine folks up and let the boss decide what we're gonna do with them."

"No please, don't. Really, we're not interested in what's going on here. I didn't even see the loons."

"Ellen!" Vic groans. "Quiet!" He wraps his arm around my chest, squeezing me to silence. "Listen, seriously, we're tired, cold and desperately in need of food, water and clothing, anything!"

"What does it look like I'm running some kind of charity give-away program here?" Peaches honks off a glob of spit into the dirt at his feet.

"Maybe we can keep them for awhile." Rooster whines. "Help us do some of the work around here. I'm sick of busting my ass. And she is kind of pretty, stuck up here in these woods, it's been awhile if you know what I mean."

Peaches shakes his head and gives the man a withering look, as if dealing with an over exuberant child. "Now don't you go and get any ideas. We ain't touching these people. Not our place. Remember Boss told us if we come up here north and do a good job, he'd make sure we'd be set for life. He gonna buy us a little plot of land and a still back home. We can while away the years, sitting in the sun, drinking and selling our own brew." His southern accent so thick it garbles the words. I could only make out something about a still, home and brew....

"Ahhh, come on." Rooster cajoles. "I'm sick and tired of working my fingers to the bone. We needs help."

"Our kidnapper is following, you don't want her here." I plead. She's an ex-Coast guard military expert. She'll be packing guns, explosives and she is ruthless. She will tear this place apart looking for us. Why don't you load us on your truck and, take us anywhere…dump us off down the road. We can make it on our own."

Then down to my last trick I burst into tears…any woman worth her weight in estrogen knows her best offensive tool is weeping. Men crumble under a well-orchestrated deluge of tears, throw in a hiccupping sob or two and they're putty in our hands. The ruse is not to be overused and only brought out as a last resort. This qualifies as a desperate measure.

"Oh, quit your crying." Peaches snorts. "Like I never seen a woman blubber before." He nods his head to Rooster. "We'll lock them in the wood shed." He yanks me roughly by the arm.

"Aww…Peaches, come on." Rooster complains. "Work, work, work, that's all I ever do."

"I said no and I mean no. Get a move on and quit your bellyaching."

~~~

Daylight narrows to a thin slit between the boards as the rasp of the dead bolt slides into place. In an attempt born in desperation, I beseech them through the closed door, "*Please,* could you give us some food or water?"

My plea falls on deaf ears and I hear Peaches chide Rooster, "The boss will be here any minute. We need to let him decide what's best to do with the two of them. Remember, we got a lot riding on this project, don't ruin it. If'en we was back home we'd just take a little ride out to the bayou and dump them for gator bait. They do things fancy up here."

I listen to their footsteps fade into the distance, only the hiss and hum of the distillery vats fills the silence left behind. "Vic, how did we end up in the hands of people more vicious then Maltby?"

"I don't know, talk about bad karma." Vic sits on the hard packed ground and winces visibly. "We didn't listen to the bear."

"The bear," I muse. "You're right, the bear tried to block our path. What are we going to do?"

"I don't know. Search around and see if there is any way to escape or something we can use as a weapon."

"Quiet, they're coming back," I hiss.

The door swings wide and Peaches stands guard with the gun while Rooster shoves a plate with sandwiches and two battered soda bottles filled with water.

"Here," Peaches points with the rifle at the food. "Eat. The boss can't come til morning, he says to feed you and keep you alive. No funny business."

Rooster throws a filthy blanket on the ground and backs away. The door is shut and locked to the sound of rattling chains. I take a dubious look at the soiled rag…maybe being naked wasn't so bad.

"Vic, it's food." I scramble on my hands and knees to the plate and pick up a sandwich.

"Elle, slow." Vic's hand clamps down on my wrist. "Remember take small bites, if you eat too quickly, you'll get sick."

"I know." My chest is heaving with the effort of self-control. I set the peanut butter sandwich down on the plate. "I know." I repeat and hand Vic a sandwich.

We take our time eating in small nibbling bites, the hunger cramps abated slightly. The water in the bottles looks grey and only slightly more sanitary than the rivers and streams, but we guzzled it down, desperate to quench our thirst.

Crawling on hands and knees we search the shed, our eyes rendered ineffective in the dim light that filters through the cracks in the wood siding. We find nothing. Any potential escape route is locked and sealed.

Bimble…(verb) walk or travel at a leisurely pace.

The rainstorm of the previous evening passed over the mountains into another valley. We woke up this morning, bodies stiff and battered to the *ping, ping, ping* of left-over raindrops sliding off the corrugated roof onto the ground below.

"Shh…" Vic says, sitting up, wagging a finger at me in warning.

I push off the dirty blanket and hear the southern twang of Peaches and Rooster. But there are other voices, new and distinct voices, one of the men has an accent but refined and cultured in comparison. I crouch down on my knees and peer though a crack in the wall. The sight before my eyes sets me reeling back on my heels in disbelief. *Oh, mother of saints and all that is good and holy…*I know the boss…and his assistant! This is not good. Damn Twinkie!

"Vic, oh my God, oh my God. I know who the boss is and what they are doing here. Ouch!" I bang my head on the cross beam supporting the wall in my eagerness to see out the hole. "Damn it, this is all Twinkie's fault. I'm sure she's involved."

"What are you talking about?" Vic asks, his voice rank with exasperation. "What in the world would Twinkie have to do with moonshiners?"

"For starters, she's Southern. Duh!"

"Just because you're Southern does not make you a hooch runner."

"Hooch runner? What? Oh for heaven's sake, listen to us."

"Quiet, they're coming this way."

"Hide!"

"Seriously, where?"

The sound of voices and approaching footsteps galvanizes me to talk faster. "I don't want them to recognize me, that will only make matters worse."

"Recognize you? Mia-bella." Vic runs a soothing hand up and down my back. "I think you need some food and rest, *quierda*. You are hallucinating. What are you talking about?"

"What I'm talking about," I hiss, annoyed he is treating me like a hysterical child. "Vic," I implore him, whispering furiously, the footsteps are right outside the shed. "When I went to Lake Placid with Twinkie, we stopped at a shop to meet her friends, Jonas and Arthur. They make this health elixir that promises to cure all kinds of ailments from arthritis to cancer. They have such a following Oprah is interested in promoting it on her Favorite Things Christmas show. That translates into millions of dollars for these guys. When Oprah promotes it, women buy it. They are sitting on a gold mine and they know it. We unwittingly stumbled into their production plant and can ruin the entire operation. From the stills to the caged loons, this is illegal and ready to blow up in their faces."

"Oh Elle, holy hell!" Vic exclaims. "What did you get us into this time!"

"Me!" I yelp, only to have my retort broken off by the rattle of the chains holding the door secure.

"Here take this duct tape. Get in there, blind fold them and bring them out." I recognize the honeyed soft-spoken voice of Jonas; apparently sweet affable Jonas is the boss. "Hurry up," he says, "I want to look them over. I have an idea of how we can dispose of them and make some cash in the deal."

"Who gives a shit? I want to know how the hell they got into our compound? The perimeter was booby trapped with a trip wire." Arthur complains, his voice harsh and clipped, the roots of his accent begun on the Jersey shore.

"I don't know, boss. Rooster, here, went and checked the traps just the other day. Didn't you Rooster? You were making sure the traps were set to hit the primer on the shotgun shells. We ringed the entire compound with them."

Rooster doesn't say a word.

"Morons," Arthur spits out in disgust. "Just tie them. We have too much riding on this operation to have a couple of potheads wander into our camp and ruin it."

Daylight floods the shed as Peaches and Rooster saunter through the door, their rifles raised in readiness. "Rooster," Peaches barks. "Take this here duct tape and bind their hands together then tape their eyes closed."

As Rooster approaches me, Vic growls, "Touch her and I swear I'll kill you." In one swift motion Rooster's skinny arm strikes like a snake and recoils, hauling me against his chest, a helpless prey caught in the snare of a predator. "I don't think you are in any position to be giving orders around here, pretty boy." Rooster says with a snide shrug, caressing my throat with a knife blade.

Vic's eyes glitter with rage; the golden flecks ignite, burning with suppressed fury. "Take your hands off her." He growls between clenched teeth.

"Make a move and I'll draw blood." Rooster threatens. He reeks of sweat, alcohol and peanut butter. I swear I'll never eat peanut butter again.

"Cut it out, Rooster." Peaches barks at his partner. "The boss is here and we gots work to do. Stop messing around with the woman."

"What is going on in there?" Arthur yells. "Get the hell out here!"

"Rooster!"

"All right, don't go and get your feathers ruffled. I'm just having me a little fun. We've been stuck up here all summer, doing nothing but making this fancy mushroom hooch." Rooster complains puffing out his chest, pantomiming his namesake. He takes the piece of duct tape Peaches hands him and covers my eyes. "When we get done with this white lightning, I'm fixing to have me a sorry-ass good time." He mutters under his breath as he tapes my wrists together. The sound of ripping tape is followed by a grunt of pain from Vic as Rooster repeats the process.

"Y'all, bring them out here in the light of day, where's we can get a good look at them." Jonas calls out.

Rooster jerks us by our arms. My swollen, bruised feet protest the walk across the sharp jagged gravel of the driveway. It must be late morning because the sun feels warm on my skin. With my body covered in dirt and hair hanging in snarled hanks covering my face, there is a chance Jonas and Arthur won't recognize me. I doubt my friendship with Twinkie would garner any sympathy and I can't help but wonder if she's involved.

"Well, they're older than I thought." Arthur says as he walks a circle around us, stopping to poke or prod an arm or a leg. "That's going to bring the price down."

"I don't know. That's a fine looking man under all the dirt." Jonas says, his southern twang accentuated by his lecherous thoughts. "He is a pretty one, almost looks familiar, like I've seen him somewhere."

Apparently, dirt, lack of food and proper hygiene make a great disguise. Obviously, they've seen Vic's movies but can't place him. Would the promise of a ransom grant us freedom?

"I don't think he swings our way, sweetheart. He seems to like the ladies." Arthur says. I hear the loud crack of a hand slapping skin.

"Get your filthy damn hands off me!" Vic erupts with a roar. "You have no right to hold us prisoners. What the hell is wrong with you?"

I hear the *woof* of a gut punch and Vic crumbles to the ground with a moan.

"Enough Rooster. We want to keep them healthy, I want a good price." Arthur instructs. "I talked to my cousin and a boat leaves out of Tampa on Friday. I want them fed, cleaned up and ready to leave by morning. On my first foray into human trafficking I don't want to arrive late with damaged goods." He gives a snort, "This is a win-win. We get rid of some meddlesome snoopers and make a little cash on the side."

"Take the tape off her eyes." Jonas commands Rooster. I wince as a layer of dirt and skin are ripped off with the tape. "I knew it!" He exclaims. "This is the lady Twinkie brought to the shop. Oh, honey child, how did you get involved in this mess?" He croons, running a finger down my cheek. "Such a shame."

"Why did you take off her blindfold?" Arthur fumes, taking my chin in his hand turning my head back and forth. "Guess it doesn't matter. Regardless, they're going. And if I remember correctly, she cleans up real nice."

"Twinkie? Is she involved in this, this…." I try waving my arm to encompass the entire compound. "What are you doing with the loons? How could you cage loons? Loons are sacred in the Adirondacks. This is horrible. What are you putting in that vile brew?" I stomp my foot in righteous indignation. "Oprah would never endorse such a product!" I rant.

"Twinkie?" Arthur shrugs. "What about her?"

"Is she part of this operation?"

"None of your business and why would we involve her?" Jonas says.

"Well, I thought she said she was your cousin and you're southern, and…and people from the south make moonshine." I fumble trying to string together a logical explanation.

"Good Lord, honey child," Jonas scoffs. "Twinkie's got enough secrets in her attic, she don't need any of ours."

What did he mean by that? Just a figure of speech? She is a bit of a fruitcake. But secrets, like what? My mind is a whirl of ideas, none of them good, moonshining, kidnapping, human trafficking, illegal sale of goods and holding loons against their will...

And then I see them, drifting, like slow moving sand in a desert storm filling the cracks and crevices of light until a solid wall of drab brown forms a line around the compound. Helmets and Kevlar vests give an alien appearance, stealth bodies not of this earth. M4 rifles held in readiness, I'd recognize them anywhere. I've seen them in my dreams, not in trepidation or fear, but relief. Because I realize a miracle is about to happen. My personal guardian angels, the S.W.A.T. team has arrived.

I feel Rooster's body go rigid, the grip on my arm threatens to cut off circulation and a strangled cry escapes his lips, a cross between a moan and a sob. "Oh, holy frickin', flippin', dadgummit, shoot!" He curses.

"What the hell is wrong with you?" The line of Arthur's mouth tightens.

"Ahhhh…" Rooster points, his face white, eyeballs bulging. In the fine hair of a split second…a click, the sound of twenty rounds of ammunition transferred from the chamber to the magazine whispers across the compound.

"What the f…?" Jonas spins on his heel, he takes one look, snatches me away from Rooster to form a shield in front of his body. A pistol appears in his hand and the cold metal of a gun barrel pushes against my temple. "Make a move and I blow her head off."

"Drop the gun and let go of the woman. This is a warning. Do as you are told and no one will get hurt." A voice laced with authority commands.

"She'll be dead before you have a chance to pull the trigger." Jonas taunts. He backs away pulling me toward a parked truck, until he trips and stumbles backward. I lurch out of his grasp, fall to the ground and roll behind one of the stills. A soft *ping* wizzes by and a hole appears in the middle of Jonas' pant leg, oozing blood. He grabs his leg and howls in pain.

Arthur screams, "Jonas!"

A deep sonorous voice calls out, "Freeze, no body move."

Peaches and Rooster squeak and drop their rifles. Arthur cries out, "Don't shoot! I'm unarmed." He raises his hands above his head.

"Everyone, hands above your head. Move slowly and carefully." The leader of the team moves forward, the word police printed in bold letters on the uniform along with his name, Corbain.

Oh, it can't be…what are the chances? Robert Corbain, the FBI agent who blazed into our house last summer on the heels of the S.W.A.T. team. He exchanges Christmas cards with me. Nothing says Christmas like an FBI agent leaning on an open gun cabinet next to a tree decorated in army camouflage. It's his idea of a joke, sends them to all the civilians he's had law enforcement encounters with during the year. I guess to make us feel safe…?

"Agent Corbain?" I ask, astonished.

"What the hell is going on?" Vic shouts. "Someone get this blindfold off me."

"Vic, it's FBI Agent Corbain and the S.W.A.T. team."

"No way."

"Yes, way, Mr. Reinz, it appears I've come to your rescue again. It pains me to ask, but how in the hell did the two of you end up in the middle of a moonshining scam?" His voice, honey thick with sarcasm. "I see that you at least dressed for the occasion."

Last summer, innocently, Vic and I were involved in a diamond robbery. Robert Corbain was the agent assigned to the case. He is a taciturn, no nonsense individual who's lot in life appears to be…rescuing me.

I feel faint, a tingly feeling comes from my legs upward, and little black dots appear before my eyes, just as I'm about to collapse, my B.S.F.F. (Best S.W.A.T. friend forever) Sergeant O'Neal appears at my side. "Ellen, easy, I got you." He reassures me as my legs turn to jelly and give way beneath me; only his steadying hand clutching my waist prevents me from dissolving into a blubbering heap on the ground. He scoops me into his arms and calls for a medic.

"Raffer, hurry up, over here. I need EMS backup."

"No, not me, take care of Vic." I protest.

"Elle, I'm fine." Vic says, his voice hoarse and cracked. He struggles to his feet, his body sways for a moment as he tries to regain his balance still blind under the duct tape.

"Sir, I insist you sit down, let us examine you and your wife so we can assess the extent of your injuries." One of the medics commands ripping the duct tape off of Vic's face.

"Trust me, the two of them are fine." Agent Corbain walks over to where we are under the care of the medics. "These two are like cats, blessed with nine lives."

"We need food, water and rest. That's all." Vic says. "And clothes, I'm so tired of being cold."

"Blankets over here." O'Neal barks to the tactical emergency medical team. "Miss Ellen," he admonishes. "What have you got yourself into this time?" He asks, a twinkle lights up his hazel eyes. "If it wasn't for you and your husband we might be out of a job. Just when things get quiet, you come and throw the mountains into a fever pitch of excitement." He lowers me gently onto a blanket laid out on the ground, covering my body.

"Mr. and Mrs. Rienz, I have to ask," Agent Corbain says. "Could I have overestimated your innocence? How do you show up at two crime scenes and still claim to be blameless?"

"Bad karma?" Vic says with a shrug.

"My crazy step-cousin, Maltby kidnapped us and we've been lost in the woods for days. It's only by accident that we stumbled into the moonshiners camp. We have nothing to do with them, trust me." I protest.

"Oh, this just gets better and better." He shakes his head in disgust. "I can't wait to hear your story."

Off to the side, Rooster, Peaches and Arthur are handcuffed and lead away. Arthur begs to be allowed to ride in the ambulance with Jonas.

As the drama recedes, the sun climbs higher in the sky breaking out of the canopy of trees. A hermit thrush's flute-like song filters through the forest and one of the caged loons gives a haunting call. I heave a great sigh and relax into O'Neal's arms, pulling the wool blanket closer. Against my bruised and naked skin the scratchy wool feels soft as silk.

"Ellen, are you in pain?" Sergeant O'Neal asks, running his hands gently over my body on the outside of the blanket.

"No, everything hurts but no major injuries. I'm just tired and hungry. Please, could we have some water?"

"Water!" O'Neal commands and catches a bottle in midair. "You remember the drill?" He asks, holding up the water bottle.

"Yes," I nod. "Slow and small sips."

"Good girl." He smiles. "You're getting to be a pro at this rescue business."

I give him a withering look. I've always had awkward moments growing up. Unfortunately, the older I get…the awkward Klutz-Ellen moments are turning into life-threatening catastrophes.

Vic crouches down next to me, wrapped in a matching charcoal grey blanket. "Mia, *querida?*"

O'Neal helps me into a sitting position, keeping a tight grip on the water bottle to prevent me from guzzling it down.

"Vic, I can't believe it, we're rescued. Those men were going to sell us, like slaves into the human trafficking market! Or kill us!" My voice rises as the full extent of our predicament crashes down upon me. I burst into tears, wet messy sobs, streaking my face with rivulets of dirt. O'Neal and Vic tense at the outburst, their eyes widen, O'Neal looks like he needs a Rolaid.

"Can we please go home?" Emotionally and physically exhausted, I whisper. "I just want to go home to my house, take a long hot bath. Eggs, I want eggs and toast, a cup of tea and something sweet, like one of those scones from the bakery in North Creek. You know the ones, with the apricots and cranberries." I'm babbling now, past coherent though, past caring.

Even though I'm sandwiched between the warmth of Vic and O'Neal's body, I'm shivering with nerves and cold. "Elle, Buttercup…" Vic kisses the top of my head. "Soon, soon, we'll be home. Cyrus and Porky will be ecstatic, Porky will eat everything in sight and Cyrus will spend half the day chasing his tail."

I sob then hiccup on a giggle in spite of myself, grateful to him for trying to make me smile.

"First, we have to take you to the hospital for evaluation." Sergeant O'Neal explains. "You're probably suffering from exposure and dehydration which requires medical care."

I sniffle and wipe a hand across my face. "How did you find us?"

"We didn't, this was a S.W.A.T. call for an illegal moonshine operation. Because moonshiners are known to booby trap their stills it was decided to call out the S.W.A.T team to project law enforcement."

"You were just an added bonus." Agent Corbain adds drily.

"So, no one was looking for us?" I ask.

"I wouldn't say that. Half the damn county is out looking for the two of you." He replies. Before I have a chance to answer, my response is cut off by the braying of a dog, loud and insistent. The howling reminds me of a hound on the scent of a fox. Yet carried over the howling, I hear someone calling my name.

"Mrs. Rienz, Mr. Vic. Where are you? Darrell said there was a radio call that said they found you. Weasel, honey, tell those policemen in that fancy gear, it's imperative we get to them.

Those poor city people lost in the woods for days. God only knows what kind of condition they are in. Darrel, where the hell are you, boy! Get over here now!"

It's Adele, my larger than life guardian angel, come to save me. I look to Sergeant O'Neal, he snaps his jaw shut and blows out a long sigh. "It's the search and rescue team."

"Adele Watson?" I say.

He nods, "It's been all over the news, everyone has been searching for you." He says, a chagrin look on his face. "And we were the lucky ones to find you. Boy, is this going to be a mountain of paperwork to untangle. This Adele and her friend have single handedly organized a massive search for the two of you."

I frown, who in the world is Adele's friend? Then I hear, "Ellen, girl. Where are you? We been traipsing across these here mountains for days. I swear by the Lord, God Almighty, if she ain't here I am surely going to pass out from exhaustion. Why won't these soldiers let us through? Come on, boys, I'm Ellen's dearest friend in the entire world."

"Twinkie?" My eyebrows shoot up in surprise. "Adele and Twinkie, together?" I'm incredulous and horrified at the thought.

Sergeant O'Neal nods, "They've been on the news putting out the word. All I know is, they are going to be pissed we found you before they did."

Vic groans. "Oh, please no, not the two of them together. How much can a man endure? How can the ducks line up with dropping shoes?"

My sweet husband is known for mixing metaphors. "Vic, it's *get your ducks in a row* and *wait for the other shoe to drop*." I correct him.

"Whatever." He waves me off impatiently. "Adele and Twinkie are coming."

The yelling and barking reaches a crescendo. A marching band during a Fourth of July parade makes less noise than Adele and Twinkie. The S.W.A.T. team members try to form a blockade around us to protect our privacy. It won't work, some things you just can't stop.

"Oh, goody." Corbain chimes in. "The reinforcements have

arrived. Every nut-case and weirdo in the mountains comes out of the woodwork when the two of you are in town."

"Who you calling a nutcase and a weirdo, buster?" Adele calls out. "I can hear you. Weasel, honey, we got us some attitude to deal with here."

"Ma'am, I'm sorry but you have to stand back. Only authorized personal beyond this point." A S.W.A.T. team member instructs.

"Who you calling *unauathorized*, sonny boy?"

I like being near the top of a mountain. One can't get lost there.
Wislawa Szymkprska

I reach for the water bottle in Sergeant O'Neal's hand and take a sip. Wiping my mouth with the hem of the blanket, I say in a calm voice, "You know, trying to keep them away is useless. They are a force of nature. Like a category 4 hurricane barreling down the coast, an F-5 tornado destroying everything in its path, a blizzard with whiteout visibility. There is no avoiding the storm, once in the eye of a hurricane, you dig in your heels and ride it out."

"She's right. Adele is pitching a fit." Vic says. "We can only hope Weasel didn't bring his shotgun. If it ends up in Adele's hands, this could get ugly."

Sergeant O'Neal sighs, "The decision is up to you. Are you well enough to cope with that tidal wave of personalities? The State Forest Rangers have been working with them, trying to direct their efforts in a positive way. I heard that search and rescue dog of yours wouldn't leave the scent. They put him to ground near a mountain lake and he must have followed your trail here."

Vic and I exchange glances. I mouth to him, "What search and rescue dog?"

He shrugs his shoulders. "Cyrus?" He whispers back.

"No way." I dismiss the idea as preposterous.

He raises an eyebrow in question. "Who else?"

"Here they come," warns O'Neal. We watch the Para-military team part like the Red Sea in biblical times. Instead of avenging Egyptians in chariots this tide is lead by the New York State Forest Rangers flanked by Adele, Weasel, and Twinkie. In front of the pack, braying like an old hound dog is Porky Pellinger, straining at the leash held by a police officer who looks a lot like Adele's nephew, Derek, but different. We find out later that Darrel is Derek's older brother, both nephews of Adele and Weasel. At the back of the SAR team is our son Josh, dressed in a neon green hi-vis jacket with the words Search and Rescue printed across the front. My heart catches in my chest every time I see him. His likeness to Vic is uncanny. We make eye contact and the tension lines of worry relax on his furrowed brow. He waves, giving us the thumbs-up, choosing to stay in the background, avoiding a confrontation with Adele and Twinkie. I blow him a kiss resisting the urge to run and throw my arms around him. But in my present state of undress, and the fact I stink to high heaven, some things are best left for later.

"Oh my stars," Adele exclaims. "Would you look at the two of you? You look like a couple of those aborigine tribe people. What in the name of heaven and earth happened to you? You look like something the cat dragged in then decided to spit out because it was vermin."

I close my eyes and repeat what I've come to call the 'Adele mantra'. "She means well, she means well." She has a unique way of expressing it.

Weasel nods at us and a satisfied look settles on his face. "Mr. Rienz, Mrs. Rienz." He says tipping his Harley Davidson baseball cap in our direction. "It's good to see you again." As if we were out for a Sunday afternoon stroll and stopped on the sidewalk to exchange pleasantries.

Twinkie pops her head up under the arms of a hulking S.W.A.T. officer; she chimes in, her voice breathless with emotion. "Thank the Good Lord we found you, Ellen. I was beginning to think you were a goner leaving that gorgeous husband of yours a widow. I knew he would make it through the wilderness unscathed, being such a brave hunk of manhood." She almost swoons, waggling her eyebrows at Vic in a suggestive come hither manner. The message gets lost in translation due to the smudged mascara under her eyes; she looks like a raccoon after a hard night of raiding the campground. "But you, poor sweet sugar," she turns her attention to me. "I didn't give you much hope at all. You being so frail and all."

"*Frail?*" I squeal in outrage. I've been called many things but never frail.

"I plumb wore out my Danner hiking boots. I didn't give you a prayers chance in hell. Look at my pink laces, I'm going to have to buy new ones!" She thrusts her foot out as evidence. Her once perfect boots are now scuffed and caked with mud. The bright pink laces tattered and snarled with burrs. In fact, the entire polished and coiffed Barbie doll façade of Twinkie Wannamaker is shockingly disheveled. Her yoga pants cut and snagged from running through thorny underbrush and covered in patches of mud. The long-sleeve plaid shirt with the L.L. Bean logo is so wrinkled she must have wadded it up in a wet ball and forgot to shake it out. Platinum blonde hair has slipped the confines of her ponytail, hanging in limp tendrils around her face. She shoves a lank piece of hair behind her ear then points a finger at us, demanding an explanation. "What happened to the two of you?" The tone of her voice implied we created this situation for no other reason than to aggravate and vex her. "I called your land line for days but you refused to answer. God knows cell phones don't work up here."

"I told you to call her back or she was going to end up on our doorstep." Vic hisses at me in admonishment.

"Shhh, good thing she sounded the alarm." I hush him, trying to figure out how we all ended up in the moonshiner's camp.

"So when you ignored me for four days," Twinkie drones on, "I decided to march right over and give you a piece of my mind, for not being neighborly and all. And what do I find but no one home and the dogs were acting all crazy. Being suspicious-like, I called Adele."

"You two know each other?" I'm astonished but not shocked. What's the saying, like-attracts-like.

"Of course." Adele blurts out. "I've been living and working in these mountains my entire life. Hell, I used to babysit her little brother." Adele gives a dismissive snort, "Her daddy and my daddy built the hotel on Long Lake, excepting her Daddy swindled my daddy out of his fair share of the money."

"Now that there is all water under the bridge." Twinkie says.

"Too bad that water did suck him under the bridge." Adele grumbles.

"Yes, ma'am," Twinkie chimes in. "Adele and me, we go way back. And we're all on the SAR team, that's search and rescue to you civilian folks."

I hear Vic mutter, "Well, I'll be, wonders never cease to amaze me."

"So, wait," I say. "I'm confused. The S.W.A.T. team is here to confiscate the still from Arthur and Jonas and ironically we stumbled into their path. The Search and Rescue team followed our trail down the mountains and walked right into the moonshiners camp?"

"Yes, that's about right. See, this here is my dog, Dixie. Once she gets on a scent you can't shake her." Weasel points to a large russet colored bloodhound with sad droopy ears, plopped down by his feet. "But Porky locked on your scent and put poor Dixie to shame, I never seen anything like it. He saved the day."

Even in my befuddled state, I noticed all of them wearing the same neon green SARs jackets as Josh. Twinkie had hers tied around her neck in that careless drape, so popular among the wealthy set with their popped collar polo shirts and matching sweaters. Adele's jacket is tied at her waist to cover her ample derriere. Weasel wore his leather Harley Davidson vest over the top of his jacket. Apparently, they are members of the SAR's team. I look at Josh, he smiles and shrugs, "Yes, they are some of our best." He steps forward to embrace Vic and I, holding tight for a long moment. "Everyone was worried sick when you disappeared. Thank God, we found you." He cocks his head to the side and chuckles, "Even if you do smell."

I swat his arm. "Disrespectful child."

Agent Corbain interrupts, "Ladies and gentlemen," he stands with hands on hips challenging anyone to defy his authority. "The ambulance has arrived and we need to get these people to the hospital and treated for exposure. You can spend time with them later, but first they need medical evaluation."

"Wait." I hold up a hand. "Someone has to go get Maltby. We left her tied up on a mountain clearing about four miles back."

"Maltby? What's a Maltby?" Adele asks.

"My cousin…err… step cousin, the woman who kidnapped us."

"That crazy lady shooting at everybody up in the woods?" Adele asks. "How in the world did the two of you get hooked up with that nut?"

Twinkie interjects, "She has the other half of the S.W.A.T. team holed up in the hills until they can flush her out."

"How can she shoot anyone? We left her tied up. She was unconscious with a broken wrist. She escaped?"

"Well, Buttercup, I'm not sure grapevine and box elder are the best materials for handcuffs."

"You tied her up?" Corbain asks.

"Yes, after the bear…"

"Bear?"

"Well, she fell down the rock wall and knocked herself out, so we decided to tie her up…"

"Never mind. We'll get your statement later."

"So between this Malbe, Mulberry *and* the mushroom moonshine makers, the police have had their hands full rounding everyone up." Weasel says. "I've never seen so much law enforcement."

"I told you every nutcase and lunatic comes out of the woodwork when the two of you come to the mountains." Agent Corbain retorts.

Adele snorts. "Who are you calling a nutcase?"

"Certainly not you, madam." Corbain smiles benignly at Adele.

"Things are generally pretty quiet up here…or were until you and Mrs. Rienz moved in." Weasel agrees, hands shoved in his pockets as he leans back on his heels. "You sure do know how to shake things up."

"What do you mean, mushroom moonshine?" Twinkie asks, suspicion creeping into her voice. "You aren't talking about Jonas and Arthur."

I point to the paramedics loading Jonas into an ambulance. It took four men to load his body onto a medical gurney. He is moaning and groaning, crying like a baby, clutching his leg, screaming, "I need pain meds, now, something strong! Help me!" He pleads.

"Jonas," she whispers. "Oh, my God, what happened?"

I bite my lower lip. "I'm sorry, Twinkie, Jonas and Arthur are not very nice men. The mushroom elixir was nothing more than moonshine hooch. They were a fraud, deluding innocent people and they were going to sell Vic and I into the human trafficking market."

"Seriously?" Twinkie recovers her composure quickly. "I don't believe you." She scoffs. "Where is Arthur? I'm going to get to the bottom of this." With a huff she storms off after the gurney.

"Hey, Amigo," calls out a gruff gravely voice. "You and Chica, owe me big, this one is for the record book."

Ike limps up dressed in jeans, hiking boots and a fleece jacket. He looks exhausted.

He hobbles over to us, drops the hiking pole he's leaning on and wraps Vic and I in a heartfelt bear hug. "If the two of you don't start living normal, uneventful lives, you are seriously going to kill me. I'm not getting any younger and this took ten years off my life." He leans in and hisses in our ears. "I've been hiking my ass off all over these mountains for the past four days only to find you naked, half dead and starving. What the hell!" His voice gains pitch and volume fueled by anger and fear. "After all the security systems we've installed, I find you in a moonshiners camp after escaping that lunatic survivalist. How in the fricking hell did you cross paths with her? She's up that mountain shooting anything and everything that moves with rounds from a M4!" He swears, taking the Lord's name in vain. "I need a new job, I'm getting too old for this shit." He wraps his arms around us, tears in his eyes. "Thank God, you're alive."

Josh comes over and takes Vic by the arm, nodding toward the road. "The ambulance is here to take you to the hospital." He says. "Can you walk or should we get a stretcher?"

"We'll walk. Right Elle?"

"Yes." I nod. "I can walk."

Josh points to Ike's ankle. "I'm suggesting the EMT's take Ike along with you. He's been walking on that sprained ankle for two days, refusing treatment. It's time to have a doctor look at it."

Ike frowns and grunts.

I'm escorted to the ambulance by two of the hottest men I know and my S.W.A.T. buddy, Sergeant O'Neal. Every day has a silver lining…

"Oh, and just so you know," Josh adds. "Trey and Tara along with Lani, Jason, Hanna and Bridget will be waiting at the hospital for you."

The entire enchilada so to speak…

Of course, our children would be waiting for us. But *Bridget?* Bridget is Vic's housekeeper on his California ranch. She is an Irish banshee rolled in to a protective mama bear when it comes to Vic. She is a whirlwind of energy and righteous determination. My stomach clutches in terror, Bridget *and* Adele in the same room? Oil and water, black and white, pickles and ice cream, certain things don't mix. Maybe being lost in the woods wasn't so bad…*gosh and begorarah meets hell on wheels…*

It's a heavy burden to look up at the mountain and want to start the climb.
Abby Wambach

The admitting doctor took one look at our family and friends and declared a moratorium on visitors until further notice. Lani broke through the ranks, jogging along side my gurney as we were wheeled in, ignoring the warnings. Dazed and disoriented from the bright lights and bustle of the hospital, I managed to assure her we were suffering from just a *little* post lost-in-the-wood trauma. She failed to see the humor in that.

It was late evening before we were admitted and settled into our room. Vic's assistant, Juls handles all of his personal affairs from the West Coast. Arrangements for a private hospital suite and permission for our beds to be pushed together was arranged. All publicity and legal issues were dealt with lightning speed and efficiency. Juls is the modern day equivalent of a magic genie in a bottle, make a wish, as long as you don't ask for a pink elephant, she makes it happen. Operating with a competent no nonsense attitude and a dry sense of humor, she keeps Vic's ego in line, and humble. Although paid handsomely for her service, she deserves every penny and is like a member of our extended family.

~~~

The initial physical examination revealed we're suffering from the effects of exposure and malnutrition. The doctor ordered rest, a bland diet and IVs for hydration. A nurse leads us to our room, hands us a stack of large fluffy white towels that smell of bleach and detergent, and small bag of toiletries. Holding her nose, she points, shower first and then, and only then will she start the IVs for hydration. Cleanliness is paramount to avoiding infection. I know we smell bad but…*jeez*.

It doesn't seem possible to weep over mini bottles of shampoo and tiny bars of soap, but I did, they smelled heavenly. Against hospital protocol we locked the bathroom door and helped each other out of the hospital gowns. I reach up and untie Vic's hideous gown, letting it slip from his shoulders onto the floor. His fingers deftly undo the hard little knots of ribbon that hold my gown on, soon a small pile litters the floor, fabric stained brownish grey where it touched our filthy bodies.

I recoil at my reflection in the mirror, hair snarled and matted, face streaked with dirt and I smell really bad. "Oh my gosh, is that me?" I point giggling. "Aren't we a pair?"

"Wow, we'd pass for a couple of cave dwellers in a museum display." He leans into the mirror for a closer look. "Amazing what a few days without basic hygiene will do for you. Whew, not good."

"I can't decide if I want to shower first or brush my teeth. I feel disgusting."

"Brush your teeth in the shower." He reaches into the shower, turns on the faucet and adjusts the water temperature. "Just right." Pushing the curtain aside he steps in and lifts his face groaning in pleasure as the warm spray washes away the initial layer of grime. "I never thought water could feel so good." The tile floor of the shower turns sludgy brown as the dirt sluices off his perfectly sculpted body. He holds out a hand, "Mia, come join me." Not needing a second invitation, I grab the bag of assorted hygiene products and join him. I gasp as the hot water hits my body, and I slowly turn in a circle letting the delicious spray massage every part of my bruised body. Eyes closed, face tilted, I run my fingers through the tangled, knotted mess of my hair as the water washes away the aches and anxiety of the past few days. One hand on his waist for balance I pick up the shower gel.

Presenting two bottles I ask him, "Which would you like?

270

What we have here is only the finest in hospital care cosmetics flown in exclusively from Paris, France."

"Probably both and a few bars of soap to get rid of this dirt and grime." He grins.

I wipe the water out of my eyes on a towel and order him to stand still. Those bold dark eyes gaze down at me, and I smile coyly. He may be exhausted but he's not dead. I empty the entire bottle of shampoo in my hand and begin to methodically massage it into his scalp, beginning at his temples and working over the top of his head, around the sides, circling my fingers round and round rhythmically. His long dark lashes fan across his cheeks, and his lips part a little, "Oh, Elle, that feels so good. Don't stop." His expression is one of blissful contentment.

I lather the back of his hair, combing my fingers through the matted locks hanging wet and heavy on his shoulders. I didn't realize how long his hair has grown this summer, its usually tucked in a man bun or pulled back in some fashion.

"Turn around, lean your head back and rinse." I command and he obeys. Lovingly, I caress his cheek, and he opens his eyes, gazing at me tenderly. I lean forward and kiss his lips. His hands join the duet, skimming my slick body, moving to my hips, creeping south around to my behind.

"Hey, no fondling the help." I feign disapproval. "That could be grounds for sexual harassment."

"Buttercup," he declares. "You are so lucky at the moment I don't have the energy to show you the true meaning of sexual harassment." His fingers tighten on my butt pulling me closer to the physical proof of his threat. One hand moves up to the nape of my neck, and his lips are on mine. I gasp with surprise as his tongue hot and hard is in my mouth. My fingers curl around his wet hair as his kiss deepens. "When I get my strength back, I'm going to..." the scintillating words get lost, muffled as his mouth nuzzles my neck, and all I hear is 'seven shades of Sunday'. He's going to *what*?

Oh... "Listen, amigo, I'm not sure this is the time or place. How about a rain check?" I tip my head in a flirtatious manner.

He smiles slowly, his lips curling into a sensuous smile full of licentious promise. "What will you do to me?"

"Oh, I can think of things."

"And what kind of things can I do for you?" he asks, nipping and swirling, creating a trail of pleasure in his wake.

"Trust me, I have a list."

"I like lists, maybe we should get started." He growls in my ear.

"No, no, no!" I start to panic. He can't be serious. As entertaining as the idea may be…steamy hot water, all soapy and slicked up…the image of me straddling his body, back pressed against the shower wall, head flung back, hollering away in ecstatic passion…*and* a team of nurses along with a security guard busting down the door comes to mind. *I don't think so…*

"What about the nurses?" I whisper frantically.

"We can invite them in."

"Not funny!" I slap him on the ass.

"Ouch!" He yelps. "Okay, I'm kidding, at the moment this amigo has nothing in the tank." The truth is, Vic is the living, breathing embodiment of a chick magnet, testosterone oozes from his pores. Until his illness this summer I've never known him to have an empty tank.

"Turn around and let me wash your hair." He commands. The scent of lavender shampoo perfumes the air. Using slow deep strokes his strong fingers massage my scalp. The shampoo forms a wet sleek blanket of thick curling bubbles streaming down my back. I've let my hair grow longer this summer, perfect to style into a long thick braid for hiking.

He takes a washcloth and squirts some gel on it. His hand starts at my neck and moves down my arms, sliding across my breasts lathering them with extra care. Leaning forward, he takes my nipple into his mouth and sucks hard, his wet hair tickling me.

"Hey, you're tickling me."

"I know." His hand moves to my hips. The cloth glides smoothly down one leg and then up the other, the sudsy surface caressing my butt. The friction of the soft cloth skating over my skin makes me tingle. He washes my face with his fingers, his thumbs skimming over my lips, my cheekbones then gently wiping the water from my eyes with the washcloth.

"My turn." I say taking a fresh washcloth from a shelf next to the shower stall. I hold it under the spray of the shower, letting the hot water saturate then squeeze out the excess and add soap. I start with his neck and move across the plane of his marvelous shoulders then work my way down to his chest, taut with corded muscles. "Turn around." I command and he complies by leaning both arms against the wall. I love watching the play of muscles tile down his lean back to the firm hard cheeks of his buttocks. The cloth, slick with soap, glides over his smooth skin, a golden bronze from the summer sun. I take extra care scrubbing his legs, paying close attention to the cuts and scratches on his long limbs, removing any and all dirt to prevent infection. When satisfied with my work I wrap my arms around him, planting soft kisses up and down his back. He turns, wrapping his arms around me, tucking my head under his chin, holding me tight in his embrace. The shock and exhaustion of the past few days overwhelms us. Our bodies shake, quivering in relief as the reality of our ordeal crashes down upon us. "I can't believe how lucky we are," he whispers into my hair. "Elle, we could be dead or..."

"I know." I put a finger to his lips and nuzzle into the hollow of his neck breathing in the heady scent of Vic, clean and slick, as rivulets of water cascade down his body. I could stay here wrapped in his arms, warm, safe and protected, forever. We hold each other savoring the feeling of skin on skin, wrapped in a silent cloud of steam, a cocoon to stave off the outside world, a moment to catch our breath and begin healing.

"Mr. and Mrs. Rienz?" A nurse politely knocks at the door. "This is Connie, your nurse. We need to get your IV's started soon. Are you almost finished?" She asks. "Do you need any help?"

"Coming." I call out to her. "Just give us a minute to towel off and figure out how to tie these hospital gowns."

I can hear her laughter through the door. "Take your time, I'll be back in a few minutes."

Vic wipes the water from my face with his thumb, "Hey," he whispers, tipping my chin back and gazing into my eyes, "By the way, you saved us. It was your survival training that kept up alive and away from Maltby. I am so proud of you."

"Always a pleasure to come to your service…" I say, standing on tiptoe to kiss him.

~~~

Vic fell asleep as Connie was putting in his IV. He was exhausted. I lingered in the twilight land between dozing and awake, too keyed up to fully relax. My head bursting with unanswered questions. How did Maltby escape our makeshift bonds with a broken wrist, where did she have guns stashed and how long can she hold off law enforcement? Jonas and Arthur's miraculous mushroom concoction is nothing more than glorified hooch? And what will happen to the loons?

When we arrived at the hospital earlier, a medical team swooped in, poking and prodding and drawing blood. When satisfied we were not on the brink of death, little white plastic ID bracelets were attached to our wrists, a room was found and orders for an IV drip to improve our hydration status. The lab tests came back negative for giardia. We drank only small amounts of water squeezed from moss and found one stream flowing with clean water. Thankfully, the water wasn't contaminated.

I place a hand over my stomach to quell the rumbling. Apparently after four or five days without food your digestive system stops functioning properly and your body adapts to feeding on itself for sustenance. Therefore, if you eat a large meal in that state it could shock your system causing heart and breathing problems, seizures, paralysis and even death. The doctor ordered a liquid diet for the next twenty-four hours along with IV's. We'll be allowed to eat small amounts of food, progressively adding more day by day. *Bummer…*

To fall asleep, I used a trick from childhood, counting backwards from a hundred. 100…99…98…weariness seeps into every pore. For the past several days there has been little sleep aside from short naps snatched on the run. Bone deep fatigue exacted from days of running and hiding take their toll and I fall off the edge of consciousness into the abyss of deep dreamless sleep. I never heard the nurses coming into the room to change the IV bags every few hours, never felt the warm hands prodding the tender flesh of our wrist checking our pulse and respiration, our silent guardian angels of the night.

*Nobody trips over mountains. It is the small pebble that causes you
to stumble. Pass all the pebbles in your path and you will find you
have crossed the mountains.*
Anonymous

The grey light of morning filters through the thin gauze of
the hospital curtain. Brightly colored balloons shimmer in the
dim lighting, bobbing and weaving caught in the draft from the
air conditioning unit. Mixed in with the balloons, a line of flowers
sits in pretty attendance on the windowsill as a testament of love
from family and friends.

The sun barely crests the horizon when the voices start in the
hall outside our room. My state of awareness drifts in and out of
sleep, a sleep so deep I surface for a few moments only to fall
back under the enchanted spell of slumber.

The incessant buzzing continues, the exact words
unrecognizable but the tone and inflection of the voices identify
the speakers. Our family is here. Through the thick hospital door
I hear a nurse say, her voice strict and authoritative. "You have to
wait. Doctor's orders. Please be patient." The nurses are having a
difficult time holding our loved ones at bay. They are done
waiting and not to be denied.

A nurse with short blonde hair and a nametag identifying her
as Gretchen, slips in, pirouettes and flattens herself against the
door, arms and legs spread wide in a melodramatic poise as if
holding back an angry mob. "Whew," she says wiping her brow.
"Your visitors want to see you, they're ready to break down the
door." She apologizes, "I'm sorry but we have strict orders not to

let anyone in before the doctor does his morning rounds. Thankfully, he's due any minute. How are you feeling?" She asks, briskly moving about the room pushing back the curtains to a beautiful Adirondack morning.

I smile at Vic and reach a hand out to touch his cheek. "Grateful to be here with my beautiful husband." I whisper to him and then say to her, "Hungry!"

"Me too." Vic chimes in, his voice ripe with longing. "Can we have real food today? What I wouldn't do for bacon and eggs, coffee, a Danish pastry…orange juice…toast and butter."

"I'd love a bagel with cream cheese. Any chance of a Twinkie in the kitchen?" I'm giddy over the thought of food, my mouth waters and my stomach rumbles in response.

"Obviously, the two of you are feeling better." Gretchen laughs, setting down a tray stacked with alcohol wipes and cotton balls. She pulls on a pair of rubber gloves giving them an extra snap for effect and proceeds to remove our IV's. "Dr. Butler will be in soon and assess your diet. My guess is that he will want you to wait a bit longer. After several days of food deprivation its' best to start the refeeding process slowly. It's really in your best interests." She glances anxiously at the door. "I hope he arrives soon. That horde is getting rambunctious out there. I don't know if I can hold them back much longer." She laughs in good humor, collects her tray and slips out the door.

"Elle, how are you feeling this morning?" Vic asks, tracing a fingertip along my chin. I hitch up my hospital gown and slide to his side of the bed, wiggling my butt to spoon his hip. Without the IV attached, I'm free to wrap my arms around him and let my fingers skim over his chest enjoying the hard plane of muscle underneath. Only Vic can look handsome, even sexy hot, in a hospital gown.

I sigh. "I feel woozy, lightheaded and hungry. I ache all over and my feet are killing me. Other than that I feel great." I snuggle closer into the crook of his arm, enjoying the warmth of his body. "How are you?"

He leans in and kisses me, playfully biting my lower lip. "I'm still tired. I don't know if I've ever felt so tired in my entire life."

"I forget this is your first kidnapping. The feeling of

helplessness, terror and food deprivation are foreign to you. You get used to it after a while. Kidding!" I exclaim with a ruthful grin. I take his hand and, glancing through my lashes at his chiseled face, I give into the urge to kiss him, his stubby jaw tickles my lips.

"You might have mentioned the Klutz-Ellen thing before we got married. I'd have been better prepared, taken out more insurance, hired extra security. I wonder if there is such a thing as S.W.A.T. insurance?" His chest rumbles under my head as he chuckles.

I slap at his hand. "Hey, it's not my fault."

"It never is, Mia, it never is."

The door swings open and Dr. Butler back steps into our room, holding a chart out in front of him like a shield, he glares at our family and points with his free hand. "I said no one, and I mean no one, gets in until I give the okay." He booms in a gruff voice. "That includes you, Mrs. Watson, I don't care if your sister was my babysitter and changed my diapers when I was a baby. I mean no one. My responsibility is to my patients." With that he slams the door and turns his attention to us. "Whew, they are a persistent bunch, I'll give you that. We haven't had so much commotion since the traveling rodeo lost its bull. The escaped bull chased the clown down Main Street, hooked the clown with his horns and pitched the poor guy into the city water fountain. Broke both of his legs." He shakes his head, opening our charts, one-by-one and flips through the pages. "Okay, let's see what we have here." He nods as his eyes scan quickly over the pages. He gives a quirk of his eyebrows and says, "A quick review of your medical records shows your lab tests have come back within the normal range. Your electrolyte balances are stabilized that's why I discontinued the IVs. Another day or so and you'll be fit to go home. But for now let's keep you off your feet as much as possible except for using the restroom and a short stroll down the halls. We'll continue the liquid diet for lunch and maybe for dinner soft-boiled eggs and toast."

Vic groans and feigns a pout, not his fantasy food. I love soft-boiled eggs, my favorite sick food as a child.

"We don't want to rush the refeeding schedule too soon. By

tomorrow afternoon we'll have you back on a regular diet, keeping the portions small." He looks up from his scribbling in the chart and finally asks, "So how are you feeling?"

"Aside from being tired, hungry and everything hurts, just fine. We want to go home." Vic says.

"Maybe tomorrow?" I ask.

"We'll see. I don't make promises I can't keep."

I look around the room and sigh, as pretty as the bouquets of flowers and balloons are, it's still a hospital room. Square, dull, linoleum floors perfumed with the faint smell of disinfectant. It's not home. I long to be home, I miss our dogs. Speaking of dogs, the thought just occurred to me, what was Porky Pellinger doing with that police officer, Darrel. The one who looks just like Adele's nephew, Derek?

"Dr. Butler?" Vic clears his throat to get the doctor's attention. "We have so many questions that need answering."

Dr. Butler holds up a hand to stop the flow of inquiries. "Before I let your family in, the authorities want to speak with you." He takes his glasses off and carefully places them in his shirt pocket then straightens his tie. "The two of you certainly have attracted a lot of attention. The FBI wants to talk to you. Apparently the agent knows you?" He shrugs. "A Robert Corburt, Corbo, something like that."

"Oh no, Corbain! I thought we were done with him yesterday. What more can he ask?" I hiss at Vic.

Vic rolls his eyes in despair. "That entire incident at our house last summer. It wasn't our fault." He blows out a deep sigh. "Then he finds us with those moonshiners. He might not be so quick to think we're innocent this time."

"This time?" Dr. Butler asks, his face incredulous. "You make a habit of getting yourself in these situations?"

"No! We didn't do anything wrong." I protest.

"Well, brace yourselves, you have a long morning ahead of you. As an authority of the law I have to let Corbain conduct his investigation. After that I can't hold your family back any longer." He cocks his head and smiles. "We'll see how you fare and then we'll discuss how eager you are to go home with your 'caregivers'." He stresses the word 'caregivers'. With a dismissive salute he tucks the charts under his arm and walks out the door.

"Robert Corbain." Vic exclaims, his eyes wide with suspicion. "The FBI. Do you know something I don't?"

I feel a sense of foreboding sweep over me. "No! How could I, you were with me the entire time." I smooth my hair wishing for makeup and concealer, a little female body armor. It wouldn't matter, Robert Corbain sees through everything... *holy mother goose, we're screwed.* Thank goodness Vic instructed Juls to contact his attorney to protect our rights and privacy.

*Doubly happy, however, is the man to whom lofty
mountaintops are within reach.*
John Muir

No polite knock or a request to enter, Robert Corbain thrusts the door open using the flat of his hand. The door bounces and ricochets off the wall with a muffled *bang!* There is silence in the hall, our family freezes, no one speaks, no one moves, caught in the stare of the iceman. Corbain turns on them, his eyes cool and gray, spark like the edge of a knife blade. He holds his index finger up in warning, indicating he's in charge…and they *will* wait. He slams the door shut on their stunned faces and marches in, his stride determined and a scowl etches furrow lines on his forehead. He zeros in on us like a fox on a cornered bunny.

The man is a master of disguise. I met him last year at the Adirondack Canoe Classic where he was working undercover, posing as a volunteer. In a wardrobe purchased off the racks of the local Salvation Army Store, he appeared to be a dumpy middle-aged man walking with a slouched posture and ingratiating demeanor. Our consequent dealings with him over a *little* diamond smuggling incident…revealed our assumptions about the man to be completely wrong.

He stands before us, ramrod straight, in a well-tailored suit with his hands on his hips. His eyes narrow as he takes in the sight of us cuddled together on a hospital bed, with an unwavering stare, he says, "Well, well, well, what do we have here?" He shakes his head and cocks one eyebrow. "Imagine my surprise to find the two of you in the woods with moonshiners. Mr. and Mrs. Rienz, we meet again." His voice thick, laden with sarcasm.

*Jeez…*of all the rotten luck. "Agent Corbain," I say, adjusting the bedcovers to make all 'lady parts' are covered. Those silly hospital gowns have a way of riding up and open, it never hurts to double check. "It's so good to see you again. We didn't have a chance to chat and catch up yesterday in all the confusion. Gosh, it looks like you've been working out. You even have a tan. You don't look nearly as dumpy as you did last summer." *Oh sweet mother of all that is good and holy, when I get nervous, I babble. So screwed.*

"Ellleen," Vic squeezes my hand in warning. "Careful, the wheels of justice, move like a dozen of this or six of the other."

I turn on him in exasperation. "No, it's *the wheels of justice grind exceedingly slow* and it's *six of one or a half dozen of the other*…oh, forget it."

"See," I point in triumph to Corbain's aviator glasses. "See," I repeat. "Now today he looks like an FBI agent, sensible suit, button-down shirt, modest tie and *aviator* glasses. If he looked this way last summer I wouldn't have gotten in so much trouble."

"Oh boy," Vic mutters, shaking his head.

"You look terrific." I compliment Corbain.

"Yes, Mrs. Rienz, it's so good of you to notice." He pushes his jacket back revealing a pistol holstered under his arm. "Actually, I have you to thank for my state of well being."

"Oh really?" I beam at him giving Vic an elbow to the side. "See?" I say with a snarky sneer on my face.

"Oh yes. Who else can I thank for making the law enforcement community traipse all over these mountains chasing a barricaded suspect who is a military survivalist holed up with enough munitions to blow up half the county? Add in a few moonshiners masquerading as herbalist healers, if that's not enough I find the two of you at the end of the trail!" His voice rises, "How the hell do you manage to get yourself entangled in these disasters? Don't you have anything better to do with your time? There isn't enough law enforcement in the mountains to keep up with your escapades." With each word, the pitch of his voice escalates, by the end he's talking through clenched teeth.

Yet he goes on…"The cost of the S.W.A.T. teams alone has placed us seriously over budget. Three years in a row! Don't you have a home in California? Maybe you could spend some time out there, see what you can stir up! Leave the good people in the Adirondacks alone for a while; give us time to catch our breath. Summers are too short, we can't keep up!" He throws his hands up in exasperation, his chest is heaving, and he's winded from the exertion of his tirade.

I raise my chin; look him in the eye. "It's…not…my…fault!" I say defiantly.

"Elleeen," Vic warns me, his voice like cold liquid gravel. *Oops*…I'm in trouble.

"Mrs. Rienz, I understand you knew the sniper." Corbain pulls up a chair and sits, taking a moment to regain his composure. When he speaks, the tone of his voice is neutral yet cold. He asks, "If you would be so kind, may I ask how did you cross paths with this female war machine? We have a few leads as to her identity but I was hoping you could help connect the dots."

"Maltby Magalano. She was my stepmother's niece. Apparently, she had some childhood vendetta for me that I never realized. My father used to joke that my stepmother's family had mob connections. They were a rather bizarre bunch. Where is Maltby?"

"At the moment, on a slab in the morgue."

"Oh…"

"She was holed up in a makeshift bunker atop one of the mountains. Unfortunately, she refused to surrender or give up her arms. She was neutralized last night."

"Oh…you mean she's been killed?"

"Yes."

"This is so bizarre." My emotions are in conflict, I'm relieved she is no longer a threat to us but a part of me feels sympathy for the girl no one understood. Even with the numerous citations she received in the Coast Guard, my guess is that Maltby never fit in and for some reason she blamed me in part for her pain.

"I have a question for you." Corbain says, "When we recovered her body, she was naked and covered from head to toe in a rash that looks like poison ivy. From the scratches on her body, it appears she almost went crazy from the itching."

"Uh-oh." I grimace.

"I thought you said it was box elder that we used to tie her up." Vic accuses me. "Not poison ivy!"

"I thought...?" I shrug my shoulders.

"You tied her up with poison ivy?" Corbain asks, a look of delight crosses his face. "Oh, this is priceless."

"Well, in our defense..."

"That's going to be weak." He comments drily.

"She was hunting us down with a bow and arrow. So we lured her up a rocky ridge." Vic says, sticking to the facts. "She got too close to the edge and fell off, knocking herself out. It looked like she had a broken wrist." I noticed he left the part with the bear out, smart thinking, this man thinks we are bat-shit crazy already.

Vic continues, "So to slow her down, we tied her up with what ever we could find, grape-vine and apparently, poison ivy."

"Hold out your hands." Corbain commands.

Dutifully obeying, we hold out our hands, palms up.

"Why don't you have a rash?"

"I shrug my shoulders. "I had a slight encounter with poison ivy last year. Maybe I developed an immunity?"

Vic says, "I tied her up using the grape-vine so I had little exposure."

"So, you're related to this lunatic?" Corbain asks, looking down at his notes. I hear him mutter, "Figures, the apple doesn't fall far from the tree."

I start to speak but Vic pinches my arm to silence me. He senses my anger seething, fearful I'll say something to imply guilt, Vic says. "They are not related by blood."

"How did you reunite with her?"

"She posed as my brother, using an old voice mail message she spliced together. She invited us to dinner at a house my brother was supposedly renting on Alliance land. I haven't seen him in years so I was happy to receive his invitation."

"We walked right into her trap." Vic says. "I had received anonymous threatening letters over the last six months. I didn't want to alarm Elle so I hired a security specialist and private detectives to track and trace whoever was sending the letters. They were never able to find anything. Maltby outwitted one of the top security teams in the country simply by having access to personal family information. She baited the trap so beautifully using Ellen's brother we never saw it coming. I can't believe I was such a fool."

"So you ended up at the house she rented, and…" Corbain waves the pen in his hand encouraging us to fill in the details.

Vic and I related the sordid details of our saga. In the retelling it sounds incredulous even to our ears.

Corbain jots down notes at a furious pace, shaking his head, stopping only to clarify facts.

"So this woman," he pauses to look at Vic, the expression on his face reads, you, great big Mister Hollywood hero taken down by a mere woman. Granted, a 6'1" amazon of a woman, but the fact remains she was a woman. Out loud he says, "So essentially you are lost in the woods, naked and afraid?" He laughs and slaps his knee, amused at his joke. "Too bad you didn't have a camera crew with you. It could have been an episode for a TV reality show, make yourself a little money on the side."

I cross my arms and give him a sardonic look that doesn't faze him a bit.

"So then you escaped a para-military stalker and walked right into a moonshiner's camp?" He taps a pen on his notes in impatience.

"We were lost, no food or water for days with a crazy lady stalking us!" I exclaim. "How much worse could it get?"

"So what were Jonas and Arthur doing?" Vic asks, rubbing the back of his neck to hide his irritation.

"Apparently, they were concocting this health brew with an alcohol base that was totally illegal for the permit they obtained."

"What about the loons?"

"This is where it gets interesting. Somehow they came up with the idea of using loon eggs and balsam needles in the elixir to add the health essence of the Adirondacks."

"That's ridiculous!"

"They were making a killing. They forced the loons to mate

in captivity. A couple zoos got hold of the story and want to know their secret. But Jonas and Arthur are holding out for a plea bargain."

"When I was in their store there was talk of negotiating a contract with the Oprah Winfrey Christmas Favorite Things show."

"Yes, that's why they needed to get rid of you. They were sitting on a golden egg and you were about to kill the goose."

"Apparently." Vic fumes. "They were going to sell us! If the S.W.A.T. team didn't show up we'd be on a plane to Florida and a boat out of Tampa."

"We're old." I say. "Who'd want us?"

"Speak for yourself." Vic grumbles. He has a vanity streak a mile long, goes to great lengths to hide his age. It helps to have an army of personal trainers, nutrition consultants, hair stylists and skin esthetician. It's a Hollywood thing...and part of his screen persona.

I give him a withering look.

"What, you're still hot!" He defends himself. "I'm sure there is an old oil sheik out there who would love to get his hands on you. You know, cheap...because of our age..." His face turns red as he realizes his blunder. "I..I..I'm sure..." he starts babbling to cover his honesty.

"Are the two of you done bickering over your age and beauty?"

I open my mouth to protest and snap my jaw shut realizing he is right. "Fine." I give Vic a pointed look that says this conversation isn't over.

"Mrs. Rienz, two years ago you were kidnapped by a hermit obsessed with a curse from the 1800's, last summer you hired a murderer and this summer..." He leaves the sentence dangling in the air. "Do you see where I'm going with this?"

I blow out a sigh, feeling a headache brewing behind my eyes. "I know. Its nuts." I admit.

"You will finish the investigation and we are free to go home?" Vic asks. He gives Corbain a piercing look, deepens his voice to the sonorous growl of Sentar, warrior king of *Firebrand,* cocks an eyebrow and says, "I have a lawyer on retainer but we won't need legal counsel, correct?"

Now, generally, the Sentar, warrior king look and voice stop most mere mortals in their tracks. Vic's made a ton of money on *the look*. Millions of people flock to the box office just to see *the look*. He's famous for it. It's graced the covers of magazines, cereal boxes and comic books.

Corbain looks up from his notes, snorts in disdain and drawls, "Well…" He pauses, "My friends, I can't decide if I'm deporting you to California or placing you under house arrest with ankle monitors. I'm beginning to think you're a risk to the community. Have a good day." He stands up and walks out the door, leaving us with no illusions as to who is king of this territory.

Oh, for the love of Pete…

It isn't the mountains ahead to climb that wears you out, it's the pebble in your shoe.
Muhammad Ali

"Why can't you be like other mothers?" Lani whines. "Other mothers knit, bake cupcakes for bake sales. They belong to book clubs, go out to lunch, have a career or do yoga."

Our family has broken through the barriers of hospital staff and invaded our room.

"Umm…" I raise a finger trying to interject. But she is on a roll. Once the preliminary hugs and 'gosh, we were so worried, we love you so much' were finished, Lani launched into a tirade of acceptable things a mother should be doing. Apparently being kidnapped (twice), lost in the woods (without clothes), captured by moonshiners and human trafficking do not make her list of acceptable mother past times. Even the calm presence of her fiancé Jason failed to bring her off the lofty perch of righteous daughterhood. He stands next to her running his hand up and down her back in a soothing motion. His dark eyes under his glasses look confused. Has he never seen this side of my daughter?

My son, Trey is absolutely no help. He simply stands, his arms crossed and nods at each accusation Lani throws in my direction. Then she turns on Vic.

"Ever since she married you!" She jabs a finger at him, branding him as the root of every evil that has invaded my life the last three years. "There has been nothing but craziness. I'm mean, when we were growing up…the Klutz-Ellen thing was awkward but not life threatening! It has got to stop. Look, the two of you have grandchildren. You're *old*!"

Vic and I gasp, "Old?"

Jason winces. Josh, Claire, Izzy and Ansel stand off to the side. Josh appears shell-shocked, probably stunned he is biologically linked to the nut cases in this hospital room. But unless I miss my guess, his wife, Claire is biting her lips, almost drawing blood in an effort not to laugh. (I always liked her.) Ansel peers from under his baseball cap, meets my eyes and gives me a thumbs-up. Ansel, the poor darling, we fear has inherited my clumsy traits; his feet and arms are a daily source of tumbles and mishaps, even at this young age.

"My wedding is less than ten days away." She runs her hands through her long dark hair, causing it to stick up like a wounded hyena. "What was I thinking to have the most special day of my life up here in the wilds of the Adirondacks, away from anything civilized. Planned by two adolescent geriatrics who can't stop screwing each other long enough to realize other people have lives!"

Ouch! Now that is downright uncalled for.

Claire claps her hands over Izzy's ears but not before a giggle escapes her lips. The expression on Vic's face, he's in retreat mode and not interfering with the run away bridezilla freight train. He shrugs his shoulders and nods his head in Lani's direction, as if to say… 'hey, she's your daughter'.

Not to be left out of the hue and cry, Vic's daughter, Hanna chimes in, "Dad, you lecture me on being responsible all the time. Nagging me on how to behave, my friends, what cars I get into and yet, *you*? You have an FBI file and an agent who calls you by your first name. Seriously?"

"Bocce." Lani says in a needling tone one uses for five-year-olds. "Outside in the fresh air, tossing those little balls on the grass. You like being outside, right?" Questioning me as if I were a senile octogenarian.

"Hanna?" Vic protests. "It's not how it looks."

"Oh, really?" She folds her arms across her chest, rocks back on her heels giving Vic a haughty look. "Mom drags me out of school telling me I have to leave for New York because my father is missing. Gosh, how many times is this now? Normal people don't get involved with the S.W.A.T. team. And by the way," Hanna points down the hall, gloating, "You should know, Mom is waiting outside in the hall. She wants to talk to you, *in private*. She was packed and ready to leave for location. Which she delayed because…you were to be in California as my guardian until we came back east for Lani's wedding." Hanna leans in, her face close to Vic and she hisses. "She is not happy. 'Maureen O'Hara' not happy with a Spanish attitude. You know the mood, arms crossed, foot tapping, steam coming out of her ears, temper tantrum, throwing things, angry. You may wish the lunatic sniper finished you. It's..not..going..to..be..pretty!"

"Oh crap," Vic groans. Sophia Delong, Vic's ex-wife is world famous for her temper, on and off the stage. I'm terrified of her.

"Your mother's here, in the hospital?" Vic's eyes dart around the room looking for a hidden door, a secret escape hatch. I watch his eyebrows go up as he sizes up the window and the distance to the ground below. "She postponed a film shoot to bring you here?"

"Yep." Hanna nods, a smug expression on her face. "She's here and dying to have it out with you." Hanna is almost giddy with the fun of chastising her father. "She's pissed."

Vic frowns, "Language, please." Hanna just smirks.

Ansel, oblivious to the tension in the room climbs up onto our bed. "Papa Vic did you see any bears in the woods?" Vic, relieved to change the subject says, "Yes, it was the strangest thing, Ansel. There was this bear, we would see it at different times of the day. It would appear and disappear, sometimes blocking or leading us in a direction, as if showing us the way. And the one time we refused to follow its lead, we walked into a very bad place."

"The bear was almost magical, like something out of a fairy tale." I add, pulling Izzy onto my lap. "I'm sorry we worried everyone but we were tricked and held captive by a person with a serious mental illness."

"Ella-ma," Izzy says. "Why didn't you just stop and hug a tree. That's what Daddy taught Ansel and I to do if we are ever lost in the woods? Stop, stay put and make friends with the nearest tree. We should always wear bright clothing, have a trash bag in our pack to keep us dry and a whistle to make noise so people can find us."

"Thank you, Izzy. That is very good advice. Next time I am lost in the woods that is exactly what I will do."

"You have a good memory, Izzy." Claire complements her daughter.

"Well, I'm just glad all us locals were on hand to assist with the search."

I start in surprise as Adele, Weasel and *Bridget* slip into the room after giving the family a few moments of privacy. *Oh, no…Adele and Bridget, together.* This is not going to be good.

"Yes sireee. It's a good thing the locals were prepared for a search and rescue operation. Between the SAR and State Forest Rangers, we got the job done." Adele chimes, visibly puffing her chest out. She gives Bridget a superior look, as if to say no help from outsiders. Weasel nods in agreement, one arm slung across Adele's shoulder.

"By the grace of the good Lord," Bridget adds in her Irish brogue. "We got here just in time to organize the food and answer the phones, keeping everyone's strength and spirits up. What with the whole fool county running around in the woods like chickens with their heads cut off, they forgot the importance of a support team." Bridget thrusts her chin out in Adele's direction, defying the other woman to challenge her importance.

"A little barbeque would have gone a long way to rally the energy reserves." Adele counters. Adele believes a good barbeque is the closest food on earth that resembles the biblical manna Abraham received in the desert.

"Faith and begora, how could you move around in that God forsaken wilderness with that evil brew rattling around in your bellies. A good stew is what was needed."

"It all comes down to field work." Adele insists. "Time on the trail, out with the dogs, that's how you find a person."

"Speaking of dogs," I jump in eager to divert the imaginary daggers flying back and forth between Adele and Bridget. "How did Porky Pellinger end up being a search and rescue dog?"

Adele tugs down the hem of her black Harley-Davidson t-shirt, stretched tight from too many washings. It was bought when Adele was several sizes smaller. "You remember my nephew, Derek, the policeman up in Saranac Lake?" She says proudly. "He has a brother, Darrell who is part of the Saranac search and rescue team." I nod trying to keep pace with her explanation. I'm suspicious the search and rescue team might be a synonym for local social club. It seems everyone in the mountains is on a search and rescue team or related to someone who is. Which says a lot for the dedication of the locals. There are standards and qualifications to participating in such organizations.

"Anyway, Darrell has been training this new dog for the last year. We never saw the dog, did we, snookums?" Adele asks Weasel and he nods in agreement. "To make a long story short, the darn fool dog took off and Darrell has been half out of his mind looking for him." Adele smacks her head in mock retort. "The fool dog was right under our noses." Bridget snorts and rolls her eyes in exasperation. Adele gives her a scornful stare and continues, "We never put two and two together realizing the dog you found was Darrell's lost dog. Wouldn't have thought the dog could travel so far through the woods and survive."

Bridget gives an audible sniff, raises her eyes to the ceiling, in Celtic body language she's saying, "Any *eejit* with half a brain could figure that one out."

Adele glowers at her, just as she is about to open her mouth and retort, Vic cuts in with a question. "How did you know where to find us?"

Josh breaks through the group and steps to the front. He raises his hand for quiet, declaring his willingness to recount what happened during the search. He has Vic's lean build, high cheekbones and dark unsettling eyes. "Twinkie alerted Ike that no one was home and the dogs were running loose around the property. Right, Twinkie?"

How the hell did Twinkie sneak into the hospital room? A glance shows her working her way forward from the back of the assembled group.

Lani interjects, "Mahjong, you could play mahjong. It's a great game for your golden years." Jason pats her arm, his face visibly pale, probably wondering if it's too late to cancel the wedding, realizing he'll soon be legally related to a bunch of nutters.

I'm worried about Lani, she looks exhausted, her eyes bleary and reddened. As much as I love her I'm about ready to buy her a one-way ticket back to California. If she dares bring up the Red Hat Society…it could gravely hamper our relationship.

Twinkie gives Lani a quizzical look before she answers Josh. "Yes, sir, that I did. I feel it is my civic duty to keep an eye out for my neighbors. 'Specially when they are as good-looking as Mr. Rienz. And his friends." She smiles up at Vic and her eyes rove over to Ike, her little pink tongue darts out and she licks her lips. Vic puts a restraining hand on my arm as I rise up out of the bed ready to do serious damage to her face. Ike's face flames beet red, causing his russet hair to look pale in comparison.

"Anyway, piecing together the information from Ike, we followed your trail to the house Maltby rented and promptly lost it." Josh supplies. "People in the Allegiance are very close knit; they don't like rental properties within the confines of their boundaries and tend to watch strangers very closely. Maltby and the van were noticed. By luck or fate the police traced the rental van by a gas purchase caught on a surveillance camera. There wasn't much around the area but some hiking trails. So Search and Rescue coordinated by the State Forest Rangers began a perimeter search centering our resources on the roads leading to the trailheads. The next break came when a National Grid helicopter pilot surveying the power lines noticed a floatplane parked on a remote lake, with no signs of life around it. We made a grid of the area and identified the plane as a rental unit. After drop off at the point, Porky picked up on your scent, he was relentless in his pursuit."

"Never seen anything like it," Weasel pipes in. "No dog ever topped my Dixie in trailing a scent. Porky wouldn't rest until he found you. We had just about given up hope, getting late in the day and all. You see as the sun sets the ground cools and the trail can drift, making it more difficult to follow. But scent will pool, like ripples when a stone is thrown into a pond or when someone stops to rest."

"Bingo." Lani says. By now everyone is ignoring her,

realizing her banter is only a coping mechanism for stress.

"The SAR's dogs are an integral portion of any Search and Rescue Team." Leaning against the doorframe stands a tall, rangy man wearing a green uniform with an embroidered patch on his arm identifying him as a Forest Ranger. He has startling blue eyes, the color of the sky on a crisp October day. He removes his hat, runs a hand through his chocolate brown hair. "Hello, my name is Officer Langtree, I am with the New York State Department of Environmental Conservation. I hope I'm not intruding. I wanted to stop in and see how you were doing." He walks over to the bed and extents his hand to Vic and I. "You led us on a merry chase. How are you feeling?"

"Very well, thank you." Vic says.

"Wow, a forest ranger." I gush. (I've always had a thing for forest rangers, rugged men who dedicate their lives to protecting the great outdoors...in uniform. *oh my...yum!*) "I thought the forestry department dealt primarily with forest management and wildlife."

"Actually," Officer Langtree says pulling on his full beard, probably a nervous quirk. At six feet he weighs in close to two hundred pounds, tall, lean with the weathered skin of a man who spends a great deal of time outdoors. "The New York State Forest Rangers are sworn police officers authorized to enforce all state laws, with emphasis on Environmental Conservation Law. So we are a leading force on search and rescue missions."

"How interesting." I gush. Vic gives me a look, bordering on jealousy.

"When a call comes in for a search we start with a sound sweep where all the searchers call out, whistle or make some noise at a prescribed time, then all are quiet listening for an answer. Until we realized there was an unstable suspect involved. This required backup to contain her before allowing us to finish the Wilderness Search. We followed the trail to the moonshiner's camp and found you under the protection of the S.W.A.T. team and FBI."

Vic pinches the bridge of his nose and frowns. "What a rotten mess."

I look away and bite my trembling lower lip, wondering if I

could have done something to prevent this terrible situation.

"In the end the S.W.A.T. team was divided, half to deal with the moonshiner's camp and half to guard the SAR team as we conducted our field work to locate you. It was a busy day to say the least." Officer Langtree comments.

"What about the loons?"

"The loons were transported to a local wildlife rehabilitation facility to evaluate their health and with any luck be returned to the wild in a timely manner and at appropriate locations."

"Sewing classes, then you could help me finish my wedding dress." Lani interjects into the conversation completely ignoring Officer Langtree.

"How is the dress coming along, dear?" I ask, shrugging my shoulders in askance to the Forest Ranger. "I can't wait to see it."

"The pieces are scattered across my design table at home. I was planning to work on them this weekend, instead…" She gives pause, "I'm in the mountains chasing my mother, lost in the company of a para-military specialist and moonshiners. I'm sure this happens to all the brides." Her fiancé, Jason leans over to reassure her but in the course of throwing her hands up in the air, she bonks him on the nose sending his glasses skittering across the linoleum floor.

"Ouch." He cries out holding the bridge of his nose as a thin trickle of blood coats his fingers.

"Oh, Jason, are you all right?" She covers her mouth with her hands. "Look! I've broken the groom. The wedding is ruined." She turns on me. "You're in no condition to finish the organizational details. We'll just have to cancel." She clutches Jason's arm. "That's it, we'll elope. I really didn't want a big wedding."

I watch my daughter come unhinged in front of me. "Lani, darling," I plead. "I have most of the wedding details already taken care of. I will be home in a day or two and that leaves us plenty of time." I pull a tissue from the box on my nightstand and hand it to her. "Look," I point to Bridget and Adele. "We have Bridge and Adele. With the two of them in charge there is nothing we can't accomplish."

Adele and Bridget size one another up, the scrutiny as

intense as a confrontation between Ulysses S. Grant and Robert E. Lee.

"Are you sure? You promise?" She asks. Jason wraps his arm around her, the other hand holds a handkerchief to staunch the blood trickling from his nose.

Smiling, I hold Vic's hand up. "We promise, everything will be perfect for your wedding on July 26th. After a little rest, Vic and I will be back in full swing. Furthermore," I tease, "it's been my experience there is nothing that can't be fixed with a checkbook and a pen. Between Adele, Bridget and the size of Vic's checkbook, this wedding will come off without a hitch."

Vic chuckles, "I'll second that, and I'm happy you've chosen our home to celebrate your wedding."

"Thanks, Mom and Vic." Lani sniffs and blows her nose on a handkerchief Bridget hands her. "Between the wedding and almost losing you…again," she gives me a despairing look. "It's been very emotional."

"Come here and give me a hug." I say, folding her in my arms. "Everything will be fine." She returns my embrace, holding on long and tight, an anchor after days of uncertainty.

"Yes, everything will be wonderful." She nods.

"Oh, Lani-blaini, you're such a drama queen. It's just a wedding." Trey teases. Tara gives him an elbow to the side. He has the grace to look chagrined.

"No need to worry." Twinkie says, a parody in pink spandex exercise clothing, consulting her cell phone. "Hamish will be in after his political speaking engagement on the 20th. Might tie me up for a few days but other than that I'll be over bright and early to help with the preparations. On the wedding day don't think of me as a guest but a helping member of the family. And just an FYI, Hamish likes his Glenfiddich scotch, neat. Where are you registered at again, honey-child?" Twinkie directs her question to Lani. "I want to be sure to pick out something real nice for you. Do you like pink?"

My jaw drops, Vic and I exchange glances, we hadn't intended to invite Twinkie to the wedding, let alone Hamish. I admit I'm intrigued to meet the man married to Twinkie. I shrug my shoulders and sigh. It seems whether I like it or not Twinkie

Wannamaker is my new BFF…and technically she did help save my life. Does that mean I'm indebted to her… *like forever?*

"How lovely. We can't wait to meet Hamish." I say, and not wanting to appear rude, I extend the invitation. "Officer Langtree, why don't you join us at the wedding? I have a few nephews interested in Forestry, you will be like a folk hero to them."

Never follow someone else' path unless you're in the woods and you're lost,
and you see a path. By all means, you should follow that.
Ellen Degeneres

Vic

Vic swings the hammer anchoring the last nail into the weathered board siding. He steps back to admire his handiwork, pleased with the results. While not a carpenter by trade or talent he enjoys working with a hammer, nails and wood. Admittedly, at first, he was less than enthusiastic about the project. Elle greeted him a few mornings ago with a cup of coffee, holding a picture of a rustic bar made from old barn siding. She gushed "I found this on Pintrest. It would be a perfect touch to our Adirondack wedding. You are so talented with a hammer and nails. And it would give you an opportunity to be involved in the wedding preparations."

Really? Apparently, all the toting, hauling and rearranging he had done the last week didn't count. Not wanting to disappoint her, he used the picture as a design reference and enlisted Ike's help. It was Ike's suggestion they rummage through the garage where a treasure of old wood was found. The previous owners had neatly arranged two stacks of barn board, set aside for a future project. There was enough wood to create the façade of the bar and the rest was constructed with new lumber painted a distressed gray to match the old boards.

Several cans of paint sit open on a tarp next to a group of signs painted in a rainbow of colors. The signs are cut to look like trail markers and listed the various libations and beverages available on the day of the wedding. Shiny silver tubs are stacked, waiting for the local brewery to deliver. Elle has a vision of beer bottles poking through heaping beds of ice, their tall necks floating along resembling miniature icebergs called bergy bits.

To himself, he thinks, its just beer, as long as it's cold does it matter? With a shrug he reaches into a small cooler he had brought down from the house.

He tilts his head back and admires his handiwork. It turned out pretty good if he does say so himself. With a sigh Vic settles into an Adirondack chair for a long deserved rest. A man needs a moment to relax now and then. He twists off the cap and takes a long swig from the beer, he lifts the bottle in a mock toast. He thought he and Ike would celebrate the completion of their project. Unfortunately, Ike had an appointment to pick up a motorcycle for a job. Some woman over in Lake George wants an antique Indian motorcycle refitted for her husband's birthday next month. It's a short deadline, so Ike will have to hustle to complete the order on time.

"Oh well, Ike, your loss. Guess I'll have to drink the beer myself, such a shame." With a sigh he leans back in the chair enjoying the warmth of the summer sun, the satisfaction of a job well done and, the quiet. Since coming home from the hospital, the Camp has been under siege, a three-ring-circus of estrogen-fueled activity in preparation for the wedding. Between Elle supervising or refereeing Bridget, Adele and Twinkie, he's hardly seen her. What is it about a wedding that makes women nuts?

He was happy Lani chose to have her wedding at Camp but won't be sorry when the affair is over. The ensuing chaos has left little room for his fantasy of a relaxing summer. It's been fun but he won't be sad when everyone packs up to go home leaving the Camp to Elle and himself.

He sits in silence for a few minutes, thinking over events of the past few months and realizes he should have handled the situation differently. By hiding the letters from Maltby he tried to protect Elle. And in doing so he underestimated her strength and placed her in jeopardy. Marriage is a partnership, working through problems and difficulties together. Maybe it was time for him to do something brave, like step up to the plate and see what it felt like to really trust someone, stop playing the strong macho man all the time. He and Elle are committed to each other, a team. After being on his own for so long, it's hard for him to relinquish control.

"From now on, Mia bella," he murmurs. "It's you and me, no more hiding secrets from one another, no matter what."

How lovely on the mountains are the feet of him who brings good news....
Isaiah 52:7

True to my word, by the day of my daughter's wedding, the house and gardens stand in perfect readiness. Pausing for a moment, I take in the scene and congratulate myself. *Whew, I knew I could do it!* Thankfully, temperatures hover in the low eighties and the sky is vivid blue dotted with cumulus clouds.

By three o'clock in the afternoon the guests assemble on the lawn as the bride arrives in a carriage drawn by a pair of sleek Frisian horses. Their feathery black fetlocks move in an even gait down the gravel drive leading to Camp. As the wheels spin over the bridge a bell is rung, the traditional Adirondack custom of announcing the arrival of a guest to camp. Today the bell rings out with joy to herald the entrance of the bride.

Jack's brother, Patrick, and I wait at the portico of the house, ready to escort her to the lakeshore where a minister stands under a rustic arbor of roses, ivy and pine boughs. Lani had asked her Uncle Patrick to give her away, Patrick being the closest in age, looks and temperament to her father. Uncle Patrick is of Lani's past, a link to her father and family history. Vic and I agreed and gave our blessing.

The day smells of balsam and summer. A heavy sheen of velvet humidity hangs in the air, heightened by the fragrance of fresh grass clippings and flowering gardens.

Lani is breathtakingly beautiful as only a bride can be. I watch as her dress floats like the flared petals of a flower over the freshly mown grass. Small pearls are delicately hand beaded throughout the bodice and skirt, each opalescent piece shimmers like a jewel caught in the sunlight. After all the hard work of ripping apart my old dress, the pieces were sewn into an underskirt, invisible under her exquisite creation. One of Grandma Fiona's precious hair combs holds her hair gathered into an upsweep of black curls that tumble down her back.

Originally Lani wanted to recreate the style of the Great Camps. But after doing extensive research, she recoiled in horror at the stiff layered creations of the day. Dresses with tight corset bound bodices; long puffy sleeves and high necklines graced the fashion scene of the Victorian era. The final result of her fashion genius, dresses inspired by the Great Camps of the 1890's, but in a more forgiving design.

Vic and the groomsmen wear starched collar shirts, light wool jackets with patches on the elbows and tight calf length knicker pants held up with suspenders. One of those tweed caps popularized by newsboys in the 1920's, sets perched jauntily at a cocky angle on his head. Frankly, I don't know any article of clothing that doesn't look terrific on his lean frame. I admit I swooned a bit when I caught sight of him in his knickers and tall-laced boots. His skin glows a tawny bronze from the summer sun, hair pulled back in a sexy man-bun, he looks quite dashing.

~ ~ ~

Jack's normally boisterous family quietly takes their seats, looking comfortable in their woolens and tweed. Being Irish, a search into their wardrobe wasn't very deep. A long-armed reach to the back of a closet produced a good facsimile of a turn-of-the-century estate garb, toted in a modern well-worn, well-loved version.

Across the aisle, Jason's Midwestern family sit stiff and bewildered, their eyes wide in wonder, examining each tiny detail of the wedding, grappling to understand the history behind the Adirondack lifestyle and our rustic home. They are a people of the plains. More accustomed to wide-open spaces and constant wind, little but horizon to obscure their vision, now in a place of craggy mountains and towering forests of balsam, cedar and fir.

Except for Jason. Jason's home is wherever Lani is...his face glows with love as his eyes lock on hers. With Patrick on one side and me on the other, we move forward at our musical queue, the first notes of Pachelbel's Canon in D. Arm and arm we lead the bride down the processional aisle, a linen covered pathway, a blaze of white dotted with galvanized buckets of baby's breath. One-by-one, the bridal party moves toward the lakeside and waiting minister. We pause, shake hands with the Reverend, exchange pleasantries and greetings.

My heart awash with happiness, I hand Lani over to her future husband, step back and join Vic at the edge of the altar.

The exchange of vows is brief yet heartfelt, there's not a dry eye among the assembled guests including myself, unabashedly weeping into Vic's handkerchief.

After the ceremony, the wait staff dressed in period costumes serves champagne and hors d'oeuvres. Guests mingle freely amongst each other, chatting and congratulating the newlyweds.

As the late afternoon sun creeps closer to the horizon, evening descends pulling a lavender curtain of cool air over the lake taking with it the heat and humidity of the day. The Camp is cast in a golden glow as legions of candles and oil lanterns are lit. The electricity turned off in favor of candlelight, to an era gone by, to a time filled with silence and quiet nights. Strings of votive lights hang from tree branches on twisted knots of twine glowing like a miniature fairy village suspended in the air. A waxing moon, close to full, sheds a pale illumination over the surroundings.

The main house, clear of everyday furniture is set for intimate dining, small bistro tables are scattered throughout, covered in white linen and fine china. Food stations are placed in strategic locations to encourage guests to wander and mingle as they sample the abundant fare. A farm to table theme predominates the foods served. Local fresh greens and vegetables, homemade pastas and sauce, artisan loaves of bread along with grass-fed beef, free-range chicken and venison round out the menu.

Adele and Weasel insisted on setting up their BBQ bar as a wedding gift to the newlyweds. Ribs, beans and coleslaw lend a festive picnic air for those inclined to sample a heartier fare.

My earlier prediction of trouble between Bridget and Adele working side by side proved correct. Even before Vic and I were discharged from the hospital the battle lines had been drawn. Bridget insisted her long-standing service to Vic and his family based on some next to non-existent blood relation trumped Adele's family service to the Camp over the past fifty years. We arrived home to find the two of them locked in a dead heat of wills, neither budging. The slamming, banging of cupboard doors, pots, pans and cleaning equipment reached a crescendo of ear-piercing level, threatening to destroy house and property. Ike retreated to the boathouse and Cyrus refused to come out from under the bed. He's mourning the loss of Porky Pellinger. Porky is happily reunited with his owner, Derrell, who promised to bring him over for a play date.

Always the peacemaker and because few women can resist his devilishly good looks and Latin charm, Vic devised a plan to keep both woman happy and out of each other's way. It was genius in its simplicity, divide and conquer, each with their private domain to control. Adele would supervise the food at the wedding and Bridget was in charge of…everything else. Barring an unforeseen disaster, such as a Category 4 hurricane named Bridget-Adele, the risk of backlash between the volatile personalities proved to be minimal.

The focal culinary presentation of the day is the wedding cake. Curls of pendant frosting topped with glittering arches and spires of sparkling crystal sugar rise layer by layer into a tower of white magnificence. The shimmering edifice of confectionary extravagance created by a local bakery is a nod to the opulence of the gilded age. Almost too fantastic to cut and eat, a creation of artistic rendering. Centered on a bed of velvet green moss amidst tendrils of ivy and white roses, the cake rises from a forest of small marzipan pine trees, a fairy castle set in a mystical woodland setting.

If the cake alone doesn't satisfy the most ardent sweet tooth then a walk down to the campfire is in order. Under the direction of Ansel and Izzy a s'mores bar was designed that would knock the socks off Willy Wonka. An Adirondack pack basket full of sticks, cut and whittled to a fine point stand ready for toasting marshmallows to a soft golden brown goodness. The sign reads *S'mores and More.* A long slab table covered in burlap holds the 'fixings': Graham crackers, vanilla wafers, chocolate covered cookies, peanut butter and mallow cups, peppermint patties and of course, sprinkles.

Through the narrowed slits of weathered barn board I spot Twinkie standing by the bar. Twinkie, a vision in pink is latched onto my husband's arm, shamelessly rubbing her breast on him. *In broad daylight…for goodness sake!* Vic catches my eye across the terrace, his face a mask of polite desperation. Not wasting a second, I hoist the long train of my dress up in one hand and charge over to save my man.

"Twinkie, darling." I drawl in the most down-right dripping with honey sweet voice I can muster at the sight of her breast plastered against my husband's arm. "You have been so helpful this past week I don't know what we would have done without you." I sidle up and wedge myself between her and Vic. I claim my prize stud muffin by sliding my hand over his chest, dawdling over a button as if contemplating what lay beneath the fine fabric of his shirt.

"Why, thank you for noticing, Ellen." She beams. "I surely did enjoying running over here and being a part of this marvelous party."

And that she did, every morning before we barely finished coffee, up the porch steps she came trotting, in her hiking boots- with *brand new* pink laces. There was Twinkie, banging at the patio door, yelling, "Yoo-hoo! Hey, you all, the day's a wasting, let's giddiup. We got things to do!" If we wanted a few moments of peace, we needed to be up before Adele, Bridget and Twinkie brigade arrived. Not that I'm complaining, between the three of them, there was little work left undone. Adele and Bridget tossed Twinkie back and forth between them like a cute little pink poodle trained to do their bidding. She loved being a part of the preparations, bringing me to the point I've secretly harbored, that Twinkie is lonely. For all of her gaiety and forced joie de vivre, living alone in that big old Camp must be awfully quiet.

To relieve her of any imaginary responsibilities, I insist. "Twinkie, make sure you relax and enjoy the party. You've earned it. Did you try the signature cocktail, the Adirondack Barkeater? It's made with dark rum and is positively delicious, I'm feeling quite tipsy."

"Oh, yum!" She leans her head back and snorts out a loud high pitched giggle that causes Jason's Aunt Patty to stop with a drink halfway to her mouth and stare. I mutter to myself. "I bet they don't have too many Twinkie Wannamakers in the Midwest. Maybe we can loan her out for a while." And then I feel guilty for thinking such unkind thoughts. Ever faithful, Twinkie hasn't missed a day of helping and believe it or not, she's starting to grow on me. I have a penchant for attracting colorful characters. In her shocking pink sheath dress with matching heels, she is a vision. She took one look at the Victorian inspired clothing, scoffed and said, "Honey child, certain fashion statements were meant to be dead, buried and *never* resurrected."

"Ellen, I was just telling your gorgeous hunk of a husband what an *amazing*," she stresses the word, amazing, "wedding we put together." She croons looking up into Vic's face, flashing him a coy smile and fluttering her eyelashes. Twinkie runs a hand up his chest only to have it caught in the vise-like grip of mine.

"Speaking of gorgeous husbands, where is Hamish? We are simply *dying* to meet him. Aren't we, Vic, honeybuns?" I simper and smile.

Poor Vic, obviously uncomfortable with the rising tide of female estrogen blooming between us, mumbles, "Yes, yes, where is he?" Vic cranes his neck scanning the crowd, desperately looking for any means of escape or distraction.

"You are just too sweet," Twinkie leans in for what I perceive to be a quick kiss on the cheek and she plants one, square on my mouth. Not a touch-and-go peck on the lips but a linger with a little twist before she lets go. *Holy hell…* Vic sputters and coughs. To my dismay his eyes grow wide, the tiny golden flecks flicker in excitement. My cheeks flame and in revenge I tweak one of his nipples. He yelps in surprise and looks chagrined.

Twinkie releases her hold, smiles broadly and flags down a tall genial looking man. He is in a heated discussion with our son, Josh, while our grandson, Ansel uses his father's arm as a piece of playground equipment, practicing his chin-ups.

Hamish Wannamaker is well polished, wearing the air of a successful southern businessman in his tan linen suit, white shirt and bright tie-obviously the colors of his alma mater. I can't remember which college Twinkie said he attended, Old Miss, University of Georgia, something like that.

"Hamish, darling, come on over here and meet my friends." She waves at him. With a grin on his face, Hamish claps Josh on the back and saunters over.

"Vic and Ellen, it's a pure pleasure to meet my wife's new friends." He extends a hand and pumps Vic's arm up and down with enthusiasm. "She can't stop talking about you, nothing but good things. Yes, sir. That's the God's honest truth."

He takes both of my hands in his and gives me the once over, "And aren't you the prettiest thing this side of the Mississippi, not counting my sweet wife." His green eyes twinkle with mischief. I pull back just a tad, fearful he's moving in for a kiss. I remember Twinkie's *little* joke about being swingers at the breast cancer luncheon. You can't be too careful, don't want to send the wrong message.

"It's a pleasure to meet you, Hamish." I say graciously, slowly wiggling my fingers out of his grip, which is strong and firm. His body is that of a football player gone soft, settling into middle age.

"Twinkie has been such a help to us this week. Hasn't she, Vic?" Vic nods and I feel him backing away, trying to distance himself from the Wannamakers. I tighten my grip on his arm.

"Aaa, yes. So how long will you be staying in the mountains?" Vic asks.

"Just through the weekend, I'm afraid." Hamish says, running a hand through his thinning blonde hair, perfectly cut in feathered layers conforming to the shape of his head. He wraps an arm around Twinkie playing the perfect doting husband. "Unfortunately, I have political obligations and business commitments, duty calls, you know. But my little honeypot knows how to keep busy. Don't you, sugar?"

A pained look crosses Twinkie's face at his casual mention of leaving so soon, but she straightens her spine and smiles up at him. "Yes, I do. I'm getting very good at it." An undercurrent of sarcasm invades her voice.

"Say, has anyone ever told you," Hamish holds up a finger pointing at Vic, "You look remarkably like that movie actor guy. The one who plays in those fantasy movies, what the heck were they called, Twink? We just saw one last winter. I can't think of the title for the life of me."

Damn… I knew we needed to be careful about hiding Vic's identity.

Vic smoothly slides into his rehearsed speech, "You know, I get that a lot…"

Twinkie cuts in with a playful slap at Hamish's arm. "Yes, I know the movies, that *Firebrand* series. No, he looks nothing at all like him, silly." She says, taking Hamish by the arm, steering him toward the bar. "What would a famous Hollywood actor be doing up here in the wilds of the Adirondacks."

Hamish shrugs, "Well, whatever you say. But the resemblance is uncanny."

"Let's leave these people to mingle with the rest of their guests. It was so lovely chatting with you." Twinkie walks her fingers up Hamish's arm in a coquettish gesture. "I'm starving. I want you to try Adele and Weasel's BBQ and tell me it doesn't rival Mama Lolita's back home." She walks away, luring Hamish with the back and forth sashaying of her backside, but not before leveling us with a smug look and a sly smile. She knows. *Damn…damn…and double damn.*

"Your hand is inside my shirt." Vic murmurs against my ear. "Are you trying to tell me something?" He teases.

"Oh, I'm sorry." I flush with embarrassment and snatch it away.

"Well, I'm not." He pulls me into his embrace, and kisses me. His eyes are dark and needy.

"I must say you look dashing as a wealthy industrialist from the 1890's. Although I do admit to having a penchant for a man in a tuxedo."

"We can make that happen." He croons, running a finger down my face, caressing my chin. The arm wrapped around my waist slips lower. "I haven't worn one since our wedding."

"Gosh, it's been over two years." I whisper in his ear. "Any regrets?"

"Not a one, Mrs. Rienz." He whispers wickedly and smirks at me. "I think a private celebration for two is in order." He waggles his eyebrows up and down in a lascivious manner.

"Stop it! We have to behave. I need to stay focused on the reception and our guests, don't distract me…until later." I preform my own eyebrow dance.

"I don't think you need to worry, it would take a group of spoiled ten-year-old Boy Scouts high on marshmallows and stolen beer to break through the ranks of Adele and Bridget." He kisses the corner of my mouth. "I think you're covered."

I put a finger on his beautiful sculpted lips to silence him. "Later, darling, later."

"Is that a promise?" He smiles at me in a way that is so sexy I feel weak in the knees.

"Absolutely!" I say with a wave of my hand, but my attempt to escape his nefarious thoughts of seduction are thwarted.

He grabs my hand to stall me. "Before you go, I suggest you look at the band your daughter hired for her wedding."

With effort I turn my attention from him and focus on the musicians. *Holy moly.* "Oh my, not what I expected!" I exclaim.

"Keep looking, it gets better."

Under a makeshift tent four men stand on an outdoor stage constructed of rough-cut lumber. The band members are dressed in Scottish garb: kilts, black shirts, work boots and high knee socks or kilt hose. Keeping to traditional Scottish Highland dress, the bass player has a small single edge knife sticking out of the top of his hose. I recognize the *sgian-dubh* dirk from a series of Scottish historical novels I enjoy reading. All the band members wear a small black leather pouch called a sporran, conveniently positioned in front of their groin. Despite their unusual appearance and odd accompaniment of instruments: bass guitar, fiddle, accordion and bagpipes, the music is surprisingly sweet and mellow. Lani and Jason take the floor for their first dance as a married couple, cheek to cheek, laughing at some private joke. I watch them, my little girl grown up and married. Vic sensing my melancholy holds out a hand, "Shall we join them?"

We dance on the lawn, gliding along on the wings of an old melody, something old, but the name eludes me. It doesn't matter; the sweet notes compliment the emotions rising within me. I sigh, wishing to savor the memory caught on my heart.

The blessing of fine weather, family and friends gathered under an Adirondack moon at a house created for just this type of occasion, is serendipitous. I run a finger across the lips of my sweet husband, grateful to him, always gracious in bringing our blended families together.

"You look beautiful." He bends, kissing me, his lips linger and savor.

"Quite the complement from the handsomest man on the dance floor."

"I beg to differ on that point." Claire says whirling by in the arms of Josh.

Josh stops to execute a graceful spin, "Like father, like son?" He says with an arched eyebrow.

"I guess you'll have to share the limelight." I tease.

"Gladly." Vic says, winking at his son.

All of a sudden the tenor of the evening changes, excitement builds from the sidelines, the bagpipes strike a haunting chord. A woman emerges from the shadows of the stage. Tall, statuesque, wearing the same black shirt as the men, but an amazon of femininity in high leather boots over black fishnet stockings. The hem of a red and black tartan kilt sweeps the ground behind her in a long train. The front of the skirt cut short to expose a portion of her comely thighs. She leaps onto the center of the stage twirling a flaming hula hoop over her head, the glowing orb slips to the center of her body where the rotation of her hips defies gravity until the fire flickers out and the hoop falls to the ground, casting a haze of spent smoke. She is a creature of the night, a filament of sky and clouds conjured up by the music.

She accepts a set of drumsticks tossed from the bass guitar player and takes her place behind a large snare drum. With arms held aloft, she commands the stage and proceeds to beat out the rapid staccato of a highland tune. Jet-black hair, streaming down her back caught up in tiny braids swings through the night, keeping time to the frenzy of her drumsticks. She holds court, the huntress taking authority of the large snare drum. The silver tipped ends of the drumsticks leap to and fro casting a hypnotic trance over the wedding guests. She shrieks an unearthly yodel, a call to the violin and fiddle who take up the challenge with gusto.

She is frighteningly magnificent…and I recognize her. I clutch Vic's arm, shocked, just as I'm about to speak, Lani steps into the dance circle and holds her hand up for attention. Under the hammering thuds of the snare drum she channels the spirit of her Gaelic ancestors and launches into the precise foot movements of an Irish step dance. Her upper body held stiff and her skirt caught high in her hand, years of childhood practice resurrect muscle memory reborn in askance of the ancients to bless her marriage.

"I can't believe she remembers how to do that!" I whisper in a hushed voice. Jack's family has surrounded Lani, clapping and hooting out encouragement.

Jason joins Lani in the final throes of the dance. Soon, a circle is formed; family and friends dance hand to shoulder forming a spiral around the newlyweds. Until a resounding thump of the drums ceases the wailing chords of the accordion and fiddle. The night rendered silent. The quiet is brief, nothing more than a pause, and the band moves into a serene melody. Couples melt one into another, gathering close to the slow rhythm of a waltz.

I loop my arm through Vic's and escort him to the sidelines of the dancing, stopping to point at the female drummer. "Do you recognize her and the bass player?"

"Yes! At first I thought I was crazy but you recognized them too?"

"I can't believe it. Those two musicians are our mystery campers in the woods! How cool is that!"

Vic tilts his head and studies the musicians. "It would seem so. The drummer is our mystery hula-hoop twirler and her boyfriend, or whatever, is the bass guitarist. I hired two private investigators to search for them." His voice amused. "They were high on the list of suspects. I was convinced they were part of some diabolical plot to harm us."

I nod, understanding his confusion. "They are just innocent

musicians. Nothing more."

He shakes his head back and forth, not conceding guilt. "They were suspicious, but I had little evidence, it was purely based on their *unique* appearance."

I hug his arm to my chest. "I'm glad we know their identity. I think they are very interesting. I must admit I'm enjoying the entertainment. I wonder how Lani found them?"

He shrugs, "Good question, where do you find a flaming hula-hoop twirling snare drum playing woman who wears tall black boots and fishnets, accompanied by Scottish bagpipes?"

"Only in the Adirondacks." I quip.

Vic points. "Look, Lani is calling you over."

The wedding guests, with sparklers in their hands form a human arch, leading the happy couple to their waiting car. Taking my hand, Vic escorts me to the head of the line where shouts of good luck and congratulations send the departing couple on their way.

As Jason holds the door of the SUV open, Lani turns and tosses her bouquet of mountain wildflowers into the arms of Trey's girlfriend, Tara. With a conspiratorial grin on her face, Lani calls out to her brother, "You're next!"

Trey places an arm around Tara's waist, gives Lani a wink and a thumbs up.

Now what was that all about…oh, holy matrimony. Are we in for another wedding?

Wander often, Wander always

My feet ache and I'm dying to get out of this dress. It must be past midnight. The moon, almost full leaves the stars hanging like faded polka-dots in the sky. The guest have gone home, the chairs are stacked, the tables cleared and food put away. All that remains is the lingering air of a party well enjoyed. Tonight memories were formed bit-by-bit, piece-by-piece, the remnants of happiness each guest left behind. I hear the screen door bang shut as Vic lets Cyrus out for a long overdue walk. The cool dew on the grass soothes my aching feet and the night air rejuvenates me. I should go to bed but I don't want the evening to end. All the emotions of the day have set my body humming. I want to savor the memory of family and friends brought together under the veil of wedding happiness. The cottony dark of the night like its own sort of prayer gathers all around me. Vic comes to stand beside me. He stops and puts something down on a table before wrapping me in his arms. Neither of us speak, letting the quiet enfold us in her indigo embrace.

"I put Cyrus back in the house." He says, kissing my forehead. I turn in his arms and realize he's changed his clothes. Even in the dim light I can see he has exchanged his 1890s garb for a black suit. I think he's wearing a tuxedo! The thin ribbon of a black bowtie peaks out from under the open collar of a white shirt, waiting to be tied. Casual, yet very elegant.

"I can never tie these things." He says holding up one end of the tie.

"What are you wearing? A tuxedo? Why did you change?" I

ask reaching up to finger the lapels of his jacket.

"I believe I promised you a private celebration complete with a tuxedo and champagne." His mouth so close to my ear it tickles. He reaches down and holds up a bottle of champagne.

I remember his offer made earlier in the day, at the time high on champagne and dark rum I agreed. I didn't think he meant tonight! After two glasses of champagne, I'll agree to almost anything, I need to be more cautious. When I see the tattered, worn sleeping bag, a souvenir of our teenage years folded into a tidy roll on top of the table, I know I'm screwed, literally.

"Now?" I ask in faux righteous indignation. "Seriously?" Knowing the answer even before the question pops out of my mouth. He's going to give me the line... 'I'm all keyed up so I can't sleep and you know what relaxes me the best' routine. "Umm...?" I murmur.

He grins and whispers, rubbing his nose against mine. "I know you're tired. But it's such a beautiful night. I thought we'd go for a midnight boat ride out on the lake...and stop for *awhile...*" His voice drifts off as he plants soft kisses down the side of my throat to that sensitive hollow spot. Even through my exhausted haze, desire blooms deep in my belly and I can't resist him. *Damn it, damn it...he's done it again!*

He is resplendent in the moonlight. Standing long, lean and tan, his white shirt glows against the black suit. Those brown eyes that set my pants on fire. He steps back, holding his hand out to me. I breathe in the honeyed night air of the mountains, ripe with balsam, the tang of dried pine needles blanketing the ground, the whiff of shoreline ploff wafts from the water below. Who am I but a mere mortal to resist the song of an Adirondack evening and Vic? He leans forward until his eyes are level with mine and he places the barest whisper of a kiss on my wrist, sending a small shiver curling up my arm. My hand folded in his strong fingers, intertwined we stroll down the path to the lake. A nighthawk calls out its sharp *peet...peet* from low in the trees and I'm beguiled under the spell.

The wooden classic Chris Craft boat bobbles in the water of the boathouse making soft *thunk, thunk* noises from the movement of water. Vic helps me into the passenger side and walks around the boat untying the rope with sharp confident movements. He hops in the driver seat and flips the switch for the blower, the hum fills the cabin of the boat before he turns the key and the throaty roar of the engine springs to life. With a soft shove the boat drifts away from the dock and out into open water.

The boat, the *Kitty Marie* is a vintage wooden Chris Craft. A descendant from the line of boats manufactured by a company in Detroit who became well known for their sleek high-end racing boats built between 1910 and 1920. Wealthy boat owners of the day included the likes of Henry Ford, William Randolph Hearst and later Dean Martin, Katherine Hepburn, Frank Sinatra and Elvis Presley. The boats were made of mahogany, Ford built engines and considered to be among the best available back in the day. Easy to operate, a must for their "weekend sailor" owners. In some circles, ownership of a classic wooden Chris Craft was considered to be *de rigueur*, very haute.

Our boat came with the purchase of the house, for Vic it was love at first sight. Nothing makes him happier than spending an afternoon puttering and tinkering around in the boathouse.

With a soft *putt, putt*, the boat cruises away from the dock. The vista in front of us sparkles like champagne. The stars, so random and perfuse, wink and glow like sugar crystals scattered on the velvet black. A view of the lake fills the entire horizon. The boat bobbles, floating on this rippling orb of mercurial silver, suspended on a web of watery animation. The night beyond is hushed.

We coast along to a quiet cove at the end of the lake watching the few remaining lights along the shore blink out, leaving the water cast in the silvery midnight glow of the moon. Vic's arm holds me against his warmth; my head rests on his shoulder, the feeling is pure contentment.

He cuts the engine and the boat drifts on the water, the lake smooth as skin. He stands up and drops the anchor into the deep inky water, turning he pulls me into his arms, gazing down at me.

"I think this is the first time we have truly been alone for weeks."

I nod mutely. "Yes, between Lani's wedding and our

recovery, the house has been overrun with people." I snuggle deeper into his embrace. "This is nice. Good idea, sweetheart."

"Oh, there is more to come." His eyes glow with amusement and something darker, something that takes my breath away. "I thought we'd spend the night adrift on the water, I've never made love in a boat."

"You? You're joking?" I gape at him and turn, glancing over my shoulder at the small passenger seat behind us. Dubious, I say, "I'm not sure we'll fit. Kind of like putting twenty college students in a Volkswagen, only a floating one."

"I like a challenge." He kisses me, more heated this time and our tongues meld and twist in a slow sensual dance with each other. "But first we have to get you out of this dress. Did I tell you how beautiful you looked today?"

"You forgot to say how graceful I am." I tug his earlobe and tease.

He throws back his head and laughs, the echo boomerangs across the water. "Your lack of grace is all part of the charm."

"You say that now, wait until you try getting me into that tiny backseat."

"Turn around." That voice of his, so low, and sexy as hell, sends a shiver up my spine. Willingly, I scoot around and turn my back to him. His hands move to my hair. Gently he pulls out each hairpin, one at a time, his fingers make short work of the French twist. Soon my hair tumbles over my shoulders, grazing the top of my breasts, modestly exposed in the low décolletage of my dress.

He sweeps my hair over my shoulder and trails a finger down the hollow of my neck then lower tracing the neckline of my dress, dancing from breast to breast. He licks his lips and plants a tender kiss at the base of my neck. I shiver in anticipation.

"So beautiful," he says as he finds the clasp and with infinite slowness, he lowers the zipper, all the way down my back, peeling the dress to my waist and deftly flicking open the hooks of my bra. The feeling of being naked in the night air, completely out in the open is intoxicating. I close my eyes and tilt my head, giving him easier access.

He nuzzles my neck. Gently he cups my breasts, toying with

them, while his thumbs circle over each nipple.

With one hand on my breast, the other caresses my ankle and makes the slow tantalizing journey up my leg. He runs his hand across my thigh and skims my stomach, over my belly, and down to the apex of my thighs, his thumb flecks the core of my desire. I stifle a moan.

"Stand up a bit." He commands and I comply. His hands travel to my behind and he finishes pushing the dress down over my backside, kneading and caressing.

"*Vic...*" I gasp.

"Shhh…" And with those words he sweeps the dress from my body. I shiver in the cool night air.

"Clothes, yours." I whisper, our breath mingling as I plant a soft kiss at the open V of his dress shirt. With sure, steady fingers I undo the buttons, kissing each inch of flesh exposed.

He groans, and with one swift move lifts me over and onto the sleeping bag spread over the backseat. He stands, precariously balanced and in one swift efficient motion dispenses with his pants so that he's gloriously naked, his bronze skin glows in the light of the moon, like some mythical god on loan, and he's all mine.

He crawls back to join me and the small cabin is eclipsed by his size. I wiggle around to give him more room, and end up facing away from him with my hands on the gunnel of the boat. Turning I see him settle in the seat and he grins…a salacious, wicked, tempting, 'I love what I'm seeing' grin. "Elle, what are you doing?" He laughs.

"Ouch," I cry out as a muscle cramp seizes my upper thigh, causing me to fall back onto him.

"Oh, Elle," he groans, twisting his hips in encouragement. "Are you trying the reverse-cowgirl move on me?" His words are soft and close to my ear. I'm almost lying on top of him…and I feel him hard against my bottom. "A new move to spice things up?"

"What! No!" I almost shout. "Are you kidding? One o'clock in the morning, floating on a boat that resembles a wobbling, bobbling cork in the water, wedged into a seat made for munchkins, no, this not the time for experimental sex positions!"

"Why not," he leans down and peels off my lacy panties, scant protection from the night air or his roving hands. He pushes my legs wider apart.

"Whoa, partner, I'm not sure I want to cowgirl anything."

"It will be fine, trust me."

"No, no, no…none of that 'save a horse ride a cowboy' stuff. I need to know exactly what you are thinking. No kinky stuff. I'm a straight shooter, buster."

He laughs, "It's not kinky at all. Reverse cowboy means…"

"Well, as lovely as all that sounds, I'm thinking we stick with something familiar…you know, the old tried and true version. With our luck we'll have a repeat of last summer's rodeo, the one where you bucked me off into the lake."

"That was spectacular, wasn't it?"

"From the man who did the launching, not the woman who was hurled head-first into the lake."

"Ah…you silly wife of mine. Here let me help you turn around." He murmurs, placing his hands on my hips and rotates my body so I'm straddling him.

"Much better." I say, as I slowly sink onto him, my hands fisting in his hair, my hips swing and sway, at the mercy of his rhythm. He grabs my hips to still me.

"Oh Elle, oh Elle, let me catch up," he breathes and starts to move, the feeling so intense that reality blurs and nothing matters but the blinding passion that cleaves us, bound to one another beyond reason and comprehension.

And at the end of the day, your feet should be dirty, your hair messy and
your eyes sparkling.
Shanti

The bobble of the boat on the soft ripples of the lake wakes me hours later, cold and cramped. Across the quiet water, the first rays of sun rise above the mountains, teasing the shoreline in a faint bath of gold, announcing the arrival of a new day. Vic slumbers contentedly underneath me. He sleeps like a man without a care in the world, not like a man squished on the small seat of a boat with his head propped on a lifejacket for a pillow. Over the gunnels of the boat I watch dawn filling the horizon in streaks of pink and gold. Morning comes early in the mountains and the birds begin their wake up chorus. Exhausted, we slept through the night lulled by the motion of the boat. I glance up from Vic's chest to examine his face, soft and relaxed in sleep. His arms are draped loosely over my breasts, and I try to match his breathing, caught in that half-awake, half-asleep land of dozing. The sweet rocking of the boat refuses to release the deep hold of slumber. It feels delicious to lay here with the early rays of sun warming away the chill of night air. I lean up and kiss the day old stubble on his chin, causing one eye to quirk open and regard me.

"Mrs. Rienz, you took undo advantage of me and plum wore me out." He drawls.

I snort. "I seem to remember this being your idea, you couldn't wait to hop back here."

"Actually," he says stretching. "We fit better than I thought.

You are quite the contortionist, madam."

"Ha, speak for yourself." I sit up pushing the hair back from my face. "Hey, we forgot about the champagne. I'm thirsty. Can we open it and toast the new day?" I snuggle further into the worn flannel pulling the faded sleeping bag tighter as he slips from underneath me, oblivious to the cold.

"Of course." He reaches under the seat and produces the bottle and two glasses. With a flourish of his hand he extracts the cork with a faint *pop*, catching the overflow, not spilling a drop. He pours the pale pink champagne into each glass and hands one to me. Taking up the other, he toasts, "Voilà! For you, my dear wife, two years of marriage and loving you for as long as I can remember...and always."

"To the love of my life and champagne before seven in the morning. Thank you." I say, accepting the flute of sparkling bubbles, enjoying the faint tickle in my nose, as I smell the bouquet. The flutes give a faint *clink* as we tap them together.

"A toast to Lani and Jason. To a happiness that lasts through the years."

"To Lani and Jason."

"And to summer."

"To summer in the Adirondacks." Vic adds, tapping his glass to mine, sealing the toast.

"To Maltby and all the ghosts of the past, may they rest in peace?" My voice hoarse with emotion.

He nods soberly. "Amen."

I lean back and let the beauty of the lake infuse my soul and muse on the complicated intricate balance of life. We float companionably, cradled in the sleek wooden boat that creaks comfortably beneath us. The breeze so soft, it barely riffles the water. Cool but comfortable, the temperature is somewhere in the low sixties. I hold up the champagne flute and watch the bubbles sparkle in the morning light, not a bad way to start the day. I smile pensively. "We have six weeks of summer left before you leave for your next film location."

"I plan on spending them right here, swimming, sailing, eating, drinking, and loving you. Period, end of sentence, no adventures, right?"

"Sure, I mean, maybe we can fit in a hike up a mountain or two, or three. Nothing too strenuous, that would be fun, right?"

"You're killing me, Elle." Vic says, "I need a rest."

"Hey, you didn't work that hard last night." I quip, giving him a playful slap on the arm.

He stretches, rubs his face, and grins at me. "We can fix that…" His hair is mussed and falls damply on his brow. I reach over to push a stray lock off his forehead, the dark locks are flecked with gray and the skin around his eyes is creased, but the impression is less of age than of exposure. He is going to make one hell of a good-looking old guy.

"I think we finish the champagne and troll this boat home. As it is, we are probably going to be doing the walk of shame. Bridget and Adele are up at the crack of dawn. Judging from the angle of the sun, they'll be meeting us at the dock with breakfast."

"You think?" He asks hopeful.

"Call them."

"I didn't bring my cell phone, wouldn't work anyway." He frowns with regret.

"Just as well, I prefer the two of them don't find me with my knickers off." I hold up my tattered panties and wag a finger at him. "These poor delicate undies never had a chance, did they?"

He looks rueful and shrugs his shoulders. "Doubtful." He glances over at me with a malicious grin. His eyes are dark like a midnight sky.

"I don't know about you but I need a shower, a cup of coffee and food. And we have a house full of guests that need our attention."

"Heard that excuse before and with a little coercion I've managed to change your mind." He runs his nose along my jaw and softly kisses my throat, my cheek and my temple before leaning back to gaze deeply in my eyes. "Shall I continue?"

I feel the familiar tug of pleasure and before my body takes control, I grab my dress from the floor of the boat. With a finger I tap him on the chin and say, "No, means no, my darling." The smile that flickers on my lips ends in a yawn. It is tempting to curl up next to him, let the boat rock us back to sleep.

He strokes his hand down my back reassuringly. "Truth be told, not sure my back is up for another go around." He grins. "It was worth a try." When I glance back, he's sliding his legs into his pants quickly doing up the fly before he changes his mind.

I hold up my dress, sighing, what was lovely yesterday is now a damp crumbled mess, and smells like mildew.

Okay...here's the question, could I walk up to the house in the sleeping bag and nothing else? The thought of wiggling my body back into that damp dress is demoralizing. It was a struggle yesterday, in this tiny confined space I'm labeling it...*mission impossible*. I wiggle into his tuxedo jacket and roll up the sleeves, dry, warm and completely covered. It works.

Across the lake our house tucked between the trees is barely visible, hidden in a shroud of pines. The veil of clouds softens the morning as the sky fades from pale grey lavender to a golden pink. Vic turns the key and the boat roars to life, there goes any pretense of sneaking up quietly. I rest my elbow on the side of the boat and take in the cedar-covered islands that dot the lake and the birds winging their way through the early summer sky. The boat cuts through the smooth surface leaving behind a trail of frothy white wake. At the edge of the bay lay the narrow triangle of land called Arrowhead Point. Leading the way into the dock a small scattering of red and green buoys mark the rocky shoal where submerged rocks lay hidden.

I close my eyes enjoying the feel of the choppy swell beneath the boat and fresh breath of morning air. When I open them the *Kitty Marie* begins making its approach to the dock. The sunlight muted and dappled on the lodge, not yet piercing through the trees. The jagged shoreline is cloaked in pines whose feathery branches skim the water and rocky precipices of granite rock rise above the lake surface, forming an uneven bumbled look to the shore. Encircled by a vista of lush green mountain peaks the lake is secluded and almost magical in the early morning mist. I shield my eyes to get a better look and see an osprey cresting over the towering white pine standing sentinel next to the house. The osprey moves slowly and beautifully in a flat plane, gliding along without seeming to move, just the barest ruffle of its wing feathers.

Trailing either side of the dock a small stretch of beach separates the shoreline from the carpet of grass leading to the house. Everything is silent, not a flicker of movement to be seen. As we come into shore, Vic cuts the engine. The boat glides slowly in on the current. I move to the port side of the boat and grab the line in preparation to dock.

On the far edge of our property where the line between grass and forest blurs I see Cyrus, rolling on his back, all four legs up in the air in joyous abandon. But who is with him? I shield my eyes to get a better view and my heart lurches in my chest, and begins to pound.

"Vic," I compress my lips to stop their trembling. "Look over there." My voice is a breathy, squeaky whisper.

"What?" He finishes tying the rope to the dock cleat. He scans the house and lawn. He shrugs his shoulders. "I don't see anything."

"Shhh…" I take a deep breath trying to bring my surprise under control. I pull him closer to me, point and say in a hushed voice. "Over there with Cyrus. Do you see her?"

Half hidden by the low growing brush, visible only because of the dappled sunlight filtering through the leaf canopy of the trees is a girl. From a distance, it is difficult to discern if she is a child or young woman. A long dress scattered with pale flowers pools on the grass around her bare feet. Ethereal, almost white blond hair hangs unbound. She is stretched out on the grass, laying full length next to Cyrus, her back to us, not seeing our approach to the dock.

"Holy shit!" Vic whispers. "Who is she?"

"Do you see her?"

"Yes, of course." He answers.

"That's my ghost girl."

Vic jerks his head back in surprise. "Get out! No way." He leans forward placing a hand over his eyebrow to get a better look. "I'll be a son of a bitch. And I didn't believe you. Elle, I'm so sorry."

"We didn't drink too much champagne, did we?"

"No."

"So I'm not drunk and you're not drunk and both of us see a

323

young pale girl lying on our lawn playing with Cyrus."

"Yes. Who is she? Could she be one of the wedding guests?"

"No, I know all the wedding guests. That's my ghost girl. Maybe we should ask Cyrus." I answer in hushed awe.

At the mention of his name, Cyrus' ears perk up and he rolls to his side, alerting the girl. Blithely lithe, she springs to her feet and with a wisp of movement she is gone, leaving only a patch of matted grass as proof of where she once lay. In the beat of an eye blink, she's vanished, leaving us in shock.

Ghostly specter, illusion of our imagination or creature of the forest, who is she? The incongruity of the situation strikes me. I'm standing on a dock, slightly buzzed on the fumes of beautiful pink champagne and the words to a poem by W. B. Yeats, *The Stolen Child* comes to mind. I memorized it in high school. The poem is based on Irish legend and concerns faeries beguiling a human child to come away with them.

> *Where dips the rocky highland*
> *Of Sleuth Wood in the lake,*
> *There lies a leafy island*
> *Where flapping herons wake.*
> *There we've hid our faery vats*
> *Full of berry*
> *And of reddest stolen cherries*

I don't remember the words exactly…over the years I'd recite the poem in the woods at night when the children were younger, it was within the realm of spooky ghost stories over the campfire. It evoked the image of changelings, a child believed to be a fairy child left in place of a human child who had been tempted and stolen by the fairies off to fairyland.

How amazing, in the throes of panic, I still remember this poem.

> *Come away, O, human child!*
> *To the woods and waters wild*
> *With a fairy hand in hand,*
> *For the world's more full of*
> *Weeping than*
> *You understand.*

On the shores of the lake, beneath the sheltering trees of our home, it would seem our adventures are yet undone. Under the blanket, I shiver, and feel a chill curl up my spine. I slip my arms around Vic, welcoming the security of his strength to subdue the sense of disquiet threatening to engulf me. I inhale deeply and exhale slowly, changelings, fairy tales and children that disappear into the woods...*oh my!*

The end...or not!

The sequel to *Audacity of an Adirondack Summer* will be a Christmas fable set in the deep woods of the Adirondacks. A tale of mysterious goings-on, snowstorms, dogsleds and ice skating on frozen lakes. Add in a wedding and all the elements of a modern day fairy tale dance off the pages. Look for book four of the Adirondack for Ladies series, *The Audacity of an Adirondack Christmas*.

L.R. Smolarek

Acknowledgements

I would like to thank my husband, Jim for his unflagging support and enthusiasm and providing me with the odd bit of reality when my imagination runs wild. Thanks for forty years of not turning tail and running every time I say, "I have an idea…"

To my beautiful daughter, Megan, my partner in crime, be it on a ski slope, hiking trail or a shopping spree…we work well together. She edits, corrects and challenges me to stretch my writing skills, truthful enough to tell me, "Change this, it doesn't work."

To my Pittsburgh family, the best cheerleaders ever! You are so smart and so funny and you give me great advice, a quality that makes me particularly proud. Thank you for your love and support, I couldn't love you more.

To my book club, you have been reading books as a group for almost 45 years, before book clubs were even a 'thing'. Your wealth of experience and literary prowess inspire me to think smarter, write stronger, in life and not just on the pages of my books.

The knitting ladies of the Embraceable Ewe yarn shop, our Tuesday night knit and gab fests provides me with laughter and many ideas for future plots. Someday Grandma Genevieve is going to be the heroine in one of my books.

To the best proofreaders ever, thank you for your time, sharp eyes and on point comments: Sarah S, Lisa Geier, Kim Wear and my ADK pal, Teresa C.

To my editor, Beth Jaminson for guiding my wandering writing hand and helping me turn a manuscript into a book that is a readable reality.

The Western New York chapter of Romance Writers of

America, your knowledge and dedication to the craft of writing inspires me with awe, such a savvy group of women taking the art of romance to a higher level.

To the real Porky Pellinger (Pittinger), a sweeter dog was never known even if you did eat Lululemon yoga pants and cell phones for breakfast.

And to my wonderful friends, Irene, Paula, Bonnie, Donna, Arlene, Gerry, Debbie, Wendy, Barb, Diane, Debi, Janet, Kathy F, my beautiful daughter in law, Sarah and to my sister, Caroline and almost sisters, Sue and Sally... how blessed am I?

Hats off to the New York State Forest Rangers, the real heroes of search and rescue in Adirondack Mountains.

To the Adirondack Mountain Club and the 46R organization for helping maintain the respect and stewardship of this magnificent mountain environment.

A portion of the profits of this book will be donated to conservation and education endeavors in the Adirondacks.

Finally, to my readers, to whom I owe the greatest debt of all, I am sending you the most sincere and profound thanks for reading my stories, for yakking it up with me on Facebook, and for coming out to book signings. It is my sincere hope you have as much fun reading as I do writing. For a book without a reader is nothing more than a bunch of pages flapping in the wind.

Sincerely,

Linda R. Smolarek

About the author…

Who doesn't love balsam scented forests, long hikes and quiet paddles across the lake?

Come along and be part of the adventure. Award winning author L.R. Smolarek loves mountains, beaches and anything that can be considered Outside! She travels in a 24 foot RV with her husband and two spoiled Yorkies, who think they are part grizzly bear. Hiking the high peaks and paddling down rivers and streams provides inspiration and meeting of the most unlikely host of characters. She spins her passion for the outdoors using a heroine not afraid to wear hiking boots by day and stilettos at night into romantic novels. And yes, she has been chased by a tame deer, several times and known to carry knitting needles in the most unlikely places.

Settle back and enjoy, the beach read has come to the mountains. The 'Adirondack for Ladies' novels are laugh-out-loud comedies with a hint of mystery, overflowing with good-looking men, a zany damsel, always in distress and a heat factor of…*sizzle*.

Follow L.R. Smolarek on Facebook at
www.facebook.com/Adirondackaudacity or her website:
www.adkwriter/wix/adirondackaudacity.